Paranormal Romance
by Jennifer Ashley

Immortals

THE CALLING
THE GATHERING
THE REDEEMING
WOLF HUNT
More to come!

Shifters Unbound

PRIDE MATES
PRIMAL BONDS
BODYGUARD
WILD CAT
HARD MATED
MATE CLAIMED
PERFECT MATE
LONE WOLF
TIGER MAGIC
FERAL HEAT
WILD WOLF
BEAR ATTRACTION
MATE BOND
More to come!

THE
REDEEMING

IMMORTALS
BOOK 5

JENNIFER
ASHLEY

Chapter One

Los Angeles, September

Samantha hated being demon bait.

She sat at a high table near the bar in Merrick's Venice Beach demon club, wearing a form-hugging, short black dress, black thigh-high stockings, and four-inch heels she'd had to practice walking in.

It had been Samantha's job for the last two weeks to perch on a high stool, cross her long legs, and wait for Merrick or one of his demons to offer her the illegal drug Mindglow. So far no one had pushed her to do anything more than order a second martini.

Tonight was typical for Merrick's. Every table was full, the clientele waiting eagerly for the demons to come in and choose their marks for the night. A few people sat alone at the bar, including a man with hunched shoulders, who stared morosely at the line of empty shot glasses in front of him.

At eleven o'clock, a door opened in the back and Merrick's demons strolled out. Beautiful and sensual, both male and female demons greeted the humans with promise-filled smiles. The demons' auras swirled like dark purple smoke as they touched their victims, deciding whose life essences they would taste that night.

Laws in all states said a demon had to have a human's permission to feed on his or her life essence — that elusive substance that made a person *alive* rather than a collection of biological parts. Like the laws that kept vampires from draining their victims dry, rules stated that demons couldn't siphon off all life essence and leave a person dead. Demons, being demons, constantly sought ways around the permission clause. The black market for life essence was huge and profitable. Hence Mindglow, the demon's coercion drug, and Samantha's current assignment.

Merrick, the club's owner, a well-formed man in a pristine gray five-thousand-dollar suit, glided to Samantha's table and gave her his broadest smile. "Ah, Sam, I knew you wouldn't resist returning to Merrick's. Is tonight the night I convince you to partake in the glory of me?"

Samantha's nostrils curled at the unmistakable scent of the netherworld, something ordinary humans couldn't smell. It was the tiniest bit of sulfur and dry air, the scent of power and arrogance.

Modern demons didn't consider themselves evil, unlike Old Ones, the powerful demons who'd walked the earth in centuries past. Samantha had once fought an Old One — not by herself, but with a group of witches and Immortal warriors — and she could attest to the evilness of the ancient ones. The whole experience still gave her nightmares.

The demons at Merrick's were lesser demons who'd learned to adapt to living in the human world. If they stepped out of line, they could be arrested, carted off to jail, and tried for crimes like taking too much life essence or coercing their marks to use Mindglow.

Samantha pasted on a vacant smile as she looked up at Merrick. "Maybe."

He had dark eyes, like most demons, all the better to suck in his victims with. *Not victims*, Merrick would insist. *Clients.*

"I live in hope," Merrick said. He reached out and traced her cheek, and Samantha did everything she could not to flinch.

"I'm still not sure."

"You never have to worry with me, Sam, my dear." Merrick's touch became softer, trailing to her bare shoulder. "I can make it as pleasurable as you like, or if you like it to hurt . . ." He broke off as his finger moved to her cleavage.

"No," Samantha said quickly. "I'm not into that."

"No. You're obviously a sweet, gentle soul." Merrick's pupils were wide, eyes black all the way across, betraying his hunger.

Samantha's half-demon senses picked up the pheromones he sent her way. He was trying to relax and arouse her, make her accepting of his touch. Samantha kept cool by remembering the young woman her partner Logan had found in the alley not far from here, her body drained of life, helped along with Mindglow.

Merrick hadn't caught on yet to the fact that Samantha was part demon. She'd learned through painful experience how to mask that part of her—then again, Merrick was possibly distracted to her true nature by his efforts to look down the top of her dress.

"I'm nervous," Samantha said. "I know it's supposed to be the best experience ever, but I'm just not sure."

Merrick moved to stand behind her and massage the nape of her neck. "You know, my pet, I've let you sit at my best table for two weeks running while you've tried to make up your mind. Most girls would have taken the plunge by now. What must I do to convince you?"

Offer me the Mindglow, already, damn it.

Samantha contrived to look bewildered. "It's not like I don't *pay*."

"Yes, but sweetheart, there are so many clamoring to get into my club. I have to turn them away while you sit here night after night. It's bad for business, my darling."

Samantha pouted and reached for her purse, which was just large enough to hold her badge and gun. "Fine, I'll sit at the bar then."

"If you wish. My bartender likes you. I'll have him give you a couple of drinks on the house."

Samantha let out what she hoped sounded like an inane giggle. "Are you trying to get me drunk so I'll go upstairs with you?"

"Of course not," Merrick said, voice a purr. "It's not as good when you drink too much—for either of us."

"What about drugs?" Samantha asked. "Is it better when you're high?"

"No." Merrick's voice was firm. "It's the best when you're aware and alert. Trust me, you want to feel everything."

"I could have sworn I heard it was better when you have a buzz on."

"You heard wrong," Merrick said. Samantha let her expression fall in disappointment, containing her disgust while Merrick traced his finger along her collarbone. "But there is something that enhances the experience, makes you less afraid. It's not a drug—more like an herbal tea."

Oh, frigging finally.

"What's that?" Samantha asked, trying to look guileless.

"Come upstairs, and I'll show you."

Not the best scenario. Upstairs, Samantha might find herself trapped before Logan could get to her. Though she was strong and had a gun, she was wise enough to know she couldn't take on a dozen demons by herself.

"I still don't know . . ."

She found her face pinched in a viselike grip, Merrick forcing her to look at him. "What are you trying to pull, Samantha?"

Samantha's first instinct was to break his grip and come up fighting, maybe giving him a kick in the balls along the way. But she hadn't staked out this place this long to blow it, and she remained still. "Nothing. I just want to be absolutely sure. You say the herbal tea will make me less afraid?"

She sensed his pheromones drifting over her, trying to relax her. Samantha resisted, and she knew he felt that resistance.

"All right, damn you," Merrick growled. "But only because I like you so much." He snapped his fingers, and one of the demon waiters came over. "One dose," Merrick said to him.

Samantha dropped her gaze so Merrick wouldn't see triumph in her eyes. She'd have to sit here until the waiter actually came down with the stuff, then Logan and his backup would raid the club, and Samantha could go home and slip into more sensible shoes.

Merrick smiled his most charming smile, and she sensed his arousal, his growing hunger. "You won't regret it, love. Because you're so special to me, I'll make it extra sweet—"

He broke off when a woman at a table near the door screamed.

Merrick jerked his head around as two male demons near the club's entrance suddenly burst out of their human forms. Their clothes ripped as muscles bulged and their bodies elongated into leathery skinned monstrosities. Everyone started screaming, scrambling to get away from them.

"What the hell?" Merrick started for the demons, signaling to his bouncers, who were already moving.

Whoever these demons were, Samantha knew Merrick hadn't authorized them. Demons appearing in demon form were bad for business. They were supposed to seduce humans by being beautiful and sensual, promising an experience better than sex.

"Out!" Merrick charged them, his arm extended as he pointed at the door. "I'm not having this in my—"

Merrick's words choked off as one of the demons grabbed him by the throat and tossed him aside. As the bouncers ran at the two rogue demons, they knocked over tables and grabbed for people with powerful swiftness.

Damn it. I was so close. But just as Samantha reached for her purse, ready to go for her gun, the hunched-over deadbeat at the bar came to life.

A deadbeat no more, he unfolded himself into seven feet of warrior in a brown leather duster, a bronze sword in each hand. His granite-hard face bore a pentacle tattoo high on his cheekbone, and his hair was flame red. He glanced at Samantha with eyes like patches of blue sky, and her mouth went dry.

Tain.

Merrick scrambled up, grabbed Samantha as she stood, stunned, and pushed her toward the back of the club. "Get upstairs and stay there."

Samantha tottered on her too-high heels, barely hearing him. That couldn't be Tain in this club. Tain the warrior who'd taken her breath away a year and a half ago, when they'd battled the deadly Old One—a demon so ancient no one knew its true name. Tain had walked away after his long recovery from that battle without even telling Samantha good-bye.

Tain shouldn't be in Los Angeles, and certainly not in a low-level club like Merrick's in Venice. He was off wandering the world, or else in that magical realm they called Ravenscroft. Wasn't he?

"Go on," Merrick snapped at Samantha. "Get upstairs and stay safe. I'd hate to see your cute little ass in tiny pieces."

The club's employees herded their clients the same direction, while the rogue demons proceeded to wreak havoc.

This had gone far enough. Samantha broke herself out of her shock, yanked open her purse, and closed her hand around her small .22. Not a lot of firepower, but she was out of options.

Merrick stared at the gun in amazement when she drew it out. "What the hell are you doing with that?"

"It's your lucky night, Merrick," Samantha said.

Merrick gaped a second longer, and then rage mottled his face. "You double-crossing little bitch, you're a *cop*. Damn it, I *liked* you."

As the words left his mouth, Samantha's partner Logan barreled in through the front door, followed by his backup. Logan tossed his weapon to a uniformed cop and morphed into wolf form, snarling as the demons leapt at him.

Tain lifted his swords and crossed them above his head. Lightning streaked up the blades, dazzling the dark club in pure, white light. The demons turned from Logan as the lightning streaked from the swords straight at them, aware too late of this new danger.

The lightning caught the demons and slammed them upward, crashing them into the club's black ceiling. Lights burst and showered the people huddled below with fine glass. Fire crackled through the demons, filling the club with the smell of roasting meat.

Then the lightning vanished, and the two demons fell straight to the floor, stone dead.

The club went silent. Logan stood a foot from where the dead demons had fallen, his lupine nose wrinkling in distaste, his clothes scattered where he'd ripped out of them. The rest of Merrick's clientele huddled in clumps or emerged, dazed, from under the tables or behind the bar.

Tain did nothing. His gaze was remote, blank, as though he couldn't see the club, the huge werewolf standing in the middle of the floor, or the demons he'd just killed.

Merrick swung on Samantha, his eyes blazing red with fury, and tried to knock the pistol out of her hand. She dodged him, keeping hold of the gun, and Merrick punched her full in the face.

Samantha's head snapped back. She righted herself, blood coming from her nose, kept her weapon trained on Merrick, and fired.

The shot sent Merrick backward across a table, but demons were hard to kill. Merrick rolled to his feet, blood all over his suit, and leapt at Samantha.

Samantha leveled her gun at him once more, but before she could fire, but Merrick was pushed away from Samantha by two swords crossed against his throat.

Merrick snarled and shifted into demon form, completing the ruin of his suit. He lunged with the strength of a volcano, but Tain, almost negligently, jammed the blades into Merrick's neck. Merrick gurgled, clawed at the swords, and slid to the floor in a pool of blood.

Samantha's nose still bled, and a deep cut in her cheek stung, but she barely noticed. Tain stepped back in silence, lowering swords that were stained black with demon blood.

Merrick had returned to his human form where he lay at Tain's feet, his beautiful suit in shreds. Blood streamed from the gash on his neck, but he was still alive. Demons were *damned* hard to kill.

Samantha limped to Merrick, trying not to slip in his blood. She pulled out her handcuffs with shaking fingers and snapped them around Merrick's wrists. "Merrick, I'm arresting you for possession of Mindglow. You have the right to remain silent . . ."

Anger flared in Merrick's eyes. He muttered, "Bitch," then fell back, his expression resigned.

Samantha felt warmth at her back and turned to look up at the man she hadn't seen in a more than year. *One year, four months, and one week*

She's fought next to him in the battle with the Old One, a vicious ass-kicker of a demon who'd wanted to watch all humankind suffer for his entertainment. Tain had at first been the demon's follower—maddened, powerful, tortured. Samantha had helped set Tain free and restore his sanity, but she wondered if he would ever be healed.

"Tain," she whispered.

He placed his fingers on her face. She felt a sharp pain, then a pull that was almost sensual. Warmth pooled in her belly, and her nipples tightened against her skin-tight dress.

Samantha recognized the feeling—she'd had it after the battle when Tain had healed her broken arm. He'd done it dispassionately, while she'd been bathed in a glow of his power that was nearly orgasmic.

He lifted his hand away, and Samantha touched her cheek, finding it whole and uncut, the blood dry. Tain said nothing, only flicked his blue gaze over her skin as though making sure her wounds were closed.

"Do you remember me?" Samantha asked him.

Tain's unruly red hair reached his collar, strands brushing his impossibly handsome face. She'd met his four brothers, all of them breathtaking, but Tain had seemed to her the most handsome, with his sculpted face and lake-blue eyes.

He also had a presence that could knock her off her feet. Samantha's knees wanted to bend, not so she could worship him, but so she could press her face to the fly of his jeans and feel what lay beneath…

Tain pinched her chin between his fingers. Merrick had done the same, but while Merrick's presumption had angered her, Tain stunned her to silence.

Tain leaned down and growled into her ear, his voice holding the faint Welsh lilt she remembered, "Stay away from me."

Then he released her, turned on his heel, and strode out of the club.

Chapter Two

"Exactly what the eff happened in there?" Logan asked Samantha hours later.

They sat in Lieutenant McKay's office at the paranormal division headquarters downtown, Logan lounging in his chair, long jean-clad legs stretched out in front of him. He had sand-colored hair, a tall, lean body, a hard face, and gold-brown eyes that became even more golden when he shifted to his wolf.

Samantha shrugged at Logan's question. "Merrick's rivals decided to stage a hit, tonight of all nights."

Demon gangs regularly fought amongst themselves and expected the police to keep out of it. Vampires did the same, although these days a vamp called Septimus kept most things under control in this part of the country.

"No, I meant the *other* guy," Logan said. He twined his hands behind his head. "I saw the rogue demons slide into the place, which was why we came running."

"Bad timing," Lieutenant McKay said. She was one-quarter Sidhe but hadn't inherited their height or much of their powerful magic. She had a small, wiry body, black skin, and close-cropped, tightly curled hair that she liked to dye orange-red. "At least you had presence of mind not to let Merrick get away in the fuss, Sam. We have him on possession of Mindglow at least."

"But not dealing, unfortunately." Samantha sighed. "He can claim his rivals planted anything we find in the club."

"True, but he'll be cagey about it even if we can't get a conviction. Merrick will be out of the Mindglow picture for a while."

"Can we get back to the other guy?" Logan sat forward, bringing the heels of his motorcycle boots to the floor. "I've never seen magic like that. Plus he sliced his swords into Merrick's neck like hot knives through butter, and demons have damned thick necks." Logan turned a sharp glance on Samantha. "He jumped in front of you to protect you, even though it was obvious by that time you knew how to bring Merrick down on your own."

Samantha tried not to move uncomfortably. She didn't want to talk about Tain. Not yet. "Maybe he doesn't like demons." *The understatement of the year.* One had tortured him for hundreds of years and driven him completely insane.

"So he just happened to be in the right place at the right time?" Logan asked, his eyes flashing gold.

"Could be he got a tip-off that Merrick's would be attacked tonight," Samantha suggested. *Nothing to do with me being there. He didn't even recognize me.*

"Right," Logan said. "So he not only killed the demons but snagged Merrick for us in the bargain. Too much of a coincidence for me. I'd say he went in there with some kind of agenda."

Samantha tried to keep her expression neutral. "Why don't you bring him in and question him then?"

"Why don't you?" Logan countered. "He jumped to your aid fast enough. I'd be interested in what he has to say."

"So would I," Lieutenant McKay said. "Killing demons is still considered murder, though we could make a case that this man did it in defense of innocent humans. If he knows something about Merrick or his rivals, I want to hear it."

Samantha thought back to Tain's hot touch on her skin, his rough voice. *Stay away from me.*

"I think you're both optimistic," Samantha said. "Nothing to say we can find the guy again."

"Try anyway," were the lieutenant's encouraging words. "Tonight didn't go exactly as we hoped, but it could have been worse. Go home and sleep, both of you. We'll clean up the mess in the morning."

Dismissed, Logan and Samantha went to their lockers, collected their things and walked out together. Samantha felt Logan's speculative looks as they departed, her partner too astute for her liking.

The Los Angeles night was cool, late September finally taking the edge off the shimmering summer heat. Samantha dragged in a breath of air, pretending to herself that it was fresh and clear, not Los Angeles-polluted.

Logan gave Samantha another one of his discerning glances as they walked through the parking garage. "You all right? You took a good punch in there tonight."

Samantha touched her cheek where Merrick's rings had torn the flesh. Tain's magic had completely healed the wound.

"I'm fine. I just need some rest."

"Want to go for pizza, maybe a movie? Some mindless, fake violence to help us forget about the mindless, real violence?"

Samantha managed a smile, but she knew that if Logan got her relaxed on beer and pizza, he'd persuade her to open up about Tain, and she wasn't ready. She didn't know how long it would be before she was ready, if ever. "Thanks, but what I really need is a hot shower and a soft bed."

Logan shrugged, the movement swift, restless. "Turning wolf makes me jumpy. Enjoy your shower and rest, and I'll see you tomorrow."

"If you go out, be careful." The streets of Los Angeles had calmed down a little in the last year, returning to their usual frenetic pace, but that didn't mean they were safe.

Logan gave her a little grin, the wolf lurking in his eyes. "I'm always careful, sweetheart."

They'd reached Samantha's vehicle by then, a used Toyota pickup. Nothing glamorous for detectives in the LAPD paranormal division. Logan had a pickup as well, but in his spare time he rode a Harley he lovingly tinkered with—days off saw him flying on his bike through mountains and the open desert far to the east of the city.

They said good night and parted. Samantha started up her truck and pulled out of the garage, then made her way slowly out of downtown, always tricky with narrow streets and cars backed up on the freeway ramps. She made it to the 10 heading west and tried to let the drive distract her. She liked driving, in spite of the constant stream of L.A. traffic and the challenges every route brought. Tonight, though, her thoughts couldn't focus, and she was relieved when she reached quieter streets.

The complex that housed Samantha's apartment in west L.A. was decent, with a pool and cherry trees that bloomed in the spring. Her mother had invited her to live at home again in Pasadena, but Samantha's demon father had returned recently, after spending the first twenty-five years of Samantha's life away, and Samantha was still coming to grips with the new dynamic.

Her apartment welcomed her with art posters that gave the generic walls color, comfortable furniture, and a shorthaired black-and-white cat called Pickles. As Samantha closed the door, Pickles leapt from the back of the sofa to the kitchen counter, purring like crazy.

"Cupboard love," Samantha said as she set down her duffle bag and scratched him under the chin. *"I love you, so feed me."*

Pickles shamelessly butted his head against her hand until she picked him up and cuddled him. She set him down again, and he raced expectantly to his food bowl, which she filled with dry cat food.

"I slave, you master," she quipped, but her heart wasn't in it.

While Pickles ate, Samantha showered, letting the hot water and steam in the glass-walled stall relax her. The aroma of soap and lavender permeated the bathroom, and she leaned her head on the glass and breathed it in.

She knew when she went to bed she'd see Tain in her mind—the tall man who'd invaded her dreams for more than a year. She also knew that seeing Tain tonight hadn't been such a big coincidence. His older brother Adrian owned a house in Malibu, and his other brother Hunter and his wife currently resided there—Adrian was living up in Seattle with his own wife. Samantha knew from Hunter's wife, Leda, that Tain visited them from time to time. It was more surprising that Samantha hadn't run across him before this.

She'd resolved not to be bothered that Tain had come to Los Angeles several times and hadn't asked after Samantha, but she couldn't lie to herself anymore. It hurt.

Tain and his four brothers were Immortal warriors, created eons ago, each born of an aspect of the mother goddess and a human man. Their original purpose had been to keep the world safe from the most dangerous creatures— the Old Ones—ancient demons and vampires. When the power of the Old Ones began to fade, so did the calls for the Immortals for help. Now the brothers were all but forgotten.

Seven hundred years ago, Tain had been captured, hidden, and endlessly tortured by an Old One called Kehksut, and his brothers and the witches they'd fallen in love with had battled the demon and gotten Tain free. Samantha had played a part in that battle, and she still had nightmares about it.

Tain had been so maddened by the demon's torture— Kehksut had flayed him, waited for his Immortal body to heal, then done it again, over and over for seven hundred years—that he'd tried to destroy the world to end his own torment. Only the combined effort of his brothers, the witches, and Samantha had restored Tain to freedom and sanity.

Now Samantha's boss wanted to interview Tain. Perfect. Samantha supposed she could call Leda and ask her or Hunter to drive Tain to the LAPD. Samantha wouldn't even have to attend the interview — Logan and McKay could ask Tain about his knowledge of Merrick and the demon underworld by themselves.

Samantha shut off the shower but stood still, letting water trickle from her skin. Unbidden came the memory of Tain rising to face her tonight in the club, his blue eyes like winter skies, and the warmth that had cascaded through her body when he'd healed her.

Shivering, Samantha grabbed towels and dried off. She turbaned her hair in one towel, wrapped another around her torso, and walked out to the kitchen, craving hot coffee and all the microwave food she could handle.

Tain was sitting at her kitchen table.

Samantha jerked back, stifling a scream, and the towel tumbled from her head. Trickles of water dripped down her bare back, chill on her hot skin.

Tain had folded his big body into her kitchen chair, his red hair still mussed from the fight, the ends singed. He rubbed Pickles under the chin with a broad forefinger as her traitorous cat purred up a storm.

"What are you doing in here?" Samantha's voice came out harsh and wrong.

Tain didn't stop rubbing Pickles as his blue gaze took in every inch of her towel-clad body. The gaze unnerved her, and not only because she was all but naked. Samantha saw darkness behind the blue, a hint of madness, which maybe had been too engraved on him to be easily erased. She'd sensed the darkness at the club, and it was stronger here, now that she was alone with him.

"I wanted to talk to you," Tain said. His voice held a lilt, slightly musical with faintly rolled r's.

"Most people knock on the front door," Samantha said, nervousness sharpening her words. "Or are the rules different for Immortals?"

"I did knock."

"I couldn't hear you. I was in . . ."

"The shower." Tain raked his gaze over her again, and Samantha tightened her hold on the towel. "You left the door unlocked."

"No, I—" Samantha broke off. He might be right. She'd been so tired she'd slammed the door, thrown down her stuff, and started the cat-feeding ritual, distracted by thoughts of him. "That doesn't mean you get to walk right in."

"I came because I need help, and you're the only one I could think of to ask."

Samantha stared in surprise. "What, your four Immortals brothers and their kick-ass witch wives aren't good enough?"

"Not that kind of help. I need police help."

Water slid down her face from her wet hair, and Samantha swiped it away. "Stay there." She turned her back and walked quickly to her bedroom, feeling his gaze on her all the way. Samantha closed the door firmly behind her but couldn't quite cut off the sensation.

When she emerged, dressed again, Tain was feeding Pickles tidbits from a can of cat treats. Pickles purred hard, his Geiger-counter buzz filling the room.

Last year, during the battle, Tain had lifted Samantha twenty feet off the ground with his magic, a drop that could have seriously injured or even killed her. He'd not dropped her only because she'd talked fast at him, and he'd become intrigued by their banter—the demon who'd imprisoned Tain had been the cause of Samantha's fall. Now the Immortal who'd so terrified her sat in her kitchen playing gently with her cat.

"His name's Pickles," Samantha said, her voice strained. "Because he likes to eat them."

"That's not what he thinks his name is," Tain said.

"What does he think it is?"

"Master of All He Surveys."

Biting back a hysterical laugh Samantha drew out the chair across the table from Tain and sank into it. "I thought your brother Hunter had the affinity with animals."

"Don't all cats think that's what they should be called?"

He sounded perfectly sane, and except for the spark buried deep in his eyes, he looked sane enough to the untrained eye. He wore jeans and a short-sleeved black T-shirt, and he'd tossed a long leather coat over the back of her couch. His forearms were mottled with scars, though they didn't look as bad as Samantha feared they would. Silky, red-gold hair had grown in across his skin, softening the marks of torture.

"Why were you at Merrick's tonight?" she asked abruptly.

"Two reasons. One of them was to see you."

His eyes were steady when he said it, no lying. Pickles put his paw on Tain's hand, and Tain resumed rubbing the demanding cat's jaw. "I saw you go into Merrick's last night. Surprised me, until I spied your partner waiting down the street, so I figured you were staking out the place. I got there early tonight and planned to follow you when you left."

"How did you even get into a demon club?" Samantha asked, still shaken. "What, they didn't notice you were an Immortal warrior with two long swords?"

"I can hide my aura if I want to," Tain said calmly. "And they're short swords, not long. Late Roman bronze."

"Yeah, well, I'm sure you have a fascinating collection of weapons."

Tain didn't rise to her banter. "You aren't very good at pretending to be a demonwhore. You smiled at Merrick, but it wasn't in your eyes."

Samantha snorted a laugh. "Merrick didn't notice. He was too busy staring at my cleavage."

"I didn't like him doing that." Tain's voice was quiet but with a hard note in it, matching the anger deep in his eyes.

Samantha shrugged. "Have to admit, it almost worked. He was ready to give me the Mindglow."

"He never would have touched you. I'd have stopped him."

Samantha's heart gave a strange beat, but she tried to make her voice light. "And ruined a perfectly good undercover investigation? I was *this* close to bagging him for Mindglow." She held up her forefinger and thumb.

"Merrick is dangerous. Leave him alone."

"I arrested him, in case you didn't notice. Merrick's in custody at a hospital, though he has the best lawyer in Los Angeles, so I'm sure he'll go home as soon as he's healed. Demons make terrific lawyers."

Tain watched her with the stillness of a wild animal before it strikes. "Stay away from him."

Samantha spread her hands. "Moot point. Assignment's over, and we probably won't get him. You said you wanted my help. With what?"

Tain dug out a few more treats for her greedy cat and watched while Pickles ate them. "You've been staking out demon clubs in Venice and Santa Monica, and so have I. That's the second reason I went to Merrick's tonight."

Samantha rubbed her damp hair. "You know, before you left the club, you distinctly told me to leave you alone. What changed between then and now?"

Tain studied his hands, the white scars on the backs of his fingers stark against his brown skin. "I don't want to need your help," he said. "I never wanted to see you again, after Seattle."

"After I saved your ass in Seattle, you mean."

To her surprise Tain gave her a hint of a smile, one that made his eyes warm like a summer sunrise. If she'd thought him handsome before, the smile made him devastating.

Tain exuded power and sensuality, all contained as he sat at Samantha's table teasing her cat. What would it be like to make love to a man like him, his heady power tempered for her? He'd warm her in the dark while she waited for the flash of smile that made him absolutely beautiful. Samantha didn't want to admit it to herself, but she was demon enough that the hint of darkness she sensed inside him would make it all the more exciting.

"My Immortal brothers had something to do with defeating the Old One," he said, still with the trace of smile. "Not to mention the goddesses."

"So they helped me out a little. You left, you know, before I was able to thank you for healing my arm."

The smile faded. "Nothing I didn't do for anyone else."

"Adrian told me your magical talent was healing. I'm surprised you're not running through the world curing AIDS and cancer and everything else."

"It doesn't work quite like that," he said in all seriousness. "If it did, I would."

They studied each other for a moment in silence, before Samantha cleared her throat. "Let's get back to the question at hand," she said. "What was it that you wanted my help with?"

Tain's eyes flickered in relief at the change of subject. "In the last couple months several demon prostitutes have gone missing in the area around Merrick's club. They're very young women, freelance, not associated with the clubs as far as I know." He leaned forward, his eyes taking on that unnerving intensity. "But they're disappearing, and I want to know why."

Chapter Three

Samantha's surprise returned. She got up and started coffee, definitely needing a caffeine fix. "I'd think you'd be the last person worried about the well-being of demon prostitutes."

She heard silence behind her and turned to see Tain watching her with an indecipherable expression. "You mean, because I was tortured mercilessly by Kehksut?" he asked in a deceptively mild voice. "And now I should hate all demon-kind?"

"Something like that."

Samantha waited for the machine to finish and took two mugs of steaming coffee to the table. "I have sweetener if you want it."

Tain shook his head, wrapped his strong hand around the mug, and took a gulp of the coffee.

"Damn, you *must* be all powerful," Samantha said as she watched the swallow move down his throat. "You didn't even have to blow on it."

She'd hoped to prod another smile from him, but his look turned grim. "If I'd wanted to destroy all demon-kind in revenge I would have killed every demon in that club tonight—the attackers, Merrick . . ."

He left it hanging but Samantha heard the unsaid word . . . *You.*

"Good thing you need my help then," Samantha said, swallowing her nervousness. "And that I looked so good in that dress."

Tain's gaze flicked over her again, although now she wore a fairly shapeless sweatshirt and loose jeans. "You did, yes."

Samantha's face heated. She had no business thinking sexual thoughts about him, but then, he was a hard-bodied man with intense blue eyes, and he'd made her feel so incredible when he'd healed her. What woman, half demon or not, could help it?

"So why *are* you worried about these prostitutes?" she asked quickly. "They usually solicit for the clubs, for bosses like Merrick, although some go out on their own. As long as there's no actual sex involved, and no complete essence draining, it's legal."

"Four girls have gone missing in the last two weeks," Tain said.

Samantha's eyes widened. "That many?" She hadn't heard of the disappearances, not that she necessarily would. Los Angeles was a big city—she worked for the western division of the paranormal police, which handled what went on in Venice—and many people wouldn't bother to report missing prostitutes, especially demon ones. "But maybe it's not such a mystery. They might have decided to move to a different part of the city, they might be lying low because they're pregnant or sick, or they might have decided to get out of the game. It happens."

Tain gave her a stubborn look. "It feels wrong. I can't explain more than that."

Samantha sat back. "Well, if you were anyone else, I'd say you were worried for nothing. Since you're a big bad Immortal warrior, I won't. I learned the hard way what happens when I don't pay attention to an Immortal's feelings." She let out a breath and reached for her coffee. "It won't hurt for me to look into it."

"Thank you."

Tain's lips were stiff as he spoke the words. She wondered how long he'd debated with himself before deciding to seek her out and ask for help.

"Why come to me?" Samantha asked after they'd sipped coffee in silence a few moments. "Why not go to the police yourself? Our paranormal division is big—you wouldn't have had to talk to me at all."

Tain met her gaze with his piercing one. "Because I knew you'd believe me."

Damn, his eyes were beautiful. They were like pieces of the sky, so blue they could make her cry. Samantha pictured looking into those eyes up close, while he slanted his head to kiss her . . .

Her heart beat faster, and she spoke swiftly to cover her confusion. "You could have come to the police department and asked for me, you know. You didn't have to follow me home."

"I didn't follow you home."

That relieved her. She hadn't had the prickly sensation of someone behind her after she'd left the station, although Tain could probably track like a panther.

"How did you find me then? Magic?"

Tain's face softened into his devastating smile as he lifted the coffee to his lips. "No. I just called Leda, and she gave me your address."

***

A few hours later, Tain leaned his head against the wall of his tiny shower and let the water beat on his body.

He hadn't wanted to go to Samantha. He'd never wanted to see her again, with her dark soul-searching eyes and her beautiful face that floated in his dreams.

After I saved your ass in Seattle, she'd said, and he'd wanted to laugh and laugh.

She'd never know how well she'd saved him—her voice, her words, and her *presence* had yanked him out of the darkness, where he'd lived for centuries. She'd wrenched his focus away from the demon who'd held him captive, and that break had allowed Tain's brothers to band together to save him.

In the end, everyone seemed to have expected him to sweep Samantha into his arms, but Tain had barely been able to touch her.

When he'd healed her after the battle, their connection had been powerful. She'd melded to him in a way he hadn't felt in eons, their essences connecting while his magic knit her bones.

He'd sensed the tug of joy that surged through her body, and the temptation to take her and run had overwhelmed him. He hadn't been able to get away from her fast enough.

A year and more had passed since that day in late May when he'd finally gained his freedom. He'd supposed the memories of the battle and Samantha would pass, but fifteen months later, they were as fresh as ever.

The water started to cool, his hot water reserve gone, but Tain remained in the shower, letting the needle-sharp spray batter his flesh. Samantha was half demon, and he felt the siren call of that species pull at him. Never again, he'd vowed. He'd survived his captivity by retreating into madness, by grabbing on to the pain and twisting it into something he could take.

Never again.

He shut off the faucet and stood with his forehead against the wall, his naked body covered with beads of water. He wanted so much for Samantha to be in here with him, where he could press his mouth to her skin, run his hands up the curves of her body, feel her breasts in the cup of his hands.

Tain indulged himself in the imagined sensations, but too soon dark memories of madness and pain seeped through and shoved them away. He'd managed, with the help of his brothers, to heal somewhat over the past year. He'd learned to go still when the blackness punched at his gut, as it had fighting the demons tonight, to breathe deeply until it left him.

But there were the times he didn't tell his brothers about, when he couldn't stop himself folding into a ball, screaming with pain that threatened to squeeze the life out of him. He drifted to the bottom of his shower now, wrapping his arms around himself, not feeling the chill of cold water on his skin. He clenched his teeth to contain the roar of anguish that wanted to escape him. His teeth nicked his lip, and hot blood filled his mouth

You are mine. Kehksut's voice whispered in his memory. *You belong to me, body and soul. I will use you as I please, and you will love me for it.*

"*No!*" The word shot out of Tain's mouth along with droplets of blood that swirled down the vortex of the drain.

Tain's cheek burned, his pentagram tattoo like a badge of fire. The mark had saved him from being lost forever, keeping a tiny part of himself beyond Kehksut's reach.

Samantha had zeroed in on that piece of him with her voice and her defiance. After she'd made a chink in his defenses, Tain's brothers had torn him open the rest of the way and dragged him kicking and screaming into the light.

His brothers, damn the four of them, still loved him and watched over him. They wanted him to be all better, and it hurt Tain that he couldn't be back to normal for them.

He closed his eyes and fought the pain. Finally, finally, the darkness began to recede, and he dragged himself to his feet, snapping off the water and looking down at his body.

After episodes like this he was always surprised to find no blood on himself, that his scarred skin remained unbroken. He reached for a towel with a shaking hand and mopped water from his face.

He'd spent the last year looking for people to help and heal, righting the wrongs he could to make up for the horrible things he'd done under the demon's thrall. The missing demon prostitutes had caught his attention because the situation was unusual, bringing Tain something new to focus on.

Demons were not chaotic people; they were precise and methodic and rarely did anything without calculation. Four girls missing for no apparent reason showed a flaw in the system, and an anomaly could mean trouble to more than just the demons.

Tain regarded himself in the misted mirror as he plied the towel. Every inch of his body was scored with scars. His face had been spared, partly because of Tain's power-infused tattoo, partly because Kehksut had wanted Tain's looks to remain unmarred.

Tain had Immortal flesh, ever renewed, and because he hadn't been tortured every few days for a while now, the scars had faded into faint white lines. His seven-foot body rippled with muscle, unbroken. He was still a warrior.

He held the towel around his neck, remembering Samantha emerging from her bedroom, damp from her shower. He'd seen a lush, long-legged woman with slim arms and rounded breasts, beautiful black eyes staring at him in startled amazement from under slick black hair.

Tain had hardened then, and he was hardening now, his cock rising quickly from a thatch of dark red hair. His penis bore no scars either — the other part of him the demon had never cut.

Tain had craved to be with Samantha in Seattle, and he wanted her now. But the thought of sex was so overlaid with the memories of torture he wasn't certain he'd ever be able to make love to a woman again. If he dared take Samantha to bed, would the pain make him crazy, and would he hurt her? Samantha wasn't just a woman, she was part demon — no telling what Tain would do to her, reacting to the natural darkness within her.

Best to never find out. Tain would thank her for her help and walk away. It was the only way he'd survive contact with her.

Tain finished drying himself, dressed, and went out into the cool dawn streets of Los Angeles. It took a long time for his erection to fade.

***

"Whatcha working on?" Logan turned a plastic chair around and straddled it backwards, gazing at the profusion of files on Samantha's desk. "That's not the Mindglow case."

"I know."

Samantha had been sifting through reports of missing demon girls, then through police records to see if any of those women had been arrested for soliciting. So far, she hadn't turned up much.

"How long have we been partners, Sam?" Logan asked her.

Samantha opened another file. "A year or so."

During the terrible happenings last year, the police department had basically shut down and let the vampire and demon gangs take over the streets, fighting each other without interference. Laws keeping vampire and demon activity under control had gone to hell, and people had been hurt and killed.

When Samantha had returned home from Seattle, the city had been busy trying to get back to normal—as normal as Los Angeles ever got—and Lieutenant McKay had begged Samantha, who'd been let go during the crisis, to come back to work. They needed every detective they could get their hands on, she said. Samantha decided that diving back into what she was good at would help her recover, and besides, she needed the paycheck.

McKay had paired her up with Logan Wright, who'd recently moved to Los Angeles from Minnesota. Logan was a Were—a wolf. He was smart and laid back, exactly the kind of person Samantha needed to spend her ten-hour shifts with. Logan never pried or asked nosy questions; he simply worked on cases or drove the two of them around the city with the quiet enjoyment of someone who liked being on the road.

Logan came from a pack in Minnesota he never talked about. Werewolves weren't Samantha's specialty, but she knew enough about them to know one didn't move far from the pack without good reason. Werewolves had difficulty emotionally leaving the close-knit confines of their families. Yet here was Logan, whistling tunes and driving Samantha around the freeways of Los Angeles, seemingly without a care.

Samantha had found herself making friends with Logan, not telling him her secrets but gradually working through the fears that had swirled through her since Seattle. But she'd never been able to mention Tain.

"A year is a long time in this job," Logan said. "Something's happened, Sam, so spill it."

Samantha closed the folder and looked up at him. "I got a tip I thought I should look into."

"A tip." Logan's wolf eyes narrowed. "About what? This red-haired guy, the killing machine? Do you know where to start looking for him?"

"No." Tain had left her apartment without disclosing where he was staying, saying Samantha could leave a message with Leda if she needed to reach him. "But I talked to him."

Logan's brows climbed. "Yeah? When was this?"

"Last night after I got home."

Logan sat up straight. "Shit, Samantha. Were you going to bother to tell anyone? Were you going to bother to tell *me?*"

Samantha busied herself gathering the folders into a neat stack. "I don't think he knows anything about Merrick's gang wars, or cares very much. He's the kind of man who will gladly let evil demons kill other evil demons."

"Shouldn't you let McKay question him before you decide that?"

Samantha sighed and slammed the last folders to the pile. "All right, if you'll stop second-guessing me and buy me a pizza, I'll give you what he *did* tell me."

Logan conceded and paid for lunch at the pizza place across the street. Over the pepperoni and sausage, Samantha told him about Tain's surprise visit and his report of the missing prostitutes. She left out the part about finding him sitting at her table when she came out of the shower, not to mention her physical and emotional reactions to him.

Logan listened, leaning his elbows on the table with his usual nonchalance, but she saw the interest on his face. "We should question Merrick," he said. "He's got an eye on all the demon businesses in that area. Owns half of them."

"He's still in the hospital." As Samantha had predicted, the D.A.'s office had already dismissed Merrick's case, saying they didn't have anything that would stick. "McKay and I had time this morning to ask Merrick only one question before his lawyer got there, and he didn't even answer that."

"We don't have to make it an official inquiry," Logan said, peeling a pepperoni from his slice and dropping it into his mouth. "Just a friendly chat. What hospital?"

"You're saying *we*."

"Doing Mindglow stakeouts for months on end is getting on my nerves," Logan said. "I need a new hobby. Besides, if the girls worked the streets near Merrick's, who's to say it's not connected?"

Samantha let out a breath. "To tell you the truth, I'd welcome the help."

"That's settled then." Logan wiped grease from his hand and held it out for her to shake. "Partners in crime-solving."

She grinned as she took his hand. Logan always knew how to defuse a moment. "I thought we already were partners."

"Okay, partners in crime-solving for cases we aren't assigned to. We'll get suspended together."

"You're all heart, Logan."

Logan winked at her. "That's why the girls love me."

***

After lunch, they went to the downtown hospital specializing in demon care only to discover that Merrick had been released that morning, right after McKay and Samantha had tried to question him. Demons healed quickly, but Samantha hadn't thought they healed *that* quickly. Merrick's neck had been nearly severed.

Logan didn't comment when Samantha suggested they drive all the way to Venice, to Merrick's club. Merrick lived in the penthouse above it, and he'd likely be home convalescing.

Venice—named by its developer back in the 1920s for the little canals that crisscrossed the area—was a different place during the day than it was in darkest night, when the vamp and demon clubs did their business. Tourists and locals in T-shirts and shorts streamed down the colorful streets to the beach. Blue sky arched overhead, the September sun warm.

Merrick's club was closed, the smoked glass doors shut and locked. Samantha banged on them, Logan standing just a little behind her left shoulder.

"We're closed," the bartender said as he pulled open the door a crack. "But you know that."

"I want to talk to Merrick," Samantha said, flashing her badge and ID.

"He's busy. Talk to his lawyer."

The bartender started to shut the door, but Logan put his foot in it and gave the demon man a warning look.

"Not about last night," Samantha said. "This is unofficial. By the way, you don't happen to know who those demons were that busted up the place, do you?"

"Nope."

"Or whose clan they belonged to? I'd like to have a chat with them as well."

The bartender's eyes narrowed. Like all demons, he had a handsomeness that went deeper than physical attraction, one that compelled a person to look into his eyes and crave what he had to give.

"Merrick really is busy talking to someone else," the bartender said. "He's pretty pissed off at you, anyway."

"Because I arrested him? I'm surprised he didn't see it coming."

"Yeah, well." The bartender turned as someone called to him from the darkened interior. "What do you know?" he said, turning back to Samantha. "I'm supposed to let you in."

Logan looked uncomfortable as they ducked inside, uneasy in a place created by demons for demons. Werewolves were creatures of intense life magic, and large doses of death magic made Logan's fur itch.

He looked as though his fur was itching badly as they followed the bartender through a private door and into an elevator that took them up four floors above the club. The bartender ushered them into a sunny penthouse, which contained a wall of windows showing the panorama of the beach and dark-blue ocean.

Merrick, on the sofa, was indeed speaking to someone in his lush living room. Tall and broad-shouldered, his life magic a physical force, Merrick's guest turned from the windows, sunlight glinting on his red hair. Samantha halted in the doorway, and Logan almost ran into her.

"That's him," Logan said with a growl. "The guy from last night."

Samantha made herself enter the apartment, though she moved numbly. Tain stood with perfect nonchalance, but he had the dark glint in his eyes again. Obviously being in a place permeated with death magic made him even jumpier than Logan.

Tain flicked his gaze over Samantha, his eyes as blue as the ocean behind him. This man possessed powerful magic and incredible strength. He could do anything to her, to Merrick, even to Logan, without any of them being able to stop him. Samantha knew she should be afraid—and she was—but at the same time Tain commanded her attention, her fascination, and wouldn't let it go.

Tain moved his stare to Logan. "You're a werewolf."

"No kidding," Logan answered. "Who are you?"

"The man who so thoughtfully busted up my club," Merrick interrupted in his usual smooth tones. "Wonderfully good for business, fried demons."

"When your rivals busted up your club, you mean," Logan said. "We pretty much saved your ass, Merrick."

Merrick gave Logan a cold look and gestured for Samantha to sit down. "Tell me what you're doing here and why my lawyer shouldn't start a suit for police harassment."

"I wanted to talk to you about something completely different," Samantha said. "Maybe if you help me on this, I'll forget about the Mindglow."

"And what Mindglow would that be?" Merrick asked in perfect innocence.

Samantha restrained herself from rolling her eyes. "Maybe you could help out of the goodness of your heart."

Merrick smiled. "My evil demon heart?"

"That's the one."

"I already asked him," Tain interrupted. "He says might be able to help."

"Oh." Samantha blinked. "I see."

"Why don't we sit down and discuss it?" Logan asked. Logan was a master at easing a tense situation, which made Samantha wonder anew what had wound him up enough to leave his pack.

Logan led Samantha to a chair, glancing up uneasily, as though expecting the ceiling to come crashing down on them any moment. Samantha alone of the visitors didn't cringe at the press of death magic, although she could feel it.

Merrick lounged on his sofa, pretending to be perfectly at ease. He wore a casual but finely tailored suit, the scarf around his neck hiding his injury from the previous night. The living room was comfortable and showy at the same time, with satin-soft leather chairs and shelves filled with crystal sculptures. The Hockney over the sofa appeared to be genuine.

Samantha and Logan sat down, but Tain remained standing, turning his back on them again to gaze out the floor-to-ceiling windows to the vast Pacific beyond.

"Your *friend* here says the missing prostitutes were freelance," Merrick said. "And they might have been. But I knew one of them, a little sweetheart from the Lamiah clan, out on her own."

Samantha jumped, and at the same time Logan asked, "Where can we find someone from this Lamiah clan, to ask about her?"

Merrick gave him a smug smile. "One is sitting right here. Our dear Samantha is Lamiah."

Tain turned and shot Samantha a sharp look, and Samantha tensed. "How did you know I was Lamiah?" she asked Merrick. "That my father is, I mean."

"You are too, Samantha, my dear. There's no getting away from your roots. When I learned to my horror last night that you were not a little morsel I could eat up, but a police detective, I had my lawyer do some research on you, you half-demon vixen. How exciting to find you come from my own clan."

Logan's eyes narrowed. "Wait a minute, you mean you two are related?"

"No," Samantha said quickly. "Clans are made up of many different families. The families that formed clans in the distant past weren't necessarily related by blood. They came together for protection or for strength. According to what my father's been trying to teach me, that is."

"But we still have a connection," Merrick said, his smile in place.

"And a matriarch," Tain broke in. "All demon clans have matriarchs. She might know something about the missing girls."

Merrick laughed again. "You're kidding, right? No demon matriarch is going to talk to *you*, Immortal one. You with your stink of life magic."

"What is she going to do?" Tain asked, blue eyes steady. "Kill me?"

"Such wit," Merrick said. "Is everyone at home like you?"

Merrick didn't know the half of what Tain's family was like, Samantha reflected. "Why did you let Tain in here if he reeks of life magic?" she asked him. "Which I agree, he does." Magic sparkled under Tain's skin, power so strong he could take out the building with one flick of his finger.

Samantha had learned in her job that life magic didn't necessarily mean *good*. A life-magic creature was sustained by life and light, unlike vampires and demons, who lived by feeding on death. Samantha had lived and worked in Los Angeles long enough to know that good and evil didn't always fall into neat categories.

"I'm guessing Tain healed you this morning, didn't he?" Samantha asked Merrick. "That's why you were released from the hospital so quickly."

"Correct," Merrick said. "*Some* people are willing to pay for answers."

"I'm not paying you anything, Merrick. I'm a cop. You help me because I tell you to."

Merrick shook his head. "I'm disappointed in you, Sam. You tricked me into thinking you liked me. I almost fell for it, you know. I'd decided to make you one of my own."

Samantha did her best not to shudder. "No thanks." When a demon took a human as his own, it basically meant he became her Dom. He took care of her and gave her everything she wanted—cars, jewelry, a job—and in turn she gave the demon her life essence whenever he needed a fix. Demon women did likewise with human men. Samantha had seen demons subs, glassy-eyed men or women who would do anything for their masters.

"Of course, I'm not about to ask you now, you two-faced bitch," Merrick said.

Tain lifted his hand and sent an almost casual trickle of white magic from his fingers to wrap around Merrick's throat. Merrick's next words were choked off and he started to gasp, then to claw at his throat. Still he managed to shoot Samantha an interested look. "Oh, is *that* how it is?" he managed to rasp.

"Returning to the point," Logan broke in firmly. He sat forward on his chair, leaning his elbows on his thighs. "Why do you think we need to talk to a clan matriarch, not just the girl's family?"

Tain lowered his hand, and the light around Merrick's throat vanished. Merrick rubbed his neck, sucking in deep breaths.

"Because it might have been an honor killing," Tain rumbled.

Samantha raised her brows. "The clan objecting to the girl taking to the streets on her own?"

"The Immortal one is possibly right," Merrick said, his voice still hoarse. "Brawn *and* brains, can you believe it?" He cleared his throat. "The clan wouldn't so much object to her selling her services as not selling them for the benefit of the clan. Plus, some families can be very old-fashioned, especially about their women, and like them to stay close to home. Then again, a gang boss might have grown angry at her for striking out on her own."

"And that boss was not you?" Logan asked.

Merrick shrugged, his voice restored. "Any young woman who works for me or in my clubs is treated well. They never desert me."

"Do the demons who work for you come from different clans?" Logan asked. "Or only yours?"

"I welcome people from all clans, and we manage to be close, despite familial differences. I like to say that Merrick's place is a little clan away from clan."

"Very funny," Samantha said.

Merrick gave her a deprecating look. "Are you this diplomatic interviewing all your witnesses? You could take a few pointers from your werewolf friend. See? He's not even breaking into fur and claws."

"I find no need to be hostile," Logan said mildly. "Yet."

"Set up the meeting," Tain broke in. Samantha sensed his impatience, could almost see it rippling from him. "Contact Samantha when everything is in place. This interview is over."

Merrick contemplated Tain a moment, his eyes speaking volumes. "Not quite yet, my friend," he said. "There's something else I need from our dear Samantha. Something of utmost importance."

Chapter Four

Tain had to get out of the room. Not only did the death magic of this entire building pound at him, but there was Samantha.

Her black-hued aura enclosed her like silk; her coffee-colored eyes did their best to draw him in. She suppressed her demon side, obviously uncomfortable with it, yet Tain could see it in her, darkness waiting for any excuse to get out. He knew Merrick could see it now too—Merrick kept looking at Samantha as though he wanted to devour her. Tain couldn't blame him, as much as Merrick's focus on her stirred him to rage.

"What is it?" Samantha asked, her skepticism plain. "This thing of utmost importance?"

Merrick rose and strolled to a desk on the other side of the room, shuffled through some papers, and brought a few sheets back to Samantha, thrusting them at her.

"I've been getting these delightful messages for the past couple weeks. I'm used to volatile letters from demon haters, and I dutifully turn the missives over to the police. But these are different."

Samantha took the sheets and read each one, her brows drawing into a becoming frown. She passed the papers to Logan, who looked them over and then handed them to Tain without Tain having to ask.

The messages were simple. On each sheet, letters cut from newspaper headlines spelled out, *Your doom is coming.*

"When did you get the first one?" Samantha asked Merrick.

"Two weeks ago. On the 23rd of August, to be precise. The other two arrived about five days apart."

Tain scanned for any magic clinging to the papers but found none. He felt the hatred of whoever had cut and pasted the letters lingering on the sheets, but many people hated and feared demons.

"Why warn you?" Logan asked. "If they want to come after you, why put you on guard?"

"I imagine they're trying to frighten me," Merrick said. "A pathetic attempt. I'm not frightened by cutouts from newspapers. Take them if you want—test for fingerprints or DNA, or whatever it is you do."

"Do you have the envelopes?"

Merrick fetched them—postmarked Los Angeles, though Tain wasn't familiar enough with the city to pair the zip code with a particular area.

Logan took the papers and envelopes and tucked them into his pocket. He and Samantha rose to leave, but Merrick said, "Sam," and beckoned her aside.

Tain was not about to walk out of the room and leave Samantha with Merrick, and he saw that Logan wouldn't either. Both men waited tensely in the open doorway while Merrick murmured something into Samantha's ear.

Samantha reddened but otherwise didn't look distressed. She turned away from Merrick without a word, not even a good-bye, and squeezed past Tain and Logan to walk out to the elevator.

"What did he say?" Logan asked her as they emerged from the back door of the demon club and into the sunshine.

The September air was warm, and Samantha's face took on a sheen of perspiration. She wiped at the droplets on her upper lip, but Tain wanted to still her hands, lean to her, and lick the moisture away.

"Nothing helpful." Samantha's black hair shimmered as she stopped at a small black pickup brushed with Logan's life-magic aura.

"What did he say that was *un*helpful then?" Logan asked.

Samantha looked at Logan and Tain, and then shook her head. "Could the pair of you possibly exude any more testosterone? It was about my father, and no, I'm not going to tell you what."

Logan let it go and opened the driver's side door. "Can we drop you anywhere?" he asked Tain.

Tain looked at the vehicle, at Samantha's hair shining in the sunlight, at the way her eyes creased in the corners with her half smile. He imagined sitting in the cab of the truck, breathing in her scent, watching her turn to say something to Logan, feeling her dark aura brush him. He'd tangle in it and never want to stop.

"No," he said abruptly, and turned and walked away.

***

The young demon woman was called Nadia. She stood with her hands cuffed behind her back and gazed with disdain on her captors as they discussed what to do with her. Her long black hair had been cut off and thrown away, her clothes disposed of.

At first they'd taken away her ability to assume her demon form, and at the moment, Nadia was too weak and sick to do anything but glare. Now, they *wanted* her to change to her demon form, and because they wanted her to, she refused.

Demons were difficult to kill, but not impossible. The methods Nadia's captors discussed showed they'd done their homework—they debated burning her, or beheading her, or tearing out her heart. Nadia stood with her chin lifted, though her body was cold with fear. These people knew how to kill.

Her captors wore masks, and the room was dark, but she knew there were two women and a man. Outside the room, more men lurked, and they had guns. Nadia would be mown down if she tried to run, and though the bullets might not kill her, they'd injure her enough that she'd be unable to get away.

"We could send her back as a warning," one of the women suggested.

"We could send her *head* back as a warning," the man growled.

"There have been too many warnings," the second woman broke in. Nadia didn't like her—her voice was far too chill and dangerous. "We need to stop warning them and start moving."

"Are we ready for that?" the man asked.

"We're ready enough."

"Just hurry up and kill me," Nadia snapped. "I'm getting bored."

The man grabbed her by what was left of her hair. "We'll do what we want, demon bitch."

She spit in his face. He threw her on the floor and kicked her. "Change," he snarled. "Show us what you really are."

Nadia knew they wanted her to change because they wanted to slice off her head while she was in demon form and display it like a trophy.

She refused. If they killed her, the human police would find her like this, looking human, beaten and tied, and be appalled. Sympathy would be with *her*, not her captors. But if her captors displayed a slain demon carcass, people might rejoice, or at the very least say she had it coming.

"Stop," the woman said sternly. "We'll do it tonight, in front of her sister."

Nadia's rage surged. "You leave her out of this, you stupid fucks."

The man stopped kicking her. He backed away, leaving Nadia bruised and hurting on the floor. "Yes," he said almost reverently. "She will be witness."

Nadia lay curled in on herself, a cold fear in her heart that had nothing to do with the certainty of her own death.

***

Tain prowled the streets as the sun went down, preferring the teeming darkness of the city to returning alone to his tiny apartment. Leda and Hunter had invited him to stay with them in Adrian's Malibu house, but Tain had declined.

Spending an evening with Leda and Hunter and their infant son could soothe him, especially whenever Tain held his energetic and fearless nephew between his large hands. He marveled at the child's innocence and innate strength, sensing in small Ryan a power that would eclipse his parents' one day. But though Tain could banter with Hunter and enjoy Leda's warm friendliness, there was still some part of him they never could reach.

Worse than that, Tain didn't trust himself around them. What would happen if he succumbed to the dark madness that still lurked in his mind? Tain was stronger than Hunter—he'd emerged from Kehksut's torture possessing more power than the rest of the Immortals put together. Hunter and Leda wouldn't be able to stop him, and there was baby Ryan, so small and vulnerable. If Tain succumbed to darkness, his family would suffer for it. Best he stay as far from them as possible.

The haunting streets of Los Angeles better suited his moods. The city had many different spectrums melding into one another—opulent neighborhoods for billionaires existed blocks away from gang-controlled slums. People from every human race found a home here, and magical species also converged, especially those who preferred a nighttime existence. Vampires and demons were most prevalent, along with other death-magic creatures.

Werewolves preferred open country, as did the Sidhe and other magical beings more tied to nature. Why Samantha's werewolf partner Logan was in Los Angeles was anyone's guess, and how the man tolerated working with a half demon was another puzzle.

People, human and otherwise, generally left Tain alone, whether he sat by himself on the bus or wandered while city lights began to gleam in the dark. They knew danger when they saw it, and the tall man in a duster, jeans, and motorcycle boots radiated danger with a capital D.

Tain's wandering took him up Wilshire Boulevard to MacArthur Park, a place where vampire and demon territory overlapped. If trouble happened at night, it would be here or nearby.

Tain could dampen his glow of life magic if he wanted to — something he'd learned during his years as Kehksut's prisoner. He'd learned many things as Kehksut had turned him into a monster, and now the most dangerous thing in MacArthur Park tonight was Tain.

Last year, if he'd chosen, Tain could have imprisoned his brothers forever and let the world go to hell. He'd never told them that. He let them believe they'd saved their baby brother with their collective power, that he was all right, that he just needed time to readjust.

He smiled grimly. His brothers could never understand the torment, both physical and mental, he'd endured. Recovering from endless torture wasn't the same as getting over a bout of the flu — if Immortals ever got the flu.

Tain spotted a vampire crossing a narrow street, the creature's dark aura like a smudge around his body. The vamp ducked into an alley, and after a moment, Tain sensed his gloating.

Vampires paid a stiff penalty for accosting humans outside legitimate vamp clubs, and for drinking a human's blood without consent. But the law didn't forbid the undead from preying on each other, and in the back streets there was little enforcement of the "consent" rule.

Tain jogged across the street into the alley the vamp had disappeared down. He saw the vamp fairly soon—he had his hand around a woman's throat, and was holding her against a wall. She was naked, struggling, and Tain smelled a hint of brimstone. Demon.

The demon woman fought pathetically, surprisingly not changing to her demon form to try to rip the vamp's head from his shoulders. The vampire had his fangs out, but he was no longer only interested in her blood—he likely planned to rape her, kill her, or both.

Tain shed his duster and drew his short swords from their crossed sheaths. "You have three seconds to run," he told the vampire in a calm voice.

The vamp whipped his head around and looked Tain up and down. His lips drew back from his fangs, his eyes bottomless pits of blackness. "What the hell are *you*?"

"One Mississippi . . ." Tain began as he advanced. "Two Mississippi . . ."

The vampire continued to stare. The demon girl hung limply in the vampire's grasp, wretched and terrified.

"Three Mississ . . ." Tain let his power glow, white snakes of it twining around his sword blades.

The vampire's eyes widened. He dropped the demon girl and spun toward Tain, assuming a fighting stance.

"No, I really meant *run*." Tain pointed one of his swords at the vamp. Blue-white light shot from its tip, striking the vampire fully in the chest and sending him flying. The next burst wrapped around the vampire, picked him up, turned him around, and gave him a hard shove.

The vampire finally got the idea and fled down the alley, the sound of his footsteps quickly swallowed by city noise. The demon girl tried to slip into the shadows in his wake.

"Not you." Tain wrapped white magic around her and gently held her in place. "Let's have a look at you."

The woman shrank against the wall, arms crossed over her body in an attempt to cover herself. She was naked except for a pair of underwear that had seen better days, and someone had cut off her hair. Her dark eyes were haunted, the hands that cupped her shoulders brown with dried blood.

"I left it," she said, tears trickling down her cheeks. "I left it. I didn't know what to do."

Tain sheathed his swords. He retrieved his duster and wrapped it around her shivering body, letting his healing touch close the small abrasions on her face.

"What are you doing?" She cringed from him. "You're life magic."

"I don't pick and choose those I heal." Tain brushed his fingers over her hair, but stopped himself from sliding his magic directly into her demon aura. Some things he still couldn't bear to do. "What happened to you?"

"My sister . . . I can't leave it."

"Leave what?" Tain gentled his voice, his Welsh lilt pronounced, and traced his finger over the bruises on her throat the vampire had left.

"They killed her," she said in a choked voice. "They were supposed to kill me. I couldn't stop them."

"Couldn't stop who? Who did this?"

She tried to wipe away her tears, but her hand shook too much. "You don't care. You're life magic."

"I do care," Tain insisted.

The demon woman fell silent, weeping in quiet hiccups.

Samantha, I need you.

The thought came out of nowhere, as though someone had put it into Tain's mind. With it came an image of Samantha's smooth face, her dark eyes, red lips curving into one of her sardonic smiles.

Tain did need her, right now at least in her capacity as a detective in LAPD's paranormal division. This was the kind of problem she could solve.

"I'm going to summon someone who can help you," Tain said.

Or whatever was the jargon for telling Samantha to come. In the seven hundred years since Tain had been taken prisoner, the world had changed. Gone were buildings of stone heated by burning peat or wood, rooms that were warm only near the fire. This city had houses of brick, thin wood, and stucco, yet the buildings were cool against the summer heat and flooded with artificial light. People now cooked without fire and washed away the remains of their meals in a complicated mass of pipes.

Seven hundred years ago, Tain might have summoned a half demon with his magic — now he pulled out a cell phone and flipped it open. Leda, who'd given him the phone, had programmed Samantha's number into it for him.

When Leda had handed Tain the phone, she'd smiled and said, "I'm going to teach one of you Immortals to use a cell phone if it's the last thing I do. Keep it on you and stay in touch."

Tain didn't like the annoying little devices, but he humored his new sister-in-law. It took him two or three tries to figure out which buttons to push, but soon he heard Samantha's breathless voice. "Hello?"

"Samantha," he said, one hand lightly on the weeping girl's shoulder. "I need you."

***

Samantha angled her truck across the end of the alley and stopped, letting its headlights flood the narrow passage.

She'd been driving home when her cell phone had rung, and she'd pulled into a convenience store parking lot and answered. When she'd heard Tain say, *I need you,* her heart had squeezed with near pain. She'd instantly imagined him saying that to her in the darkness of a bedroom, his hand on her hair as he lay against her.

I'm crazy, Samantha told herself as she got out of the truck. *He hates demons. He's touched me with his healing power, and I'm reacting to that. Nothing more.*

She kept her hand on the butt of her Glock as she hurried down the darkened alley to where Tain crouched on the filthy pavement, facing a young woman huddled in his duster coat. Samantha felt a brief stab of envy. She'd love to be the one wrapped in a coat that held Tain's warmth while he gazed at her so intently

The envy evaporated when she got a good look at the young woman. She was a demon, but her demon-beautiful face was covered with scabbed-over cuts, her hair crudely chopped off in uneven hanks.

Samantha knelt next to Tain, gentling her voice to not startle the young woman. "What happened?"

"Her name is Nadia," Tain said.

Nadia had been crying, tears streaking the dirt on her face. "I don't know who they were."

Tain related in a few brief sentences how he'd followed a vamp down this alley and found her. "She won't talk to me."

Samantha found that surprising. If Tain had draped his coat over Samantha's shoulders and given her comfort, she'd be pouring her heart out to him.

Samantha slid her ID and badge from her pocket and held them so the girl could see. "I'm paranormal police. You need to tell me what happened to you."

"Not here," Nadia said, her voice hoarse. "They took me, and Bev. They killed Bev and sent me back to take it home."

"It?" Samantha glanced at Tain, but he shook his head. "Take what home, Nadia?"

"I left it over there." She pointed with a grimy finger down the alley.

Samantha started to rise, but Tain said, "No, let me."

He strode swiftly through the trash-strewn alley until he stopped a few yards away. He stared at the ground a moment, then leaned down and picked up a small canvas bag.

Tain carried the bag back to them, holding it out from his body as though it might explode. Samantha caught a stink of death and terror.

Nadia moaned and covered her face. "I couldn't stop them. I should have stopped them."

Tain unzipped the bag and pulled it open. Samantha gasped and took a step back, bile rising in her throat. A heart lay on blood-stained cloths inside, black and horrible.

"It's Bev's," the girl sobbed. "My sister. They killed her."

***

"This one is going to keep us up all night," Lieutenant McKay said in her office. Samantha had brought Nadia and the grisly evidence back downtown, and Nadia had been given medical attention, clothes, and something to eat.

Samantha had half expected Tain to leave as soon as they reached the paranormal division headquarters, but he'd accompanied her to McKay's office. He'd said nothing, simply followed Samantha upstairs.

"Forensics has the heart," the lieutenant said. "But there isn't much doubt that it came from a demon woman. A killing like that must have made a mess, difficult to clean up. We'll search the buildings around there. This Nadia is from the Lamiah clan, she says, so we'll have to question their rival clans." McKay sighed, looking tired. Demons clans were notorious for closing ranks and being uncooperative.

"Her sister was probably killed far from there," Tain said. "Perhaps they teleported Nadia to the alley, choosing one at random."

McKay focused on him, her dark eyes no-nonsense. "And who are you exactly? First, you post yourself in Merrick's club in time to stop an all-out gang war, and then you just happened to find this girl in an alley near MacArthur Park?"

Tain's gaze flicked up and down the small Sidhe woman with black skin and red-orange hair, a flash of irritation in his eyes. He was a being far stronger and more dangerous than McKay could ever understand, one who could wipe out the entire room by twitching his pinky. Samantha watched Tain tamp down the darkness inside him deliberately, burying his power under stoic grimness.

"I'm a demon hunter," he said.

"Demon hunting is illegal," McKay shot back.

"Demons follow your rules because it's to their benefit," Tain said. "The rules let them drink the life essences of fools and live in comfort among you. But they are death magic, and when the balance shifts, they become the masters. Never forget that."

"I don't," McKay said. "Samantha is half demon, though, and pretty reliable."

"Even she has the potential to turn, and she's more powerful than she understands."

Tain rested his full gaze on Samantha, the one that made her feel the weight of his life magic. She folded her arms, as though that would shut it out. Why did she find it harder to face him here, in her boss's office, on her own territory, than it had been last year when he'd wrapped magic around her that could have instantly killed her?

"Excuse me," Samantha said, keeping her voice from shaking. "Could we make this *not* about me? A beaten-up demon girl found with her sister's heart in an alley is a little more serious than my heritage."

McKay nodded. "You were right about the demon prostitutes who went missing around Merrick's. Nadia admitted she was a streetwalker with her sister, but she can't tell us who captured her or where they held her. She says her captors wore masks and black clothes, and she couldn't tell if they were vampire, demon, or human. Their true natures were cloaked, probably with a spell."

"So *are* we looking for demon hunters?" Samantha asked.

McKay gave Tain a pointed look. "It seems so."

Tain returned the look. "Not the same kind of demon hunter as I am. These young women were tortured, and neither my brothers nor I would do that. Our kills are clean."

McKay's expression was carefully blank. "Maybe I should talk to your brothers."

"They don't live here," Samantha said quickly. "Well, except for Hunter and his wife. But they're not responsible. I already know that."

"But they might be a good resource. Samantha, I'd like you and Logan to ask Tain's brother about what he knows regarding demon hunters in Los Angeles. I'm going to try to set up an interview with someone in the Lamiah clan — find out if there is a clan war brewing, which we do *not* need. We're still recovering from the gangs getting out of hand last year." McKay shook her head. "The clan matriarchs are damn touchy. It's anyone's guess whether they'll let any of their demons talk to me or tell me the truth." She fixed Samantha with a look. "Samantha, you're Lamiah clan, you say. Perhaps you could put in a good word for me?"

Samantha lifted her hands in protest. "I have no contact with the demon side of my family — they don't exactly like half-bloods. I've never met any of them except my father."

Even that was tricky. Samantha's father, a demon called Fulton, had turned out to be not so bad, for a demon, but Samantha still walked on eggshells around him. She, her mother, and Fulton had made good progress this year at finally becoming a family, but it was slow going.

McKay rubbed her hand over her close-cropped hair. "It could be another good resource, Sam. We don't want this spiraling out of control. If your father could ask around in his family if anyone knows anything about these kidnappings, or whatever they are, I'd be grateful. Young girls disappearing from the streets is not good, demon or no."

Samantha let out a breath. "Got it. Ask Tain's brother about demon hunters; ask my father to talk to the Lamiah clan."

McKay gave Samantha a curt nod and told her to go home and get some sleep. Tain walked out with Samantha all the way to her pickup, opened the door for her, then went around and got into the passenger seat without invitation.

Samantha put her key in the ignition with force. "Somewhere I can drop you off?"

"I want to make sure you get home all right."

"I usually do. I'm careful, I'm a cop, and I'm armed."

"But someone is cutting out demon hearts," Tain pointed out. "And you happen to be a demon."

He had a point. Samantha had been forced to leave squeamishness behind long ago in this job, but what had been done to Nadia and her sister would stay with her for a long time.

"All right then," she said in a light voice. "Buckle up."

Samantha started the truck and shot down the ramps and out of the garage, but Tain never reached for his seatbelt. *He's an Immortal,* she told herself. *Why should he?*

She drove quickly through almost empty streets but slowed her truck as they hit freeway traffic, still thick even this late. "I only have half a demon heart," she said, continuing their conversation. *The half you're never going to let me forget.*

"Not your fault," Tain said absently. He looked out the window, his blue eyes flickering as he took in what they passed.

"Generous of you." Samantha swerved around a car that had come to a complete halt in front of her.

Tain didn't answer. Samantha's demon side cringed from his overwhelming life magic, barely contained in her small vehicle, while the human part of her was drawn to the warmth of his hard body so close on her little pickup's bench seat. Tain rested his arm between them, which ensured that Samantha kept both hands firmly on the wheel.

"Where do you live?" she asked. "Or are you staying with Leda and Hunter?"

Tain didn't look at her. "I have my own place."

Samantha waited for him to tell her where that was, but he fell silent again. "I always did like cryptic men," she said.

"You should like me, then."

She shot him a sideways look. "Was that a joke? Tain the brooding Immortal warrior made a joke?"

He lifted his brows. "You expected I'd sit home and reflect on my tragic, tortured past—what's the expression Leda uses—twenty-four, seven?"

The glint in his eye was half humor, half anger. At least Tain had decided to look at her fully.

"I guess I'm just wondering if you're all right," Samantha said.

Tain looked away again. "I'm not."

Cryptic, right. "So why did you come to Los Angeles? To be near Hunter?"

"Here's as good a place as any to find out what I'm supposed to be."

"You know who you're supposed to be," Samantha said nervously. "You're a big bad Immortal warrior people call on when there's trouble."

"No, that's what I *used* to be." Tain's voice was gravel-harsh, as though it had broken along with the rest of him. "What am I now?"

The quiet question worried her, so Samantha kept her tone light. "In other words, you've come here to find yourself?"

"Maybe."

"Some people find themselves by going to Tibet, climbing mountains, meditating with a guru . . . "

"Seems like a lot of work."

"I was joking."

Tain's rare smile flashed for an instant then was gone. "No one has to go very far to find themselves. The hard part is what you do once you've looked in the mirror and accepted the scars."

She wondered if he meant the literal scars on his body or something much deeper. "So, helping figure out what's going on with these girls is kind of a pit-stop for you?"

He gazed at her without expression, and Samantha realized that a man who'd been hidden away for seven hundred years might not understand the reference. "I mean . . ."

"I know what you meant." Tain shrugged large shoulders, which rippled muscles in places Samantha shouldn't be looking at. "It's something to keep me busy."

"Bullshit," Samantha said in a mild voice. "When you were at the club last night, you could have taken down every demon in the place—Merrick, his rivals, the bartender—everyone. If you wanted to keep busy, you could enjoy yourself destroying demons and demon clubs. You didn't even kill Merrick when you had the chance. Why didn't you?"

Another shrug. "I needed to talk to him."

"Bullshit again. You could have questioned him then killed him, but you didn't."

"Not worth the bother," Tain said.

Samantha drew a breath and asked what she really wanted to know. "Last year, you could have killed *me*. I was at your mercy, and I couldn't have escaped." Traffic had stopped, and she looked at him fully. "So why didn't you?"

Chapter Five

Tain's tone never changed as he answered. "You were innocent in that struggle. My brothers were using you, and so was my mother."

Samantha shivered. During the battle, the goddess Cerridwen, Tain's mother, had briefly infused Samantha with incredible power that had helped defeat the Old One. Samantha still had troubling dreams about it. "I was happy to help. I was ready to take you down, whatever the cost."

Tain chuckled, a grating sound. "You couldn't have taken me down."

"I was willing to die trying."

Samantha felt his gaze touch her though she'd resumed watching traffic, which had picked up speed. "Why?" he asked. "All you had to do was run away and save yourself."

Samantha made herself shrug. "I had nothing to lose. If your brothers couldn't stop you, what was left for me?"

"You have a home and family. I'd think that was something to lose."

Samantha pulled off the freeway at her exit, turning through the few blocks that led to her apartment complex. "What are you trying to get me to say? That stopping you was in my own self-interest? Well, it was. It was my butt on the line, too. Besides, Amber and the others were compelling."

"Yes, my brothers' wives," Tain said in a resigned tone. "Very compelling women."

"I like them."

"They've made my brooding, arrogant brothers happy," Tain said, sounding almost human. "They're changed men."

"They're not lonely anymore." Samantha pulled through the gates into her apartment's parking lot and stopped. "Being alone is a hard thing, believe me. But I guess you'd know all about that."

"Oh, I was lonely, Samantha," Tain said, opening the pickup's door. "But never alone."

He was out of the truck and walking around to her side before she could comment on this statement. She slid out while he held the door, another gentlemanly gesture.

"Well, here we are," she said. "How are you going to get home?"

"I'll walk you upstairs first."

"It's a gated complex with a security guard. I'll be fine."

"Someone out there knows an effective way to make sure a demon stays dead," Tain said firmly. "I'll walk you upstairs."

Samantha wasn't used to being protected. Logan watched her back daily, but that was different—he wouldn't stop her from doing her job, and he assumed she'd watch his back at the same time. Samantha had always taken care of herself, and her training for the police force meant she had the physical wherewithal and expertise to do so. Tain hovering on guard at her shoulder as they went up the outside staircase was a new sensation.

"There are thousands of demon women in this city," she said. "Are you going to walk them all home too?"

"I would if I could."

Tain waited until had Samantha unlocked the door, then he pushed in ahead of her. Pickles jumped down from the counter and ran at Tain, meowing pathetically.

"I obviously never feed him or pet him." Samantha dropped her purse and briefcase on the sofa and shut the door. "He probably hasn't eaten in at least ten minutes."

Tain took the bag of food from its place on the counter and topped off the cat's bowl, while Pickles pranced around him, tail high.

"You'll spoil him rotten." Samantha clattered her keys to the counter and kicked off her shoes, determined to not show Tain how much he unnerved her. "By the way, I'm home now."

Tain straightened up, put the food away, and started to leave, not saying good-bye. At the door, he swung back, his face hard. "The glamour," he said. "It's very good."

Samantha blinked. Tain the warrior stood at her door, the cat-feeder and healer gone, the dangerous Immortal being back. "Glamour?" she stammered.

Tain's eyes darkened as he came to her, making Samantha back into the counter. This close, his impossibly tall body made her feel small, his life-magic brushing her like a crackling net. His face was too handsome, the pentacle tattoo on his cheek almost glowing with his power.

"The one you keep up to hide your demon self," he said.

"I don't . . ."

Samantha stopped, not knowing how to answer. Lesser demons chose their physical appearance in childhood, she'd learned, instinctively mimicking whatever parent was closest to them—in Samantha's case, her mother. Half demons without strong magical skill lost their ability to change from human to demon form as they got older, apparently. Samantha would look human the rest of her life—no morphing into claws and scales like Merrick did.

Tain brushed his fingers over her chin, his hand fever hot. "It's very, very good. Difficult to say what you truly look like."

"I look like *this*," Samantha said nervously. "I don't use a glam."

"It's what demons do—draw in the unwary by being beautiful, coaxing them to give up their life essences to you."

Beautiful. Samantha's heart beat faster. "I don't feed off life essences. I prefer cheeseburgers."

Tain didn't laugh. "I have an overwhelming life essence. It must be difficult for you to resist it."

"More like an overwhelming ego." Samantha tried to keep her voice steady, but she was shaking. Tain's eyes darkened, his fingers biting down.

"I don't know what *ego* means," he said. "Everything is new to me, including your language. But I know what I'm drawn to."

"You think *I'm* enticing *you*?"

"Aren't you, Samantha?"

Tain brought to the surface Samantha's secret fear that she was indeed trying to entice him—that her demon nature reached out to him without her consent, wanting the essence that poured from him, with hungry intensity. Samantha fought demons like Merrick because she didn't want to become like them, didn't want to live to feast on others.

Tain went on, "It would explain why, ever since I first saw you, I've been struck by the need to kiss you."

He had? "That's not my fault . . ."

She trailed off as the blue of his eyes was swallowed by black, and his hot breath touched her lips. A fraction of an inch separated their mouths, and Samantha's body began to respond as it did when he'd healed her—a rush of heat, the need to melt to him, the stir of intoxicating desire.

Tain closed his eyes as his lips touched hers, the lightest featherlike brush. His hand went to the nape of her neck, his large palm warm.

Samantha tried to draw a breath and found nothing. Nothing but heat, the hot firmness of his lips on hers. He opened his eyes again, the blue of them pulling her into their depths, making her want to tell him everything, even if it killed her. She touched his arm, pulling him closer.

He slid his tongue between her lips, one tingling stroke. Samantha chased it with her own tongue, her fingers locking behind his neck. The ends of his hair tickled her fingers, and she rubbed the rough silk of it. She felt his powerful life essence waiting below the surface, beckoning her, enticing her as he'd accused her of enticing him.

"Stay," Samantha whispered. "Please." She needed him here, with his wild life magic. She wanted to make love with this amazing man who was strong enough to end the world. She wanted his body on top of hers, his solid arms cradling her. What couldn't she face with a man like Tain to hold her at the end of the day?

"No," Tain kissed her again, harder this time, his teeth scraping. Samantha pulled him closer, wanting to rub herself on him, to feel his hard body against hers, to lick his skin and love the taste. He had so much strength, shaking with it as he held himself back.

Her fingertips slid toward the tattoo on his cheek, seeking it without realizing. Samantha felt the hot sparks of his life essence, the ink that marked him containing so much power . . .

Tain jerked his head up and pushed her from him, breaking the contact.

Samantha tried to take a step back and found the countertop digging into her spine, her breath coming harsh and fast. Tain curved over her, trapping her within his body heat, his mouth a rigid line. "I told you to stay away from me."

"You insisted on coming up here." Samantha's heart slammed with fear, but her need for him remained high. "And then you kissed *me*."

"And now I'm going."

Sudden emptiness ached in her chest, along with anger and sorrow. "Good. Don't let the door hit your ass on the way out."

Tain only looked at her, his eyes like flint, his face unmoving. Samantha wanted to scream and rage; she wanted to burst into tears of relief. There would never be anything between them, never mind how he made her feel.

Tain hated demons, was making his whole life about hating demons. The only reason he'd helped Nadia tonight was because he'd felt sorry for her—because he was, deep down inside, a healer. But a demon had destroyed him, and Tain had no room in his messed-up life for a half demon who was eating her heart out over him. Some things weren't meant to be.

"Go on, then," Samantha said, folding her arms across her chest. She could feel her heart pounding, her breasts tight. "I'm not stopping you."

Tain gave her one more look, his body over hers, pinning her. He could kill her so easily, could rip out her heart as had been done to Nadia's poor sister. No one would find Tain if he didn't want to be found, no one could control and tame him. A demon had tried to tame him for seven hundred years, and Tain hadn't been contained even then.

Samantha saw it in his eyes, the need to kill, to rid himself of all that had hurt him. She saw the pain too, the darkness behind the blue, the rage. Tain wanted to kill to ease his pain . . . just as he wanted to heal.

It was tearing him apart.

He growled low in his throat, jerked away, snatched up his coat, and strode to the door. Cool night air breezed into the apartment as he walked out, his duster swirling around him. The door slammed, and he was gone.

Pickles jumped up on the windowsill with a disconsolate meow, staring out over the dark parking lot.

"Let him go, Pickles," Samantha said, tears filling her eyes. "He's not worth it." Her words ended on a groan, and she rubbed her hands over her face. "*Damn* it."

Pickles didn't answer. Samantha moved to close the blind and saw Tain with his distinctive stride moving from the parking lot to the street beyond.

"Damn," she said again and let the blind rattle closed.

***

Tain returned to the alley where he'd found Nadia, too pent up from his encounter with Samantha to go tamely home. His body throbbed from the kiss, his arousal still rock hard.

He never should have touched Samantha, never should have implied to her he was in danger of succumbing to her. She might be only half demon, but all demons learned early that they were irresistible, and spent their life honing their talent for luring victims. Samantha had seemed surprised that she possessed the siren's pull, but her obliviousness didn't negate the fact that Tain wanted her.

When he'd started looking into the problem of the missing prostitutes, he'd told himself it would be logical to ask for Samantha's help. She knew the city, and troubles like this were her job. Now Tain realized he'd simply wanted to see her again.

Samantha had been right; he could have gone to the police and reported his concerns to anyone there. He hadn't needed to seek her out specifically.

But he had, and now he was paying for it. Tain had been thinking about Samantha since Seattle and pretending not to, pretending he had no use for a half demon to whom he owed his life. And yet, as soon as he'd arrived in Los Angeles he'd found a way to see her again.

When Samantha had entered Merrick's last night, in that skin-tight black dress that made her legs a mile long, Tain had known he'd made a grave mistake. No more pushing the gorgeous woman out of his head—she was there to stay.

Tain tried to distract himself from these thoughts by looking around the alley, but he found nothing he hadn't seen before.

He gave up on finding anything more, flagged down a taxi, and gave the driver Hunter's address in Malibu. He didn't have any money with him, but Hunter would be good for the cab fare, and Tain would pay him back the next time Hunter dragged him to an ATM and explained how it worked . . . again.

Adrian had set up a bank account for Tain and deposited a substantial sum into it, saying Tain deserved it after all he'd been through. Tain had thanked his brother but rarely used the account, partly because the bank's damned machines regularly ate his card, partly because he'd never in his life had much use for money. Easy enough to get along without it, and Tain didn't have the need for opulence that Adrian seemed to.

A black limousine stood in the driveway of the long, low house on the Malibu hill. The limo held the distinct taint of vampire, and Tain's skin crawled when he passed it. The driver in the limo was certainly vampire and clutched the steering wheel defiantly as Tain stared at him.

"Tain." Leda Stowe smiled in delight as she opened the front door and squeezed Tain with a one-armed hug. Her other arm cradled baby Ryan, who was blowing bubbles with his own spit.

Leda twined her fingers through Tain's and dragged him inside, handing off Ryan to him. "Look who's here," she said brightly to the two men in the living room.

One was Hunter, next brother in age to Tain. Hunter had tawny hair, intense green eyes, and the Immortals' build. He was no stranger to tragedy—his first wife and two children had been brutally murdered by a demon long ago. He'd found peace now with Leda, but Tain observed that Hunter watched his wife and new son with a fierce protectiveness.

The other man in the living room was a vampire. Not just a vampire—an Old One, which meant he was ancient and strong. The vamp had dark hair, bottomless blue eyes, and a death magic aura that made Tain sick to his stomach. He never understood why Hunter let such a being into his house, but his brothers and the vampire Septimus had become friends of sorts. Hunter had taken the life-magic barrier down, obviously, to allow a death-magic creature like Septimus to enter. Otherwise, the vamp never would have made it inside.

"Ah ha," Hunter said, looking at Tain. "Mystery solved."

Chapter Six

"What mystery?" Tain hefted the baby in his arm, instinctively keeping his nephew far from the vampire.

"Septimus here came banging on the door at midnight," Hunter said. "He wanted to know why I was harassing one of his vamps earlier tonight in a downtown alley, but I haven't been out all day."

Septimus broke in, his voice too smooth for Tain's liking. "The vampire from my jurisdiction complained he was accosted in an alley by a tall man with an incredible life-magic aura, plus a sword."

Hunter grinned. "So Septimus naturally thought of me. But it was you, wasn't it?"

"Yes."

"Any particular reason why?" Septimus asked Tain.

"He was bothering a demon girl," Tain said, his words clipped.

Septimus arched dark brows. "A demon girl?"

"Who'd been tortured and nearly killed, and forced to watch her sister brutally murdered. I didn't think she deserved to be sucked dry by a vampire on top of it."

Leda, Hunter, and Septimus stared at him. Ryan made contented noises, enjoying the safety of Tain's arm.

"She isn't sure who did it to her," Tain went on, with a pointed look at Septimus.

Septimus shook his head. "None of *my* vampires are responsible."

"How can you be certain?"

Septimus's mouth flattened to a grim line. "When vampires get out of line, I'm usually the first to hear about it. I've heard nothing."

Tain knew the reason Los Angeles was relatively quiet these days regarding vampire and demon battles was that Septimus controlled the entire vampire population — with his power as an Old One, he dominated all other vampire lords and their underlings. He'd also taken advantage of the chaos the year before to start power bases in other cities. He'd made a deal with Adrian to keep the Los Angeles vampires contained — in return, Septimus was allowed to continue his long and sin-dark life, and Adrian left him alone.

"Maybe no one's told you yet," Tain suggested.

"Demons do fight amongst themselves, you know," Septimus said. "Clans battle for domination."

Hunter broke in. "But those are simple, straightforward fights. The demons either gather weapons and do battle, or they sneer at each other at formal luncheons."

"Demons have an honor, of sorts," Septimus agreed. "I've not heard of them torturing and killing women of rival clans, at least not these days."

"Civilized demons?" Leda broke in. "Samantha is civilized, and her father's not bad, but . . ."

"Welcome to the twenty-first century," Septimus said with a cold smile. "Demons have discovered the comforts of the modern city — why dwell in a death realm when you can live in a mansion in Beverly Hills?"

Tain was finished with the discussion. "Just make sure it's not the vampires," he said to Septimus. "Hunter, there's a cab outside waiting to be paid."

Hunter shot Tain an exasperated look. "You lost the ATM card again, didn't you?"

Tain shrugged and turned away, finished with the conversation "It's somewhere."

Hunter heaved a sigh, rose from where he'd lounged on the couch, and stalked past Tain to the front door. "I'm gonna have to explain it all over again, aren't I? In words with one syllable."

"Time was, an Immortal didn't pay for anything," Tain said, handing Ryan back to Leda and following his brother. "People were happy to give us a drink or a ride for nothing."

"Yeah, well, this is Los Angeles, and nothing's free. The world forgot about us while you were away."

The chink of darkness that ever lurked in Tain's mind rose up that moment with a terrifying suddenness and swallowed him whole. One second he was walking behind Hunter toward the bright cab, the next, his mind spun him into suffocating blackness.

Hot pain, endless pain, then the burn of healing, made horrifying because he knew that his reward for healing himself would be more pain. He'd been trapped, powerless, terrified, and at the same time wanting the pain as punishment for what he'd become.

Kehksut had taken everything from him. Tain should have been with his brothers all those years — fighting, drinking, chasing women, having stupid one-upmanship rivalries. He should have been with his family who loved him, no matter what. Kehksut had peeled everything warm and loving from him until Tain couldn't even now lie back and bask in the joy that filled Leda and Hunter's home.

"Tain? You all right?"

He found Hunter's green eyes in front of him, a worried frown on his brother's face. They were standing in the driveway, the cab pulling away, taillights flashing in the night.

Tain dragged in a breath. "I'm fine." He heard himself distantly, as though he watched the scene from afar. "Why didn't you tell the cab to wait for me? I only came up here to ask you about demon hunters."

"Leda said to send it away, because you're staying for dinner. Didn't you hear her?"

Tain knew time had passed while he stood in his stupor — it always did, but he never knew how much. "No."

Hunter's frown deepened with the frustration of a strong man who hated to admit he couldn't fix everything. "It still gets to you, doesn't it?"

"It always will. I accepted that a long time ago."

"I don't accept it, damn it," Hunter growled. "I didn't bust my ass pulling you out of that demon's power to lose you again."

Tain spread his arms, hearing the love in his brother's gruff gone. "But you did pull me out. I'm here, free. My brain will catch up after a while."

Hunter lowered his voice, glancing inside at Leda who was smiling at a glowering Septimus. "When we formed the circle to rescue you, when we joined, I felt some of what had happened to you. I took it inside myself. So did our brothers. I saw what you'd gone through."

But what they'd experienced taking Tain's pain into themselves had been the merest fraction of what Tain had endured. Tain had deliberately latched on to the crack of light his brothers had made for him and kicked his way out of Kehksut's power. It had been his choice.

"I know you hurt yourselves to get me free," Tain said. "I'll always be grateful — you know that."

"It's not about gratitude. I can't stand to see you blank out like that. Like my baby brother is still lost, and I can't help anymore."

Tain shook his head. "Believe me, anything I suffer now is only a millionth of what I went through before. Trust me on this. I'll get over it."

Hunter shot him a skeptical look, but he'd learned when to drop the subject. "We'd better get inside. Leda will come looking for us if we don't get our butts in there."

"Why are you having dinner now?" Tain asked as they walked back into the warm, light house. The living room was gigantic, covering one entire wing of the house, with the large dining room and kitchen filling one corner of the floor. "It's after midnight."

"Because Leda decided to fix it now. Don't even think about refusing."

Leda swung around from the kitchen, cuddling Ryan. "That's right," she said. "Septimus will join us and then give you a ride home."

Septimus looked pained. "I don't need food."

"You drink wine—I've seen you." Leda gave him a cheerful smile. "You can always wait in the limo if it upsets you that much."

Amusement trickled through Tain's darkness as Septimus, the supreme vampire lord of one of the largest cities in the world, deflated before Leda's insistent look, and obeyed.

**

Tain learned the reason for Leda's insistence that he stay when he volunteered to help her with the dishes. He chose to wash dishes mostly to get away from the uneasy looks Hunter kept slanting him. Septimus too watched him closely, in a way Tain didn't like.

"So," Leda began brightly. "You've talked to Samantha. How is she?"

Tain studied the water slicking his scarred hands as he held one of Leda's good plates. Throughout the meal Tain had tried unsuccessfully to shut Samantha out of his mind, and now the sensation of kissing her earlier tonight rose up and slammed him in the gut.

Samantha had tasted too good, her hands strong as she'd laced them around his neck. He'd thought even a half demon would taste like death, but Samantha's spice had been heady.

"She's in good health," he managed to say, relying on a polite phrase from the dim and distant past.

Leda handed him a scrub brush. "No, I mean *how is she?*" *Beautiful. Dangerous.*

Tain knew that Samantha wasn't Kehksut, the demon who'd flayed him then turned into a beautiful, seductive woman and forced him into sex. Kehksut was dead, the ancient being's evil magic gone. Kehksut had been death magic incarnate—Samantha was alive, warm, generous, sensual.

Tain knew he'd made a mistake avoiding sex in the last year. Kehksut had so warped sex for him Tain feared he wouldn't be able to stand the touch of a woman. He had no way of knowing what he would do if he tried to take a woman to bed—would he go insane and hurt her, maybe kill her?

But maybe he should have eased back into it, found a woman so far the opposite of Kehksut that he could remind himself how gentle and pleasurable sex could be.

But he hadn't, and now he came to Samantha like a starving man. If Tain made love to her, he wouldn't be able to hold back. He was drawn to Samantha and her dark beauty, something in him crying out for her.

Hunter came to the kitchen and leaned his elbows on the breakfast bar. "Give in, brother. Leda's not going to be happy until she's got you paired off."

"Don't be a smart-ass," Leda said, but with affection in her voice. "I think Tain and Sam were made for each other. I always have."

Because Leda was happy, she wanted everyone in her world to be happy. Tain recognized that. Leda and Hunter were to have gone to Ravenscroft right after Ryan was born, but Leda had put it off, saying she wanted to wait until Ryan was a little older.

Tain knew the true reason was that Leda didn't want to leave while Tain was in Los Angeles. He could be rude and tell her he didn't need a babysitter, but he kept his silence. Hunter and Leda were trying to be good to him, and the least he could do was let them.

Leda persisted for a while, but after a few more evasive answers from Tain, she let the topic drop.

Tain rode back downtown in the smoked-glass windowed limousine with Septimus, each of them watching the other. Septimus didn't even bother trying to make small talk. Tain's skin crawled with Septimus's death magic, but he liked knowing that his life magic made Septimus uneasy in return.

Septimus insisted on dropping Tain off at his apartment building, the limousine crouching on the street until Tain went all the way inside. Tain knew Septimus waited partly to satisfy Leda that Tain had arrived home safely. Septimus's other motive was to discover where Tain lived, especially because the converted motel that housed Tain's apartment was in Septimus's territory.

The quiet of Tain's one-bedroom apartment welcomed him, the darkness soothing. Tain liked the dark—this century's artificial lights grated on his nerves.

He'd bought candles, cheap votives and tea lights, and strewn them about the room. He drew the shade against the streetlights outside, lit the candles, then stripped off his clothes and sat in the middle of the floor to begin his nightly meditation.

As he feared, the mind-quieting of the meditation didn't come easily. Instead his brain only conjured the image of Samantha, the scent of her, her lips red with his kisses, her dark eyes betraying hurt when Tain told her *no* and walked away.

***

"I know it's not easy for you," Logan said to the demon girl Nadia. "But we need to go over it again. I want to find something to help us figure out who did this to you and your sister. And possibly other girls out there too."

Nadia reclined in a bed at the clinic, sheets pulled over her hospital gown. A nurse had trimmed away the hanks of her shorn hair to even it up, but the young woman's scalp still contained a few bald patches. Burns decorated her arms and cheeks.

Nadia was twenty-three, the file in Logan's lap told him. No parents. Nadia had left her clan two years ago to work in a club in Santa Monica with her sister. Tiring of answering to the stringent demands of the club owner, the two of them had taken to the streets to sell the pleasure that came with letting a demon sup on life essences.

Logan usually left dealing with demons to Samantha, the wolf in him hating all death-magic creatures. Yet he'd grown enraged when he'd looked over Samantha's notes this morning, and he decided he wanted to find the person — demon, human, vampire, or otherwise — who had done this to Nadia.

Nadia's eyes were pools of darkness in her white face, but she was pretty — probably demon glam, Logan reasoned. Right now, though, she looked pathetic and exhausted.

"I told you," Nadia said, making her voice hard. "I barely saw them. Mostly I was tied up in a closet."

"An ordinary closet? Not a cell?"

"There were brooms and mops, pipes in the walls. Like something in a maintenance room. I tried to use a broom handle to break open the door, but it didn't work. Hard to do with my hands and feet tied."

Logan closed the file. He'd been told he'd grow hardened to the plights of victims, especially in Los Angeles, a city that drew those who wanted to prey on others — though Logan had seen nothing so far that compared to what werewolves could do when the pack turned against one of their own. Logan hadn't grown calloused in the last year, however, so he spent a lot of time aching in compassion for people like Nadia, even if they didn't appreciate it.

"I want to get these bastards, Nadia."

Her dark eyes widened. "You're life magic. Why would you want to help a demon? And why did that other guy — the red-haired one — want to help me? Who the hell was he, by the way? He was definitely full of life magic."

"I'm not sure myself about him," Logan had to answer.

"So why do you care so much?"

Logan stretched out his long legs and folded his arms. "This is my town," he said, drawling like an Old West sheriff. "I want to keep it clean."

"Bullshit, werewolf."

The wolf in Logan started to growl, but that was only his life magic with its hackles up. "I want to find out who did this to you and your sister," Logan said. "There's a difference between a good fight with a death-magic creature and . . . this."

Nadia deflated, her eyes moistening. "I'm going to get them for what they did to Bev."

Logan nodded, telling the beast in him to shut up and sit down. "I don't blame you. But let *me* get them, all right?"

Nadia sank back to her pillows, her face fine-boned and vulnerable. "I can't help you—that's what I can't stand. They gave me something that took away my strength. When I was in the closet, I couldn't change into my demon form. Then, later, they wanted me to change, because they wanted to kill a demon, not something that looked human."

"Which means they weren't after you in particular, but demons in general."

"Yes, but it was my sister *in particular* who was killed."

Nadia's face crumpled, and she looked like nothing more than a young woman who'd stumbled into tragedy. Logan couldn't stop himself from reaching out to brush back the shorn ends of her hair. Nadia gave him a startled look from her streaming eyes, but she didn't shrink away.

Logan was glad now that Samantha had roped him into this case. He decided then and there that he'd do anything— *anything*—to get the bastards that caused this helpless young woman grief.

Chapter Seven

Tain lay full length on the living-room floor, his eyes open, having long since given up on his meditation. Any peace of mind eluded him tonight.

Dawn seeped through the window, silence descended, and time slowed. The presence of a goddess began to fill every space of the apartment, like a perfume permeating a close room.

Tain.

Though Cerridwen only manifested as a white light above him, Tain felt her love and warmth flow around him, her healing magic seeking out his hurts.

Cerridwen had helped Tain heal little by little over the past year, boosting his Immortal life magic to complete the healing of his flesh. Sometimes, like tonight, Tain shied away from further healing. Somehow, he needed to hurt. He didn't always want comfort.

"Why did you let it happen?" he asked the light. "My brothers didn't come for me until the end, but at least they tried. You stood by and did nothing."

The light retreated the slightest bit, and Cerridwen remained silent, as usual. Tain hadn't really expected an answer. He'd asked the question many times since his escape from Kehksut, but had never received a response.

Cerridwen's sorrow heightened until Tain could barely stand the crush of it, and to his surprise, she spoke.

I let it happen so you would be strong enough to defeat the ancient one. Your imprisonment and pain gave you strength. Now you are greater than all your brothers put together. It had to be thus.

She spoke an ancient Celtic language — her voice musical and flowing, but Tain couldn't feel the peace of it.

He answered in the same language. "Are you saying you let me be tortured *on purpose?*"

It had to be, or your brothers could not have come together to save you, and the world would have been lost. One of you had to have the strength to kill the Old One — even all of you together wouldn't have been able to defeat him, the most ancient and powerful of his kind.

"One of us? Why was *I* chosen? What the hell made me so special?"

Tain had always known that Adrian and Kalen were far more powerful than he was. Tain, Hunter, and Darius had been closer in strength. The three had often fought death-magic creatures together, and had time and again awakened after a long, post-battle revelry with little memory of the party they'd so enjoyed.

Tain had only ever thought of himself as a warrior with a magical talent for healing. However, because he couldn't heal Immortals, he, Hunter, and Darius had always had to suffer through the hangovers.

We drew lots, Cerridwen said. *It was to my great sorrow that I won.*

Tain sat up. "You drew *lots?*"

It was the only way, the goddesses and I, to decide which of you would gain the strength. We didn't have the fortitude to make such a decision, so we left it to Fate.

Tain got to his feet, power crackling from him in rage. "Do you mean I suffered for seven hundred years because *you drew the short straw?*"

Yes.

Tain roared in anger, light exploding from him. He wouldn't have wished what he'd suffered on his brothers, but the full betrayal of it struck him. He and his brothers, the indestructible warriors, had been pawns in a game of the goddesses.

"You should have asked us," he snarled. "You should have let *us* decide who would go."

We couldn't bear to stand by and watch you choose who would make the sacrifice. The decision of who would go to Kehksut was made before any of you were even born.

If Cerridwen spoke the truth, that meant everything Tain and his brothers had ever done, had ever endured, from their birth to the time of Kehksut's death, had been part of a long, elaborate scheme. Tain had suffered torture, Hunter had lost his wife and children, Kalen had endured a terrible punishment. Darius had been kept a prisoner by the goddess Sekhmet, and Adrian still blamed himself for Tain's capture and imprisonment. But all along it had been the goddesses who'd planned every move and watched their sons suffer one by one.

"Do my brothers know?" Tain asked.

No. Please, never tell them.

Another wave of power boomed from Tain. "Get out of my head. Get out of my *house!*"

My son . . .

"I said get *out!*"

Tain slapped his magic at her, a whiplike tendril that wrapped the white light that was Cerridwen and shoved her away. Cerridwen stilled in shock, her grief pressing at Tain like a dark wave. Then she dissipated and was gone.

Tain rose from the ground and whirled through his apartment, blasting pieces out of the brick walls with white-hot magic. He stopped and thumped back to his feet, shaking in rage, then he pulled on his clothes and slammed out the front door.

His neighbor, a lanky man with a long dark ponytail, poked his head out of the next apartment, eyes round. "Hey, man, you all right?"

"Fine," Tain snarled. He snaked a gentle tendril of healing magic at his neighbor. "Sleep and forget."

The man started to yawn and said, "Take it easy," before he went back inside.

Tain walked out into the dawn, creatures both mortal and magical melting from his path.

***

"Good morning," Logan said cheerfully as Samantha hopped into the police car Logan had halted outside her apartment complex gate. "Glad to see you this bright and early. Me, I never got to bed."

Samantha pushed her damp hair out of her eyes as Logan slid into Los Angeles traffic. Logan had called her as she was getting out of bed to tell her they'd been summoned to a disturbance near Union Station and that he'd pick her up on his way in.

"Why do they need detectives?" she asked, grabbing the coffee Logan had stuck into the cup holder for her. She sipped the dark brew, wincing at its bitterness. "Uniforms are supposed to handle stuff like this. What's different about this one?"

"Because this one involves your friend Tain."

Samantha came all the way awake. "Tain? Shit, what's he done?"

"Remember those demons that attacked Merrick's place? Turns out they were from the Djowlan clan—I think I'm saying that right. Tain walked into one of their clubs a few hours ago, kicked out all the human customers, and is holding the demons hostage, including the one who ordered the raid on Merrick's."

"You've got to be kidding me."

"He says he's not letting them go until one of them tells him what happened to Nadia. And that he's only *thinking* about letting them go. There's been fighting, but he's got them cornered and scared shitless."

Samantha rubbed her forehead as though that would clear the fog from her brain. "But Tain said he thought demon hunters did it, not demons."

"Guess he changed his mind."

"Crap. And McKay wants me to . . . what? Talk him out of there?"

"That's her idea."

"What makes her think he'll listen to me?"

Logan gave her a sympathetic grin. "Lieutenant McKay says you have to make him listen, and that everyone's counting on you."

"Gee, thanks," she said.

Logan chuckled, but without much humor. "I'll be right here with you, partner."

Samantha's gut ached as they dodged through traffic. The coffee swam in her stomach like sludge, and she thrust the cup back into the holder.

Samantha reasoned she could always call Hunter, but then, Hunter was no friend to demons and might see nothing wrong with Tain taking his revenge. Hunter's first wife and kids had been slain by demons, and his reaction upon seeing them was to kill without asking questions. When Hunter had first met Samantha, he'd stuck the point of his sword against her chest—Leda had talked for a long time before Hunter had conceded to let Samantha live. Hunter might decide to join Tain for some demon bashing, and then Samantha would have *two* Immortal problems.

The club Logan pulled up to was typical of the downtown demon clubs—very businesslike and modest on the outside with only a small logo above the door to say what lay inside. Samantha recognized the place as one run by a demon called Kemmerer from the Djowlan clan. Kemmerer had kept things fairly quiet and clean in the last year, not because he was a moral citizen, but because he couldn't afford to have the paranormal police shutting him down.

The circle of police cars in front of the club and along the side alley destroyed the quiet look of the place. Most of the cops were uniforms from the paranormal division, with some backup from the regular division.

Samantha climbed out of the car and approached the officer in charge, showing him her ID. "Did the guy inside say he'll negotiate with me?"

"He hasn't said anything at all," the officer answered, rubbing his close-cropped hair. "Your lieutenant says you can talk him down, so I'm to let you in."

"I'm going with her," Logan announced.

"I wish you wouldn't," Samantha said. "At least not until I know what's going on. If Tain hasn't slipped back into insanity, I might be able to reason with him."

"*If* he hasn't slipped back into insanity?" Logan asked, incredulous. "That's it. I'm coming with you." He slid his Sig from his shoulder holster.

"Please don't shoot him. You'll just piss him off."

Logan's jaw tightened. "But it might distract him while you get away. Sorry, sweetie, I have a wolf's protective instinct. Doesn't matter that you're not pack or mate, you're my friend and partner. He even looks like he's going to hurt you, he's going down."

"I outrank you. If I tell you to stay put, will you?"

"Nope."

Samantha let our her breath. "All right then, but if you get killed, don't come crying to me."

Logan gave a grim laugh. "You betcha."

It *was* smart to let Logan come in with her, Samantha reasoned, even if the two of them together were no match for an Immortal like Tain. If Tain had retreated into madness, they were screwed. Samantha had seen what he was capable of, and she never wanted to see that again.

Her heart ached. Last night Tain had bent to kiss her as though he couldn't stop himself. The warmth of his kiss had lingered in Samantha's dreams, and she felt it on her lips still. She'd wanted him last night, and the light of day hadn't changed that.

But she wanted whatever she had with him to be normal—as normal as things could be with an Immortal. Friends if they couldn't be lovers. Samantha was half demon; Tain was a rampaging, angry demigod, and they were probably always meant to be star-crossed.

Logan kept his weapon drawn, and Samantha drew hers. The guns might not work on Tain, but there were demons in there too.

The first thing Samantha noticed when they went inside was the smell. Demon musk, overpowering and awful. When demons wanted to seduce, they sent out pleasing pheromones to trap the unwary, but these odors had nothing to do with seduction. The demons in here were terrified.

Three demons, males, in human form, lay inert in the vestibule. They were large men in business suits and had gone down in the act of drawing weapons.

"Not dead," Logan said as he checked them. "Just out."

Samantha stepped over the motionless bodies, and proceeded with Logan through the heavy door to the main club. All the lights were on, which made the club's vast open space, three stories high, look strange and a bit seedy. Seduction was easier in half darkness.

Tain sat on a wooden chair from one of the tables in the middle of the open floor. He'd tilted the chair back, and reposed almost negligently, his arms folded, his duster brushing the floor.

The walls above him were covered with demons. They hung limply against the brick, some right side up, others upside-down, all pressed there by Tain's magic. About half of the demons had reverted to their monster-from-hell forms; the others retained their human forms and expensive clothes — suits for the men and slinky dresses for the women.

The one thing they all had in common was fear. Waves and waves of terror poured down at Samantha and made her want to be sick.

One of the female demons saw Samantha and shouted down at her. "Help us! Please!"

Samantha walked steadily forward, but when she was about six feet from Tain's chair, her feet ceased moving of their own accord. She tried to take another step, but couldn't. Logan stopped beside her, frowning, feeling the same thing. Whether Tain had erected a magic barrier or simply spelled their feet not to move, Samantha couldn't tell.

"Tain," she said quietly.

When Tain flicked his gaze to her, Samantha took an involuntary step back, her throat squeezing shut.

The darkness in Tain's eyes was vast, drowning out the blue. Whatever had been human in him was gone. He was a god today, powerful, deadly, and consumed with rage so intense it had swallowed everything sane inside him.

"Go back outside, Samantha," Tain said clearly. "Tell them I wouldn't negotiate."

Samantha's heart pounded in fast, dull beats. "I can't do that." She wished her voice sounded stronger, but it rasped. "My lieutenant expects me to bring you in and save the day. I have the feeling my future promotions will be riding on this, so how about you do me a favor and come outside with me?"

Dark magic flashed out of him. "Don't try to cajole me." He gestured to the demons on the walls. "Do you want to know what they told me?"

"Tell me outside. McKay will want to hear it, too."

"I don't work for law enforcement. Your procedure is too slow, and I like to be direct."

No kidding. "Well, barging into a club and sticking everyone up on the walls is certainly direct," Samantha said.

Tain gave her a flint-hard stare. "Put away your guns. This isn't a TV show, and someone might get hurt."

"All right." Samantha made a show of taking one hand from her Glock and stowing the pistol in the holster at the small of her back. Logan slid his Sig back into his shoulder holster, his eyes white with his wolf's anger.

"There, gun gone." Samantha showed Tain her empty hands.

"Don't patronize me. This one . . ." Tain shoved a demon in a black business suit higher up the wall than the others. "Is Kemmerer. He sent the demons against Merrick's club. He said he's trying to expand and wants the beach towns. He considers Merrick fair game."

Shit, not good. If Merrick found out Kemmerer was after his territory, Merrick would go on the warpath, and the clan battles would begin.

"I asked him about Nadia," Tain continued. "He admitted to grabbing Nadia and her sister off the street, but he claims he had nothing to do with the torture and murder. What he did was sell the two girls to the people who wanted them."

Samantha looked up at the defiant Kemmerer, her loathing nearly matching the anger she saw in Tain's eyes. "Slavery is illegal," she said to Kemmerer. "By demon law as well as human."

Kemmerer glared down at her, still the indignant club owner who'd been invaded. Idiot.

"Are you sure you want me to let him go?" Tain asked her.

Samantha itched to tell Tain to knock Kemmerer's head against the wall a few more times, but she let out a breath. "We have to do it by the book, or we can't make the charges stick."

"It would be faster if I ripped off his head. I can do it for you." Tain held up his finger and thumb as though the demon's neck were between his grip. Kemmerer's defiance turned to fear, and he made strangling noises.

"I wish I could let you," Samantha said, meaning it.

"I'm strong enough to kill everyone in this room," Tain said in a calm voice that was somehow more frightening than his rage. "I can do it without even breathing hard. They made me strong on purpose, and here I am, so powerful they don't know what to do with me. What would they do if I became uncontrollable?"

Samantha had no idea what Tain was talking about and wasn't sure she'd like it if she did. Logan shot her a sideways glance, and Samantha shook her head the tiniest bit.

"Should I test this?" Tain asked, as though half to himself. Kemmerer rose higher, the gurgling in his throat becoming more pronounced.

Samantha looked at Tain's eyes. The darkness had receded, and now they were lake-blue again. The surface looked quiet, even calm, but Samantha sensed that beneath that surface lurked a roiling, churning pain more vast than she could imagine. Tain was trying to relay to her what he was going through, giving her a glimpse of the anguish that surpassed all anguish in the world.

It was the most frightening thing Samantha had ever seen. She could think of only one thing to do. She pulled out her cell phone and started scrolling through numbers.

"Who are you summoning?" Tain asked without much interest. "Your SWAT team?"

"No," Samantha said, thumb hovering over the button that would complete the call. "Leda. All I have to do is push this, and she knows everything."

Chapter Eight

"Oh, Samantha." Tain's voice remained powerful, but it was tinged with the slightest bit of amusement and respect. "You play dirty."

"Against Immortals? I've learned to."

The wild magic subsided the tiniest amount, Tain sounding more normal. "Put away your phone. I'll leave with you. Just you," he said as Logan straightened up. "If you promise to set up a meeting with the Lamiah clan matriarch, I'll walk out with you, Samantha, without hurting anyone."

"A *meeting* with the matriarch?" Samantha asked. "That sounds very tame. You mean you won't just burst into her mansion and blast everyone senseless?"

Tain shrugged as he rose from his chair. "These are thugs who live by manipulating humans with their magic," he said, waving a hand at the hanging demons. "The clan leaders are somewhat more civilized. The matriarch will hear me if nothing else."

"I'll see what I can do," Samantha said with caution.

"You will do it. I'll walk out with you now, and you'll take me beyond your circle of police and leave with me."

"They won't let you go," Samantha said. "The cops will follow us and arrest you."

"Don't tell him that," Logan growled at her. "No way am I letting him take you hostage."

"They won't follow me," Tain said. "They'll forget about me once we pass. What your partner and your boss decide to do with the demons in here is their own business."

Samantha dropped her cell phone back into her pocket, still wary. "Fine."

"Samantha," Logan said. If he'd been wolf, his hackles would have been up and rippling.

"We don't have much choice," Samantha told him. "I agree with Tain that Kemmerer is a shithead. Do with *him* what you want."

Tain walked to Samantha, his duster moving with his stride. When he reached her, he turned her around and put his hand on her shoulder. Samantha hoped he couldn't feel her shaking.

The demons still hovered in midair. Would Tain let them fall, or would he turn around and strike them dead as he went? Samantha felt tension shimmering through Tain's body, the towering rage she'd seen in him held back with Herculean effort.

"What happened to make you do this?" she whispered to him.

"Walk."

Samantha led him out past Logan, heading for the main entrance. She stepped over the demons sprawled in the vestibule and out into the balmy early morning.

"Don't shoot," she said to the waiting uniforms, her hands spread. "I'm bringing him out."

The uniforms didn't lower their weapons, and as Samantha walked by, their eyes glazed over. They kept their guns trained on the open door, as though waiting for someone else equally as deadly to emerge.

"Keep walking," Tain said to Samantha.

"What did you do to them?"

"Simple magic. They'll remember rushing here to arrest the demon leader for kidnapping Nadia and her sister, and Logan will take, as you say, the kudos for it."

"And what will we be doing?"

"Talking to your father."

Samantha and Tain had walked beyond the circle of police vehicles without any of the uniforms or the officer in charge noticing. The street was relatively quiet after that, the people there focused on watching what the police were up to. Their eyes didn't track Tain or Samantha as the two of them walked by.

"What did you have in mind for transportation?" Samantha asked, her jaw clenched so her teeth wouldn't chatter. "My truck is at home, and I can't take Logan's car and leave him stranded."

"That's all right," Tain said, his hand warm on her shoulder. "I don't mind taking the bus."

***

They took a taxi. Samantha found it surreal to be sitting next to Tain and his swords in the shadowy backseat of a musty-smelling cab at seven in the morning, while the driver sped them up the Pasadena Freeway.

As he'd done in her truck last night, Tain sat close enough that Samantha could feel his warmth and smell the scents of the night that clung to his coat. His intense life magic could knock her out of the taxi, and she marveled that the driver didn't seem to notice.

"Why did you let me lead you out of there?" Samantha asked Tain in a low voice.

"I was finished." He sounded so logical, so calm now.

"What made you go into that club the first place?"

Tain looked out the window, passing lights flickering yellow-white bands across his face. "It was the club closest to the alley where I found Nadia. I wondered why whoever had captured her had chosen to release her there, and I figured that alley was probably where they'd snatched her in the first place."

"Good deduction," Samantha said. "I'm sure Logan will be happy to interrogate Kemmerer. What happened to Nadia truly pissed Logan off."

"And me."

That's the trouble with being paranormal police, Samantha thought. *Sometimes our true natures want swift and final justice. But we have to work within the law, while people like Tain are outside it.*

The taxi dropped them at the end of the driveway of Samantha's parents' house in Pasadena, a quiet neighborhood showing no signs that last year it had been overrun by demon gangs. Her mother's geraniums grew undisturbed in the front garden in the early morning light, and the stucco house with the tile roof and small windows was calm and welcoming.

Samantha's father lived here with her mother now. For a long time Samantha had hated Fulton, believing him to have coerced and abducted her mother, as demons did. She'd come to understand, though, that Fulton had fallen in love with Joanne, her mother, and had kept away only because he knew Samantha hadn't been ready to accept him as her father. Samantha had been skeptical and angry, but when Joanne had disappeared last year, Samantha had seen exactly how much Fulton loved her and worried for her.

Samantha and Fulton had worked together to find Joanne, and Samantha had watched her parents embrace with the frantic joy of two people who'd believed they'd never see each other again.

The past year had been difficult, but Samantha had gradually come to know the man who was her father, and Fulton to understand Samantha a little. Joanne had never been so happy, and for her sake, Samantha was willing to try.

Fulton answered Samantha's knock and greeted her with delighted surprise. He was a demon male who'd made himself look about thirty-five, but Samantha knew he was more than a hundred years old. He was dark haired, brown eyed, and handsome.

"Your mother popped out to the store for more milk while I cook breakfast," Fulton said over his shoulder as they followed him in. He picked up a spatula he'd left on the hall table and headed back to the kitchen. "I'm mastering banana pancakes."

"My favorite," Samantha said.

"I know. Joanne told me. I wanted to practice."

That her estranged father would try to make her favorite childhood food made Samantha's eyes sting. She and Tain followed him into the kitchen, where Fulton frowned at a griddle as it heated on top of the stove.

"This one's different," Fulton said, but Samantha knew he wasn't talking about the griddle.

"This is Tain, Hunter's brother," Samantha clarified.

"I thought he might be one of those Immortals." Fulton glanced at Tain, his expression guarded. "I've never felt life magic so concentrated before. Makes me sick to my stomach."

"He'll behave himself." Samantha shot Tain a look, which he ignored.

Samantha explained about Nadia, and Tain's wish to talk to the Lamiah clan matriarch. While she spoke, Tain wandered about the kitchen, studying everything from the clock on the wall to the stovetop griddle. Fulton flipped pancakes, scowling when Samantha told him how Nadia's sister had been killed.

"That was done by someone who knew precisely how to kill demons," Fulton said. "A demon can't recover from his or her heart being torn out."

"Not many people can," Samantha said dryly.

"Vampires can," Fulton said. "They die when a stake is driven through their rotted hearts, but that's more symbolic than biological. They're the only race that can be killed by a metaphor."

Samantha didn't smile. "It's my job to know how to kill a demon if necessary. But the average person on the street doesn't have that knowledge or ability."

"We're not looking for the average person on the street," Tain said. He'd moved to the French doors that led to the small backyard and looked out at Joanne's collection of succulents and colorful annuals. "Demons know how to kill other demons."

"Vamps know how to kill demons too," Fulton said. "I'd bank on vampires doing this."

"Vampire activity has been subdued since Septimus took over," Tain said. "While demons still fight for domination throughout the city."

Fulton looked stubborn. "It doesn't sound as though Nadia's death is the result of a demon gang trying to muscle out another demon gang. This was a deliberate act of murder, and sending the girl's heart back was a signal. A message to other demons."

"That doesn't rule out the possibility that one demon clan wants to declare war on another," Tain said, turning from the window. "That is why I wish to speak to your matriarch."

"I think you should let him," Samantha said to Fulton. "I'd like to hear what she has to say as well."

Fulton shook his head. "Child, you know so very little. What's been done to Nadia and her sister is an abomination. If our matriarch thinks another demon clan has committed an atrocity against the Lamiah, she will declare war, and you do not want to be in the middle of a demon war. What happened last year is a schoolyard scuffle compared to what an all-out demon war would do. There hasn't been one in centuries."

Samantha felt a qualm of unease, but she pressed on. "The matriarch might already know who is doing this and point me in the right direction. Then I make an arrest and stop a war before it starts."

Fulton let out his breath, resting his fists, one still clutching the pancake turner, on the counter. "That is the other thing you don't understand, Sam. I can't simply take you to the matriarch. You have to be accepted into the clan before you're allowed to even get near her."

"But I'm your daughter. Doesn't that make me of the clan Lamiah?"

Fulton straightened up and slid another finished pancake onto the stack warming on the back of the stove. "You're not of full blood."

Samantha's irritation rose. "And that's bad, I take it?"

Tain broke in, his rumbling Welsh accent filling the room. "Demons are very old-fashioned. Trust me on this. I was taught about demons by a master."

Fulton dribbled more batter onto the grill. "It's difficult for some demons to accept that we now mate with non-demons. Less than a hundred years ago, a demon could be slain if he even married outside the *clan*. His mate and any offspring would also be killed. Times have changed, but still it is difficult for demons to accept intermarriage."

Samantha's uneasiness rose at her father's flat statement — *His mate and any offspring would also be killed.*

"If demons weren't allowed to marry outside the clan, didn't that lead to inbreeding after a while?" Samantha asked Fulton. "Receding chins, genetic diseases, that kind of thing?"

"Demon clans are huge," Fulton said. "And not all the families are related. But yes, learning about genetics was one reason for lifting the ban on intermarriage. That is, it's acceptable for demons to mate with humans, but marrying across clans is still discouraged and carries a stigma for the mated couple and their children."

"What happens if the Lamiah clan decides not to accept me?"

Fulton looked quickly back at the griddle, scraping his plastic turner under the firming batter. "That's up to the matriarch."

The way he carefully avoided Samantha's gaze as he finished the pancakes told her that things could get bad for the rejected half-blood demon.

"Nothing will happen to Samantha," Tain said, his deep voice breaking the silence. "I won't let it."

"You won't be there at all," Fulton said, looking up at him. "The clan matriarch will never allow someone as full of life magic as you anywhere near her."

"That's what Merrick said," Samantha added.

Fulton scowled. "Merrick. He's scum of the earth. Stay away from him."

"I know he is. That's why I arrested him. It's kind of my job, Dad."

Fulton turned quickly away. Tain watched both of them, his expression revealing nothing.

"The matriarch will see me," Tain said to Fulton after a moment. "The easiest way to do this is for you to bring me in with Samantha. I'll follow the matriarch's rules, but she'll meet me."

Tain was going to insist, and Samantha decided not to argue with him. The idea of having Tain at her back when Fulton presented her to the matriarch appealed to her.

"She might decide to take it out on me," Fulton said still focusing on the pancakes. "Maybe forbid me to see my wife and Samantha."

"She won't," Tain said.

Fulton finally turned around, his dark eyes moist. "I take it you've never met a clan matriarch, Immortal. You couldn't have, or you wouldn't be so cocky."

"Perhaps not," Tain said.

"Tain killed an Old One," Samantha said. "One of the most ancient and powerful demons that walked the earth. Perhaps it's the matriarch who shouldn't be cocky."

"I heard about that," Fulton said. He looked sharply at Tain. "But when you meet the Lamiah matriarch, you might wish you were back doing battle with that Old One."

***

Samantha's mother returned not long after that, happy to see Samantha and intrigued to meet Tain. Tain even agreed to a breakfast of pancakes and bacon and ate heartily — maybe tearing up a demon club first thing in the morning gave an Immortal an appetite.

Fulton finally agreed to try to set up the appointment with the matriarch and told Samantha what they'd be expected to do and even wear if the matriarch accepted.

Mission accomplished. Samantha finished breakfast with her family and called another taxi for her and Tain.

"Are you sure I can't drive you home?" Fulton asked as they all went outside.

Samantha shook her head. "You did enough, fixing breakfast and helping with the matriarch. Call me once you know?"

Her father nodded. When the taxi arrived, Samantha hugged her mother, promising to return to visit soon, and she and Tain climbed in the back.

"I think my father started crying while we were talking about what the matriarch might do to him," Samantha said as the taxi rolled away from Pasadena, heading west. "He must be very worried about the consequences of this meeting."

Tain's harsh gaze suddenly softened, making his face more human. "He wasn't crying because of that."

Samantha gave him a puzzled look. "What then?"

Tain's blue eyes became more gentle than she'd ever seen them. "He was crying because you called him *Dad*."

***

Before Samantha and Tain could meet with the clan Lamiah matriarch, Merrick's club in Venice burned to the ground.

It happened at mid-morning, two days after Samantha and Tain had talked with Fulton, when anyone who worked at the club, which closed at five a.m., would be gone or sleeping in apartments above it. Samantha and Logan went to the call, watching from the perimeter while firemen directed their hoses onto the club and the buildings close around it.

The demon employees who lived in the building—the bartender and several of the female demons—huddled in blankets outside the ring of police barricades. The young women were crying, the bartender watching the fire with a stunned look on his face.

"Where's Merrick?" Samantha asked the bartender, but he shrugged as though he couldn't manage enough energy to answer.

"He didn't get out," one of the women sobbed. "He pushed me down the stairs and got me to the door, but he didn't come after me."

"Damn it." Samantha shoved her way to one of the firemen who'd stepped back to drink some water. "Did Merrick make it out?" she shouted at him. "The owner? One of the girls thinks he's still in there."

The fireman shook his head, looking grim. "We tried to get to him, but we couldn't. The middle floors are completely gone, and the ladder trucks had to back off."

Samantha gnawed her lip. She didn't like Merrick, but she didn't necessarily want to watch him burn to death either. If he reverted to his demon form, he might make it— demons were tough—but smoke inhalation could take down most forms of life except vampire.

"Hey!" one of the firemen bellowed. He backed up to where Samantha stood with the other fireman. "Someone just ran in there. Asshole. It's a death sentence—for us too, because now we have to try to get him out."

"No." Samantha stopped him. "You don't need to go after him. He won't die in there."

The two firemen stared at her in surprise, but Samantha had seen California sunshine on flame-red hair and knew exactly who'd run into the fire.

Chapter Nine

Tain found Merrick in his living room, the demon reclining on a leather sofa and sipping a glass of brandy. The walls were bare, the expensive artwork gone.

Flames and smoke rampaged in the rooms surrounding this one, but the living room was an oasis of relative calm. Merrick had employed some kind of magic to seal himself into safety, but the spell wouldn't be strong enough to keep the fire back for long.

"Now I know I'm in hell," Merrick said when he saw Tain stride in, straight through fire and the magic barrier. "And not the good kind."

Tain didn't answer. Smoke seeped under the doors on the other side of the room, the fire starting to break through Merrick's magic.

"Are you here to save me?" Merrick asked, unruffled. "Or to make certain the fire does its job?"

"Samantha wants you out."

"Sweet girl, our Sam. What do we do? Run out through it? That's fine for you. You can survive a burning building falling on you."

Tain folded his arms. "Whenever you're done with your drink . . ."

The magic shield cracked like breaking glass, and fire roared through the open door. Merrick threw aside his brandy and leapt to his feet. "What now?"

The window that had afforded the beautiful view of the sea and pier was already broken. Tain kicked away melting, jagged shards and stepped up to the cleared sill.

"You've got to be kidding me," Merrick said, eyes wide. "We're at least fifty feet up."

Flame roared through the room, engulfing the opulent leather couch on which Merrick had just been sitting. Without a word, Tain picked up the protesting Merrick, slung the demon-man over his shoulder, balanced a moment in the window, and stepped off the sill.

Merrick screamed obscenities. Tain threw a handful of white-hot magic at the ground to slow their fall, but he still landed hard, going down with Merrick's weight. Tain rolled and came back to his feet as the building's bricks began popping out with the heat.

Paramedics dragged Merrick out of the way, he collapsing against them and groaning. Tain tossed off his ruined coat and scrubbed his hand across his grimy, cut face.

Samantha hurried to them, her dark eyes round. She reached for Tain, her cool hand contacting his hot skin, an impulsive gesture of worry and caring.

"Are you all right? I saw you jump."

Tain waved off the paramedic who was trying to get him to sit down and be examined. "Merrick will live." He glanced at the demon the paramedics were easing onto a stretcher. "But I think he wet himself on the way down."

"I would too if you jumped out the window with me. You damn near gave me a heart attack." Samantha's eyes were watering, probably from all the smoke. She blinked them clear, then looked at him in horror. "Tain, your *hair*."

Tain put his hand up and came away with a handful of brittle, charred lumps. "Doesn't matter. I'll cut it off."

"I like your hair." She sounded wistful.

Tain held out the clumps out to her, the corners of his mouth lifting into a smile. "You can have it if you like it so much."

Samantha put her hand over her mouth, and tears leaked from her eyes. "You are such a shit. I know you can't be hurt, but . . ."

"I *can* be hurt. I hurt all the time."

Again, the cool hand on his wrist. "I hate seeing you like that."

Tain looked into dark eyes that dragged him inside her. He hadn't spoken to Samantha since she'd left the taxi they'd shared from Pasadena two mornings ago. Tain's basic urges had wanted him to go with her into her apartment and stay, but he'd made himself turn away, returning to prowling the city.

He'd wanted her in his own apartment in the small hours of the night, as he lay on his bed and stared at reflections of city lights rippling across his ceiling. He wanted her to be with him, her head snuggled on his shoulder, her silken hair spread over his chest while his neighbor's music thumped through the wall.

Tain craved Samantha like a starving man. He feared the hunger at the same time he embraced it. He didn't want the emotions that had begun to stream through him in Seattle to continue, and at the same time, he didn't want what was nudging its way to his surface destroyed.

Samantha's voice had cut through the nightmare of his mind the night of that final battle. *I prefer to go out kicking and screaming,* she'd said, her voice crisp. And then she'd given him an all-over assessment and told him frankly that she liked what she saw. Samantha had been terrified — Tain had tasted it in the air, and yet she'd looked him in the eye and told him to get over himself.

For the first time in centuries, a spark of interest had crept into Tain's dark, tormented world. A half-demon woman, of all people, had finally snapped his bonds.

Tain touched the corner of Samantha's mouth, wiping away a smudge of soot. He stroked again, the softness of her like rose petals against his fingertips.

The chaos around him vanished—the stench, the shouting, the fear of the fire's victims. Tain saw only Samantha, her dark eyes, her red lips slightly parted, her skin beneath his touch.

Samantha swallowed, her slender throat working. "We should go talk to Merrick," she said, voice cracking.

Tain traced the corner of her lip with one finger, something tight inside him loosening. Then he lifted his hand from her, though he still held her gaze.

Samantha swallowed again and stepped back, turning her burning black eyes away from him.

Tain's heart bore a little ache as he followed her to the ambulance where the paramedics had carried Merrick on his stretcher, an oxygen mask over his mouth and nose. Merrick's hair had burned too, leaving him half-bald and scowling.

"Hi, Merrick," Samantha said in a cheerful voice. "Glad to see you made it."

The demon mumbled something, the words lost behind the mask.

"Any idea what happened?" she asked him. The no-nonsense policewoman was back, the demon seductress hidden away.

Merrick nodded. They'd bandaged burns on his hands, which made his fingers clumsy as he fumbled with his suit jacket. "In the pocket," he said under the plastic mask.

Samantha took a pair of latex gloves from her pocket, pulled them on, and dipped her fingers into the ruined silk of Merrick's coat. She pulled out a piece of paper, which she unfolded.

Tain read over her shoulder. In letters cut from newspapers and magazines, the message read, *Thy Doom is Here.*

Merrick slid his mask to his forehead. "Found it this morning as I was closing up. I didn't know what the hell it meant, but I guess I do now."

Samantha folded the paper and dropped it into a bag for forensics. "I'll have it checked for prints or anything else that can help us, but I'm not hopeful. Do you know how the fire started?"

"Explosion of some kind, I think in the room right under my bedroom. It spread fast. I didn't know fire could move that fast."

"It can. Especially if it was helped along by fuel or magic. Or both."

"No kidding." His sarcasm carried beyond the oxygen mask. "Please tell me you're going after the bastards."

Samantha nodded, looking competent and confident, another thing she was good at. "You'll be happy to know that Kemmerer of the Djowlan clan is in jail. He sold Nadia and her sister to their captors."

"I heard." Merrick oozed satisfaction in spite of his life in ruins around him. "Did he tell you who the captors were?"

"He didn't know. They took good care to keep from being seen. We had a telepath do lie detection on him, but he's telling the truth. He doesn't know. And lo and behold, he's been getting the same kind of 'doom' letters you are. I have the feeling these captors and letter senders are one in the same."

"Good work, detective," Merrick said in a dry voice.

"Don't push it. The fire is a pretty good way to hide any traces of Mindglow we might have found if we searched your club."

"Oh, please. I'm not blithering stupid enough to burn down my own club to get rid of evidence."

"I know." Samantha patted Merrick's shoulder. "I was teasing you. I'll get whoever's doing this, I promise you that."

Tain believed her. Samantha wore a determined look, and Tain had the feeling she'd do any kind of crazy thing she could think of to bring down the perpetrators. Which meant Tain needed to stick with her to keep her alive through it all.

Samantha had saved his life once. Maybe if he got her alive through this, it would make things even.

Tain knew things between him and Samantha would never be even, but the idea was one he could grasp amid the smoke and madness, a tiny lifeline to cling to.

***

When Fulton told Samantha she needed to dress formally to meet the clan matriarch, he meant it. No slinky dresses, no spike-heeled shoes, no bare legs, no bare shoulders.

Samantha had to rent a gown, a shimmering blue silk with elbow-length sleeves, a collar that hugged the base of her neck, and a long skirt. The bodice itched, and she had to kick the skirt out of the way to walk, but Fulton said it was modest enough for the matriarch.

"I feel like I'm being presented to the queen," Samantha muttered as she studied herself in the full-length mirror in her mother's guest room. Of course, in the demon way of thinking, she pretty much was.

Tain met Samantha at Joanne's house, from which Fulton would drive them to the matriarch's mansion. Fulton had made it clear that the matriarch had agreed to see Samantha only after a long debate. Fulton speculated that the reason the matriarch had granted the audience at all was her curiosity about Tain.

Tain's idea of formal was a Scottish dress kilt. Samantha stopped in heart-pounding delight when she saw him.

Whatever the Celtic man of fashion had been wearing eighteen centuries ago, Samantha didn't know, but Tain had chosen a black suit coat, white shirt, and red-and-black plaid kilt. He was a big man, but the coat fit him perfectly, tailor-made, she could tell. The kilt's hem brushed just below his knees, and his muscular calves were encased in supple black boots.

He'd cut his hair close, shaving off the hanks that had singed in the fire. Samantha had loved Tain's longish, sleek red hair, but she had to admit he looked pretty good in a buzz. The cut emphasized the sharp lines of his face, high cheekbones, square jaw, and the pentacle tattoo black against Tain's skin.

Samantha wet her lips. "We don't match. I would have worn black or something, if I'd known you'd wear that."

"Doesn't matter," he said absently.

Of course it didn't; it wasn't as though they were going as a couple. "Never mind. My father is ready to go."

Samantha kissed her mother goodbye and climbed into Fulton's SUV. Joanne wasn't allowed to accompany them, being human. Fulton didn't like leaving her behind, although it was clear he could do nothing about it.

Samantha sat in the front seat of the SUV with Fulton, and Tain took the seat right behind Samantha. Fulton made for the freeway, giving them plenty of instructions as he drove.

"When we get there, don't talk to anyone, and don't ask any questions. Don't look around the house, and don't let on that you're curious about anything you do see. Don't speak to the matriarch before she speaks to you, and then only if she asks you a direct question. If she decides, when we get there, that she doesn't want to see us at all, we leave. No questions, no arguments."

Samantha listened with growing uneasiness. "I'm starting to think this is a bad idea."

Fulton scowled. "It *is* a bad idea."

"It's her way of protecting herself," Tain said from the backseat. "Matriarchs live in constant fear of being overthrown either by a rival clan or from within."

"I suppose that's true," Samantha conceded. "I'm surprised she agreed to see Tain at all."

"She knows who he is and what he did to the Old One last year," Fulton said. "She admitted to being curious."

Fulton drove them to Beverly Hills, the SUV winding up manicured streets and past gated mansions. One particularly long, twisting road ended at a huge iron gate that looked delicate, but Samantha could see it was thick and strong.

Fulton pulled to a stop in front of a gatehouse, where two guards—both demons—sauntered out to ask them their business and then to search the car. Tain had to relinquish his short swords and Samantha the gun in her purse, though Tain made sure the guards locked everything in a cabinet in their gatehouse instead of simply tossing the weapons onto their desk.

After contacting the main house, the guards told Fulton to park in a designated lot halfway up the drive. Two more guards in an electric cart met them at the SUV and drove them the rest of the way to the house.

Samantha realized the parking area was strategically located, so that if she and her father managed to smuggle in explosives in the SUV, the vehicle lay too far from both gate and house to do immediate damage to either one.

"It's easier to get onto a military base," Samantha said as Tain helped her from the electric cart at the front door.

"The matriarch can't afford to take chances," Fulton answered. He was nervous, which showed in his walk and clipped words.

Tain kept his hand lightly on the small of Samantha's back as they moved up the shallow steps. Tain's warmth behind her contrasted to the death magic she felt blanketing the house, and she wondered how he could stand such a concentration of it.

More demon guards met them inside the front door. Fulton had warned Samantha not to look around, but she couldn't help tilting her head back as they entered the lofty main hall.

The mansion was as opulent as any movie mogul's, with glittering, empty reception rooms on either side of the hall. A wrought iron staircase wound up through the middle of the house, but it, like the rooms and the hall, was empty. The setting sun slanted through western windows, and trees outside cast thick shadows, rendering the hall dim, despite the electric chandelier turned on full, high above them.

The guards led them to the very back of the house to a small elevator and ushered them inside.

The elevator went down, not up. Off balance, Samantha reached for the nearest thing to steady herself, which happened to be Tain. Her hand locked on his wrist, and when she would have pulled away, he put his hand on hers, keeping her there.

The elevator door slid open to reveal an underground floor as opulent as upstairs. The rooms that opened off the square hall were lit with warm artificial light instead of sunlight, but they were just as empty.

The guard tapped on a closed double door at the end of the hallway. He stepped back deferentially as the door was pulled open, and a tall, thin woman with a short haircut and business suit stared out at them.

She was a demon but reminded Samantha of a severe maître d' she'd seen once in a posh restaurant that catered to CEOs and movie execs. The woman regarded the three of them with cold dark eyes, told them she was the matriarch's majordomo, and announced that the matriarch would see them now.

"Samantha, what will you drink?" came a voice from across the room. A second woman, equally as tall and thin, turned from a gilded, wheeled drink cart that was clustered with crystal glasses, decanters, and bottles. She lifted an ice cube from a bucket with silver tongs and regarded Samantha quizzically.

The matriarch was as severe as her majordomo, her salt-and-pepper hair cut short in a close, businesslike style. Her gray silk suit expressed expense as did her stately high-heeled shoes. Gold rings with small precious stones clasped every finger, and equally opulent but tasteful earrings hung from her small earlobes.

Her look said *powerful businesswoman,* one who'd been around long enough to become a force to be reckoned with. Demons could make themselves look any human age they wished, and the matriarch's deliberate choice of late fifties had been designed to command respect.

The matriarch's ice tongs hovered, waiting. Fulton sent Samantha a glance that said she'd better hurry up and choose what to drink. Samantha said quickly, "Whatever you'd like to fix is fine with me."

The matriarch gave her a look of disappointment. "Scotch and soda, then."

"All right."

The matriarch mixed the drink herself and pointedly did not offer anything to Tain or Fulton. "I heard what you did last year against Kehksut," she said conversationally to Tain as she stirred Samantha's drink with a long silver stick. "I was pleased at the Old One's death. He disrupted the balance of power among demonkind, especially here in Los Angeles."

"I was pleased at his death too," Tain said, his blue eyes quiet.

"You would be," the matriarch said. She moved her dark gaze to Samantha as she handed Samantha's drink to the silent majordomo. "You, Samantha, work to protect humans against your own kind."

"Not only humans," Samantha said quickly, taking the heavy crystal glass the majordomo brought to her. "I protect against any paranormal criminal—demon, vampire, werewolf, or otherwise. I also protect our kind against humans or other paranormals who would harm them."

"So many species, living together in our vast city," the matriarch said, her tone acid. "Celebrating diversity."

"It's the only way to survive in Los Angeles."

"Your human blood taints your perspective. Demons don't want to live with other races. We are for ourselves. The vampires can't come out into the sunlight, which gives us great advantage. The humans fear the night, which gives us another great advantage. When the lesser races kill each other off, the demons will be left standing." The matriarch gave Samantha a pointed look. "Where will you be?"

Chapter Ten

Samantha felt Tain at her back, though she'd not seen him move across the room to her. He said nothing, but his warmth behind her gave her strength.

Samantha had met demons like the matriarch before — a demon for demons. The matriarch might seduce humans and imbibe their life essences, but she would always regard them as a lesser species, made to be victims. She'd give humans as much respect as a human might give the slice of chicken on his plate. A demon with human blood likely got even less respect.

"I asked my father to bring me here to tell you about demons who are being targeted in the city," Samantha said, deciding to get down to business. "Merrick, a Lamiah demon who owns a club in Venice, received threats, and then his club was burned down. A club owner of the Djowlan clan has also received threats. And two young women from the Lamiah clan were kidnapped and tortured, one of them killed."

"I heard about the one called Nadia and her sister," the matriarch said, her voice frosty. "No vengeance will be taken. They are no longer clan Lamiah. They weren't even before the incident."

Samantha blinked. "They weren't? Nadia said she was Lamiah."

Both matriarch and majordomo looked displeased. "Their family shunned them," the matriarch said. "As should be. A demon woman who walks the streets drinking life essence for pay is a disgusting creature. Working in clubs is barely acceptable, but when the woman becomes nothing more than a prostitute, she shames her family and their clan. Nadia's parents were told to disown their daughters, which they did."

"Oh." Nadia's file had said her parents were dead, and Nadia hadn't contradicted the fact. Samantha had thought that what demons did in clubs and on the streets was perfectly acceptable to other demons. She'd had no idea some demons would view it with distaste, just as humans viewed women and men who sold their bodies with similar distaste.

"You think me harsh?" the matriarch asked her.

Samantha felt her father's warning look, but she ignored it. "I do."

"It is necessary. Women rule the clans for good reason. If males were allowed to rule, there would be chaos and destruction, and we'd have died out long ago. For women to let themselves be slaves to men is an abomination. Those who don't obey the rules shall be clanless."

Samantha wondered whether the matriarch directed the last words as a warning at her and Fulton. "Still, someone is targeting demon clubs and the people associated with them," Samantha said. "The fact that members of two different clans have received similar threatening letters worries me."

"Vampires," the matriarch said dismissively.

"Not vampires," Samantha said. "When vamps want to kill demons, they kill them. No threats, no abductions, no setting fires to clubs."

"Perhaps."

"I came to ask if you've heard anything that might help me. Have you received threatening letters yourself?"

The matriarch snorted. "Of course I have. I receive threatening letters every day of my life. I am the matriarch, and there are always those in the clan who want more power than they should."

"I think this is more than clan politics. It started with the clubs, but the troubles might spread to include all demons."

The matriarch gave Samantha a cold look. "No being can topple the most powerful clan of demons on earth. Except perhaps him." She gave Tain a sweeping glance. "You overestimate the danger, girl."

"Merrick's club burned to the ground, and he nearly died," Samantha said, her voice hard. "Nadia's sister *did* die, in a most brutal way. Are you saying all this has nothing to do with you?"

"I am. And if you were true demon, you'd understand that." The matriarch's already cool gaze turned frigid. "What is it you really want, Samantha? You are a half demon, half human, neither one thing or the other. Is it power you wish? Over demons? Is that why you work for the human-controlled police department?"

"I told you, I try to help people — both human and non-human."

"It eats at you, doesn't it? Being split down the middle? Your demon instincts tell you to do one thing; your human instincts, something else."

Fulton moved closer to Samantha, and Tain remained solidly at her back.

"I'm used to it," Samantha said, maintaining her professional tone. "I've learned to put aside my personal feelings to do my job."

"Detective." The matriarch smiled. "Would you arrest me?"

Samantha gave her a stiff nod. "If you were committing a crime, yes."

"You sound so certain of yourself." The matriarch's aura began to darken, her death magic rising. "How would you arrest me if I didn't permit it?"

"I usually work with a partner." Samantha kept her voice steady, determined not to let the woman intimidate her — or at least not to show that she did. "For tough cases, the department has powerful witches or vampires, even demons, ready to assist."

"But if you came across me alone? Or if I tried to kill your father, right here and now, what would you do?"

The field of death magic around the matriarch strengthened, and she raised her hand. Samantha stepped protectively in front of Fulton, painfully aware that her pistol was locked far away in the gatehouse. She had cuffs with her that contained a subduing magical field, but she'd have to get close to the matriarch to use them.

"Show me," the matriarch said. "Show me what you'd do if you had to arrest me right now."

Samantha sensed her father's rising anger, and she touched his hand, signaling him to keep quiet. The majordomo watched the drama with cold, glittering eyes, a faint smile on her face.

And Tain . . .

Tain did nothing. He remained near Samantha, looking utterly devastating in his kilt, his legs braced apart, his arms folded across his chest.

"I'd call for backup," Samantha said, opening her purse. "Then I'd try to subdue you."

"How?" The matriarch watched her with almost fanatic intensity. "I want to see."

Samantha drew a breath, and then let her anger take over. Fine — if the matriarch wanted to know what would really happen, Samantha was happy to give her a demonstration.

Samantha handed the majordomo her untouched drink and yanked the cuffs from her purse. "I'd call for backup," she repeated, tossing aside her purse and advancing with a swift stride. "And then I'd get you cuffed and read you your rights."

Samantha knew that, physically, she could spin the slender woman around, pin her to a wall, and cuff her quickly and efficiently. She'd done it to vampires twice her own size—they were shackled and subdued before they knew what hit them.

However, she knew she couldn't best the woman magically, and she suspected that magic was what this was all about. The matriarch was testing her resolve.

The matriarch allowed Samantha to get within three feet of her. Then she let fly her death magic, both at Samantha and Fulton. It was nasty magic, designed to kill. Samantha felt its suffocating finality, and knew the breath would go out of her as soon as the magic touched her.

She dove hastily aside, but the dark spell sought her, twisting around her like a net. Samantha brought up her hands, hoping the negation spell on the handcuffs might help a little, but the matriarch was one of the most powerful demons in Los Angeles.

Light suddenly exploded through the room as a blast of white-hot life magic burst around Samantha and the net of darkness, lifting Samantha a few inches off her feet. She landed again, hard, on her one-inch heels, her heart pounding.

The pulse of life magic tangled around the death magic and crushed it to nothing. A smell of sulfur mixed with the acrid scent of burned wire trickled through the room a silent moment, then dispersed.

Tain hadn't moved. His blue gaze met Samantha's as she turned to him, the power in his eyes making her flinch. He crackled with magic, white fire glowing around him and dimming the rest of the room.

The death magic of the place wasn't hurting him at all; the matriarch nothing to an Immortal demigod who'd destroyed the most powerful demon in existence. Tain could kill every demon in this house right now, without thought, without even breathing hard.

Samantha remembered how gentle he'd been when he kissed her in her apartment, and again when he'd touched her face at the fire, after he'd leapt fifty feet down a burning building to save a demon butthole like Merrick.

The compassion Samantha had briefly glimpsed in him had vanished. The Tain who stood here was the hardened warrior who'd lived for centuries—merciless, dangerous, and brutal.

He really could wipe out a room by twitching his pinky.

The matriarch was shaken, but she strove to hide it behind another frosty smile. "I wondered what you'd do if I threatened her," she said to Tain. "What is Samantha Taylor to you?"

"She saved my life," Tain said, giving the matriarch the full force of his white-blue gaze. "I owe her my protection."

"But she's demon," the matriarch argued. "Didn't a demon enslave and torture you for seven hundred years?"

"Even so," Tain said quietly.

"That's what I thought," the matriarch said, sounding smug. "Thank you, Samantha, for a most enlightening display. I want you to leave now."

***

Samantha followed the guards out the front door of the matriarch's house, her heart still beating swiftly. Tain strode behind her, his footfalls loud in the quiet.

The matriarch had commanded Fulton to remain behind, and her father had obeyed. Samantha hadn't wanted to leave him, but the matriarch had smiled and said she was finished with intimidation today and needed to speak to Fulton on clan business.

Fulton had given Samantha a brief hug. "It's all right, Sam. I'll be fine. I'll talk to you tomorrow."

The demon guards had met them outside the suite's door, which the majordomo, who'd remained silent the entire time, opened for them. The guards, still in human form but nervous now, led Tain and Samantha back to the elevator, up through the house, and outside.

Night had fallen while they'd been underground, and Samantha and Tain emerged to floodlights which lit the mansion and manicured gardens around it. A guard drove them in the electric cart past Fulton's SUV and all the way to the gate. One of the gate guards called for a taxi and told Samantha they'd have to wait for it outside the gate. None of them spoke to Tain at all.

The demons at the gate had obviously heard about or sensed Tain's show of magic in the matriarch's room, because the guards regarded him uneasily and dealt with them as quickly as they could. They returned Samantha's pistol and Tain's swords, the guard who held Tain's swords handling them gingerly, as though the pieces of metal might explode.

The big iron gate rolled closed behind Tain and Samantha as they walked out, the guards visibly relaxing as the two moved a little way down the street.

"The matriarch owes me cab fare," Samantha growled.

"She likes to manipulate," Tain said. "It's part of her power."

"I didn't notice you saying much in there." Samantha folded her arms over her shining blue gown. "I rented this damned dress for nothing."

"I wouldn't say for nothing."

Tain raked his gaze down her body, and Samantha's skin heated. His look could be as warm as a touch.

"Why do you think she brought us here then?" she asked.

Tain shrugged, muscles working under his coat. "To learn about you. And me. I let her learn what she already thought, nothing more."

Samantha raised her brows. "Keeping yourself to yourself, were you?"

"To her. For now."

"Not only to her," Samantha said.

His eyes were deep blue in the glare of the floodlights, and fixed on her. The black coat emphasized his broad shoulders and hard body, the straps that held his sheathed swords in place crisscrossed over his chest.

With the swords and his kilt, Tain looked like a Scottish warrior of old, one every maiden would want fighting for her. The goddesses had certainly done good work with him.

"Better that I keep myself to myself," Tain said in a quiet voice.

"Better for who?"

"The gods only know what I will do if I lose control again. Better to hold myself away, don't you think?"

He spoke in his usual musical-sounding voice, but something flashed in his eyes, a loneliness so deep and wrenching that Samantha's heart tore.

Tain had been alone for seven hundred years, ripped from everything he knew and loved, imprisoned at first by chains, then by his own mind. Now that he was free, Samantha realized, Tain didn't know how to find his life again, how to return to day-to-day existence. Everything had changed since his capture; everything he'd ever known was gone.

Samantha hurt for him, and hurt even more to know he didn't want her sympathy. "What about that Ravenscroft place?" she asked in a light voice. "Isn't that supposed to be some kind of Valhalla, where nothing can hurt you?"

Tain gave her a nod. "I was there for a time. It helped a little." Samantha saw more despair, the knowledge that even his haven hadn't wiped out his years of fear and pain. "But I can't hide forever, can I? Licking my wounds and whining about it?"

"I suppose that's a point."

"Would you hide from yourself?" Tain touched her cheek, fingers like fire. "I think you wouldn't."

Samantha tried not to lean into his caress. "I want to help you."

"You are demon." Tain's finger and his gaze drifted to her lips. "You call to me. I should back away from you most of all. You and your seductive glamour."

"I told you, I don't cast a glam." Samantha could barely stop her voice from shaking. "Half demons don't—why don't you know that?"

Another caress, this one across the sensitive skin beneath her lower lip. "I didn't know any half demons in my old life. Half demons were killed at birth."

"Oh, that's pleasant."

"The world is different now."

Samantha took a step back, making herself break his touch. "Thank the goddesses for that. I can't glam. I don't have a tenth of the magic the matriarch in there has, or even some of what my own father has."

Tain let his hand drift back to his side, his eyes dark in the ambient glare from the floodlights behind the wall. "Doesn't matter. You're twisting me around inside so much that all I dream of at night is you."

Samantha's heart squeezed so hard her breath threatened to desert her. She was sure every woman in the world would want a man like Tain, with his blue eyes and looking that good in his kilt, to tell her he dreamed about her. She swallowed. "You do?"

"I fall asleep, and you're next to me."

"Looking like the demon I am?"

"Looking as you do now, with your eyes drawing me in, your hair like silk on my shoulder."

His voice went soft, his lilt pronounced as he leaned to her. Samantha didn't back away this time, and his hot breath brushed her cheek.

She gave him a nervous smile. "In your dreams, I'm not wearing this awful dress, I take it?"

"You're bare for me. And I want you. I want you so much it burns me from the inside out."

Samantha wet her lips. "I hope this dream has a happy ending."

"I take you. And I take you again. I take you all night, coming alive inside you, in a way I haven't been alive in centuries." Tain's eyes were fixed on her, his entire focus for Samantha and Samantha alone. No distractions, only his amazing eyes and the heat of his magic wrapping around her.

Samantha couldn't breathe. Her skin was on fire, the space between her legs needy. She thought of his kiss, the smooth seduction of his lips. She wanted that again, though she knew she'd burn up and melt if his mouth touched hers.

"But then I wake up and you're gone," Tain said, his voice going bleak. "You were never there."

The emptiness in his words made Samantha's heart ache. She said softly, "I made a fool out of myself the other night, asking you to stay."

Tain's eyes went hard again. "If I'd have stayed that night I wouldn't have gone slowly. I might have hurt you. In the dream I can do whatever I want to you, but in reality . . ."

Samantha's throat was tight. "I'm no delicate flower. I went through some pretty tough training to become a cop and then extra because I'm in paranormal division. Arresting a vampire in a blood frenzy isn't exactly the same as bringing in a jaywalker—unless it's a jaywalking vampire in a blood frenzy. I survived."

"You would never survive me."

"I have already. In Seattle, remember?"

Tain's white-hot magic flickered through his eyes. "In Seattle I decided to let you go. You've never fought me in truth."

Samantha took a hesitant step closer to him. He stood his ground, a muscle twitching in his face, as though he expected a blow.

She touched his chest. His skin was hotter than any human's, and his heart beat swiftly under her fingertips. "If I asked you to stay the night again, what would you say?"

His voice remained harsh. "I should say no."

Samantha slid her fingers to the side of his neck. "Please say yes."

Tain looked down at with his fathomless deep eyes, and she saw the spark of pain and darkness deep within them. She knew he would never kiss her, especially not here on the sidewalk outside the demon matriarch's mansion. He'd never let go of the tight hold on himself to do it. So Samantha rose on her tiptoes and kissed him instead.

Tain didn't move. Samantha lightly kissed his lips, brushing the smooth warmth of them, feeling the amazing life essence of Tain. He stood rigidly as she kissed his lips again and again, then he made a low noise in his throat and scooped her up to him. He slanted his mouth over hers, furrowing her hair with hard fingers, opening her lips with a bruising, punishing kiss.

He tasted like fire, and Samantha was happy to burn. She touched the back of his neck, loving the strength she found in him, and smoothed her hand to the short silk of his hair.

Her body squeezed, imagining him inside her, his thick cock parting her and taking what he wanted. She would readily let him, because she wanted it too.

Samantha stepped daringly close to him, indulging in the feel of his body through the thin gown, the rough of the kilt pressing her skirt. Stupid dress had to be good for something.

Headlights swept over them, probably the taxi arriving. *Damn the driver's great timing.*

The guards at the gate shouted something. The headlights swerved sharply, and Tain wrenched away from Samantha as a large pickup truck slammed itself into the gates.

The iron structure was sturdy enough to take the force, and it held. Without waiting for the guards to react, two demons leapt out of the truck and started running at Tain and Samantha.

Tain shoved Samantha behind him, hands going for his swords, but the demons parted around them, sprinting up the street away from the mansion.

Samantha yanked her badge out of her evening bag. *A perfect ending to a perfect day.* "Hey! Stop, I'm a police officer—"

Tain grabbed Samantha with rough hands, and her words cut off into a surprised breath. He threw her around the corner of the high block wall just as white-hot fire lit up the night, and the roar of exploding truck at the gates rang to the stars.

Chapter Eleven

Tain got to his feet, putting himself protectively in front of Samantha. In the red, hot light from the burning truck, he saw the iron gate twisted off its hinges and lying in a mangled heap inside the wall. The gatehouse was in ruins, and the surviving guards were sprinting for the house.

Three dark vans screeched up to the now-open gate. Demons leapt out of the vehicles and ran past the burning truck into the complex. They ignored Samantha and Tain in the shadows, their intentions fixed on the Lamiah compound.

Samantha struggled to her feet, her blue dress torn and mud-stained, fury in her eyes. She tore her cell phone out of her purse and punched with her thumb.

"Lieutenant," she yelled into the phone. "We have a situation."

More demons ran through the gates as Samantha finished and dropped the phone back into her purse. She drew out her pistol and started for the gates, but Tain grabbed her arm, dragging her back. Samantha flashed a glare at him and tried to wrench herself away, but Tain clamped down, letting his full strength come to the surface.

"Let me go!" Samantha said, struggling. "My father is in there."

"He's demon," Tain said in a hard voice. "He knows how to fight. If he's with the matriarch, he's more protected than we are."

Samantha's eyes were anguished, but she finally subsided. "What do you expect us to do then? Watch them start a war?"

"No."

Tain drew one of his swords and pulled Samantha behind him as he made his way around the burning truck and into the compound.

Demons were everywhere, the ones in human form in combat gear, others in their muscular, mottled-skin forms. The demons didn't all look the same — some were large and fearsome, some were smaller and had wings, and others looked nearly human except for demonic faces and horns.

Tain wasn't expert enough to tell the Lamiah clan defenders from whatever clan was attacking. He knew the difference between Old Ones and lesser demons, but after that nothing was clear. While Tain had been in captivity, lesser demons had politicized themselves into complex clans with complex loyalties, and the world was no longer simple.

He knew he could kill all the demons — he had that power. The matriarch had known it as well and had indicated, by the little test in her lair, that she was trusting him not to. She had metaphorically stretched out her neck and waited to see if Tain would chop off her head. Tain had showed the matriarch, in return, that he hadn't returned to the world to practice the indiscriminate slaughter of demons.

The problem was, Tain didn't know whether he could stick to that resolve. The temptation to raise his hand and obliterate every demon in the place right now, which would include Samantha's father, was strong. He gulped breaths of night air, fighting the impulse.

"Well?" Samantha asked, watching the demons, pistol tight in her grip. "What do we do? Backup is coming, but these guys can do a lot of damage before then."

Tain drew his second sword. Fighting down another wave of need to simply kill everything in sight, he brought the blades together and pointed them toward the house.

Life magic flowed from the sword tips across the lawn and to the house, the magic spreading outward as it touched the mansion to cover it in a gleaming net. Tain willed his magic to change from destructive to protective, and a glow of flickering blue encased the house, throwing back the attackers who'd reached it. They yelled and snarled, picking themselves up to regroup.

The defenders inside didn't much like it either. Tain heard screams, shouts, and curses from those within. He turned away without sympathy. Better the demons suffer a little nausea from a dose of life magic than Samantha's people be chopped into pieces.

Samantha stared in awe, her face grimy in the glow of the compound's lights and the still-burning truck. "Gee, wish I could do that."

She smiled at him, the warm smile that reminded Tain how good she'd tasted when he'd kissed her. He wanted to draw her up to him, lean down, and kiss those smiling lips, savoring every bit of her. He could take what he wanted from her, act out his dreams—he was strong enough—but he knew exactly the worth of something extracted by force. Something given freely was a much sweeter gift.

The attacking demons looked around for the source of the magic and didn't take long to focus on Tain and Samantha. A demon in human form, his face fined-boned and almost delicate over his combat gear, pointed an automatic rifle at them.

"Who are you?" he demanded.

"I protect them," Tain answered calmly.

"This is our fight, mage. Get out of it."

Tain lowered his swords in silence, but the blue light remained intact around the house. It would stay until he decided to remove it.

The demon snarled in fury, brought his rifle up, and opened fire at Tain. Samantha yelled and dove for the ground, but Tain held up one hand. The barrage of bullets parted around Tain and Samantha, and then dissolved from existence with little pops of light.

The demon stared, his dirty face pale. "What the fuck kind of thing *are* you?"

"A protector," Tain said.

The demon spun away and shouted at his followers to surround Tain and Samantha.

You could so easily kill them all, the voice inside Tain whispered.

He knew exactly how. He could lift his hand and send a wave of pure death to surround and suffocate the demons. They'd drop to the ground, lifeless, and all would be silence.

But then Samantha would look at him with horror in her coffee-brown eyes. He'd lose everything she'd given him so far, every smile, every tiny bit of trust, every moment of their budding friendship. All would be for nothing.

The darkness in Tain's mind kept screaming at him, willing him to forget Samantha, a half demon, and sweep out with his magic. *These are demon-kind, and they should die.*

Samantha struggled to her feet. "You're a great diplomat," she growled at him. "Now what?"

Tain hooked his arm around Samantha's waist and pulled her up beside him. He shoved the whispering voice into a corner of his mind and concentrated on Samantha's scent and the sensation of her against him. "You could always arrest them," he said, straight-faced.

"Very funny. How are you going to get us out of here?"

Tain turned to the delicate-faced male demon. "What is your quarrel with the Lamiah clan?"

"What do you mean, what is my quarrel? My quarrel is that Lamiah trash stole my daughter and sent back her corpse! They'll die for that."

Samantha's eyes widened. "What? What happened? Why didn't you report it?"

"I *did* report it." The demon's eyes were filled with fury but also bleak pain. "I reported it to my warriors, and we're here to take our vengeance."

"I'm sorry," Samantha said quickly. "Trust me, I am. But no one in Lamiah clan touched her."

The demon pointed his weapon at her. "Of course they did. This had Lamiah clan all over it, along with those damned letters."

"Printed in cutouts?" Samantha asked.

"That's them. Did you send those?"

"Lamiah clan has been getting them as well," Samantha said. "And they've been losing daughters too."

"They'd kill their own kind to cover up a murder. Take the magic off the house and let us in there. I'm cutting out the heart of your matriarch bitch."

A demon next to him, this one in monster form, jerked his chin at Tain. "He's the one who wrecked Kemmerer's."

The delicate-faced demon's attention snapped back to Tain.

"He was there, yes," Samantha said swiftly. "Talking to the Djowlan demon who sold two Lamiah clan women to captors—likely the same captors who killed your daughter."

The second demon growled. "This bitch was there too. Half-breed. Demon tainted with human blood. The one in the kilt killed our boys at Merrick's."

Demons closed behind them, all furious.

"Tain," Samantha said nervously.

"Last chance," the lead demon said. "Stop defending Lamiah, and we might let you live."

"No," Tain answered.

The lead demon snarled in fury and shouted a command. Those around Tain and Samantha attacked.

Samantha swung around to be back-to-back with Tain, her pistol out, telling Tain at the top of her voice what she thought of his powers of persuasion. Tain sent streams of white magic from his swords to hold the demons back, but he was running out of options. He was powerful, but he had to keep the magic over the house, beat back the demons without harming them, and keep them from hurting Samantha.

Killing them all would be so much easier, the voice reminded him.

At one time Tain would have agreed. Kehksut had killed and tortured arbitrarily to prove that his power was great.

But Tain knew, had always known, that having power didn't mean only wielding death. Kehksut had never been able to take that understanding away from him, which was one reason Tain was now free. The woman fighting like mad at Tain's back was the other reason.

A smaller demon with wings sailed under Tain's reach and swooped behind them. He let out a stream of gelatinous acid that splashed up and down Tain's back and all over Samantha.

Samantha screamed. Tain swung around and swept the demon aside with a burst of magic. Samantha was already writhing on the ground, trying to claw the sleek liquid from her body.

Tain threw a final blast of magic at the demons then dropped to his hands and knees to Samantha, desperately gathering his healing magic to pour into her.

The acid was a thick glue-like substance that clung stubbornly to Samantha's skin. It would eat her flesh to her bones in minutes. The thin silk dress couldn't keep it out, and already her face was red with blood, her screams fading to hoarse sobs.

The battle receded and grew dim. Tain saw nothing but Samantha, felt nothing but her torment. Sweat dripped from him as he willed all his magic into her, picturing in his mind the interconnected fibers of her skin and muscle knitting back together.

He swore in several languages as the acid reopened the skin he'd just closed. Tain had to wash the goo off her or she'd die.

Beyond the gate, blue and red lights flashed, and a helicopter cut overhead, training its spotlight on the compound. More bullets flew, this time between demons and the paranormal police that had come to put them down.

Tain lifted Samantha and made for the gate. Police meant police cars, and one could get her to safety.

Logan stepped in front of Tain, handgun ready. "Holy shit. What happened?"

"She got acid-burned," Tain said curtly. "I need to get it off her. Do you have a car?"

"Sure . . ."

"No," Samantha said weakly. "Get one of the uniforms to take me. McKay will have your hide if you leave the scene, Logan."

"Paramedics can deal with acid burns," Logan said.

"Not fast enough," Tain snapped. "Get me a car — *now.*"

Logan swung away, galvanized into obeying. He signaled to a passing uniformed policeman and gave him instructions. In a few minutes, Tain held Samantha in the back of a patrol car, its lights flashing as they sped out of Beverly Hills to the grittier parts of town.

Tain cradled Samantha in his arms, the black grill between them and the driver throwing spangled lights over her face. He whispered rapid words of healing as he sank his magic into her, trying to slow the corrosion.

The uniform dropped them off inside Samantha's complex, and Tain was out of the backseat and halfway up the stairs before the officer could offer to help take her inside. Tain growled at him to go, and the car peeled off.

Pickles meowed and jumped onto the counter as Tain banged in and slammed the door with his foot. The cat sensed something wrong and followed as Tain strode down the tiny hall to the bathroom and cranked on the shower. Pickles sat down in the hallway and howled.

Tain thrust Samantha under the shower's spray, dress and all, and frantically scrubbed slime from her face with his fingers, her scented soap, and the water.

Heal her. Cerridwen, help me.

Tain was wet himself, his ruined clothes heavy with water. He pulled his coat off and dropped it on the floor, then began peeling the sodden clumps of silk from Samantha's body.

He knew exactly what it felt like to have his flesh stripped from his bones—the agony, the fear, the hope for death that would make the pain stop. He'd felt it every three days for seven hundred years, until his entire existence had revolved around pain.

Tain never, ever wanted Samantha to know what that had been like. He didn't want her to look into the mirror every day and see the scars from the ordeal, didn't want her to loathe herself as Tain loathed the mess of his own body.

Samantha's head lolled, a weak moan escaping her lips. The acid had burned Tain as well, eating through the back of his coat, but he barely felt it.

It took a long time. The shower water and soap at last began to soften the goo so Tain could scrape it from Samantha's skin. He ran his hands over her wet body, willing his magic to ease the burns, close the abraded flesh, make her skin whole and new.

Samantha began to come out of her stupor. She opened her eyes, which were whole and unburned, thank the goddesses, and looked wearily at the ruined clumps of silk scattered over her bathroom floor.

"Oh, great," she said, her voice faint and scratchy. "How do I tell the rental place their gown got slimed by a demon?"

Tain closed his eyes, weak with relief, and gathered her against him.

***

Samantha lay in his arms, aware of his slick body against hers, the tingle racing through her blood she realized was his healing touch. His life magic forced away the poison, healed her skin, and made her draw a deep, shuddering breath.

Tain opened his eyes, the gleam of blue shining through. "You're all right," he said.

"Think so. Not sure yet."

"Gods, Samantha." Tain's arms tightened around her, eyes closing again, his head bowed against her neck.

Samantha stroked his wet hair, something breaking inside her. Holding him was like holding a wild beast, he taming himself to allow her to touch him.

"I'm all right," Samantha said. "I am now."

Tain started to draw away from her. Samantha saw the pain in his eyes, the darkness, the need to hold on, but he was pulling away again. Closing himself to her. Withdrawing.

Samantha gripped his arm, bearing down, though she hardly made a dent in his skin. "Stay. Please."

Tain brushed her hair back from her face, his gaze meeting hers, then evading.

"Please." Samantha clutched at him, knowing she sounded desperate, but she didn't care. "Don't leave me alone."

In silence, Tain slid his touch to her breasts, fingers searching her skin for more acid. He moved his hand across her belly to her hips and round to her buttocks, touching, washing, healing.

His own clothes, sodden, got in the way, and he impatiently pushed them off. His body came into view little by little as he discarded shirt then kilt. His skin was covered with scars, deep, horrifying ones. The wounds were a year healed now, but the pain he must have endured Samantha could barely comprehend. She touched the scars on his shoulders, wishing she could heal him as he healed her.

"No," he said, voice harsh.

"I want you to be whole."

"I never can be." Tain looked down at her, blue gleaming from half-closed eyes. "He hurt me, Samantha. Over and over. He'd hurt me, and then he'd shift his form and come to me as a woman, to sex me as I healed."

Samantha swallowed, not wanting to imagine that. "It's over now." She ran her hands across his wet skin, wishing she could erase the scars, the memories. "You're free. You're finished with it."

Tain opened his eyes fully, the anguish in them heart-wrenching. "No, I'm not. It's all mixed up inside me. Pain and sex, jumbled together, until I don't think I can have one without the other."

And that frightened him, she saw. Tain the Immortal warrior, who'd spared the demons tonight because *he'd* chosen, was afraid. He could have slaughtered the Djowlans and Lamiahs alike and disappeared to his Ravenscroft place, leaving Samantha to clean up the mess. That is, if he hadn't simply killed her as well.

Now Tain was afraid.

Samantha kissed his scarred shoulder. She did it gently, barely touching him, her fingers tender. "It doesn't have to hurt," she said.

Tain stilled. Again Samantha thought of a wild animal, nervous at an unfamiliar touch. She continued to caress him, remaining gentle, before she lifted her head and kissed him.

Tain's body jerked, then he moved his lips in return, shaking, uncertain. This was nothing like the hot frenzy with which he'd kissed her outside the matriarch's mansion. Now Tain was seeking, wondering, fearing. Samantha skimmed her hand down his back, fingers slick with soap, and gathered him against her.

***

Tain couldn't move. His healing magic flowed through him and into Samantha until her skin glowed with it. Her mouth moved against his, her lips slightly parted, the moisture of her hot and enticing.

Samantha was small against his large frame, so mortal, so vulnerable, and so incredibly gentle. Her mouth was a place of warmth and quiet strength, and Tain needed her so much.

He lost all sense of time and place, much like he did when he retreated into the darkness that always waited for him. For now, there was only Samantha and her heat, their lips meeting and parting, her hands on his body, fingers tracing the scars that reminded him of intense pain.

But this time when Tain opened his eyes, he was on the floor of the shower, Samantha lying against him amid the ruins of her blue silk gown. Her skin was whole, the acid gone. She'd live, and be well.

Samantha looked up at him as the water cooled. "Thank you," she whispered. She smiled at Tain in gratitude, and broke his heart.

***

The blanket was prickly on Samantha's wet back as Tain laid her on the bed. She thought he'd follow her down, but he stood back and looked at her, his naked body dripping from the shower.

He was breathtaking. Despite the fading white lines that crisscrossed his arms, thighs, and abdomen, his body was beautiful. He must have been incredible before his ordeal, and he still was. But now Tain wore the weathered, weary look of a man whose innocence had been beaten out of him.

Samantha's skin was pink where the acid had burned it, but she'd been in such merciless pain that a little pinkness was a small price to pay. She'd known she was dying until Tain's healing magic had wrapped itself around her and pulled her back to life.

Now Tain gazed at her in silence, taking in her body from the tips of her toes, up her slightly parted legs, to her breasts, to her face.

He put one knee on the bed and got himself down full-length onto it, not speaking, not smiling. Samantha traced the pentacle tattoo on his cheekbone, her fingers brushing each point of the pentacle then moving around the circle.

Something dark flickered in his blue eyes. "That doesn't hurt you?" he asked, his voice like broken gravel.

"No. Should it?"

Again the flicker. "It's the mark of the Mother Goddess. Cerridwen put it on me when she first came to take me to Ravenscroft."

Samantha drew her palm over the tattoo, then showed him her hand. "See? No burning. No pain. Perfectly fine."

"Kehksut could never touch it."

"Good," Samantha said, her heart warming. "Then he couldn't steal all of you."

Tain took her hand and pressed it again to his tattoo. She felt his pulse in his fingers, the swift beating of his heart, as he let her touch what one of the most powerful beings of demonkind hadn't been able to.

Tain slid on top of her while he kissed her, heavenly warm, his skin still damp. He moved his strong hand between her knees—no sexy talk, no play, just need.

Samantha felt plenty needy herself. She drew the sole of one foot up the back of his leg, welcoming his warm weight.

"You make me want to go slow," Tain said softly. He kissed her chin, his lips a point of fire. "I want to go slowly, to make you more desperate." He trailed kisses along her throat, sliding his body down hers as he went, his lips and tongue finding the valley between her breasts.

Samantha jumped when his kisses reached her navel, and he licked a stray droplet of water from it.

"That would be cruel," Samantha managed to say. "Making me desperate, I mean."

"I'm a cruel man." Tain stroked her belly as he kissed down to the swirl of hair between her legs, his breath scalding. "Not nice at all."

The tension in his body, the stillness of his eyes as he worked back up to her breasts told her he was holding himself in, tempering his strength for her. Even in the shower, Samantha had sensed him trying to contain himself.

Samantha wondered, with a shiver of delight, what it would be like if Tain *didn't* hold back. She was strong, her demon side making her tougher than she looked, but Tain could do what he wanted with her. She wouldn't be able to stop him, and he knew it.

He drew his tongue firmly around the areola of her breast, then took the nipple between his teeth. He closed his eyes as he plied his mouth, his lashes dark against his sunburned skin. His teeth and tongue were gentle, scraping her only enough to make Samantha shiver for more.

When Tain raised his head again, his eyes were so heartbreakingly blue she wanted to hold on to him and never let go. *I could love this man. If he'd let me, I'd fall in love him.*

Tain's hand went to the spread of Samantha's thighs. Slowly he eased himself onto her, his body heavy, his gaze meeting and holding hers.

"Please," Samantha whispered. She rubbed her foot up his leg again, her body open and aching for him.

Tain leaned down to kiss her lips, and his cock, hard and wanting, touched her thigh.

"I can't stop this," he said, brushing her hair back from her face. "If I start, I won't be able to stop."

"Good," Samantha whispered. "I don't want you to stop."

Tain closed his eyes, lines around them tightening as he slid inside her. Her slick need let him come all the way in without impediment. He was big, and Samantha's body flushed hot as she took him.

Tain pushed in a little farther, then he stilled, opening his intense blue eyes. "You all right, love?"

The *love* would break her. He was large inside her, touching something basic and carnal Samantha never knew she possessed.

"Yes," she said, trying to control her voice. "Fine. Good."

Tain bowed his head, and moved. Samantha dragged in a breath as the whole of him came into her again, and she cried out. He kissed her, muffling the sound.

Samantha held on to him, fingertips gripping his back, rocking with him as he built up the rhythm. It was wicked and wild, erotic and stunning. This big, astonishing man had rescued Samantha from demons, cleaned her off in the shower, healed her, and was now loving her, making her feel things she hadn't known she could.

Tain's fists bunched in the bedding next to her, his arms tight and hard. He closed his eyes as though fighting his release and fighting himself.

"Samantha," he whispered.

"Yes."

When Tain looked at her, Samantha gasped again. His eyes were glowing, blue and powerful, filled with his life essence. Samantha spread her hand over the pentacle on his cheek, wishing she could touch what burned white-hot inside him.

And then she *was* touching it. Samantha was demon. Her kind had the capacity to draw the life essence—that integral *something* that made a person alive—out of others. She'd never done it. She didn't know how, and she'd never wanted to explore that part of her demon self.

Now Tain's life essence exploded into her through her fingers. Samantha cried out with the weight of it, a sheer force that lifted her off the bed.

A wave of climax swamped her at the same time, and she screamed. She saw Tain's face, blue eyes wide in concern, and then an amorphous blackness rose up and blotted out her world.

Chapter Twelve

"Samantha."

Someone sounded very worried, shook her, even. Samantha turned groggily away and burrowed back into the warmth of the pillows.

"Samantha, look at me."

A strong hand gripped her face and forced her head from the comforter. She groaned.

"Wake up, love."

Samantha liked the voice—deep, musical, and full of sinful promise. She wished he would keep talking, keep calling her *love*.

Warmth tingled where his fingers contacted her, magic that pulsed against her skin. Samantha recalled the incredible heat that had jolted through her when she'd touched Tain's tattoo, and she woke with a gasp.

Tain lay next to her on the bed, long, strong, and naked. He propped himself on his elbow, his hand softening on her face, his eyes watchful. Pickles perched on the pillow above his head, staring down at Samantha with as much intensity.

"What happened?" Samantha tried to sit up, only to collapse again and blow out her breath. "Whatever kind of orgasm that was, I'd like to do it again. Or maybe never, I'm not sure."

"You took my life essence."

Samantha pushed her hair from her eyes. "Is *that* what that was? I thought you were trying to kill me with ecstasy."

Tain gave her an odd look, his eyes watchful. "How does it usually feel when you feed on life essence?"

"I don't know. I mean, I've never fed on one before. If I did just now, it was an accident." Samantha gave a little laugh. "Believe me, if I wanted a diet of life essences, I certainly wouldn't start with *yours*."

Tain didn't smile. "The demon part of you needs to feed. You can't stop it."

Samantha shook her head. "Really, I had no idea what I was doing. I vowed I'd never subject anyone to that. I've seen humans who let themselves get addicted to demons, and it's not pretty."

"All demons need life essence to survive," Tain said, still watching her as though gauging her reaction to his words. "Old Ones, lesser demons, demons of mixed blood . . . Your touch is practiced."

Samantha again attempted to sit up, but her body was limp and warm, and so comfortable. "Listen, I know you want me to be an evil, life-sucking, death-magic demon, but that's not how I was raised. My mother treated me like a human child, and that's what I became."

Tain's voice was quiet. "You must have taken life essence before, many times. By instinct—maybe without realizing you were doing it."

"Nope, not once. If I had taken it from someone, they'd feel it and tell me. Who would let me do that without saying anything?"

His gaze was unfathomable, his body still. "Your mother, perhaps."

"No." Samantha managed to sit up this time. "I'd never do that to her."

Tain remained stretched out beside her, a tall, godlike being who'd just given her the greatest night of her life. He touched her arm, his fingers warm, comforting despite his troubling words. "When you were a child, you wouldn't have known or understood. You probably didn't need to take much, being only half demon. The fact that your mother let you do it speaks much of her."

Samantha clenched her hands, worry welling inside her. "You have to be wrong. I never took from her."

"But I'm not wrong, am I?"

"You must be." A thought gave her hope. "I haven't lived at home for five years now—where would I have gotten life essence since then if I need it so much?"

Tain shrugged, a slow rippling of muscle, but he spoke gently. "You see your mother often. And for the last year, you've had a very strong life-magic werewolf for a partner."

"Logan?" Samantha rolled off the bed and onto her feet. "No, I never have. He would have noticed. He'd have stopped me. Wouldn't he?"

Tain remained on the bed, watching her with eyes that had gone dark blue. "Maybe not if you didn't take much. Logan's a very powerful werewolf, maybe even a pack leader or close to being one. He has strength to spare."

"You're wrong," Samantha said, her breath hurting her. "About me. And about Logan. Logan's strong, sure, but he would never let me feed off him."

Tain's voice was quiet but reasonable. "He might if he knew you needed it. He must have understood the risks of working with a demon before he took the job."

"*Half demon.*"

"You aren't used to taking much," Tain said. "My life essence overwhelmed you because you got too strong a dose of it. I should have muted it for you."

Samantha balled her fists. "I don't want to take *any* dose of it."

Tain came off the bed beside her, dominating her small bedroom. The sleek little gew gaws she collected from various craft fairs around Los Angeles and the curtains she'd made from scrap upholstery dulled next to the exotic demigod and his beautiful, naked body.

"It is what you are, Samantha," Tain said in his deep timbre. "It's the hardest thing in the world, to be what you truly are."

"Are you trying to bully me because I'm demon? *I'm* not the one who kept you prisoner all those years—it wasn't *me*."

"I know." Tain caught her elbows and pulled her against his body. He smelled of warmth, sleep, and their lovemaking, and his fingers tingled with healing magic. "I know, my Samantha."

Samantha barely heard him through her clenching confusion. She wasn't like Merrick and his demons or the girls who sold themselves on the street to take life essence. She wasn't like the matriarch, cold and business-like, or her equally cold majordomo. She wasn't even like her father who'd met her mother in secret while waiting for Samantha to grow up enough to accept him.

Samantha had lived her life as a human, with human ambitions and needs. Being demon was an inconvenience, or else something that gave her insight into how to catch demon criminals.

Samantha balled her hands against Tain's chest. "I don't want this."

"I know."

She felt his magic slide through her, trying to soothe her, but she fought it, somehow needing the grief and guilt. "Please go away."

"No."

The one-word answer was typical of Tain, taciturn and indicating he'd do whatever he damn well pleased. Samantha knew he'd decided to stay with her tonight because this was *his* agenda, not hers.

"I need to get some sleep," she said, hardening her voice. "I have to go to work in the morning."

"Sleep then." Magic trickled through her, too strong to fight, numbing Samantha's anguish. Tain had to be wrong, and in the morning, after she slept, she'd prove it.

Samantha felt his lips in her hair again, his warm hands on her back. Tain lifted her and laid her on the bed, then got himself beside her and pulled the covers over both of them. Samantha saw Pickles decide that all was well and curl into a nose-to-tail ball before she slid into hazy sleep.

***

Tain stirred the charred bits in the frying pan as he heard Samantha's bedroom door open. Without turning, he felt her gaze on his bare back and the kilt he'd pulled on over his hips. The rest of his clothes had been ruined by the demon's acid and the shower, the kilt the only thing salvageable.

He also felt the weight of her beauty, her dark eyes and straight black hair, the memory of her body under his. He remembered those lovely eyes widening in horror when he told her she'd drunk his life essence—he'd assumed she already knew.

What had he expected? That Samantha would smile and gloat that she'd just imbibed from an Immortal? Her astonished look and the tears that followed had turned his ideas upside-down.

"What are you burning?" she asked.

Tain warmed at her voice, the sultry one that haunted his dreams. But her tone was sharp, the prickly, don't-touch-me Samantha returning.

"It was eggs and bacon."

Samantha came to him, took the pan off the burner, and peered at the ruined contents. "I'll grab something on the way."

She'd dressed in conservative black slacks, white blouse, and blazer, Samantha in her professional garb. Tain pictured himself kissing her while he peeled back the jacket and parted the buttons of her rather virginal blouse.

He settled for skimming his hand through her hair, liking that she let it hang loose and free today. Her face had healed completely, only a few pink lines remaining from the attack.

Samantha stepped away from him. "Can I drop you somewhere?" She'd become all business again, pretending to put what had happened between them behind her.

"I need to wait for my brother," Tain answered. "He's bringing me clothes."

"Then you'll be gone when I get back."

It wasn't a question. Tain lifted one brow at her and put the pan back onto the burner. He liked burned eggs and bacon.

"The attacking demons were Djowlan, and have been arrested," he said. "Each clan is assuming the other is responsible for the battle."

Samantha blinked, and he saw her shift thought gears back to the demon problem. "How did you know that?"

"Logan called on your cell phone."

"It survived the demon acid?"

Tain shrugged. "Guess so."

Samantha grabbed the phone from the counter, checked its readout, then slid it into its pouch on her belt. "Why didn't you wake me when he called?"

"You needed to sleep."

Tain had gone back into the bedroom after speaking to Logan to find Samantha curled on her side, her head resting on her bent arm. Her black hair had fanned out on the pillow, her even darker lashes tight against her skin. He'd stood still and let her beauty soothe his heart.

"I don't even know if my father's all right," Samantha said, worried. "We left him with the matriarch . . ."

"He called while you were showering. The matriarch had him driven home, but he'd heard you were hurt. I told him I'd healed the burns, and you'd be fine."

Samantha flushed. "I'm sure he wondered why you were answering my phone at six in the morning while I was in the shower."

Fulton hadn't sounded very surprised. In fact, Tain had sensed his relief that Samantha hadn't been left alone and unprotected. "I don't think he wondered at all."

"Terrific." Samantha swung away from him and grabbed her purse from the sofa. "I have to go. Don't give any of that burned stuff to the cat."

Tain came to her, greasy spatula and all, and touched her face, subtly and quietly sliding a protection spell around her. The spell wouldn't stop a bullet, but it would keep her from ordinary kind of harm.

"Cerridwen's blessing on you," Tain said, then kissed her forehead.

Samantha jerked away and started for the door. On the threshold she turned back. "Thank you," she said awkwardly. "For the healing, I mean. I wouldn't have survived that attack."

Tain didn't answer. In his mind, he thanked the goddesses for giving him the healing gift that had allowed him to save her life. He knew that if she'd died last night, he would have drifted back into his madness and never come out.

Samantha gave him another self-conscious look, then turned and left him. Tain watched her go from the kitchen window, enjoying the way her backside swayed under the blazer as she hurried down the stairs.

Pickles jumped to the counter to sit next to him. Tain absently slipped him pieces of blackened bacon as they watched Samantha climb into her car and roar off to join Los Angeles traffic.

***

"You look pretty good for a woman who got slimed," Logan said, leaning back in his chair. "You all right?"

Samantha's attempt to slip in quietly and bury herself in paperwork about last night's incident had failed miserably. Everyone in the department had heard about the battle, Samantha's injury, and the fact that Tain had taken her home—the uniform who'd driven her to her apartment had made sure the story whizzed around Paranormal Division at the speed of light. She'd had at least twenty congratulations and commiserations before she even reached her desk.

"I got lucky," she told Logan. She couldn't make herself look her partner in the eye, still trying to sort out her thoughts.

Now that Tain had introduced the possibility that Samantha had taken Logan's life essence, and that Logan had let her, she felt awkward with the man she'd always been able to relax with.

Samantha could plunge herself into denial, inventing all kinds of reasons why Tain had told her what he had, but something inside her knew the truth. She *had* been stealing from Logan, and Logan must have known. Why he'd said nothing was the mystery. The knowledge rose like a knife to cut into their friendship.

Equally mysterious was Tain's certainty that Logan was a wolf high in his pack, even a leader. But if a high-ranking wolf had come out to Los Angeles to work a mundane job, that spoke of big problems in the pack. She did know that much.

"It wasn't luck," Logan said, cutting into her thoughts. "It was an Immortal. One good at healing, I think you told me."

Samantha looked up at him, still avoiding his tawny eyes. "What are implying?"

"Implying? Me? I think you'll make a great couple."

"We're not going to make any kind of couple," Samantha said sharply. "He kept the acid from burning me, that's all."

"Sure thing, partner." Logan gave her a knowing look. Of course, he'd called her cell phone early this morning, and Tain had answered. He understood exactly what Tain and Samantha had done all night. "The Lamiah matriarch is calling for blood," Logan went on. "But the Djowlan matriarch is claiming no responsibility for the attack. She says the attackers were rogues who acted without her approval."

Samantha glanced at Logan's report, thankful to focus on something other than her messed-up feelings about Tain. "One of the demons who led the attack said his daughter was kidnapped and killed. Was he brought in?"

Logan looked surprised. "I hadn't heard this. We arrested a lot of demons last night, but haven't had time to question them."

"Can I talk to him? Damn it, I knew I should have called in."

"You were down, Samantha," Logan said, the teasing leaving his voice. "You needed to recover—I'm surprised you're even here this morning."

Samantha was too, but Tain's healing magic amazed her. The acid should have killed her—painfully—and here she was walking around with barely any scars.

Besides, she couldn't have stayed home after Tain's revelations, no matter how delicious he'd looked in her kitchen in that kilt. When she'd walked in and seen him in at her stove, wearing a kilt and nothing else, she'd wanted to get down on her knees, lift up the plaid, and enjoy what was beneath.

Right then, she hadn't wanted to talk about her feelings, or her inner demon, or Tain's past. She'd only wanted to make love to him again and again until she forgot her own name.

Logan took Samantha down to the cells where last night's arrests waited. Demon cells contained strong witch wards that kept demons from breaking down the doors with their immense strength. The demons from last night, however, looked defeated and subdued, not about to attempt a breakout.

The demon with the delicate face who'd confronted Tain looked up in anger as Samantha entered the interview room and sat down across the table from him.

"You," he snarled, then looked past her to Logan. "Who's *he*? What happened to your Lamiah-protecting lover?"

Samantha slid a paper encased in a plastic sheet across the table to him. "Is that like the notes you've been getting?"

The demon glanced at the paper with its cutout letters, the last Merrick had received before his club burned down.

"Like that, except the one they sent back with my daughter's body and her ripped-out heart was more specific."

"What did it say?" Samantha asked, maintaining her calm interview voice, despite her growing sympathy and horror.

"Two lines." The demon shoved the letter back at her and folded his arms. "*Another one down. The rest of you to go.*"

***

Hunter brought Tain a change of clothes, then lounged on Samantha's sofa flipping channels while Tain showered and changed.

"Did you bring the other things I wanted?" Tain asked when he emerged again.

Hunter lifted a duffle bag from the sofa beside him. "I raided your apartment. You didn't have much to raid."

"I travel light."

"A man after my own heart. Leda likes to buy mysterious gadgets for the kitchen and learning toys for the baby every time she leaves the house. I tell her we can't take any of it to Ravenscroft, but she doesn't care." Hunter rumbled but Tain noted the gleam of pride in his eyes.

"Leda's enjoying herself."

"She is." Hunter looked around Samantha's apartment with its soft chairs and the kitchen's curtains and matching towels. "This is pretty cozy. Better than the dump you live in now."

"Where I live is cheap."

"There's an extra bedroom at Adrian's house," Hunter said, sounding casual. He brought it up every time they saw each other.

"I don't need Samantha to be alone right now." Not with demons spitting venom at her and clans at war. Tain didn't want Samantha out in the city without him either, but he acknowledged that she'd be with Logan or inside the well-warded police headquarters.

"You and she can share Adrian's guestroom," Hunter suggested.

"She won't."

Hunter shrugged. "You mean she's proud and independent, like someone else in this room. You two should get along famously."

Famously was not how Tain would put it. The look in Samantha's eyes when he'd told her she'd taken life essence from her mother and Logan, like the demon she was, had been anguished.

Tain hadn't realized she hadn't known. Demons loved to suck life essences, and Samantha's pleasure when she'd taken Tain's had been intense. But instead of triumphing that she'd tasted the power of an Immortal, Samantha had been scared and stricken.

Hunter watched him, his green eyes narrowing. "Are you telling me Samantha hasn't fallen for you yet? You can't be trying hard enough."

Tain sat down next to Hunter and snatched the remote from his hand. "The last thing I need is advice about women from *you*."

"No, the last thing you need is for Leda to come down here and try to shove you two together. Seduce Samantha until she can't live without you—end of problem. Then Leda and I can go off to Ravenscroft."

"Leaving me with someone to look after me?"

Hunter looked slightly embarrassed. "Something like that."

"I'm glad you care." Tain was, in truth. Having his brothers cluck around like mother hens was preferable to not having his brothers around at all.

"But leave you alone?" Hunter went on. "Nope. Sorry. We left you alone for too long. You're stuck with us now."

Tain sat back on the sofa, flicking through channels full of curious activities people of this century considered entertainment. He and Hunter had spent hours like this whenever Tain had visited Hunter during the past year, sitting side-by-side in companionable silence in front of a television, commenting on the odd things humans liked to watch. Staying still too long made Tain restless, but he realized the importance of it, the bond strengthening between himself and his brothers.

Samantha needed life essence, and Tain had it to spare. The solution was simple. Samantha could take life essence from Tain whenever she needed to, which would never hurt him. That way she wouldn't have to worry about harming her mother or Logan or anyone else.

Is this my redemption? he silently asked Cerridwen. *To give this woman my life essence so she won't hurt the people she loves?*

He didn't think this was quite what the universe had in mind for Tain's atonement, but at the moment he didn't care. Samantha could have all she wanted of his white-hot life essence, and he'd assuage his own inner pain by letting her take it.

"Don't let me lose track of time," Hunter said after a while. "Leda's giving a lecture at six to some group about using protective witch magic. She'll kill me if I miss it."

Tain glanced at him, his interest stirring. "Mind if I tag along?"

Hunter shrugged. "If you want to come, sure."

Tain looked back at the television, where two wrestlers were enjoying themselves slamming each other to the floor. For a brief moment Tain's memories of himself, Hunter, and Darius slid through the turmoil in his mind—they'd spar then argue about who'd won. Go off to get drunk together, and try to entice ladies to choose which brother they liked best. Or Tain and Adrian would fish on the bank of some flowing river, neither speaking, watching the water and the silver flip of fish that always seemed to avoid their lines.

Tain let the memories of the past come for the first time since his release, accepting their comfort.

Tain didn't need to wonder what had opened the dam to let the memories through. It had happened last night when he'd dragged a half-demon woman back from death and made love without pain for the first time in centuries.

***

Samantha reached home that evening feeling drained. She'd been tense all day, keeping Logan at a distance and avoiding phone calls from her mother and father. Logan had known something was wrong — something more than her being nearly killed by demon acid — but hadn't asked, and Samantha hadn't said a word to him.

How do you ask your best friend if you've been sucking out his life essence?

Samantha wearily climbed the stairs and entered her apartment. It was dark, Tain gone, Pickles meowing like a cat who hadn't eaten in three days. She flicked on the lights, noting that Tain had done the dishes and put them away.

"What a dream man," she said as she closed and locked the door. "A one-night stand who cleans the house before leaving."

Samantha dumped her purse and briefcase on the sofa and went into the bathroom. She didn't notice until she was at the sink splashing water on her face that an unfamiliar toothbrush rested in the holder next to her own.

She stared in surprise, then reasoned that Hunter had likely brought it with Tain's clothes, and Tain had forgotten it when he left. Same with the razor hanging from the shower caddy.

Samantha snapped on the light in the bedroom and opened a drawer to grab one of the oversized T-shirts in which she liked to lounge around the apartment. She stopped. Half the drawer was filled with men's T-shirts, large ones, folded neatly. Her underwear drawer above it shared space with a handful of boxer shorts and rolled socks.

Samantha slammed the drawers shut and yanked open the closet. Tain hadn't brought many clothes — shirts and jeans and another duster coat — but they were hanging quietly next to hers. Above them on the shelf was an empty duffle bag.

She shoved the closet door closed and stormed out to glare accusingly at Pickles. "He's moved in."

Samantha couldn't help thinking her cat looked a bit smug. She grabbed the phone and called Leda, needing in her panic to talk to someone used to Immortals, but no one answered.

Samantha hung up, fed Pickles, then started pacing. She hated waiting to see if and when Tain would return, but that's what she would have to do.

She stared at the phone a little bit longer, then slowly picked it up again and called her mother.

***

Tain stood in the back of the small auditorium with Hunter, listening to Leda answer questions.

"Ms. Stowe," said the interviewer, a slender woman who'd introduced herself as a Ms. Townsend. Ms. Townsend wore a business jacket and skirt, had blond hair wound in a careful knot, and minimal makeup. "How do you feel about the city of Los Angeles allowing demon-kind and vampires to go on living here after they nearly destroyed us all last year?"

Hunter leaned to Tain. "I don't like her."

Tain studied the woman's aura, which was fiery red-orange next to Leda's blue and green hue. "She doesn't have death-magic," he said. "She's just an angry woman."

The group called themselves No More Nightmares, and were very interested in how normal human beings could protect themselves against demons and vampires. They'd asked Leda how she and the Coven of Light had destroyed the demon Kehksut the year before and what she'd learned from it.

Leda answered readily enough. "As a member of the Coven of Light, I learned that death magic and life magic must balance in order to maintain the status quo of the universe. Last year, there was an unhealthy dose of death magic, which resulted in the chaos that we had to live through. Once life magic was allowed to return to its normal level, harmony was restored. But we need death magic to keep the world on an even keel."

"You have a son," Ms. Townsend cut in, glancing toward the back of the room. A carrier rested at Hunter's feet, his sleeping child in it. "As a mother, don't you worry for him? Do you want him playing outside, exposed to any demon who might happen along? Or any vampire?"

"Of course I worry," Leda answered. She laughed a little. "Being a new mother, I'm paranoid. But we have guarded our house with the strongest wards, and I'm confident that my husband and I can keep him safe until he learns to protect himself." She looked out at the audience, her smile reassuring. "Demons keep to themselves, mostly. Their clans are close-knit, and few venture outside them, except in the clubs. Humans seek out vampires and demons for the thrill of it, not the other way around. Last year was unusual."

"Not all of us have the benefit of possessing witch magic," Ms. Townsend said. "What of us mundane human beings?"

"There are plenty of witches around who are happy to ward your house, your car, whatever you like. Protection is never a bad idea."

"For a fee."

The audience murmured angry agreement.

"For a modest fee," Leda corrected. "Witches have bills to pay, and supplies cost money. If a witch wants to charge you an exorbitant price, of course, you should seek another."

"Do *you* do these wardings?"

"I don't have time to do much, but I can refer anyone here to witches who do."

"Witches who practice death magic, like yourself?" Ms. Townsend snapped.

The crowd started their murmuring again, and Hunter stirred uneasily.

Leda flushed. "I admit that I have twice in my life used death magic to perform a ritual. I didn't want to, and I didn't like it, but both times it was absolutely necessary."

"Necessary?" Ms. Townsend asked coldly. "Or the easiest way to get what you wanted?"

"Necessary," Leda repeated. "The first time, it saved a life; the second time, it helped kill an ancient demon threatening the world."

"So you advocate using death magic if *you* feel it's justified."

"No, I don't advocate using it at all."

"And in fact, I believe your own coven asked you to leave after you performed this death-magic ritual."

"I left of my own accord," Leda said with a hint of frost.

"I've spoken to other witches of this so-called Coven of Light—some of them tried to cover up for you, others openly left because of the coven members who condoned what you did."

Leda started to answer, but Hunter thrust the baby carrier at Tain and strode up the aisle. White-hot magic surrounded him, and people cringed out of his way.

Hunter grabbed Leda by the hand and glared at Ms. Townsend. "What happened in Los Angeles was nothing to what would have happened if Leda hadn't done what she did. She doesn't deserve to stand here and be berated by people like you."

"*Hunter,*" Leda said.

Ms. Townsend regarded Hunter down her long nose. "I am pointing out that even those whose motives are pure can be seduced by death magic."

"Point it out without us." Hunter pulled Leda down the steps and up the aisle, Ms. Townsend watching them go with glee.

Hunter took the carrier with the waking baby as he passed Tain. "You coming?" he asked when Tain didn't move.

"No. I want to listen a while."

"You're kidding. What for?"

"It might be important."

Hunter growled, but didn't argue.

"Be careful," Leda said to Tain.

Tain gave her a reassuring nod. The two of them left, and Tain stepped into the shadows beside the door.

Ms. Townsend regarded her audience with a chill smile. "Wasn't *that* interesting? Aren't you glad I asked her to come?"

Her followers applauded. Ms. Townsend waited for the admiration to die down before she spoke in clear, strident tones. "Death magic is insidious. It comes at us when we least expect it, seducing us as the demons seduce their victims in their so-called clubs. We must work to eradicate the darkness any way we can."

She waited for the next round of applause, then launched into a speech about demons and what they did, much of it inaccurate. She brought in vampires too, talking about the laws that barely held them back from slaughtering the population.

"We need to take back the night, ladies and gentlemen. Our children need to be protected from these evil beings that our laws favor, before it's too late."

Her audience, ordinary looking men and women, cheered. The trouble was, Ms. Townsend wasn't completely wrong. The network of laws that kept demons and vampires in line worked only as long as the demons and vampires wanted them to.

Septimus was strong enough to keep the vamps in Los Angeles under his thumb, and his power extended to other cities up and down the coast. Demons harbored so much resentment between themselves and clans that an overall demon leader would likely never emerge. But if the balance of power ever shifted, humans would be sitting ducks, and these people knew it.

Tain had the feeling, as the meeting went on, that this group wasn't about to combat the problem with bake sales and sticking fliers on car windows. His hunch was confirmed when Ms. Townsend began describing the exact methods for subduing and killing a demon, including how to cut out its still-beating heart.

Chapter Thirteen

Samantha's apartment windows were completely dark when Tain reached it at eight that night, after he'd done what he'd needed to do. Her small truck sat in the parking lot, and Tain made his way quickly up the stairs, worried about why she hadn't turned on any lights.

When he opened the door, he saw Samantha sitting motionlessly on the sofa in the glare of the outside lights, her feet on the coffee table and a lump of cat curled up on her thighs. Tain exhaled in relief and closed the door, making his way to sit next to her in the dark.

"You were right," she said after a while, voice low. "About my mother."

Tain said nothing, sensing she didn't want words from him right now.

"I talked to her tonight," Samantha continued, bleak. "I asked my mother point-blank if she'd let me take her life essence, and she said yes. I asked her why, and she said she knew I needed it, and she didn't mind."

"She loves you," Tain said, keeping his voice gentle.

"That makes it worse."

Tain smoothed his hand down Samantha's bare arm, finding her cold. "I wouldn't have told you that abruptly, but I thought you already knew."

Samantha flicked a glance at him. "Because I'm demon, and that's what demons do?"

"Yes." He couldn't explain more than that.

"And you believed I'd suck dry my own mother." Samantha bit off a laugh. "Well, you were right."

Tain sat in silence for a time, uncertain. It seemed strange to want to comfort a demon, but this was Samantha. This was different.

"When I was a lad," he said slowly, "I used to hurry through tedious chores using my magic. My father would shout at me about it."

Samantha looked at him, clearly wondering why he was bringing this up now. "Your Roman soldier father? You lived with him in England, right? Or whatever it was called then."

Tain nodded. "He valued hard work and honor above all else. He considered using magic a shortcut to shirking."

"Not on the same scale as sucking out life essence," Samantha said, her voice dry.

"I couldn't control the vast power inside me, and I nearly killed him with it. I collapsed a stone shed on top of him, because I was trying to cheat while helping him repair the roof. That was the day I discovered my healing ability."

Samantha's eyes widened, and she touched his hand. "Thank goodness you had it."

"What I'd done terrified me for a long time," Tain said. "I was afraid to use my magic again. My father understood, but he never chastised me, just made me work very, very hard." He smiled, remembering the tough physical labor his father had put him through, which Tain had done without complaining. He'd been happy to do it. "My dad's dead and gone now, centuries ago."

"Sounds like you loved him."

"You didn't say it in those days—respect and honor was what you gave your father. But I did love him. Very much."

Samantha rubbed his arm. "I'm sorry you lost him."

Tain shrugged. "He was a mortal human, and grew old and died." He tried to sound stoic, but the day his father passed had left a hole in his life that had never been filled. "I would have lost him sooner or later."

"That doesn't make it easier."

Tain shook his head. "No."

The day Cerridwen had come for Tain, his father had gruffly told him to go and not to shame him. Tain had seen tears on his father's face, but the man had turned around, stiff-shouldered, and walked off into the woods.

Tain slid his arm around Samantha, unable to keep from touching her, and pressed a kiss to her fragrant hair. "Let me warm you," he said softly.

She looked up at him, her eyes holding both anguish and need. "I think I'd like that."

Tain carefully set the sleeping Pickles aside and led Samantha to her bedroom. He undressed her, and by the time she was bare, she'd recovered herself enough to help undress him.

Their lovemaking was slow this time. Tain licked her mouth, tasting the salt-tang of her sweat, then ran his tongue across her throat and breasts. He worked his way downward to press his mouth between her legs, teasing her there until she moaned. Then he rolled off her and to his back, lifted her onto his body, parting her legs to straddle him, and slid straight up inside her.

He made a low noise of passion as Samantha moved down onto him, her body taking his. He *belonged* here.

Samantha rested her hands on Tain's chest, her knees against his sides, her head going back as he rocked up into her. In the light that leaked through the slats of the window blind, he saw the glitter of her dark eyes, the faint hue of her aura like sunshine on midnight velvet. Her head lolled back, her sleek hair falling across her shoulders. The movement thrust her breasts toward him, and Tain cupped them, teasing the nipples with his thumbs as she rode him.

When Samantha started to come, he took her hand and laid it over the tattoo on his cheek, feeling the tingle as his life essence trickled into her.

"No," she moaned.

"Take it. Take all you need. You won't hurt me."

Samantha's mouth twisted. Tain knew she wanted to argue, but her climax was on her, and she cried out and ground herself against him. At the same time she drew his life essence into her through her hand on his tattoo.

The high of that was like nothing Tain had ever experienced. Kehksut had tried to make sex with his female form the ultimate in erotic satisfaction, but Tain had loathed every minute of it. He'd been trapped in pain and madness and the demon's magic, the tiny, sane part of him screaming while his body obeyed the demon's wishes.

With Samantha, everything was different. Tain was wound up tight with wanting, and he lost control in the best way, finding his hands digging into the mattress as he thrust up and up into Samantha. The white essence of him swirled over her fingers and into her body, her eyes shining with it.

"Take every bit of me," he said, voice breaking. "I want you to have me."

Samantha gasped as he pushed all the way inside her, farther than he'd dared go their first time. Samantha's eyes widened with the shock of it, and then a second climax overtook her.

Tain moaned his own release and rocked into her, still hard, until the joy of it wound its way down to sweet languor.

Heart thudding, Tain drew Samantha down on top of him, kissing her face, throat, lips. "Thank you," he whispered.

Samantha lay down on him, breaking contact with his tattoo but folding him into her warmth. He could stay here forever, in this silence and darkness that was peaceful, not terrifying. Being with Samantha was a haven, not a prison. Tain closed his eyes and let himself relax for the first time in centuries.

Samantha touched his cheek again, he still inside her, but the connection between them had gone.

"I didn't mean to do that," she said softly.

Tain opened his eyes and let himself smile. "I *hope* you did."

Her eyes were pools of darkness but held warmth, not triumph. "I didn't want to take your essence this time, but I couldn't stop it."

Tain stroked her hair from her face. "You shouldn't stop it. You crave it like your body craves food. You need life essence to survive."

"You know a lot about it."

He gave her a half smile. "I became the demon expert."

"Is that what Kehksut did to you? Stole your life essence? Over and over again?"

Tain shook his head as he threaded his fingers through her sleek hair. "He couldn't stand my life essence—it was too much for him. That's why he had to break me."

Samantha's eyes glittered with sudden tears. "I'm sorry. I'm so sorry." She was crying now, and Tain gathered her into his arms.

Samantha laid her head on his chest, hot tears wetting his skin. "I don't want to forgive your brothers for not finding you, for letting you suffer so long."

Tain had come to terms with this a while ago, knowing his brothers weren't to blame. "They tried for a long time, but they couldn't. When Adrian did find me, I was so far gone in madness that I refused to go with him. It took my brothers' collective power to get me free. And you."

It had taken a long time after the ritual had ripped him from Kehksut's power for Tain to realize he was truly free, that Kehksut was dead and had no more hold on him. Tain's brothers had expected him to bounce around rejoicing, but the scars inside him were too deep for a quick healing. They might never heal. Tain could only withdraw into himself and wander the world, waiting for the darkness to go away.

Samantha was frowning at him, her brown eyes wary. "I noticed you moved your stuff in here. Without asking me."

Tain's smile died. "I moved in because there are people out there teaching other people how to kill demons," he said. He'd moved in for other reasons, but the No More Nightmares organization was a good excuse. "In fact, I met one of them today."

***

Samantha listened with trepidation as Tain described the meeting of No More Nightmares he'd attended and their treatment of Leda. He twined his hands behind his head as he talked, which made his muscles move beneath her in all kinds of nice ways.

"The woman in charge," Tain said, "this Ms. Townsend, she had details about how to incapacitate a demon long enough to cut out its heart."

Samantha propped herself on her elbows and frowned. "That's not new. I've been hearing complaints from the demon and vamp communities about such organizations as long as I've been a cop. Someone is always passing out pamphlets on the best way to stake a vampire or behead a demon. Occasionally the fanatics go on a rampage, human customers get hurt, someone gets arrested or sued, and the group dies down awhile." Samantha traced a scar on Tain's hard chest as she spoke, hating the pain it represented but liking the strong, even beat of his heart beneath it. "Logan and I can check out what the groups have been up to lately. Maybe one of them has gotten out of hand."

"Maybe." Tain didn't sound convinced.

"I'll interview this Ms. Townsend, though. She sounds interesting."

He gave short laugh. "*Bloodthirsty* is the word I'd use."

Samantha shrugged. "I can't really blame these people, you know. Last year was horrible. The police stopped responding—my mother disappeared, demon and vamp gangs took over the neighborhoods. The only one helping was Septimus, and he could only do so much. Sounds like this Ms. Townsend and her followers are afraid the chaos will happen again."

"It won't." Tain's eyes were hard. "I won't let it."

"You're only one man, you know—I mean, one Immortal."

"I am enough. I won't let demons kill humans."

"You've reassured *me*," Samantha said. "But how will you make the other ten million people in Los Angeles believe it?"

"*You'll* convince them."

Samantha gave him a wry laugh. "You're confident."

Tain's blue eyes warmed, which started fires in her blood. "You have more power than you know, Samantha. You even saved my ass, as you like to say."

"That's different. That was easy."

Tain raised his brows. "That's what you call *easy*?"

"It was easy, because I wanted to save you."

"Why did you want to?" He sounded as though he truly wanted to know.

"You needed saving." Samantha let a teasing note enter her voice. "You were the best-looking Immortal there, and I wanted one of my own."

"I was a long way gone in madness by that time." His frown returned, the distant look that spoke of pain. "None of it seemed real anymore. Except you."

Samantha remembered how blue Tain's eyes had been when he'd looked at her through the darkness during the battle in Seattle, and then the terrible grief and sorrow in them when he'd healed her later. "If I was so wonderful," Samantha asked in a soft voice, "why did you leave Seattle without saying good-bye to me?"

His eyes were just as blue as he looked at her now. Though the grief had lessened, sorrow lingered. "Because I didn't trust myself near you."

Samantha's heart beat faster. "You're near me now."

"I know." Tain brushed her cheek with his fingertips. "I need to be here."

For how long? Until Samantha felt safe or he did? When Tain healed, and the world was safe for demons again, would he move on?

The peal of Samantha's cell phone cut through her thoughts, and she groaned. "What now?"

The phone's readout showed her it was Logan. "Can't I have a night off?" she bleated when she answered.

"You need to get down here, Samantha," Logan said, sounding more serious than she'd ever heard him. "There's been another demon murder."

Samantha's thoughts went instantly to her father, and her heart leapt to her throat. "What murder? Who?"

"The matriarch of the Lamiah clan. She was found in her own bedroom with her heart cut out."

***

"How the *hell* did this happen?" Samantha shouted to Logan as they entered the matriarch's mansion.

Tain felt the tingle of death magic touch him as he strode behind Samantha into the house, his hands on the reassuring bulk of his swords under his duster. Tain had accompanied Samantha without them arguing about it— he'd simply dressed and waited for her in her pickup, giving her no choice.

The glittering opulence of the Beverley Hills mansion was infested with a plastic-garbed forensics team roaming through it as uniformed police interviewed the residents of the house. The remains of the protection spell Tain had cast over the mansion the previous night lingered, but Tain saw plenty of death-magic wards pulsating around the door sills and windows, felt the weight of them.

Logan had met Tain and Samantha at the remains of the gate, grim, not questioning Tain's presence. Logan explained what had happened. "The majordomo left the matriarch in her bedroom at seven this evening to ready herself for dinner, as usual. The matriarch apparently always took an hour or so for herself after the business of the day and before dining, often with guests, though tonight she was to eat alone. When the majordomo knocked on the door at eight, the matriarch didn't answer. Majordomo grew alarmed, used her key to open the door, and found the matriarch dead on the floor. Heart cut out, same as the others."

"And where is it?" Samantha asked him as they strode through the hall toward the elevator. "The heart, I mean."

"No one's found it yet. Chest cavity open, heart gone. Not that *I* could tell with all the blood, but that's what the medical examiner said."

"Is her body still here?"

"In the bedroom," Logan answered. "But it's nothing you'd want to see."

Samantha squared her shoulders. "I should look anyway."

Logan shrugged. "I can't stop you."

Death magic pressed around Tain, mitigated somewhat by the presence of the police, most of them human. Whoever had killed the matriarch had not disturbed the mansion's wards at all. Interesting.

Samantha continued her questions to Logan as they rode down the elevator to the matriarch's underground quarters. "Have you started making note of who went into and out of the house all day?"

"Sure," Logan said, "But security has apparently been a nightmare since the Djowlan demons blew up the gates. The guards patrolled, but it's not the same as having a huge gate and electronic surveillance of every nook and cranny. Plus they've been cleaning up from the attack, having repairmen coming in from outside, that kind of thing."

"Does the majordomo have a list of the repair companies and the workers they sent?"

"Yes. She's a frosty bitch, but highly organized." Logan shook his head. "I imagine she has to be with this job."

They'd reached the matriarch's bedroom, and they walked inside. The body lay where it must have fallen, the stench of it terrible. The matriarch had been dressed in a white linen suit and low-heeled ivory pumps. The crisp suit made the drenched blood all the more stark, every splash sharp edged against the white.

Samantha glanced once at the chest cavity that had been ripped open, then quickly looked away. Tain roved his gaze around the body, noting that the matriarch was wearing a necklace of pearls and that her face registered shock and amazement.

"She didn't try to assume her demon form," Samantha said.

"I saw that," Logan said. "She might have been drugged first, like Nadia."

Samantha nodded. "That's possible. The medical examiner can let us know."

She turned away from the gruesome body. The entire room was neat and tidy, an empty glass sitting in the middle of a doily next to a chair that faced a television set.

"Television on or off when she was found?" Samantha asked.

Logan scanned his notes. "Off, the majordomo said. Glass was empty except for a few ice cubes, and yes, the dregs have been taken for testing. Before you ask, the door was locked and not forced. The majordomo had to open it with her key."

"So the matriarch finished her drink, stood up, and met her killer in the middle of the floor," Samantha concluded. "Either the killer had a key and walked in, or the matriarch let him or her in herself." She rubbed the bridge of her nose in frustration. "Just great. I love a locked-room mystery."

Tain looked down at the body again, noting absently that the forensic team working in the room gave him a wide berth. "No rival demon should have been able to enter the house," he said. "The windows and doors are strongly warded, plus some of my own protective magic is still here."

"So it was someone in the Lamiah clan?" Samantha asked. "Better and better."

"Or a human," Tain answered. "One of those repairmen or whatever other people came in and out of here today."

Samantha sighed, hands on hips. Tain liked the way she looked in her square-cut blazer, her sleek hair falling straight to her shoulders. When she'd gotten dressed, she'd started to scrape her mussed hair into a quick bun, until he'd pointed out the love bite he'd left on her neck. She'd flushed and let her hair drop.

"I want to interview the majordomo," Samantha told Logan. "And anyone else who admits being in this basement today, plus anyone who was even *seen* down here. Double-check the majordomo's list of who came in and out with whoever the guards say they admitted. And find a Ms. Townsend of a group called No More Nightmares, one of those anti-demon petition organizations. It's a long shot, but I'd love to know what she was doing tonight."

"Easy enough," Logan said, jotting notes. "There's something else I'd better tell you," he added, glancing at the forensics team.

"What's that?"

Logan stepped to her and Tain and lowered his voice. "A few of the demons here are saying *you* did this, or at least had it done."

Samantha stared at Logan in shock. "What? Why in the names of all the gods would *I* want to kill the matriarch?"

"Because, partner," Logan said, "the majordomo told me shortly before you arrived that the matriarch was thinking about having you take her place when she retired. Groom you for the position. The demons who live here are saying that maybe you decided to get a jump on things."

Chapter Fourteen

Samantha took a startled step backward to find Tain's strong bulk behind her. "Someone's feeding you a wad of bull," she said. "You weren't here when I met the matriarch. She hated me on sight."

"New blood, is what they're saying," Logan went on, watching her carefully with his wolf's eyes. "The matriarch thought you'd bring a dose of common sense and a taste of the outside world into an inbred culture. Her very words. Well, her very words as told to me by the majordomo."

"Shit." Samantha's head started to throb, and she rubbed her temples. "I need to talk to that majordomo. What's her name?"

"She calls herself Ariadne."

"Fine. I'll interview her in one of the reception rooms upstairs." She looked at Tain. "I suppose you're coming with me?"

"In a minute," Tain rumbled. "There's something I want to look at first."

Samantha didn't like that she felt bereft when he walked away without explanation. He'd resumed wearing jeans, shirt and coat, no more delectable kilt, but he looked plenty good even so. Strong too. She'd felt so close to him tonight, so connected, and this murder had ripped her away from him and into the real world again.

She sighed and took the notes Logan gave her, then marched upstairs alone. She wished she could send Logan home — the wolf in him must be having a hard time with all this blood, death magic, and demons. But they had to do their jobs.

One of the ornate reception rooms had a polished antique desk with serpentine legs standing in the exact center of the room. Samantha plopped her notebook on this opulent desk and lowered herself to the chair, wishing the whole house didn't intimidate her. The careful décor of this quiet room reminded her of the matriarch — her every hair in place, every finger decorated with tasteful rings.

The rings had still been on her body, along with her circlet of pearls. Whoever had done this was out to kill, in a very specific way, and hadn't bothered with robbery.

Samantha rubbed her temples again. Logan had listed the names of the two companies who'd come out to repair the security system and start rebuilding the gate and gatehouse, but it was an even bet that if the culprit had come in with them, he or she was long gone now.

Ariadne, the majordomo, who was as stiff and cool as the matriarch had been, entered the room. She refused to sit down, so Samantha stood as well.

Ariadne repeated her story of knocking on the matriarch's door and unlocking it to find the matriarch dead. She went on to relate what had happened during the day, giving the details on who had entered and exited the house and when. The repair people had stayed outside, except for those who'd gone to the basement to look at the wiring, and they'd entered the basement through an outside door in the back. The maintenance area, the majordomo said primly, was unconnected to the matriarch's apartments.

Samantha nodded and jotted notes. When she finished, she laid down her pen and gave Ariadne an even stare.

"Someone is trying to tell me that the matriarch talked about grooming me to be her replacement."

Ariadne's thin mouth pinched. "She did."

"Why?" Samantha asked, bewildered. "She didn't like me."

"No, she didn't." Ariadne looked Samantha up and down as though she agreed with the matriarch's assessment. "She thought you were disrespectful, full of yourself, and far too modern in your thinking. But she also believed that those were the characteristics of a good matriarch. She'd been thinking of retiring for some time, and planned to start training you to take over."

"How would that work, exactly?" Samantha tried to organize her spinning thoughts. "As a half-blood, I thought I wouldn't even be admitted into the clan."

Ariadne folded her hands. "A matriarch can choose whomever she wishes as her successor, though that choice must be approved by the heads of the most powerful families in the clan."

"So they . . . what? Vote on it?"

"Sometimes they vote. Sometimes they fight to the death."

Samantha flinched. "Oh."

"A matriarch has to be strong enough to defend her clan," Ariadne said.

Samantha tried to push aside her unease. "I saw that the matriarch died without the chance to revert to her demon form."

Ariadne nodded. "Which is highly suspicious, don't you think?"

Of course it was highly suspicious—that was why they were investigating. Samantha hid her irritation and asked the majordomo if anything out of the ordinary had happened that day.

"Apart from the repairs to the security system and the gate the Djowlans blew up, no."

"Why did the matriarch ask my father to remain behind the night of the attack?" Samantha asked, trying to sound businesslike.

Ariadne looked annoyed. "I really have no idea. You'd better ask him."

Samantha held on to her temper and asked a few more questions about where everyone was and what they were doing for the hour the matriarch was alone in her room, but she didn't learn much more. As far as Ariadne knew, most of the staff had been in the kitchen or dining room preparing for dinner, or out if it had been their night off. Ariadne herself had finished up some phone calls in her first-floor office then gone downstairs to fetch the matriarch.

Which left Ariadne alone during the time in question, Samantha noted. She'd have to find out who the majordomo had called and how long those conversations had lasted.

"Did the matriarch have a—" Samantha broke off, trying to think of the appropriate word. The matriarch was a widow, according to Logan's notes, but the word *boyfriend* didn't seem quite right for a woman like her. "An intimate relationship with anyone?"

"A lover?" Ariadne supplied. "Of course she did."

Samantha picked up her pen again. "Does he live here? What's his name?"

"*She* is attending a conference in San Diego."

Samantha suppressed her surprise. "She'll have to be contacted."

"I have already seen to it."

Of course you have. Ariadne had to be one of the coldest women Samantha had ever encountered, and that included the matriarch. Ariadne had been her second in command, and now the woman would be out of a job.

Samantha told her she could leave, and Ariadne took the dismissal with poor grace. Once Ariadne had departed, closing the door with a soft but firm click, Samantha sank to the gilded desk chair with a sigh.

She preferred cases with obvious culprits and motives—in most cases, Samantha and Logan could walk onto the scene, discern what supernatural creature had done the crime, or had had a crime done to them, round up suspects, and have the guilty party in jail within a day or so, sometimes within the hour. A covert murder of a high-ranking and very rich member of paranormal society, committed under the noses of the best security in Los Angeles, was not something Samantha looked forward to tackling. High-profile cases got a lot of press, and police often didn't look very good in the stories.

Tain walked in. It dismayed Samantha how much better she felt the moment he was near her again. She was used to being independent, and now she found herself watching for this tall man, listening for his step. Probably because she'd tasted his life essence, Samantha reasoned, and the demon in her wanted more. She feared the wanting would turn into a craving, and then she wouldn't be able to do without him.

Not that Tain had an average life essence. He was the son of the goddess Cerridwen, raised by a hard-working Roman soldier in Briton, and his life essence was amazing, heady, fulfilling.

Samantha sighed and laid down her pen. "The repercussions of this are going to be bad," she said. She wasn't sure if she meant the matriarch's murder or her growing need for Tain. Both, probably.

Tain remained on the other side of the large room, looking out of place in the gilded, eighteenth-century perfection of the chamber. "You mean when people realize that the most powerful of the demons can be killed?"

Samantha nodded. "The other clan demons might be eager to take over Lamiah territory while the Lamiahs scramble around trying to find another matriarch. Plus, ordinary humans might start believing that if one matriarch can be killed, they all can, thus destroying the power of the demon clans. I really need to talk to that Townsend woman."

"Only if I'm with you."

"Fine." Samantha sighed again and leaned her forehead on her spread fingers. "What is going on here? One night I'm doing a routine stakeout for Mindglow, and the next I'm chasing a demon serial killer capable of murdering a matriarch." She looked up at Tain. "Funny how all this started the day you showed up in my life again."

Tain regarded her calmly. "I'm not the one doing these killings."

That hadn't been what Samantha had meant, but she admitted that Tain did look like a demon killer with his hard body, swords at his sides, his hair buzzed short, and the pentacle tattoo marking his face. Any demon would run screaming from him, and Samantha knew she should as well.

"You took down the demons attacking Merrick's easily enough," she pointed out.

Tain shrugged, unworried. "They were on a killing rampage. I'm a warrior, but I fight to protect, not to slaughter."

"Is that why you came to Los Angeles?" Samantha rested her elbows on the desk, giving him a little smile. "To protect us against rampaging demons?"

"Partly."

His one-word answers drove her crazy. "What was the other part?"

His blue eyes fixed on her. "To see you."

Samantha lost her smile, and her heart sped. How nice if he meant he'd come because he *liked* her, not for some strange, cryptic, Immortal reason—to make up for the past or something like that.

"You know, when a demon feeds on a life essence, it gives the feed-ee a high," Samantha said after a time. "After a while it grows addicting for the victim."

Tain's gaze didn't waver. "So I've heard."

"I've seen it happen again and again in my career. That's why Mindglow is illegal—it takes away the last vestiges of a person's ability to resist a demon. A human can get over their addiction by staying away from demons for a while, but Mindglow always turns the *no* into a *yes*."

Tain folded his arms, commanding the room without moving. "You fear I'm giving you my life essence because I'm addicted to having a demon feed on me?"

"It's a possibility," Samantha said cautiously.

Tain's look said that Samantha didn't understand him at all, and he didn't have time to explain himself to her. He moved slowly across the room, stopping a foot from the desk. "You should think instead that I'm a healer who needs to be healed."

Samantha's throat was dry. "And me taking your life essence heals you?"

"For now."

Samantha had always considered herself a stolid person, able to take in horrific crime scenes and help the victims without breaking down. She channeled her compassion for the victims and her anger at the perps into making sure she did everything in her power to find the ones responsible.

But with Tain, her emotions were all over the place. Samantha knew she shouldn't trust him, and then she turned around and trusted him implicitly. Doubt and surety went back and forth with crazy rapidity, and it didn't help that she was falling in love with him.

Falling? A cynical voice laughed inside her. *You fell in love with him the day you first laid eyes on him, and it's only gotten worse since then.*

Like now — Samantha was on duty, this was a crime scene, and Tain shouldn't be here. But she couldn't stop herself rising from the desk, going to him, leaning into him. Tain slid his hands to her hips, and she rested against the solid strength of his body.

He always smelled so good, of male musk and the outdoor scents of wind and rain. Samantha had made love to this god-man, had taken him inside her and entwined with him.

Tain's breath was warm as he kissed her lips. She could drink him in all day, taste the sharp spice of his mouth, enjoy the heated caress of his lips. Samantha slid her hand to his cheek, unable to stop herself, fitting her palm over his tattoo.

His life essence came to her, less powerfully than when they made love, but still intense. Samantha didn't want to want it, but she didn't stop herself pulling a bit of it inside her, letting it fill her empty spaces.

Tain deepened the kiss, bunching her hair in his hands as he opened her mouth with his. Being with Tain had made Samantha understand why demons wanted life essence, especially one like his. Demons were creatures of the dark who craved the light; they were strong, yet needed humans who were physically weaker than they to fulfill a part of themselves they couldn't.

Tain was ten times stronger than a normal human, ten times as magical as the most powerful life-magic creature Samantha had encountered. He could crush her like a fly, yet he was healing her and making her whole.

"We have to stop," Samantha said, forcing her hand from his face. "If we don't, I'll pull you down on this desk with me, and I know we'd break it. It looks delicate."

Tain's smile was positively sinful. "I don't care about the desk."

At the moment, Samantha didn't much care about it either. "I'd get fired."

"Then I'll keep you with me and safe."

"That sounds nice." She rubbed her cheek on his shoulder. "Maybe after this case is done, I'll take some vacation. We can go—I don't know—anywhere. A tropical island in the middle of the Pacific where I can sip mai tais and watch you walk the beach. You won't be wearing anything, of course."

"Neither will you."

"But then if I spilled my mai tai, I'd be cold."

"Not with me there," Tain rumbled.

Samantha imagined him licking the droplets of liquor from her skin, and she grew a little dizzy. "This is a nice fantasy."

"I can make it reality in the blink of an eye."

She looked up at him, startled. "How? You can teleport us, or something?"

Tain touched two fingers to her forehead. "I could put it into your head, make you see it. It will be real, and it won't be."

"You're tempting me." Samantha traced the points of his pentacle tattoo. "*I'm* supposed to be the demon."

Tain only smiled again. Damn, he looked good when he did that, as though he knew her most secret desires and could make them come true. He made her want to forget all about the matriarch, the Lamiah clan, her career, and dead demons, and float off with him into his tropical fantasy.

Samantha swore she could feel an island breeze touch her skin, smell coconut oil and the sweet scent of a mai tai mixed with the salt of the sea. If Samantha closed her eyes, maybe she'd see Tain with bright sunshine on his bare backside as he strolled away from her down the beach.

The door to the reception room swung open, and Samantha jumped away from Tain. She banged into the little gilded chair which started to fall. Tain caught the chair and set it upright, looking in no way guilty or ashamed to have been caught holding Samantha.

Logan shut the door quickly behind him, his raised brows indicating surprise but not censure. "McKay wants you off the investigation," he said to Samantha.

Samantha blinked, startled out of her embarrassment. "What? Why? I've barely started."

Logan regarded her calmly, though she sensed his wolf was alert. "Because you're clan Lamiah and because of the majordomo's claim that the matriarch wanted you to take over when she retired. Serious conflict of interest, my friend."

Samantha stared at Logan in dismay. "No one really believes that, do they?"

"The press might," Logan said. "She's here, by the way. McKay. Taking over the investigation herself."

"Terrific. Making it look as though she doesn't trust me."

"Making it look as though she's protecting her favorite detective. If you are nowhere near this crime, no one can accuse you of jiggering the results."

Samantha suppressed her wave of anger, knowing there wasn't much she could do about being kicked off the case at this moment. "Yes, all right," she said, jaw tight. "I'll walk away if it's that big a deal. You can have my notes, although the majordomo didn't tell me much more than she told you."

She handed Logan her notebook, and Logan looked grateful she wasn't making a fuss. He tried to keep things lighthearted. "Go home and kiss your new boyfriend."

"Very funny."

Tain said nothing. When Logan walked out again, closing the door carefully behind him, Samantha twined her fingers through Tain's. "Will you come with me to talk to this Ms. Townsend? I want to know how a woman with diagrams on killing demons fits into all this."

Tain leaned down and said into Samantha's ear, "If I come with you, are you willing to pay a price?"

Samantha's body heated. "Possibly."

Tain smiled at her, and the faint tropical breeze came back. "I'll make sure I think of a good one then," he said, and led her out.

***

Septimus the vampire was an Old One, one of the original vampires made by a forgotten dark goddess at the dawn of civilization. He'd stayed alive all these centuries by being smarter and more wily than his fellows as well as stronger.

Once upon a time, he'd controlled vast lands, and people who'd bowed down to him as their lord and master. Now he lived in a glittering, modern city and controlled an empire of vampires — lesser vamps of course, because almost all the Old Ones were gone. Septimus enjoyed his power. He liked to keep his finger on the pulse, so to speak, of everything that went on in this city.

His lover, the beautiful Kelly O'Byrne, had made Septimus happier lately than he'd been in a long time. He was toying with the idea of making her immortal, so she could stay with him until the goddesses decided to send him back to dust.

At the moment, Septimus was in his cushy private office in the back of his very lucrative club, listening to one of his employees tell him about Tain.

"Are you sure about this?" Septimus asked him.

"I saw him," the vamp said.

"I need to be very certain, or his brothers will back me into a corner and do horrific things to me." Septimus leaned back comfortably in his leather armchair. "I'll be begging them to stake me and get it over with. And there's no telling what they'd do to *you*."

The other vamp swallowed nervously. "Tonight he went to a meeting of those No More Nightmares lunatics. Then he followed them back to their headquarters, which isn't far from here. He slipped into the building and back out again. I lost him after that, but one of my men found him later back up near Wilshire getting on a bus." The vampire shook his head as he adjusted his silk tie. "All that magical power, and he takes the *bus*."

"The ways of Immortals are strange to us," Septimus said. "What else?"

"He ends up at that half-demon cop's apartment. He goes inside and stays a while. Probably shagged her, but I didn't have a chance to see."

"I'm not interested in his sex life. What else did he do?"

The vampire consulted his notes. "He and the cop come barreling out about nine tonight and head up to the matriarch's house in Beverly Hills. The Lamiah clan bitch got her heart cut out." The vampire paused to smile. "I'm sorry I missed that."

"I know about the death," Septimus said, placing his fingertips together. "I'm only interested in Tain and what he did the afternoon *before* the matriarch's death."

"You think he killed her?"

"I don't know whether he killed her. That is why I'm asking for your report."

The vampire smiled again, letting his fangs show. "Your pet Immortal went to the matriarch's house earlier this afternoon while his girlfriend was at work. The human I have watching him during the day says the Immortal went back to the matriarch's place and got inside." His smile widened. "What was he was doing in there, I wonder?"

Chapter Fifteen

Shit. Septimus moved in his chair, suddenly uncomfortable. "I'm not asking for speculation," he said sternly. "Just facts. How long did he stay? Does your man know who he spoke to?"

The vampire had to shake his head. "No. He didn't stay long, maybe twenty minutes. Then he slips back out — no one seeing him — and walks away."

"What time was this?"

The vampire flipped through his notebook. "Four fifteen. He walks all the way down to Santa Monica Boulevard and hops a bus again. My man lost him there, but I intercepted a cell phone call between his brother and the brother's wife talking about meeting at that No More Nightmares rally." The vamp paused to shake his head. "Those people really are crazy — women getting all excited about killing demons. If they start going after vampires, I'm moving to Idaho."

"Their meetings make people feel empowered," Septimus said, unworried. "They don't want their safe little lives threatened."

"Well, they're not threatened by *me*," the vampire scoffed. "I only do humans who come to the club and ask for it." He smiled again, his dark eyes shining. "They beg for it."

Septimus restrained himself from rolling his eyes. He supposed that once upon a time he'd enjoyed having people fall all over themselves to offer their bodies for the night and their blood for his thirst, but lack of control always irritated him. Septimus liked control, lots of it.

He made a dismissive gesture. "Thank you, that's all I need tonight."

"You want me to keep following your Immortal?"

"No." Septimus leaned back again. "I'm satisfied. Your bonus will be attached to your end-of-month check."

The vamp tucked away his notebook. "You know, I'd give up the bonus if you let me have one night with the half-demon cop. I bet her blood is *fine*."

"No," Septimus said. "She's off limits."

"She's *demon*. Who the hell cares if I drain her?"

"I said no," Septimus repeated, without heat. "Touch her, and you're dust."

The vamp looked disappointed but nodded. Septimus had no doubt he'd obey, because all Septimus's vampires knew the consequence of disobedience.

Septimus sat for a long time after the vamp left, thinking over what he'd been told. Once or twice, he reached for the phone on his desk, then lifted his hand away.

When Tain had first arrived in Los Angeles, his oldest brother, Adrian, had called Septimus and said, *Keep an eye on him.* Adrian hadn't actually said, *Put a twenty-four-hour watch on Tain with detailed notes,* but Septimus liked to be thorough. If Adrian did ask for a report, Septimus would have it.

Of the five Immortal brothers, Tain worried Septimus the most. Even Hunter had some sort of shut-off switch, and he and Septimus in the last year had become friends—as far as an Old One and an Immortal warrior could be friends. Septimus knew Hunter wouldn't kill him unless Septimus either went on a mass rampage through the city or in some way tried to hurt Hunter's wife and child.

Tain, on the other hand, was a walking time-bomb. Last year, Tain had been a crazed killing machine, ready to rid the world of life magic as well as death-magic creatures. True, Tain had been instrumental in ending the battle against Kehksut, but then he'd disappeared into the blue, doing the gods knew what. A year later, the man resurfaced in Los Angeles, still with darkness swimming behind his eyes.

What would it take to push Tain over the edge? Or had Tain already been pushed and was taking his revenge, one demon at a time?

And was Samantha Taylor another piece in his vengeance game? Or did Tain have something else in mind for her? Septimus hated not understanding exactly what was going on. It made his fingers itch.

The door opened and Kelly entered, unannounced. She was the only one allowed to come and go from his club office as she pleased, and the other vamps understood that she was completely untouchable.

Kelly had been filming most of the day for an independent studio on a movie that might propel her to superstar status. Septimus had read the script, watched some of the filming, and knew Kelly was poised to take the world by storm.

Kelly's smile warmed him as she took his outstretched hand. "You look so serious, my love," she said. "What's wrong?"

Septimus took in her breathtaking smile, his blood heating. "I find myself on the horns of a dilemma."

Kelly stroked one finger across his lips, then leaned and kissed them. "You'll figure it out. You always do."

"That's why I love you." Septimus pulled her to his lap, his needs stirring. "Are you ready for me?"

Her voice went low. "Aren't I always?"

Septimus's body thrummed. He loved her scent, the way she touched him, the beauty of her. Kelly let him savor her any way he liked, and she only smiled at him and loved him back.

Septimus kissed her lips again. Then he tilted her head to one side and tenderly bit her neck.

***

Early the next morning Samantha drove with Tain to a high-rise in L.A.'s downtown financial district, not many blocks from Septimus's vampire club. The directory inside the lobby boldly said that No More Nightmares had a suite on the twelfth floor. Samantha had discovered while researching that they had a main office here and branch offices throughout the state.

On the twelfth floor Samantha and Tain walked out of the elevator to find a line of glass-fronted offices, most of them still dark. The office with *No More Nightmares, A California Nonprofit Organization* on the door had lights on inside, but the door was locked.

Samantha knocked on the glass door, showing her ID and badge through it to the startled woman who came out of the back.

The woman opened the door and peered around it. "Yes?"

"I'd like to speak to Ms. Townsend, please."

"She isn't in. I'm her personal assistant. Is this about our petition?"

Samantha didn't know what petition she meant, but it was a good enough opening. "I have a few questions for you."

The woman opened the door and let them in. Samantha noted that she didn't feel any witch wards on the doors, nothing to keep out the death-magic creatures they purported to loathe. But perhaps they couldn't do anything so blatant in a large building in downtown Los Angeles, where many death-magic and life-magic creatures worked side by side.

Tain walked in behind Samantha. The assistant stared at him, her eyes narrowing. "You're with the police?"

"I'm not," Tain answered, cryptic as ever.

The assistant flushed and looked uneasy, but she gestured for Samantha to sit in a square, hard chair in front of the desk. Tain positioned himself behind Samantha's chair, silent and still.

The woman introduced herself as Melanie Atkins. "What is it you need to know?"

Samantha began with innocuous questions—how long had the group had been active, what were their objectives, who was Ms. Townsend?

"Ms. Townsend is an amazing woman," Melanie said with obvious hero-worship. "She gives us hope for a better world."

Samantha scribbled notes. "I heard that at a meeting yesterday Ms. Townsend insulted her guest speaker—Leda Stowe—who then walked out."

Melanie looked prim. "That was unfortunate. I'm afraid Ms. Stowe took some of the remarks the wrong way. Has she complained to the police?"

"Not as far as I know," Samantha answered. "Ms. Townsend then gave a lecture on how to kill demons?"

Melanie's flush deepened. "In self-defense only. Demons are so much stronger than we are that we need all the knowledge about them we can get."

"Humans killing demons is just as illegal as demons killing humans," Samantha pointed out.

"Yes, but so often demons get away with it. Look what happened last year."

"Last year was a different story." So far Melanie had given Samantha little more about the organization than Tain had told her—this was all probably on the brochure. "I'd really like to meet with Ms. Townsend. Can I set up an appointment?"

Was it Samantha's imagination or did the woman's nervousness shoot sky high? "She's out of town."

"Really?" Samantha let the word fall. "She left quickly."

"No, she didn't. She'd planned this. A little vacation."

"Fine, then I'll talk to her when she returns."

Melanie gave her a look of suspicion. "Why do you want to see her at all? She's done nothing wrong."

"I never said she had." Samantha stood and Tain moved to stand right behind her. "Last night, the matriarch of one of the demon clans was murdered, her heart cut out, using the exact method Ms. Townsend described at her rally. I'd like to know where Ms. Townsend was between the hours of seven and eight last night."

"On a plane to Pennsylvania," Melanie said without hesitating.

"Do you mind if I look at her itinerary?"

Melanie stood up, covering her agitation with a brisk manner. "Yes, I do mind. You can't march in here and make accusations. You have to have a warrant."

She'd certainly watched her television. Samantha said, "If I can assure myself that Ms. Townsend was on a plane or in another state during the murder, then I won't have to bother her."

"*Murder*, you keep calling it. The woman was a *demon*, as you are."

Samantha tensed, and behind her Tain shifted. "Why do you say that?" Samantha asked.

"You're not full demon, but you have demon blood. I can tell."

"Really? How?"

"I have some magical ability," Melanie said, sounding proud. "I can see it in your aura."

"I'm half demon," Samantha said sharply. "It doesn't make me any less able to do my job."

"Of course it does. You'll side with them."

Melanie slid open the desk drawer and took out a piece of crystal that had thin wire twisted around it. She held it up, letting it sway back and forth as she began whispering words, and Samantha felt suddenly weak.

Tain stepped forward and wrenched the talisman from Melanie's hand. Melanie gasped and shrank away from him.

"We're going," Tain said.

Samantha didn't argue. Tain put his hand under her elbow and steered her quickly out of the office, tossing the talisman into the nearest trashcan. Out of the corner of her eye Samantha saw Melanie scuttle for it, but Tain had Samantha down the hall and into the elevator before Melanie could retrieve it.

The elevator doors closed with a thump. Samantha leaned against the wall, trying to catch her breath, as the elevator slid smoothly downward. "I think I can consider that attempting to assault a police officer," she said, wiping her sweat-coated palms on her pants. "Thank you."

Tain said nothing as they walked past security and made it to the parking garage on the other side of the street. Tain opened the driver's side door for Samantha after she unlocked her pickup, then he rested his arm on the roof and looked in at her.

"I want you to move to the Malibu house with Hunter and Leda," Tain said. "You'll be protected there."

Samantha, startled, looked up at his grim face, his shadowed blue eyes. "What? Why?"

"Because I have to go, and I might not be back in time to stay with you tonight."

Her heart sped. "Why? Wherever you're going, I'll go with you."

Tain touched her cheek. "Do you trust me, Samantha?"

A difficult question. Samantha wanted to trust him. Her initial attraction to him had deepened into something intense, and she couldn't decide whether to embrace the feeling or flee in terror from it. She wanted to embrace *him* then fall asleep in his arms after making fantastic love with him.

In the back of her mind was the worried question—if she let him go today, would he ever come back?

Samantha reached up and touched the tattoo on his cheek, letting a spark of his life-essence arc into her fingers. "I don't want you to go."

He kissed the palm of her hand. "It's necessary."

Tears pricked her eyes, and she blinked them away. "Can't you give me a hint?"

Instead of answering, Tain said, "Stay with Leda and Hunter while I'm gone. It's the only place you can be protected. Go there now."

There was nothing wrong with his arrogance. "I can't leave Pickles alone."

"I'll tell Hunter to fetch him. Hunter's good with animals."

"Tain . . ."

Tain leaned into the car and kissed Samantha with firm lips, cupping her cheek with strong fingers. "Go."

He straightened up and stepped back. Samantha thought of a dozen more arguments, suppressed them, put the truck in gear, and drove away.

Trust him. The thought swam through her head even as worry twisted through her gut. *He needs someone to trust him.*

As she drove out of the garage, Samantha looked into the rearview mirror at the stretch of concrete she'd just left, but Tain was gone.

***

"He went where, exactly?" Hunter demanded.

Samantha sat on a voluminous sofa in the Malibu house's living room with Pickles on her lap, facing the inquiries of Hunter and Leda. Leda, at least, didn't interrogate her, just made strong coffee and looked worried.

"I don't know," Samantha answered. "He wasn't about to tell me."

Her demon senses quailed at all the life magic in the house, even though Hunter had dampened the wards to let her in. Hunter's aura was almost as strong as Tain's, and Leda was a powerful air-magic witch. The house belonged to Adrian, the oldest of the Immortals, and his magic permeated it. Samantha had stayed here before, and had thought she'd be used to it by now, but she wasn't. The combination of all three life magics was formidable.

Hunter sank down on a chair, his green eyes troubled. "Adrian told me to look after Tain while he was down here, and now I go and let him disappear."

"We can't keep him on a leash," Samantha said. "He'll never be fully healed if we don't let him go whenever he needs to go."

Hunter drew his hand through his tawny hair. "You have to understand. We lost him for such a long time that all of us are constantly scared we'll lose him again. Even Kalen calls about him, and believe me, it takes a lot to motivate Kalen to communicate with the rest of us." He gave her an open look. "We love him, Samantha."

"If you do love him, you have to show him that by letting him go," Samantha said. She'd spent the drive up here repeating the same words to herself.

Pickles, oblivious, climbed up on Samantha's shoulder, his claws pinpricks through her shirt. She saw via the large mirror across the living room that he was staring with interest at Mukasa the lion pacing down on the beach.

Hunter's green eyes narrowed, and he pinned Samantha with a knowing stare. "You love Tain too."

Samantha softened. "'Fraid so." She tried a smile. "Even if he never loves me back, I can't help it. I'm trusting him, whatever it is he's up to, because I need to."

"I understand," Leda said, setting down another mug of coffee. "Believe me."

Samantha saw in her eyes the brave compassion of another woman caught by an Immortal. *They are hard to love,* the look said, *but worth every second of it.*

***

Tain investigated what he needed to in the building that housed No More Nightmares, using a little misdirection magic to keep people from noticing him. He'd become very good at that while a captive, some part of him becoming expert at hiding his true self from Kehksut.

That tiny hidden part of him had been his salvation. Samantha had reached it, allowing Tain's brothers to then bond and pull him out. He remembered the anguishing pain when his true self had emerged at last, the reluctance with which he'd been dragged back into the light.

Returning to the light meant acknowledging his torment and loneliness, facing his pain head-on instead of hiding in madness. Tain's brothers had ripped the scab from his very deep wound, and Tain had bled for a long, long time.

Tain discovered what he wanted in the building and departed, heading for the roads that led out of town. He didn't have much cash left, so he traveled the way he'd learned in the last year—he walked along the side of the highway and stuck out his thumb.

Chapter Sixteen

Samantha returned to work, assuaging Hunter's and Leda's concerns by having Logan drive her. Logan emerged from the car in front of the house when Samantha came out, and laughed when he saw Pickles touch noses with the lion Mukasa, before the two cats strolled away together.

"At least someone's enjoying his captivity," Logan remarked as they pulled out and headed down the hill. "It must be hell for you having to stay in this luxury house on the beach with better security than Fort Knox."

"The view is nice," Samantha admitted. "Though all the life magic in there makes me dizzy."

Logan shot her a look of concern. "How are you holding up?"

"I'll be all right. They're trying to keep down the magic without jeopardizing the protection."

"Any word from Tain?"

"Not yet."

Logan drove for a few minutes without speaking. He turned onto Sunset, making for the freeway, traffic quickly hemming them in as soon as they left the on-ramp.

"You know," Logan said as they inched along. "I'm not the kind of guy who interferes in my friends' personal lives. And one of the things I like best about you is that you don't pry into mine."

Samantha studied the cars packed onto the freeway on either side of them. "I figure if it's important for me to know something about you or your past, you'll tell me."

"And I appreciate that," Logan said.

"But . . . ?" Samantha turned to him. "I hear a big *but* coming."

"Something's on your mind. You look at me, then look away— like you need to tell me something, and you're not sure how. You can give it to me straight, Sam. Does McKay want to fire me?"

Samantha's eyes widened in surprise. "Good Lord, no. You're one of the best detectives in the division. Why would you think that?"

"Don't know—you've seemed jumpy around me the last couple of days."

"Well, I'm sorry if I worried you."

"What is it then? I wouldn't push you, but I'm feeling the tension. What's up? Or is it the whole matriarch dying thing?"

The traffic opened out a little, and their speed picked up to an even 30 mph. Samantha faced Logan, deciding to stop being a coward.

"Tain told me I need to imbibe life essence in order to survive. That the demon in me does it instinctively."

Logan gave her a nod. "That's probably true."

"He said I must have taken some from *you* without knowing I was doing it." When Logan said nothing, Samantha's heart gave a painful throb. "Oh, gods, he was right, wasn't he?"

Logan moved his shoulders in a shrug. "I don't mind so much."

Samantha sat up straight, her mouth open. "Are you insane? You let me do that to you without trying to stop me? Without saying *anything*?"

Logan kept his eyes on the traffic. "I thought maybe you did it to all your partners."

"This isn't funny. I had no idea . . . *When* did I?"

Logan started to smile. "You do it in tiny bits at a time, like when you touch my shoulder or shake my hand or whatever. Maybe the demon part of you can't resist the powerful life essence of a badass werewolf like me. You never take very much, and it doesn't hurt me."

"Son of a bitch, Logan. Why didn't you ever say anything?"

Another shrug. "What was there to say?"

Samantha balled her fists. "Are you kidding me? So if I were a vampire and bit your neck every time I saw you, you wouldn't mention it?"

"That's different."

"It's exactly the same," Samantha nearly shouted. "Maybe the life-essence sucking isn't as obvious as a vampire drinking blood out of a vein, but it's just as bad. How did you feel when you found out you'd been partnered with a demon?"

Logan's smile died. "Compared to being with some of the wolves in my pack, hanging out with you has been absolute bliss." The bleak anger in his eyes surprised her. "You've never hurt me, Samantha, and I was grateful I could do something for you. You were patient with me when I was a newbie detective."

"Wait a minute—are you telling me things were so bad in your pack that having a demon suck on your life essence was *better*?"

"You have no idea." Logan stopped talking as he navigated through some tricky traffic. "Let's just say I was happy to start over again."

"Wow." Samantha turned her gaze out the front window again, studying the dented trunk of the older car in front of them. Logan closed his mouth again, finished with the discussion. Samantha wondered again what on earth had happened in his pack to make him leave it—especially if he'd been high in it, as Tain had suggested—but Logan had just finished telling her how refreshing it was that Samantha didn't ask a lot of questions. When Logan was ready to tell her, he would.

She let out a breath. "It was easy to be patient with you when you were a newbie detective," she said. "You're a good cop, Logan."

"Thank you."

Samantha leaned back in the seat. "And it's handy to have a partner who can turn into a sniffer dog."

"Aw, thanks."

Samantha shared a grin with him then lost the smile. "I'm still not sure how I feel about you not telling me I took your life essence," she said. "When I figure it out, I'll let you know."

"Hey, any time you need my life essence, it's here for you." Logan gave her a sideways glance. "Although I have the feeling you don't need it so much these days."

Samantha thought about the wild, white-hot sensations she experienced when she joined with Tain, and her face heated. "Remember back when we didn't talk about our personal lives?" she asked, her voice light. "I liked that."

Logan gave her a nod and a laugh. "I'm right there with you, partner."

They turned to discussing the matriarch's murder and what Logan had discovered, which hadn't been more since Samantha and Logan had parted ways at the matriarch's mansion. Logan and McKay were still going over the statements and tracking down whatever maintenance and repair workers had come to the estate. Forensics was still analyzing and would tell them what they'd found on their end when they were done.

Samantha listened, trying to bury herself in the facts of the case, but she couldn't quite shut out the new tension between herself and Logan, nor her deep worry about where Tain was and what he was up to.

***

Tain braced himself on the hard bench backseat of a pickup as it started bouncing along on bad shocks down the I-15. He'd found rides all the way out to Barstow, then walked along the freeway again as the sun had set. The two friends in their truck saw him and stopped for him, and the driver good-naturedly told him to hop in. Tain found himself squeezed into their backseat between a large cooler and an even larger tawny-colored short-haired dog, who was currently asleep.

"So where you headed, bud?" the driver asked as the sun sank behind them. He had a grizzled beard and a head of wiry, graying hair. His friend looked much the same.

"Not sure yet." The information Tain had found at No More Nightmares mentioned a hideaway out in the deserts on the California-Nevada border, but hadn't been specific about where.

The driver burst out laughing. "Anywhere but here?"

"Something like that."

"Yeah, I hear you. I'm Ed," the driver went on. "This is my buddy Mike."

"Tain," he responded.

Ed laughed again, a roar that drowned out the screeching engine. "What the hell kind of name is that?"

"Celtic." When Ed looked baffled, Tain said, "Welsh."

"You're not American then."

"I am now." Adrian had obtained all kinds of documents for Tain that said he was an American resident of Seattle, even though Tain stayed with Adrian at the Seattle house only a few weeks at a time. Pieces of paper didn't mean much to a man who'd traveled where he'd pleased before his capture, but people these days liked documents, and Adrian had told Tain they would save a mountain of trouble. "From Seattle," Tain added.

"Well, at least you're not—*Shit!*" Ed broke off as the truck bucked hard then coughed. Then the rattling stopped, and the truck drifted to the side of the road in silence.

Traffic was sparse, the few cars giving them a wide berth as they passed. Mike hopped out as Ed popped the hood, and Tain joined Mike on the gravel.

The land here was empty, soothing. The desert stretched forever on either side of the freeway, pale gravel covered with slender-limbed creosote and smaller scrub, nothing manmade except a lighted billboard a few yards off the freeway, advertising a 24-hour casino in Las Vegas.

Los Angeles's constant smell of exhaust was gone, replaced by the clean scents of dust and night breezes. The air was pleasantly cool now that the sun had slid behind the horizon, though during the day, even in September, the temperature out here would soar into the triple digits.

Mike, who hadn't said a word since they'd picked up Tain, had his head under the hood, shining a flashlight over various pieces of metal and dried rubber hoses. He wiggled things, and then Ed tried to start the truck, but nothing much happened except clunking noises and Ed's string of obscenities.

"Let me try," Tain said.

Silent Mike gave him a look that said, *Sure, if you want,* and stepped out of the way.

Tain knew nothing about the mechanics of vehicles of this century, although he knew men enjoyed tinkering with them whether they needed to be tinkered with or not. But he could feel the engine's core, see the power snaking through it, and understood where that power was blocked.

He jiggled bits, as Mike had done, while he sank a tiny trickle of magic through the engine, unclogging the lines, fixing the gear shaft that had been slipping, and smoothing over frayed belts and various cracks in the metal.

Tain withdrew himself from the machine's belly and said, "Try it now."

Ed cranked, and the engine started up. Instead of the loud rattle with which the truck had eaten up the miles, the engine now purred, smooth and quiet. Ed's eyes widened over the steering wheel, and Mike stared at Tain.

"How the hell did you do that?" Ed bellowed out of the truck window.

Tain said nothing as he closed the hood. Mike clapped him on the shoulder and gestured him back into the truck.

Ed told him to sit in the front this time, Mike scooting over to the middle so Tain could be by the passenger door. The dog, still sleeping in the back, began to snore.

Ed pulled out after a lone car had shot by, grinning as the truck moved easily down the freeway. He pressed the accelerator and quickly caught up to and overtook the other car.

"Woo hoo!" Ed screamed. "Hey, Tain, we're heading to a place out by Vegas. Want to come? The girls there really like to party."

Mike spoke for the first time. "One of them is a vampire."

"But nice," Ed said quickly. "She won't kill you or anything."

"She can bite my neck any time," Mike said softly, and Ed bellowed with laughter.

Tain smiled along with them. A vampire might know what he was looking for, if only because she'd want to avoid it.

"Sure," Tain said.

Ed whooped again. "Hot damn. Hang on, here we go!"

***

McKay had taken Samantha off the investigation of the matriarch's murder but hadn't banned her from looking into the destruction of Merrick's club, Nadia's abduction, or the threatening letters. Samantha spread the files over her desk late that afternoon and went through it again a piece at a time, adding what she'd learned from her visit to No More Nightmares.

She wished she could have found a suspiciously cut-up newspaper and a bottle of glue on Melanie's desk, but there hadn't been anything in the innocuous office to justify Samantha asking for a search warrant. Ms. Townsend's preoccupation with methods of killing demons and her assistant's fanatic protection of her weren't criminal, per se. Samantha had to be content with putting a watch on the office and trying to track down Ms. Townsend.

She also wanted to interview Merrick again, to find out how someone had gotten a firebomb into Merrick's club without him knowing it. Logan had sniffed around the morning after the club burned down and discovered a little pile of crystals, wire, and small, fine bones. A forensics department witch had identified the pieces as accoutrements for a spell that could remotely trigger a fire. Samantha also wanted to talk again to the Djowlan demon who'd attacked the matriarch's house, and Kemmerer, who'd sold Nadia to her captors. All these threads had to go somewhere.

Plus it kept her from thinking about Tain. *Trust me,* he'd said.

Did that mean he'd come back with the culprit in tow and give him to Samantha along with all the evidence she needed? Or was he up to something Immortal she really didn't want to know about?

Samantha's harried thoughts were interrupted by her cell phone. Her hopes leapt—*Tain*—then plummeted when she saw the call was from Septimus's vampire club.

"Yes?" she said.

"Don't sound so happy to hear from me," the vampire's dark voice rolled from the other end. "I need to talk to you."

"I'm listening."

"Not on a phone half the world can tap. Can you meet me? At my club would be best."

"Your club full of demon-hating vampires? I don't think so. How about the Malibu house?"

"I want to talk to *you*, not Hunter and his charming wife. How about a restaurant later tonight? I'll set it up—I know a good place."

"No vampires," Samantha warned.

"No vamps. Just humans catering to an exclusive clientele. You'll like it."

"Can you give me a hint what this is about?"

"It concerns a mutual friend, and that's all I will say on a phone. I'll send the limo to pick you up at ten."

"No, I'll drive myself."

Septimus sighed. "I'd rather you let me make sure you get there without problems. I'll send the limo. Kelly will be there, if it makes you feel better."

"A date with a famous actress and a vamp boss? How can it get better than this?"

"Your sarcasm stuns me. Be ready at ten." Septimus clicked off without saying good-bye.

Samantha returned to her files, uneasy. A vampire had secrets about Tain he didn't want to tell her over the phone, and she had to wait until ten or so tonight to find out what they were, if Septimus would even tell her everything. This did not put her into a good mood.

She stared in irritation at Logan's and her notes until the phone on her desk rang. She snatched it up. "Samantha Taylor," she snapped.

"Samantha?"

Samantha blinked and adjusted her tone. "Hello . . . Dad. What's up?"

"I need to talk to you, privately, not on the phone."

"Doesn't everyone?" Samantha said. "Sorry, I mean, sure. Want to meet me for a quick dinner?"

She heard him consult with her mother then Fulton replied that he'd drive down and meet her at La Casa Bonita, her favorite downtown Mexican place. Samantha now had to spend the rest of the afternoon wondering what that conversation would entail as well.

Samantha reached the restaurant before her father did, being too restless to work much longer. The staff knew her because she came in so often, and they let her take a booth away from the most crowded areas. When Fulton came in, catching sidelong looks from the waitresses who weren't adverse to good-looking demons in their establishment, Samantha stood up and hugged him.

Fulton looked pleased but puzzled. "What was that for?"

"Can't I be glad to see my own father?"

Fulton's frown deepened as they sat down. "Anything wrong?"

Samantha shrugged. "You're the one who wanted to talk to me."

Fulton waited until he and Samantha had ordered, then he looked around the crowded restaurant. "Not my idea of private."

"It's the best I can do. I'm on evening shift, and all the interrogation rooms at my office have two-way mirrors and microphones. This place gets so noisy no one will hear a word we say."

Fulton looked skeptical, but once the waitress had deposited a basket of tortilla chips and bowls containing four different kinds of salsa in front of them and walked away, Fulton began to talk.

"Do you know why the matriarch asked me to stay and talk to her the day you met her?"

"I needed to ask you about that." Samantha dipped a chip in the pungent tomatillo salsa and took a bite, savoring the lemony, salty taste. "What I recall mostly from that day is demons attacking, and me getting gooey acid all over me."

Fulton gave her a concerned look. "You're all right from that, aren't you?"

"Sorry, yes, I'm fine. Tell me why the matriarch asked you to stay."

"To talk about you. She asked me about your upbringing, what you did now, why you'd joined the police. She also asked me about your mother, and what you were taught about demon-kind."

"I wasn't taught anything about demon-kind," Samantha said, dipping her next chip into roasted tomato and chipotle salsa. "I thought I was an ordinary human child for a long time."

"I know." Fulton looked chagrined. "That was my fault—your mother wanted you to know, but I begged her not to tell you until you were old enough to understand. I wanted you to be raised human, because . . . well, for many reasons."

Samantha busied herself eating her soaked chip, but the taste she'd normally savor got lost as she wondered what Fulton's reasons had been. She said, "I heard an insane rumor that the matriarch wanted to groom me to take her place. That's what the majordomo—Ariadne—seems to think."

"That's another thing the matriarch wanted to talk to me about. She asked me to put you forward as a candidate at the next clan muster."

Samantha sat back, stunned to hear him confirm it. "What's a muster?" she asked faintly.

"A gathering of heads of demon households. We call it a *muster*, an old-fashioned term, because we used to have them only when we geared up to fight some battle. These days musters are more like board meetings."

Samantha reached for another handful of chips. "The majordomo told me that the matriarch put forth a candidate, and the heads of the families approved or didn't."

Fulton gave her a nod. "Heads of families can name a candidate as well, especially if the matriarch dies before she names who she wants as successor."

"So when are you going to tell the head of our family about all this? Or did you? What did he say?"

Fulton touched his chest. "*I* am the head of our family, which is one of the most powerful in the clan."

Samantha's chips dropped from her fingers, and she grabbed a napkin to wipe them clean. "You always told me you were a lesser demon, not very strong."

"Magically, I'm not very powerful. But politically, I am. When my father died some years ago, I took his place—I was the oldest son and heir, and you are my only child." Fulton's dark eyes softened. "Your mother and I were going to introduce you to all this gradually, but the matriarch jumped the gun by wanting you as a candidate. She was right, in retrospect. You need to know."

"But I'm only half demon," Samantha protested. "Why would the clan accept me as matriarch? Not that I have any intention of taking the position."

"Because my family has plenty of clout," Fulton said without boasting. "The matriarch was also from our family—she was my great-aunt, which means of course, that you share her blood." Fulton paused, his eyes darker than ever. "I hope you will consider it."

Samantha started to raise her voice in argument, then remembered they were in a crowded restaurant. "I can't possibly be clan matriarch," she said, trying to sound calm. "The idea is insane. I can barely work magic."

"Yet you know the activities of every demon club and demon boss in Los Angeles, not to mention everything the vampires do. You defeated an out-of-control Old One alongside a powerful Immortal warrior, and you have friends among the life-magic creatures who can do amazing things. Plus, you don't take shit from anyone. I remember all the things you did to try to find your mother last year."

Fulton finished as the waitress brought enchiladas and empanadas to the table. "Please, consider it," he said.

Samantha sat back again, the steam from her enchiladas rising to caress her face. Of all the things she'd speculated her father would say to her tonight, it wasn't this. She'd thought he'd shake his head in wonder at the matriarch's declaration, maybe agree that the woman had come unhinged.

Now Fulton was sitting here calmly eating empanadas and telling Samantha he thought she should become the next matriarch of their demon clan.

"What does Mom have to say about all this?" Samantha asked.

Fulton swallowed and wiped his mouth. "Joanne always knew this was a possibility. She doesn't really understand why it must be, but she'll support you."

"That makes two of us," Samantha said. "Not understanding, I mean." She let out a breath and pinned Fulton with a hard stare. "I appreciate you telling me all this, but I can't possibly become the clan matriarch. That's all I can say."

"Please, think about it."

Samantha ran her fork through her black beans sprinkled with cotija cheese. "Something I don't understand — you said you'd wanted Mom to raise me as human. Why do you all the sudden want me to be queen of the demons?"

The look in Fulton's eyes was serious. "Because as matriarch, you will have power, and you'll be protected by that power. I married your mother because I loved her, but I defied my family and convention to do it. In the old days, a half-blood offspring would have been immediately killed. Even these days, demons have been known to murder half demons and feel justified. But if you are the matriarch, one endorsed by the previous matriarch and backed by one of the most powerful demon families in the country, you will be safe."

Samantha looked at Fulton for a long time, until he picked up his fork again and stabbed it around his rice.

"This is my life," Samantha said in a soft voice. "All I ever wanted was to be a cop. When I found out I was half demon, I worried I'd never be let on the force, but then I learned I could be in the paranormal division. It's all I ever wanted to do — it's who I am. I don't know anything about the demon clans, and I certainly don't want to be head demon." She stopped. "I can't."

Fulton reached over and clasped Samantha's hand, his touch warm and vibrant. "Please, child, don't dismiss it so quickly. If another matriarch is chosen, and she takes against you, you might forfeit your life."

Chapter Seventeen

"Is this a great party, or what?"

Ed and Mike had driven Tain through the dark desert to end up in a bar inside the Nevada border, too far from Las Vegas to be anything but down scale. The air conditioning was faulty, the interior dark, the door permanently open to the night air.

Except for the slot machines blinking in one corner, Tain could be in the kind of tavern he'd frequented with Adrian in the old days—the same disreputable characters, barmaids who were either coyly smiling or sullen and un-trusting, and patrons who either wanted to be best friends or start a fight.

Ed insisted Tain stay and meet "the girls," who came from a ranch some way up highway 95. Ed said *ranch* with a little wink.

The vampire woman was easy to spot. She came in at about ten in a belly-dancing costume, set up a portable CD player, and started swaying and twirling to Middle-Eastern sounding tunes.

The girls laughed with the regulars, which included Ed and Mike, and sized up Tain with calculating eyes. Two of the young women were demons.

The vampire finished her dance and came over to where Ed enthusiastically beckoned her. "How you doing, sugar?" Ed asked her, giving her a one-armed hug. "This is our new friend, Tain. Tain, this is Vonda."

Vonda slid her sultry gaze from Ed to Tain, then she froze, her lips rolling back from her fangs. "What *are* you?"

Ed looked surprised. "He's a hell of a good mechanic, that's what he is. We picked him up outside of Barstow."

Tain snaked a small bit of his magic out to touch Vonda. She tried to counter with a tendril of death magic then looked terrified as Tain easily brushed it aside.

"He's a witch," Vonda said angrily, stepping away from Ed and folding her arms across her bare belly. "He has to be."

Tain let his magic become soothing, healing. "I'll not harm you."

Vonda stared at him, mouth open. Tain made an *I want to talk to you* gesture with his chin, and moved to the corner near the slot machines. Vonda kept staring, then finally she followed. Ed, oblivious, grinned and gave Tain a thumbs-up.

Vonda was still wary of Tain, keeping her arms folded as though trying to shut him out, but she conceded to answer his questions. "Sure, the No More Nightmares people come around here sometimes. The guys don't let on that Amy and Sandy are demons, and the No More Nightmares people don't seem to care that I'm vampire."

"They can't sense the other two girls are demon?" Tain asked. Amy's and Sandy's dark auras were thick around them — no one with a spark of magic could miss it.

Vonda shrugged. "They don't seem to. I mean, these No More Nightmares chicks whine about demons being a menace and how they want them all gone, but they can't even tell when one walks by them."

And yet Melanie at the No More Nightmares office had known right away that Samantha was half demon. "But they leave *you* alone?" Tain asked her.

"Yeah, they do, which is weird. Sometimes I think I should go to one of their stupid meetings and tear out the throats of half of them, but it's not worth getting staked for. But I could do it."

Tain knew she could. The petite young woman in the belly-dance veils and jingling sash could take out this entire room if she wanted to.

"Where do they have their meetings?"

Vonda wrinkled her nose. "You aren't thinking of joining, are you?"

Tain shook his head. "Just curious."

"I don't know. Seriously, I don't. I don't want to know."

"Could you find out?"

Vonda gave him an assessing look. "What would I get if I do?"

Tain thought of his empty pockets, but he knew this vampire girl wouldn't be tempted by money. "What do you want?"

Her eyes darkened. "A sip of whatever kind of blood is riding through your veins."

Tain shook his head. "My blood wouldn't be good for you — too much life magic will kill you."

"I've done life-magic creatures before." Vonda's look turned coy. "Werewolves are especially good. They *say* they hate vampires, but when they really want one . . ."

"I'm not a werewolf."

"No? What are you, then? Chameleon?" Chameleons were similar to were-creatures, except they were humans who could take the form of any living being. They didn't become that creature in the same way a shapeshifter like Logan became his animal self; they were still human no matter what animal they resembled.

"Call me a guardian," Tain said. "Have any demon or vampire girls disappeared from around here lately?"

Vonda considered. "I don't know about *disappeared*, but a few have moved on. That happens a lot. Girls come and go, and they don't always leave a forwarding address."

"Is there a place around here that's different somehow?" Tain asked. "Maybe a place vampires and demons are afraid to go?"

Vonda gazed at him in sudden suspicion. "Why do you want to know that?"

Tain kept his voice gentle. "Because I don't like people who deal in fear. I want to know what the No More Nightmares people are doing and why. Is there such a place?"

Vonda gave a grudging nod. "All right, I have heard weird stories about a canyon not far from here. But if I tell you about it, you really do need to give me something in return. I don't work for free." She reached up drew and a finger across Tain's left cheek, the one unmarked by his tattoo. Her eyes grew sultry, filling with true desire.

Tain brushed her hand away. "I have a lover," he said. He tightened when he thought of Samantha, her warmth, her eyes as dark as this woman's, but filled with laughter and heat.

Vonda grinned. "Sweetie, that doesn't stop anyone here."

"It stops me." Tain's firm tone put a disappointed look on her face. "What I *will* do, though . . ." Tain took her hand again and sent a trickle of healing magic through her.

When she'd touched his face, he'd felt the taint of a weakening spell, one she strove to hide. A witch could have put it on her, or rival vampire or customer—it was hard to say—but the spell was slowly killing her. With one touch, Tain broke and removed it.

Vonda stared at him in shock. She touched her own cheek, eyes widening as she realized the spell was gone. "Thank you." The words were the sincerest she'd spoke all night. Then she smiled again. "Are you sure you don't want a little extra fun?"

She looked hopeful, but Tain shook his head. "I'm sure. Now, how do I get to this place?"

***

Samantha rode in Septimus's ultra-luxurious limousine to a five-star restaurant in which corporate presidents made international deals and big-name producers wined and dined investors. Samantha had conceded to the limo because Septimus refused to tell her the name of the restaurant, and she truly wanted to know what he had to say. Information from a vampire boss was worth a little secrecy. She'd called Logan to tell him of the meeting—liking someone to know she would be with the most powerful vampire in California—but she hadn't been able to reach him. She left him a message and, in the limo, checked her own messages and found none.

Samantha scrolled to where she'd saved Tain's cell phone number and let her thumb hover over the "Call" button. She wanted to push it, to hear his Welsh-accented voice answering. She wanted to say to him, even if she had to leave a message, *I miss you.*

Samantha sighed, turned off the phone, and dropped it back into her purse.

The wait staff at the restaurant knew Septimus, who'd booked a small private room for himself, Kelly, and Samantha. The maître d' guided Samantha through the dining room to the back as though she were a celebrity gracing them with a visit.

Septimus stood up when Samantha entered. Samantha was relieved to see Kelly O'Byrne with him as promised. The actress was sitting in the cushioned chair at Septimus's table, looking as stunning as ever. Kelly never seemed to make extra effort with her makeup or clothes, but she was always poised in her understated but hideously expensive wardrobe, ready for whatever camera might flash at her.

Kelly greeted Samantha warmly, holding her hands. She owned the house next door to Leda and Hunter, and Samantha had come to know her somewhat over the past year. As usual, Kelly wore a silk scarf around her neck to hide the bites of her vampire lover. It had become a signature look, imitated by her fans.

"Do you mind if I stay?" Kelly asked. "If you'd rather talk to Septimus alone, I can go."

Samantha squeezed her hands. "No, please."

"Ms. Taylor doesn't trust me," Septimus said dryly.

Samantha slanted him a weary glance. "It's more that I don't want to explain to my lieutenant why one of her detectives was treated to dinner at a chi-chi restaurant by a vampire boss. If I say I was here for my friend Kelly, things get easier."

"Of course." Septimus gestured Samantha to sit, and then flicked his fingers for a waiter to come and pour wine. Then he ordered for the three of them, which annoyed independent Samantha, but since he was footing the bill, she decided to say nothing.

Samantha studied Septimus as she drank her wine— which was smooth and rich. He had black hair pulled into a modest tail at the base of his neck, a hard face that still managed to be handsome, and a broad-shouldered body that nicely filled out his thousand-dollar suit. He kept his dark blue eyes slightly averted from both Samantha and Kelly, and even the waiter, because one look into an Old One vamp's eyes could mesmerize a person into doing and saying anything Septimus wanted.

Samantha found herself comparing Septimus with his pristine suit and smooth manner to a man who wore a worn duster over a T-shirt and jeans, and who didn't mind pinning people with an intense blue stare. She decided she preferred hacked short, unruly hair to the tamed style Septimus wore, a white-hot life magic aura over the inky darkness of an ultra-powerful vampire.

Septimus waited until the first course was served then bade the waiter shut the door behind him and not return until called. Septimus reached into a briefcase and pulled out a file, which he laid beside Samantha's plate.

Samantha flipped the file open. "What's this?" She expected something about the demon disappearances and deaths but instead found herself looking at a photo of Tain. He was walking away from the camera, sunshine on his duster coat and thick red hair.

The next picture was of him entering the building where No More Nightmares had an office. The following photo was one of him strolling by the gate of the matriarch's compound. Then more pictures showing Tain in various places around the city, and then pages of notes in cramped handwriting, containing dates and times.

"What is this?" Samantha repeated in a hard voice.

"A record of Tain's movements since he first arrived in Los Angeles," Septimus said.

Samantha looked up at him in angry surprise. "Why?"

The vampire took a casual sip of wine. "Adrian asked me to keep an eye on Tain, although I don't believe he meant for me to be so detailed. That, I took upon myself."

"Why?" Samantha asked again, voice hardening.

"Because Tain is unpredictable. I wanted to make sure I knew what he was up to while he was in my city."

Samantha firmly closed the folder. "He's been helping me on this demon case."

"A case he brought to your attention in the first place. I'm showing this to you for a reason, Ms. Taylor. I think Tain is more involved in it than he's let on."

Samantha's heart beat faster. "Explain."

Septimus toyed with the stem of his wineglass, while Kelly looked on, her look both sympathetic and concerned. "Tain has been seen in the vicinity of every incident you've investigated," Septimus said. "He was spotted near the locations where each of the demon prostitutes disappeared. He unerringly walked into the alley where the demon girl Nadia was returned. He was seen near the matriarch's mansion before she was found dead, and breaking into the offices of that No More Nightmares place yesterday evening."

Samantha felt brittle. "You've done a thorough job. If you know so much about Tain, where is he now? What's he up to? Do you have satellite photos?"

Septimus took her outburst calmly. "He was last seen heading east out of San Bernardino, and after that, I considered him out of my jurisdiction."

"If you're that worried about him, why did you stop tracking him?"

"I wasn't *tracking* him, as you say. I was making sure he wasn't getting himself into trouble down here while his big brother worries in Seattle. When Adrian gets worried, bad things happen to those of us of the death-magic persuasion. If Tain goes around the bend again, Adrian will hold me partly responsible."

"So you were covering your ass, is that it?" Samantha asked angrily.

"I don't like what I found any more than you do . . ."

Samantha cut him off. "Have you sent this report to Adrian? Told him Tain's committed the crime of walking the streets of Los Angeles?"

Septimus looked pained. "I haven't said a word to Adrian. I wanted to show you first."

"Why?"

"Because if it means nothing, I won't have pissed off five Immortal warriors who carry very large swords. If it *is* something . . . You're paranormal police—it's your job to take care of problems like Tain."

Samantha clenched the hand that rested in her lap. "If Tain has gone insane again—and I'm not saying he has— why do you assume *I* can take care of him? I'm nowhere near as strong as his brothers, or you for that matter."

"Because you helped him before," Septimus said in a matter-of-fact voice. "His mind completely gone up there in Seattle, and yet he looked at you, talked to you, even flirted with you, I've been told. I don't think it was a coincidence his brothers were able to restore him shortly after he met you. Or that Cerridwen chose you as the witch whose body she'd enter during the battle."

Samantha drew a breath. "I think you're optimistic about my influence over him."

"I think he's right," Kelly said softly.

Samantha glanced at Kelly, who looked sympathetic but pragmatic then back at the file, her throat tight. She didn't want these pictures of Tain near crime scenes to be anything but coincidence. She didn't want to face the fact that, if Tain went insane again, if she lost him, it would devastate her.

She thought of his phone number saved on her cell phone — if she'd called him when she'd been tempted to in the limo, would he have answered? She'd stilled her hand because of Tain's last question to her — *Do you trust me?*

I have to trust him. Otherwise my love for him is nothing.

Samantha wet her dry mouth. "What do you want me to do, follow him and drag him back to Los Angeles?"

"I wanted you to be aware what he is doing," Septimus said. "You can keep the file. Use it as you wish."

Samantha gazed at the brown folder for a long moment, then she nodded. She knew Septimus wasn't handing her the only copies of the photos and information — Septimus likely had everything double and triple backed up.

The waiters entered at Septimus's signal with perfectly prepared plates of food, but the scents, which should have been heavenly, made Samantha a bit queasy. "I'm sorry, but I don't have much appetite."

"I quite understand," Septimus said.

Samantha stood. "I have to go."

Septimus gave her an imperceptible nod and beckoned to one of the waiters. "Have my driver take Ms. Taylor home."

Samantha would have preferred a taxi, not in the mood for another muffled ride in Septimus's dark limousine. But Kelly gave her a warm hug, then the maître d' ushered Samantha out before she could argue, taking her all the way out of the restaurant to the open door of the waiting limo.

She didn't want to return to the Malibu house and a curious Hunter and Leda, so Samantha told Septimus's driver to take her back to the police department. There she could sit in isolation at her desk, study the file Septimus had given her, and decide what to do. The last thing she wanted was Hunter calling Adrian and his brothers and saying they needed to round up crazy Tain again.

No, the very last thing Samantha wanted was for what was in the file to be true—that Tain was taking his revenge on demons one at a time, starting with the most helpless and working his way up to the matriarch. She remembered how easy it had been for him to kill the demons at Merrick's club—two blasts of his lightning magic, and they'd been solidly dead. No butchering necessary.

But, she realized when she reached her desk and spread Septimus's notes and photos over it, that Tain had to be closely involved in all of this. The time stamp on one of the photos put him outside the matriarch's mansion just before her death.

Samantha stared at the photo and put her head in her hands, wondering where the hell Tain was now.

***

Ed dropped Tain off about midnight on the dirt road Vonda had indicated, but neither Vonda nor Ed would get out of his truck.

"You sure?" Ed said, leaning on his arm out the window. "It's spooky out here."

Tain gave him a nod. "I'll be fine."

"Well, alright. Give me a call if you want a ride back. See you."

Tain raised his hand in farewell, and Ed's truck screeched around and rolled away, bathing Tain in exhaust and dust.

This stretch of road was deserted, an unpaved washboard that rolled with the contours of the land. A mountain ridgeline rose high and sharp to the east, the moon filming the landscape with silver. The white desert floor showed the black outlines of creosote and stunted Joshua trees.

At the end of this road, Vonda had said, was the bad place, but she wouldn't be more specific than that. She'd never seen it, but she'd heard stories of people going there and never coming out.

By *people* Vonda had meant death-magic creatures. Tain, boiling over with life magic, walked down the road with a little more confidence.

His boots stirred puffs of white dust but nothing else moved in the stillness. It was a fine night, cool though not sharply cold, and the moon lighted everything well. But he heard no noises of night creatures—coyotes, owls, bats, snakes—only silence and the crunch of his boots on rock.

The road ended at the entrance to a box canyon, its walls rising sharply from the desert floor. Hardy thistle bushes clung to minute ledges all the way to the top. An obvious path led inside the canyon, and Tain followed it.

The canyon wound with the wash that had formed it, the very bottom of the wash's bed damp from runoff from the last rain. As the walls closed off the open desert behind him, Tain felt a faint diminishing of his magic that he at first thought was imagination. But as he went on, the sensation grew stronger, a definite suppression of the power inside him.

Perhaps this was what Vonda meant—that the strong natural magic of vampires and demons was negated here. If so, whatever field or spell hung over this place squelched *all* magic, both life and death, which was unusual.

Tain drew one of his swords and kept walking. The interior of the canyon was even more silent than the open desert—not an insect moved across the rocks. The moon, high overhead now, showed him the blank end of the canyon, a wall pock-marked with man-made openings.

He craned his head to study the sides of the canyon, finding the tell-tale evenness of cliff dwellings in natural fissures, houses that had been built hundreds of years ago, out of the reach of coyotes and wolves. He wondered if the ancient Americans had chosen this place precisely because its negating field had kept them safe from magical creatures.

Tain sensed another taint over the place that was more recent, as though someone had taken the repressing properties of the canyon and twisted it for their own purposes.

He scanned the cliffs, magically searching for any living thing. He felt as though he were trying to swim through deep water, the effort to send out even a small thread taking much strength.

His thin tendril of magic touched something only about ten feet above him, a life, single, alone, powerful. Tain also sensed that many others had been here, felt their gloating, their glee.

He thought about what Nadia had reported—when she'd been held captive she couldn't shift into her demon form or gain her demon strength. Samantha had thought drugs had suppressed her ability, but in a place like this, where all magic, including powerful demon magic, was weakened, ordinary human beings would have the advantage.

Tain pulled out his cell phone. The picture he'd asked Leda to put as his wallpaper was one of Samantha—Leda had taken it at a family gathering this summer and had sent it to Tain. Samantha's face was slightly turned to the left, but her dark eyes had fixed on the photographer. Sunshine gleamed on her black hair, and she smiled a subtle half-smile, as though she knew a secret she wasn't about to share.

Tain touched the image, feeling empty spaces inside him, before he tapped the button that would bring up his list of phone numbers.

The phone blipped, the readout saying, "No Service."

Tain thoughtfully shoved the phone back into his pocket. Another advantage to having a meeting place out in the middle of nowhere, was that no one could secretly call for help.

He scanned the ruins again and asked clearly, "Who are you?"

Tain's voice echoed around the canyon and up to the slit of open sky. After a long few minutes, a small rain of pebbles dribbled from a shelf above, and someone stepped out onto the ledge.

"You were followed."

Tain looked behind him, trying to probe for an aura, but he still felt as though he pushed through molasses. "I know that, Ms. Townsend."

The woman drew herself up, no longer wearing the smart suit she'd had on at the lecture. Tonight she wore a flowing black robe, colorless, and hiding her body.

"Who are you?" she asked.

"A traveler. Who are you?"

Ms. Townsend laughed. "I am the voice of vengeance, the hand of justice. Through me, the world will be rid of darkness, and life will shine once again."

"Will it, now?" Tain answered. "That's interesting."

Ms. Townsend looked down at him with icy hauteur. "It will be done. I have been chosen."

"Who chose you?" Tain asked.

She didn't answer. "This barren world will be green again, when all the death creatures are gone."

"This part of the world is supposed to be barren," Tain pointed out. "And death magic has to balance life magic, or there's chaos."

"There is chaos now."

"Not really."

As Tain spoke he thought through ways he could ascend the walls and snatch her, truss her up, and drag her back to Samantha for interrogation. Nothing would be easy, but he would try.

"You feel weak, don't you?" Ms. Townsend went on. "Your magic is gone. It's not beings like you who will heal the world, it is us. Through me."

Her eyes were like windows of darkness as she looked down at Tain. Tain wondered if someone channeled magic through her—if that it was possible in this place. If they could, it confirmed something he'd found when he poked around the matriarch's house by himself, something he wasn't yet ready to tell Samantha.

"I've seen what the imbalance can do," Tain said. "Now I seek to maintain the balance."

Ms. Townsend's lip curled. "Ah, yes, the so-called balance of life magic and death magic. Propaganda from the death realms so right-thinking people won't swoop down and eradicate the demons. Demons have invaded our world, running what they call *businesses* and *clubs*. They've oozed their poison into our lives, and now it will cease."

Tain drew his second sword and crossed both blades in front of him, pouring every bit of magic he had into them. Despite the dampening field, he might be strong enough to at least knock the woman off the ledge, and once she was on the ground he had more than enough physical strength to subdue her.

"No," she shouted down at him. "I am chosen!"

Sudden darkness surged behind her, and she floated out over the canyon like an enormous bat. Tain reached up with a snake of white magic, but it dissipated before it could reach her.

Ms. Townsend continued to float across the rocks, untouched, until she disappeared into the shadows on the other side of the canyon. Tain started climbing toward the ledge on which she'd stood, rocks and pebbles sliding under his feet. About halfway up, the cliff became sheer with no handholds—he'd need rope to go any farther.

Tain scooted back down in time to see glowing eyes vanish into the shadows of the cliff face below. He straightened up and brushed off his coat.

"Come out," he said. "I heard you."

Chapter Eighteen

A gray timber wolf walked out into the moonlight, a huge male with a powerful body and thick fur. It stopped a few feet from Tain and lowered itself to its haunches without fear.

Tain spoke in a low voice, aware of how sound carried in the still air. "Did you come on your motorcycle?"

The wolf made no indication that he understood, but rose and slowly walked toward the entrance of the canyon. Tain followed.

The night was quiet again, no sounds of pursuit from behind, and no hint of Ms. Townsend anywhere. As they walked, Tain felt the restraining field lessen, and his magical strength return. Not long later, the cliffs receded and a chill breeze from the open desert washed over him.

The wolf padded back down the wash to the unpaved, rutted road where Ed and Vonda had left Tain. He turned aside and led Tain over a slight rise to another wash, which was nothing more than a narrow slice in the desert floor. A motorcycle had been shoved behind a thick stand of brush, its Harley Davidson logo gleaming.

The wolf's body elongated as it rose on its hind legs, his features contorting and twisting until they resolved into those of a man. Tain turned away so Logan could grab his clothes, though Logan, like most shifters when they changed, didn't seem bothered by his own nudity.

"I got your call," Logan said as he pulled on his T-shirt. "Why didn't you want me to tell Samantha I was meeting you?"

"Because she would have insisted on coming."

Logan grinned. "True. She's one tough lady. But when it comes to strong magic, I like to go in first, and she doesn't always appreciate that."

"No." Tain smiled slightly and pulled the motorcycle from the wash, propping it up to wait for Logan to dress. Tain pictured Samantha's outrage when she learned he and Logan had investigated this place without her. "You're protective of her," he said.

Logan shrugged. "I'm a wolf. I like to take care of my friends."

There was more to it than that, Tain suspected. He didn't pursue it, but Logan's answer confirmed his idea that Logan was high in his pack—the closer to pack leader the wolf was, the stronger his need to protect.

"When you disappeared into the canyon," Logan said, "I became the wolf to follow you by scent. Then the vortex hit me, and I couldn't change back."

"Is that what it is?" Tain glanced at the ridge in which the canyon hid. "A vortex?"

Logan nodded. "You get a lot of vortexes out here in the desert—places where energy and magic collect. Some vortexes enhance magic, some cancel it out. I've never felt a dampening one as strong as this, though."

"You know a lot about what's out here," Tain said.

Logan shrugged. "I'm a biker. I explore roads other people don't."

Tain looked back at the ridge. "The Townsend woman was possessed by something, and the vortex didn't seem to suppress that."

"Well, there's definitely something weird about these No More Nightmares people."

Tain leaned against the bike and folded his arms while Logan pulled on his jeans and boots. "Something unusual about you, too."

Logan looked up sharply. "Look who's talking."

"There can't be much you don't know about me by now," Tain said. "Whatever Samantha hasn't told you, I'm sure Hunter has. But no one knows much about you. First I thought you might be a pack leader, but I'm guessing you were Packmaster."

Logan stopped. "What would make you think that?"

"Because a leader wouldn't walk away from his pack. He'd fight to the death rather than choose exile. But a second-in-command might leave—in fact, if shunned by the pack, he'd have to."

Logan turned his face to the moon, his tawny eyes glittering in the white light. "The pack is no longer part of my life. I made my decision."

"Did they force the decision on you?"

Logan sighed, his expression bleak. "It's something I'd rather not talk about, if you don't mind."

Tain was curious, but he more than anyone recognized the need to leave the past in the past. "If you promise me the reason won't hurt Samantha, I won't ask you."

Logan relaxed enough to grin again. "Now who's being protective?"

"Samantha's worth protecting."

"She's becoming pretty wrapped up in you, you know. Do me a favor and don't break her heart. If I have to punch you, I will, even though I don't think the odds are in my favor in a fair fight."

"It won't come to that." Tain had no intention of leaving Samantha until he stopped whoever was cutting out demon hearts. After that it would be her decision whether he went or stayed. If one of them ended up brokenhearted, it would likely be Tain.

Logan came to the bike and lifted his helmet from the back. "It's about six hours to Los Angeles. We'll be there by morning."

Clearly finished talking about his past, Logan climbed on the bike and slid forward enough to accommodate Tain. Tain settled his swords out of the way and climbed on behind him. Logan fired up the bike, and they took off into the night, the sound of the motorcycle ringing back up the still, silent canyon.

***

Logan walked in late the next day, reaching his desk as Samantha was eating lunch at hers.

"Where have you been?" Samantha demanded.

"The Nevada desert." Logan yawned, very much like a wolf stretching after a long night. "Ran into construction on the freeway, which slowed us way down. Then I had to take a shower, or you wouldn't have liked me sitting next to you today."

"The Nevada desert?" Samantha repeated. "*Us?*"

"Tain came back with me." Logan rubbed his eyes with the heel of his hand and logged in to his computer. "He said he'd crash at his own place and meet up with you later."

"Oh." The explanation felt anticlimactic and at the same time awakened more of Samantha's worries. "What were you doing in Nevada?"

"Looking for the No More Nightmares compound." Logan then told her an incredible tale of a narrow canyon with a magic-dampening field and Ms. Townsend floating across the sky.

"Am I supposed to understand any of this?" Samantha asked when he finished. "Is this evidence that No More Nightmares is doing the killings?"

"You tell me." Logan yawned again. "My brain is fried."

Samantha regarded him without sympathy. She'd stayed up far into the night at the Malibu house looking over the file Septimus had given her on Tain, then tucked it into her briefcase and brought it in with her this morning, not wanting Leda or Hunter to stumble across it.

The evidence Septimus had gathered was pretty damning. The photos and surveillance notes showed Tain in places where he shouldn't have been, meeting with people like the fine-boned Djowlan demon who'd led the attack on the matriarch's house. And now Logan talked about Tain hitching across the desert to track the No More Nightmares group to a bizarre canyon in Nevada.

"We can contact the county sheriff out there," Samantha suggested. "See what he knows about it."

"Sheriff in that county's a she. I called her already, and she said she'd send a couple of deputies to check it out. Humans only, I said, because of the magic-killing vortex. She laughed at me and said they weren't much for paranormal police in her county anyway."

Samantha paused. "If she said that, they might be sympathetic to No More Nightmares. Another thing to be careful of."

"Yep."

Logan turned to his computer, looking ready to bury himself in work. Samantha decided to leave him to it.

She went in to see McKay, said she needed to go out and follow up her investigation of No More Nightmares, and left without Logan. She took the file on Tain with her and made her way to the apartments in east L.A. where Septimus's notes said Tain lived.

The apartment complex Samantha parked in front of looked like a converted motel, and was as worn out as any building in this neighborhood. She climbed outside stairs to a railed balcony that ran past all the front doors on the second level, and walked briskly along until she reached number 210.

Samantha found the door slightly ajar, but when she listened she heard nothing from within. She reached into her blazer and closed her hand around her pistol before she ducked inside.

The apartment was small, with a tiny living room — empty — an equally tiny kitchen, and a door leading to a bedroom in the back. The bedroom door stood open, but Samantha heard no sound from behind it.

The bedroom was so small it could contain only the bed and the man who lay in it, facedown in a pool of sunshine. A sheet bunched around his lower body, revealing his sun-kissed back and arms, a tan from wind and weather that some red-haired men could achieve. Tain had scrunched the pillow beneath his head, fists clenched as though he'd been fighting with the pillow in his sleep. His tattoo was stark black on his cheek, his lashes curled against his skin.

His life essence called to her in a powerful surge, a need that swirled through her brain in red-hot waves. Samantha didn't want the need, had been fighting it, but now it rose up and overwhelmed her. She found herself stretching out her hand to touch his tattoo, ready to pull in and savor his magic. Plus she just wanted to *touch* him, the man who'd made her open herself to him. She needed to feel his warm skin, the firmness of his body under her fingertips.

She closed her fingers over her palm and backed a step, sweating. The demon in her growled. *Take him. It is what you are.*

This was a mistake. She turned to go.

"Samantha."

Tain's deep, accented voice slid over her, forcing her to turn back before she even made it through the bedroom door.

Tain rolled over onto his back, tucked his hands behind his head, and he regarded her with his sky-blue eyes. His torso was hard with muscle, red-brown hair dusting his chest and hiding the thin scar lines there. The sheet dipped to his hips, revealing a swirl of darker hair south of his navel.

Samantha wet her lips. "The front door was open. I thought I'd better check if everything was all right."

"I must have forgotten to close it right. It drifts open."

"This is a bad neighborhood for doors that drift open."

Tain flicked his fingers and sent a wave of magic swirling past her. The front door slammed, and the lock clicked into place.

Samantha jumped. "You don't set wards," she said, a little breathlessly. "I walked right in without feeling anything." If Tain had warded the apartment, the strength of his magic would have prevented Samantha from even poking her head in the open door.

"I didn't, in case you happened by," Tain said.

"You were expecting me?"

His blue gaze raked up and down her. "I hoped."

"Logan told me what you'd found out in the desert," Samantha said quickly.

"Is that why you came?"

"Partly." She trailed off, hugging her arms over her chest.

He doesn't need to trap me with magic. All he has to do is reach out his hand.

Tain reached for her now, his strong, scarred fingers stretched to her in wordless invitation. Samantha swallowed, then went to him and let him pull her down to the bed, into the warm goodness of him.

Tain slid her on top of him, and then cradled the nape of her neck and kissed her. His mouth was all kinds of delicious, his skilled tongue loosening her. His lips tasted of sleep and need, warmth and smoothness.

He deepened the kiss, fingers furrowing her hair. Beneath her thighs Samantha felt the solid hardness of his arousal through the sheets.

She broke the kiss, pushing at his chest, but it was like trying to move a brick wall. "I can't. I'm on duty."

Tain's heated breath brushed her face. "Then why did you come?"

"To talk about where you went last night."

Tain brushed back a lock of her hair. "Logan told you. I'm sure he left nothing out."

Samantha licked her bottom lip, which was tender from his kiss. "A good cop always follows up." Following up, checking to see if Septimus had been right, was just an excuse to see Tain, and Samantha knew it.

He traced her cheek. "You want me to tell you the part that happened when I wasn't with him."

"That would be nice."

Tain only looked at her. She could drown in his heated gaze, the one that probably had made hundreds of generations of women wilt. Samantha traced his lips with her fingertip, liking that, at the moment, she was his sole focus.

"You need more life essence," Tain said.

That was part of why she'd come, but only a small part. "I'm trying to cut back," Samantha answered, trying to sound lighthearted.

"You know you can take it from me whenever you need it."

Samantha gave him a faint smile. "Funny, a lot of people have to be seduced or given Mindglow before they'll let demons anywhere near their essence. The first time, anyway. After that, they're addicted."

He watched her in solemn contemplation. "I'm not human, and I'm not giving it to demons. I'm giving it to *you*."

"Why?"

Tain's touch drifted to her lips. "It's what I'm meant to do."

Samantha drew a ragged breath. "I never understand you."

"There's nothing to understand." Tain took her hand and started to move it to his cheek, but Samantha pulled away.

"I can't right now. Whenever I get a taste of it, I want to have sex with you."

Tain's rare smile flashed. "And that's a bad thing?"

"It is right now. I'm supposed to be working."

Tain kissed her fingertips. "Samantha, you need this. I see the hunger in your eyes. If you deny it for too long, it will kill you."

"I'd like to think I'm stronger than that."

"You're not." Tain's seductive smile vanished. "All demons need a dose of life essence to exist, especially outside the death realms."

"Another thing I don't understand about demons. I've never been to the death realms."

"Good. I don't want you ever to go. It's dangerous if you're not full demon—it's dangerous even if you are. A death realm can kill anyone who has a spark of life magic in them, if they're not under a demon's protection."

"I might not have a choice," Samantha said. "My father wants to put my name forward to take the matriarch's place."

Tain's brows twitched together. "It's gone that far already?"

Samantha shrugged. "Apparently the matriarch was my great-great aunt, and my father has enough power to tell our family who to back as the next one."

Tain went silent a moment, then he said, "I think it's a good idea."

Samantha pulled away in surprise. "Are you kidding me? Me, become the clan matriarch? I'm not even full demon, as you just pointed out."

Tain regarded her in all seriousness, tucking his hands behind his head again. "But you know this world very well, and your police training has honed your fighting skills. You are stronger than most humans, but you understand humans and don't despise them."

"You're as bad as my father. I'm twenty-seven—the matriarch was about a thousand. Much more experienced than me, wouldn't you say?"

"She didn't start when she was a thousand. I think you could be very good at it."

Samantha flopped down beside him on the bed, landing against the comfort of his body. "If I became the matriarch, I'd be absorbed into the clan, married to it and its politics. I'd wear business suits and have a majordomo and attend meetings. Anything left of *me* will be gone. Hell, if the last matriarch even had a *name*, I didn't know it."

"It was Naoma."

"How did you know that?" Samantha asked in a sharp voice, remembering the record Septimus's vamp had made of Tain at the matriarch's house.

"I saw it on the majordomo's desk, while you were interviewing her upstairs."

"You went through her desk?"

Tain shrugged, his strong shoulder brushing hers. "Perhaps I did."

Samantha knew she should admonish him, but some things were more important. "What else did you find?"

"That the matriarch had many appointments, but with the same people or businesses again and again. No one new or different for that day, no appointments for the time she died."

Samantha raked her hair back from her face. Tain's eyes had gone enigmatic again, and she had the feeling he wasn't telling her everything. One more mystery to worry about. "This case is driving me crazy. It's all about powerful women—the matriarch on one hand, Ms. Townsend of No More Nightmares on the other. Plus their staunch defenders, Ariadne the majordomo, and Melanie the guard-dog assistant."

Tain rumbled, "Against Samantha and her Immortal guardian."

She didn't smile. "I'm hardly a player in this game. Those women know what's going on, and I'm swimming around trying to figure everything out."

Tain touched her hair. "You are better than you know."

Samantha let out an exasperated sigh. "I suppose if I did become the matriarch, I'd find out who's out there killing demons, because those killers would come after *me*. Of course, I probably wouldn't know until too late whether it was demon-hunters, rival clan members, or demons from my own clan—I bet all three would try."

Tain's voice took on a stern note. "I'll not let you use yourself as bait."

"Why not? I'm used to it. I've done more than one assignment which called for me in a strapless dress and stilt-heels, where I waited to be hit on, offered drugs, or killed. Like at Merrick's club."

"You looked beautiful." Tain's purr slid over her. "I had trouble concentrating on what I'd come to do. That's why I told you to stay away from me."

"Because I'm demon?"

Another caress to her hair, his voice softening. "I was afraid my attraction to you was a perverse need to be with a demon, that my madness hadn't truly gone away."

"What changed your mind?" she asked in a light voice. "Or have you?"

"It wasn't a demon in my dreams," Tain said. "It was you."

Samantha stared down at him, stunned, her heart pounding until she couldn't think. He could melt her, keep her here, not let her leave. Samantha would eagerly stay, for the chance to hear those words his low, rumbling voice.

"I'm still technically at work." She faltered, her declaration not as adamant as she'd have liked. "See? I have my gun." She patted her holster under her blazer.

"I have my swords." Tain indicated the naked blades resting against the nightstand. "I like weapons."

"For defense."

"For defense. Another reason you'd make a good matriarch. You think of defense rather than attack. You think like a protector."

His low, velvet tones were wearing down her own defenses. "The word *matriarch* sounds so old."

"It's a term of respect. But you can be a modern matriarch—call yourself a clan leader if that makes you feel better."

"It doesn't."

Tain lifted Samantha's hand and kissed her palm. Instead of answering, he said, "You need to take some life magic from me."

She tried a smile. "Because I won't be so crabby if I do?"

"Because I want you to." Tain kissed her palm again, then caught her gaze as he pressed her hand to his cheek, right over his tattoo.

The warmth of his body came to her, and this time the tattoo seemed to burn into her hand. The flow of his life essence seared stronger than before, or perhaps Samantha was simply more needy. She gasped with it, a spark filling her fingers and flowing into and through her body.

Tain slid the sheet out from between them, and her fingers found his warm skin, taut over muscle. Samantha slid her arm around him as they lay on their sides, face to face, and she stroked down his spine, fingers lingering on the hollow at the small of his back.

Tain dipped his head and licked her neck as lovingly as a vampire might. Only Samantha was the vampire-like one now, drinking in the ecstasy of his life essence.

The demon in her rejoiced. Half-human Samantha was still wary of the process, but the beast inside her hungered for what Tain was giving her.

"Mine," she whispered. "You are *mine*."

She understood now why demons like Merrick wanted to possess their marks—they wanted to have *this* at their beck and call any time they needed it. Samantha trailed her fingers through the silky ends of Tain's short hair and then down to the firm tightness of his buttocks.

This gloriously strong and naked male belonged to her and her alone. Samantha laughed with the joy of it, tilting her head back so Tain could nibble on her throat.

His erection pressed into her thigh through her slacks, moving as though he enjoyed the friction of the cloth. She nudged him to lie flat on his back, and he obeyed, his blue eyes half closing in pleasure.

Samantha got on her knees next to him, her hand still firmly connected with his cheek. With the other hand she traced patterns on his chest, brushing the hard points of his nipples, traveling along the ridges of his abdomen.

The indentation of his navel greeted Samantha's questing fingers. She found the warm hair above his penis, then the thick heat of the shaft itself.

Tain made a quiet noise of pleasure as she clasped him. He pressed his hips slightly upward, Samantha's hand closing all the way around him.

"Beautiful woman," he murmured.

The sensations rushing through Samantha were too heady for words, so she only smiled, while Tain lifted against her hand. He touched her fingers where they rested on his cheek, his eyes warming as though her taking his essence gave him more pleasure even than her hand squeezing his cock.

He belonged to her, this elusive, taciturn warrior who came and went as he pleased. Tain's body was laid out for her, his skin damp with sweat from what she was doing to him.

Samantha continued stroking him, his shaft slick with sweat from her palm. She loved the heaviness of his cock, the satin-soft tip and the thick velvet of the shaft itself. He was so large Samantha could barely fit her hand all the way around him, the wide knob sliding between her fingers.

Tain closed his eyes and laid his head back, a half-smile on his face, his hand resting on her wrist. He was letting her play, letting her enjoy herself. He rocked his hips, but gently, as though he held himself back from full thrusts.

Tain's body tightened as she went on, his breath coming faster. Samantha liked that he contained his strength for her, liked imagining what it would be like if he didn't.

She kneaded and stroked him, twisting her hand around his shaft until he moaned with it. Samantha felt the buildup in him, his buttocks tightening as he rose through her hand.

Then he dragged her down to him in rock-hard arms and kissed her deeply, his body moving against hers in the joy of the moment.

"Keep taking me, love," he breathed. "That's it."

Tain's essence flowed into her, and he closed his eyes, a half smile on his face. Samantha kissed his throat, her body limp and warm against in his, her hand still moving on his penis.

She wondered if he'd wait for her here while she went back to work, if she would return to find him stretched out naked on the bed, smiling his sultry smile for her. A vision flashed through her mind of his thick wrists enclosed in manacles, his arms over his head, the manacles fastened to the headboard. Her captive, smiling when she returned for him, his arousal rising swiftly when he saw her.

Command him, the demon in her whispered. *He will obey.*

The need rushed up in Samantha so fiercely she gasped and tried to yank away from his tattoo. Tain clamped his hand around her wrist, keeping her palm on his cheek, his life essence pouring into her. Her palm burned with it, the tattoo searing her flesh.

"Stop," she said, her breathing ragged. "You have to stop."

Tain's eyes were closed, his mouth pressed in ecstasy. Samantha lost hold of his shaft, the blunt knob knocking her fingers. She tried to pry her hand from his cheek, but Tain was ten times stronger than she was, and Samantha couldn't get free.

His essence was white light burning her from the inside out. The demon in her snarled, and the human in her cried out in pain.

"Tain, please stop! I can't take it."

Tain didn't respond.

Samantha sobbed. "Please."

Tain's eyes snapped open. He stared at Samantha as though he'd forgotten her there, then he yanked her hand from his cheek and shoved her away.

Samantha sat up, wincing when her palm contacted the sheets. Her skin bore a bright red burn, the exact imprint of his pentacle tattoo.

"Samantha." Tain's eyes were wide with concern. He reached for her.

Samantha rolled off the bed to her feet, cradling her hurt hand. "I have to go."

He stood up, seven feet of naked male in front of her. "Let me see."

Samantha slowly held out her hand. He took it and kissed her palm, lips caressing. His healing magic sank into her, erasing the pain, and when he released her, the mark was gone.

"I have to go," Samantha repeated, closing her hand.

The remorse in Tain's eyes cut her to the heart. "Goddess, Samantha, I never meant to hurt you."

"I shouldn't have come here. I should have just . . ." *Trusted him,* her cynical side finished.

Tain scraped his hand through his short hair. "I told you in the beginning you should stay away from me. This is why."

Samantha's heart ached, tears burning her eyes. "It's too late for that, don't you think?"

He was still mostly erect, his body tight with need. "I thought I could go slowly. I thought I could teach you—I thought I could control it. Gods damn my arrogance."

The dark horror in Tain's eyes worried her. Samantha pointed a shaking finger at him. "Don't you dare disappear again, because you think it's better for me. Don't you dare leave me to get through this alone."

Emotions flicked through Tain's eyes, none of them easy to read. He stood looking down at her, stricken, making no move to touch her or to stop her.

"I'll come back," Samantha said. "After work, I'll come back, and we'll talk. You'll be here, right?"

He shook his head. "I don't want you to come back here. You need to go to the Malibu house."

"Wherever it is, we need to talk—privately."

Tain swallowed, his body tense, and he nodded.

Samantha let out her breath and made herself turn away. She wiped her eyes with the heel of her hand, squared her shoulders, and walked out of the bedroom.

At the front door, she felt him behind her, his large hands on her shoulders. He leaned down and kissed her hair, his lips warm and gentle. She sensed the power in his hands, his shaking as he deliberately held himself in check.

Without looking at him Samantha unlocked and opened the door, and walked out of the apartment. Behind her she heard the door very faintly close, and the lock click into place.

***

After Samantha had gone, Tain dressed, went into the living room, placed his votive candles in a circle, lit them with a tiny brush of magic, and tried to meditate. But his heart was beating too hard, his thoughts too jumbled for any kind of peace.

He was a fool for thinking he could have something real with Samantha. She'd been right that letting her drink of his life essence would become too heady for him to resist— today when she'd naturally slowed the taking, he'd sped it up, unable to stop himself, wanting her to take from him.

Tain had lost all perspective on how to be human and gentle. Kehksut had been hideously strong, liking to receive pain as much giving it. Tain had grown used to not holding back his strength—in fact, he'd pretty much forgotten how.

Since coming to Los Angeles, he'd run into situation after situation where he'd had to stop himself hurting others.

Giving his essence to Samantha was supposed to mitigate the terrible things Tain had done in the past. And now he'd hurt her as well.

Cerridwen, help her, he sent silently.

She needs you, came the whispered answer, and Tain slid into dreams.

He was in a faraway land of long ago that smelled of peat fires, damp, and cold. Tain was seventeen years old, strong and skilled, and he wanted to be a soldier like his father. All his life he'd wanted to wear Roman armor and march with the soldiers back from Britain to the greatest city in the world, conquering territories as they went.

Rome was a fabulous city, so the legionnaires from the nearby garrison had told him, full of riches from places far across desert sands. In Rome a person could find olives from Spain, fish from the Mediterranean, silks and spices from the East, gold from Egypt. Tain had spent his childhood dreaming of the day he could leave the farm he tended with his father to seek the warm climes of Rome and the blue, blue waters of the southern seas.

His father had trained Tain to use swords, having retired from the army to a farm in Britain where he raised his son. Tain's father had saved money for years to have the local armorer make two bronze blades for Tain, and then Tain had taken lessons from his father in how to use them. As a boy, he'd run off every chance he could to the woods to fight battles against soldiers who didn't exist and ghosts of his imagination. As a young man, he still retreated there to practice.

One night in his seventeenth year, he'd come across a real vampire, an encounter that changed his life.

Chapter Nineteen

Tain had known the woman was evil as soon as he looked at her. She'd dressed in an exotic silk gown and had twisted ropes of jewels through her braided dark hair. She was breathlessly beautiful. But Tain sensed her aura like black ooze, tainting her and canceling out her beauty.

This female vamp had come to the soldiers weeks ago as a camp follower and had killed several men before escaping into the wilds. The vampire had been waiting for Tain in the woods, probably smelling his blood, where Tain took his swords to practice every day as soon as his chores were done.

"Thanks be to Minerva," the vampire said when Tain approached her. "You have come to save me."

Tain rested the blade of one of his swords across his shoulder. "Have I?"

"You're a clever young man and can get me back to camp," she said in perfect imitation of a distressed young woman. "I'm the wife of one of the officers there."

"No, you aren't," Tain said. "You are the woman who killed some of my friends."

The vampire dropped her pretense. "You're an intelligent one, aren't you? I thought you a mere pig farmer, but I see I was wrong."

The vampire woman came closer, the stench of darkness that clung to her sharp. She was truly beautiful—no dirt or mud marred her lovely skin, her hair was gleaming and soft, and the jewels she wore glinted in the moonlight. Tain had no doubt the jewels were real, nor any doubt she would kill any man who tried to take them from her.

"You want my blood," Tain said. He held out a muscular arm. "Why don't you take it?"

The woman's dark eyes flickered, uncertain, and she took a quick step back. "You stink of life magic. Why would you let me drink from you?"

"Because you're hungry. How long has it been?"

Her sultry look vanished. "Ten days."

"I can let you drink if you don't drain me. Do you promise?"

The vampire woman stared at him in astonishment. "You would make this bargain with me?"

She'd killed soldiers, and she was strong, but Tain saw the illness in her, her aura torn and tainted. Ever since Tain had accidentally hurt his father and discovered his healing ability, his instinct to use that healing power was strong. There was something wrong with this vampire, and the young Tain thought that, if he could help her, he could train her to spare others.

"How long ago were you turned?" he asked.

She gave him a startled look, then whispered, "Six months."

"Against your will."

"Yes." Tears flowed from her red-rimmed eyes, and he saw her horror at what she'd become.

"You can take blood without killing if you do it a little at a time. I will show you, but you cannot kill any more soldiers."

"You would protect me?"

"Only if you promise."

The vampire closed her mouth, her face contrite. "I promise."

"Very well then." Tain held out his arm.

She came to him, sinking to her knees in the mud and decayed leaves on the forest floor. She lowered her head to Tain's outstretched arm, her eyes filled with need.

The bite hurt, but not as much as Tain had thought it would. He felt the blood flow into her mouth, a sensation much like that when he had intercourse, but not quite. He understood now why the soldiers had died lying in bed with this woman—the sensations of sex and her taking their blood on top it must have been too wonderful to stop.

The vampire woman raised her head and hissed, his blood staining her fangs. "What *are* you?"

"A pig farmer, as you said," Tain answered calmly.

She shook her head. "Your magic is too strong—you think to kill me with it. Are you Sidhe?"

"No." Tain had glimpsed the beautiful race of Sidhe when he'd journeyed to the far north with his father, seen the white-hot heat of their life-magic auras shimmering in the cold. When he'd told his father about them, his father had snapped that Tain had a wild imagination, that the Sidhe didn't exist.

Tain knew better. He knew that the stories of Sidhe, demons, and vampires were true—he had living proof in front of him.

The vampire hesitated, her hands uncurling. "You don't know what you are, do you?"

"I am Tain, son of a Roman centurion."

"You're not human, boy." The vampire got to her feet. "You are filled to the brim with life magic, the strongest I've ever felt, even more than a Sidhe." She held out her hand. "Come with me. I'll take you to my master, and he will tell you what you are."

"I'm no one special," Tain answered with conviction.

"You're wrong." The vampire moved closer to him, brushing her hand across his unmarred face. "You're very, very special. My master will want to meet you."

"Who is your master?"

"A demon. A great one, an Old One, from the mists of time. He is powerful. He can make you great too. Do you want to be great, boy?"

Tain thought about the way he lived — the backbreaking work clearing and plowing fields, the sword lessons, the quiet nights listening to his father's stories of his days as a soldier. Tain had always meant to leave home when he was ready, but parting from his father to have adventures in Rome was one thing; disappearing into the night without a word was something else.

"I don't want to meet him," Tain said. "Drink and sustain yourself, or go."

"You will come with me."

Tain felt the woman's death magic sliding into him, trying to twist his thoughts to obedience. He saw flashes of the pleasure she could give him — her body, her blood, her power. Tain easily brushed aside the enticing visions, seeing her as she was — a starving vampire, weak and pathetic.

"No," Tain said. He felt strange compassion for this woman, who hadn't chosen to become a killer. She couldn't help what she was, any more than a wolf could help stalking and killing a deer. He held out his arm again, the bloody holes she'd left already closing. "Drink of me, and heal yourself."

The vampire attacked him instead. Tain sidestepped and brought up his sword, scoring her across her shoulders. The vamp screamed and whirled for another attack, lunging for his neck, claws poised to tear out his throat.

Tain had his second sword out, crossing it with the first, and the woman's momentum propelled her right into them. One jerk, and her head fell, severed from her body. She folded in half and landed across the carpet of leaves.

Her body decomposed before Tain's eyes, becoming the dead thing she truly was, the stink turning his stomach. After only a few minutes she'd dissolved into dust. Tain swallowed his regret that the encounter had ended this way, then shouldered his swords and walked home.

By the time Tain reached the small house he shared with his father, the bite on his arm had completely healed, and the vampire's blood on his blades had dried to dust and disappeared.

"I killed a vampire in the woods," he announced to his father. "The one stalking the soldiers. She's dead now, so they'll be safe."

His father had looked at him sharply then turned away, but not before Tain had seen the tears in his eyes.

Tain's dream shifted. Three months after he'd slain the vampire, his father had told him to dress in his best tunic and follow him. The year was the ninth in the reign of the Emperor Domitian, and Tain assumed they were going to the Saturnalia celebration at the nearby camp.

Instead his father led him to a clearing encircled with standing stones, odd upright boulders that sang of magic in the moonlight. The older man regarded Tain sadly then moved from him and sank to his knees in the middle of the stones, lifting his sword hilt-first. "Cerridwen, hear me."

Tain watched in surprise. His father had never shown an inclination to worship the strange gods native to Britain—like a good soldier, his father sacrificed to the warrior god Mars, and also to Minerva for wisdom, and to Zeus for strength.

Wind blew through the circle, sending leaves and twigs swirling through the standing stones. Tain sensed a stab of intense magic, brighter and hotter than anything he'd felt before.

When the light died, a woman stood in the clearing. She had wild hair as red as Tain's own and wore a glimmering cloth that encircled her hips and covered her breasts. Tain darted forward, fear in his veins, as the woman reached down and touched his father.

His father was crying. Tears streaked his weathered face, and he gazed at the woman with a combination of adoration and sorrow.

"I did what you asked," he said in a broken voice. "I raised him the best I could. My love, why did you never come back to me?"

"Because he couldn't know me until it was time." The woman's voice was rich and full, with a musical accent.

"Time for what?" Tain strode forward, his heart pounding. "Who are you?"

"Tain, she is your mother," his father said softly.

"My mother was a Gaul, a slave."

"No. She is a goddess."

Tain looked at the red-haired woman, and the life magic that flowed from her hit him with a hard impact. He remembered the vampire hissing when she'd tasted Tain's blood, declaring that Tain had more life magic than even a Sidhe.

"Why did you never tell me?" Tain demanded of his father.

The woman, Cerridwen, turned to him. Her eyes were like fire, yellow orbs that made Tain both want to run away and stand gazing at her forever. "I wanted you to have a simple life, my son. Simple happiness before you must face what is to come."

"What will come?" Tain asked, his voice hard.

"Danger," Cerridwen said. "Darkness. Things from which I cannot protect you. You are a warrior, Tain, one of the greatest warriors in the world. But you must be trained."

"My father trains me."

"To fight with swords, yes. You need to learn so much more, how to defend the world from the darkness that walks it, how to use both your gift of healing and your powers of destruction."

"I'm to go to Rome and join the army. I am already past old enough, but I didn't want to leave Father until I found someone to help him."

His father shook his head. "No, son. You must go with her now."

"And if I choose not to?"

"You will come," Cerridwen said. She stretched out her hand, and Tain found himself walking toward her, though every muscle in his body screamed for him to stop.

His father watched, eyes wet, as Cerridwen reached out and pressed her palm to Tain's unmarred cheek.

A sudden, sharp pain seared through him, and Tain couldn't pull away. His father cried out, but Tain held his ground, looking into Cerridwen's beautiful and powerful eyes.

When she took her hand away, he saw a black outline on her palm, a five-pointed star within a circle. He knew in that instant who he was—not the son of a slave woman and a Roman soldier, but a demigod who'd been raised as a human. His father was still his father, the chosen lover of a goddess.

Mist shimmered between two of the standing stones and when it cleared, four tall men stood there.

"Your brothers," Cerridwen said. "They've come to take you home."

Tain hated them on sight. They were all big men, as tall as Tain but older, their bodies heavier and more muscular. One had dark hair and wore an armband in the shape of a snake. The second had tattoos covering almost every inch of exposed skin. The third had intense gray eyes and a look of arrogance; the last had tawny hair, green eyes, a wide grin, and a large sword strapped to his back.

"Hey, baby brother," the fourth one said in flawless soldier Roman. "I'm Hunter. Nice to meet you."

"How can they be my brothers?" Tain turned an accusing stare on Cerridwen. "Are they your sons?"

"They are your half-brothers, of a sort. They were all born of a human father with an aspect of the Mother Goddess of the world as their mothers."

"We'll take you to Ravenscroft," the one called Hunter said. "And I'll teach you to be as much of a shithead as Adrian is."

"Leave him be," the one with the snake armband said.

"Big brother's pet," Hunter growled, but with a smile.

The smile made Tain feel a little better. The four of them reminded him of the garrison soldiers: rough, foul mouthed, and close-knit, although that didn't mean Tain wanted to get to know these men any better.

"Go with them, Tain," his father said.

Tain turned to the only person he'd ever loved, the only person he knew how to love. "I can't leave you, Father."

"You have to. The Roman soldiers will never leave you in peace if they learn how magical you truly are. Go and be who you need to be."

Tain was several inches taller than his father, and he bent his head to look into his father's eyes. "There's more than that, isn't there? More than going with these people to train. What aren't you telling me?"

He saw fear flicker in his father's eyes and sorrow beyond measure. At the time, Tain had only thought his father sad that his son had to leave him. With distance, knowledge, and time, even in the dream, Tain knew his father had been told of the pain and darkness Tain would have to bear. And still his father hadn't tried to stop Cerridwen taking Tain away.

"Father, why?"

"I'm sorry."

His father wept openly, his body crumpling in on itself as he looked upon his son for the last time.

Two mortal years after Tain had left for Ravenscroft, his father had died of a cancer. Tain had returned to find him dying, his body wasted. Tain had flooded him with healing magic, but it was far too late, and all he could do was soothe the pain and let his father die in peace.

Tears rained down Tain's face as he looked at his father's still and lifeless body. He'd realized then what being Immortal meant—that he would lose every person important to him. He'd go on, and they'd die. Like Samantha.

The chirp of Tain's cell phone jerked him out of sleep, and he jumped awake. He found himself flat on his back on the living-room floor in his shabby apartment, breathing hard, his face wet, the candles guttering.

Tain wiped his eyes as he sat up and plucked the phone from the table with a shaking hand. It was Samantha. She sounded strained and awkward, and she started speaking before he could say a word.

"Hello, Tain. Remember when I said I didn't have enough for a search warrant for the No More Nightmares' office? Well, I do now. Melanie Atkins, the super-assistant to Ms. Townsend has been murdered. Heart cut out, just like the others."

Tain started to answer, but Samantha hurriedly said that she just thought he ought to know, and hung up. Tain remained sitting on the floor, staring at the phone, lost in thought. Then he rose, took up his swords, and left the apartment, heading for the matriarch's mansion.

What he'd seen there and in the desert canyon connected, and he thought he knew now the secret the dead matriarch had been hiding from her clan.

***

The previously quiet office of No More Nightmares now teemed with police. Samantha ducked under police tape to join Logan and Lieutenant McKay in the front where Tain and Samantha had interviewed Melanie. Logan told Samantha as soon as she entered that Melanie had been found in a large supply closet in the back.

"More of a supply room, with the photocopier in it," Logan explained. "She was stretched out on the floor in front of the copy machine, very dead, heart cut out."

"I never sensed she was demon," Samantha said. "Was she?"

"Possibly part demon," Logan said. "The scent was very faint. I never would have smelled it if her body hadn't been wide open—she might have had one grandparent who was demon."

"Yet she worked for No More Nightmares," Samantha said. "Interesting."

"Maybe she didn't like her own demon blood," McKay suggested. "Thought railing against demons would make her more accepted by humankind, maybe?"

Samantha shook her head. "That wouldn't have worked. If the humans in No More Nightmares found out she was demon, they'd be even angrier at her betrayal. It's hell being half-blood."

"Tell me about it," McKay said. "I'm a short part-Sidhe. Don't think that doesn't get me into trouble."

Logan laughed, but with strain.

"Can I take a look?" Samantha glanced toward the knot of police in plastic gear in the back.

"Logan and I have, but suit yourself," McKay answered. "Three heads are better than one."

Melanie's body was much like that of the matriarch, untouched but for the bloody, gaping hole in her chest. A woman knelt next to the body, taking swabs from it and placing them carefully into tubes.

"Logan said you didn't find the heart," Samantha said to her. "Like with the Lamiah matriarch."

"Nope." The forensics woman looked up. "Maybe they use it for rituals."

"Not if they claim they're against death magic. But who knows?"

"Who knows?" the woman repeated, wiping another swab through the dead woman's mouth. "These people are nuts." The forensics woman was a witch, fire-magic, Samantha knew. Technically she was life magic, but those against death-magic creatures often had it in for witches as well.

Samantha turned away without answering and sought Logan. "I hate that this happened," she said to him. "But it's a good excuse to go over these offices with a fine-toothed comb. Beginning in the file room."

Officers had already started to box up files and the few PCs in the back. Samantha looked around at the mountain of folders and grimaced.

"Finding Ms. Townsend and questioning her might be easier," Logan suggested.

"Oh, you never know what interesting details files hold," Samantha said with conviction. "I assume you're already looking for Ms. Townsend?"

"McKay is on it," Logan answered. "That Nevada county sheriff might be more willing to cooperate now that Ms. Townsend is a murder suspect."

"Yes, if she discovered that her faithful assistant was part demon, she might have lost it and taken out the knife." Samantha glanced around the room and the crowded office outside. She'd thought Tain might come downtown, interested in a connected death, but she didn't see his tall form among the police.

"There's another similarity between the two women's deaths," Logan said, bringing Samantha's attention back to him. "Neither of them struggled."

Both women had been on their backs, but they hadn't fallen that way. The expressions on their unbruised faces had been ones of surprise, not fear.

"Melanie probably didn't have enough demon in her to be able to change and fight," Samantha mused. "But the matriarch certainly did. It was almost as though they let themselves be killed."

"Drugged?" Logan asked.

"Maybe, with something like Mindglow," Samantha said. "You take that, you smile and let others do anything they want to you."

"Does it work on demons?"

"I think so, but I'm not sure. On the other hand, we know someone who would know."

"Our friend Merrick," Logan said.

"Exactly. Want to pay him a visit with me?"

Logan shot her a look. "Oh, I'd like nothing better."

Samantha led the way back out, told McKay what they meant to do, and got the nod to leave. As they rode down the elevator to the ground floor, Samantha folded her arms across her chest and frowned at the numbers lighting as they descended.

"Tain not showing up doesn't mean jack," Logan said to her.

Samantha turned her scowl on him. "Did I say anything?"

"You don't have to, partner. I know you called him about this, but Tain doesn't work for the police—he does what he damn well pleases. I'm happy he's interested in the case and giving us information, but I don't expect anything from him beyond that."

"I'm worried about him, that's all. We had a fight." Samantha broke off, knowing that wasn't quite true.

Not a fight. A revelation. We can pretend all we want, but what we have isn't normal, and it isn't what either of us needs.

That thought triggered another: *What do I need?*

The answer was *Tain*, but they couldn't go on as they had been.

The elevator doors rolled open. Samantha and Logan walked through the lobby and out of the building. Police cars and vans lined the streets, attracting the curious. It had attracted more than the curious, Samantha saw, spying a long black limousine a little way down the street.

Samantha told Logan she'd catch up with him, made her way to the limo, and tapped on its back passenger window.

The window slid down to reveal Septimus sitting in deep shadow, well out of the way of any stray beam of sunlight.

"Did you come to watch the police in action?" Samantha asked him.

Septimus gave her a faint smile. "I was following your Immortal. One of my underlings alerted me that he'd gone back to the Lamiah matriarch's mansion."

A qualm stole through her. "So why aren't you at the matriarch's mansion?"

"I was, then he spotted me and commandeered my limousine to drive him down here."

Samantha looked back at the building. "He went inside? I didn't see him."

"He's there." Septimus pointed upward. "On the roof."

Samantha turned and stared up at the skyscraper, shielding her eyes against the afternoon sun. "What is he doing on the roof?"

"I couldn't say," Septimus answered. "You may look through my driver's binoculars if you like."

"No." Samantha turned away, hearing the limo's window glide up behind her, muffling Septimus's chuckle, and ran back along the street and into the building. She impatiently waited for an elevator, then dove inside and pushed the button for the roof, which had been unlocked for the police investigation.

The elevator let Samantha off in a maintenance room, where an open door on the far side led to the roof and blue sky. She went through this door cautiously, hand on her pistol.

Tain grabbed her by the arm and pulled her out and around the corner of the little maintenance building. He had one of his swords in his hand and a look of fury in his eyes.

"What the hell are you doing here?" he demanded.

"My job. It's a crime scene. Why are you here? And why did you go to the matriarch's?"

"To block a portal to one of the deeper death realms."

Samantha blinked at him. "Portal to a deeper death realm?" She frowned, trying to make sense of what he was telling her. "The matriarch would have a portal to the Lamiah death realm . . ."

"This wasn't the Lamiah realm," Tain said, anger in his eyes. "It's much deeper, and older. Another portal to the same realm comes out here."

"At No More Nightmares? They're supposed to be demon haters."

"Demon sacrificers," Tain said.

"What?" Samantha stared, her thoughts whirling. "Is that what they're doing with the hearts — some kind of sacrifice?"

"Yes," Tain answered grimly.

"What about Nadia's sister? Her heart was sent back."

"I don't know." Tain's eyes gleamed with rage, and with his shaved hair, black tattoo, swords, and scarred body he looked more frightening than the scariest gang banger Samantha had ever come up against. "Maybe it was found wanting."

Samantha wet her dry lips. "I'd swear the No More Nightmares office has no death magic in it. You didn't feel any, either. They aren't sacrificing there."

"The office is a front for the people who truly believe they're suppressing demons. But the temple is here on the roof."

Tain gestured with his sword. Beyond the building, Los Angeles spread out around them, a gleaming, glittering sprawl of city under a hot sky.

On the far side of the roof was a low shed that looked like a shelter for electronics or plumbing. For a moment Samantha felt nothing from it, and then a wave of death magic blasted out of it, strong enough to knock her over.

Tain caught her with a firm hand and shoved her back into the maintenance room as he shot life magic at the shed to counteract the threat.

"So these demons beyond the portal," Samantha shouted over the sudden noise, "are they pissed off at you?"

"Oh, yes," Tain said, and he smiled, just as demons, dozens and dozens of them, poured out of the portal into the late afternoon sunshine.

Chapter Twenty

Tain drew his second sword and stepped back outside to face the approaching horde. "Call Hunter," he yelled over his shoulder. "Tell him to get his ass down here."

Inside the maintenance room Samantha pulled out her phone and punched keys with her thumb, her pistol in her other hand. "Why didn't you call him when you got here?"

Tain flashed her an annoyed look. "My damn phone stopped working."

"Didn't you charge it?"

Tain didn't answer, but she thought she heard him mutter something like, "Fucking technology."

"Hunter?" Samantha yelled into the phone, then stopped as a terrible noise sounded behind the elevator doors.

The phone went dead. Samantha shoved it back in her pocket just as the elevator exploded open and belched demons through a hole of complete darkness.

Samantha sprinted outside, heart pumping, and made for Tain.

"Change of plan," she panted.

The roof was thick with demons. The attack on the matriarch's house had been done by only a score or so demons of one clan; this was an all-out assault by an entire death realm.

Samantha had seen demons insane with bloodlust before, attacking and ripping apart anything they could get their hands on. Whatever Tain had done at the matriarch's mansion, these demons were now intent on ripping *him* apart, and probably wouldn't mind if they took out Samantha along the way.

Samantha knew her pistol would be almost useless against them, but the bullets might at least slow a few down. Tain, however, wasn't fighting. He had his swords crossed and all the lightning energy within him directed at the shed.

Sealing the portal, Samantha realized, but it still left about a hundred demons on this side, and many of them could fly. Thinking of the horrific pain the acid-spitting demon had caused, she planted herself hard against Tain's back, staying within his protective magic.

"Do you think you could start fighting them off anytime soon?" she yelled at him.

"There are thousands more behind them, and they'll come through if I don't plug the hole."

"Damn it, Tain, what did you do to make them so mad?"

"Cut off their main portal and desecrated a shrine to their master."

"Oh, is *that* all?"

Tain swept a last blast of life magic at the shed, which folded in on itself and crumpled into rusted pieces of metal. Tain swung around and directed another waft at the elevator inside the maintenance room. Demons screamed and dove at him and Samantha, talons and fangs bared, but any demon caught in the lightning from Tain's swords died instantly.

"Wait a minute," Samantha shouted. "A shrine to *what*?"

"An Old One. The matriarch was trying to increase her power by sacrificing to him."

"But someone killed *her*. That doesn't make any sense."

Tain didn't answer. He grunted with effort, and the light from his swords grew brighter. The black portal began to shrink, swirling in on itself like an inky vortex. Demons dove for it, a few making it back inside before the portal shuddered, and then exploded into shards.

The maintenance room shook with the impact of the colliding magics. Cement blocks burst into gray shards, and pipes screeched and broke, spewing geysers of steam and water. The walls of the maintenance room groaned. Then, like the shed, the whole thing collapsed into a pile of stone, metal, and dust.

The remaining demons screamed and fixed on Tain and Samantha, their rage shaking the air.

"You know that was our only way out, right?" Samantha said, coughing.

"Do you trust me?" Tain was gazing down at her, his blue eyes intense.

Samantha tried to find her breath. "Oh, gods," she said faintly. "Why?"

"It's a yes-or-no question, not a *why*."

She swallowed, her throat dry. "Are you saying you have a clever plan for getting away, but you don't have time to explain, and I have to go along with it?"

Tain gave her one of his cryptic nods. "Yes."

"You can fight them though, can't you?" Samantha's voice was sharp with worry. "You're strong and Immortal. This is what you do."

"Put away your gun and trust me," Tain said.

Samantha's heart beat faster. "You're crazy, you know that?"

"I know." Tain sent her a feral smile. "Put it away."

Samantha slid her gun back into its holster, her body throbbing with fear. "Now what?"

"You hang on to me, and hang on tight," Tain said. "Do you understand? Wrap your whole body around me if you have to. Promise?"

Tain held his swords warily, examining the distance between the horde of demons, the two of them, and the edge of the roof. Samantha followed his gaze, and her eyes widened. "Tain, you can't fly."

"No," he agreed.

Tain sheathed his swords in one smooth motion, and then grabbed Samantha and sprinted past the demons, who swooped after them in glee.

"I know I'm going to regret this," Samantha shouted, but let Tain lift her into his arms.

At the last minute Samantha wrapped her legs and arms firmly around Tain before he launched himself off the roof and into empty air.

***

Tain expected Samantha to scream, but she didn't make a sound. *Cerridwen, give me strength,* he prayed. Then he shot all the magic he had in him straight at the ground several hundred feet below.

The demons that could fly dove after them. Tain hoped they didn't catch up, because he couldn't spare any magic to fend them off. If he moved his focus, his descent wouldn't slow, and he and Samantha would make a spectacular splat on the ground. Even an Immortal might not be able to survive it—Cerridwen might think it kinder to let the puddle her son had become die.

Wind rushed in Tain's ears at a sickening speed. His magic splintered and sprayed, as though he scraped his hands along concrete at high speed. Below them traffic spread out of the way of his shaft of white-hot magic, and he saw Logan bound into the street in his wolf form.

Tain sensed the death-magic pull of another portal opening, and he looked up to see it form, dense and black, high over the building. The demons who'd been chasing them whooshed into it, as though being sucked inside by a giant vacuum.

Before the portal snicked shut, Tain felt it—the aura of an Old One, gloating, angry, powerful. The seductive pull touched him, and to his horror, Tain's first instinct was to follow the demon home.

"Tain," Samantha said in his ear, her breath warm against the wind. "I love you."

The demon's pull lessened. Over the adrenaline of the tumbling fall, Tain's body tingled, a fire coursing through his veins, beating back the touch of the Old One.

Tain redoubled his efforts to get them down safely, his arms aching, his body roiling with the magic that streaked through him. Samantha burrowed into him, her warmth giving him a point of focus, his need for her canceling out the demon's siren call.

Finally, gradually, Tain felt their descent slow, his downshaft of magic acting as a cushion. His magic gathered below and now sent a shockwave back to meet them. Fifty or so feet from the ground, the wave flowed around Tain and Samantha, cocooning them in a bubble, which decelerated them until Tain's feet gently bumped the pavement.

Samantha raised her head, her eyes black pools in her colorless face. "Are we down?"

"Yes."

Samantha made no move to let go, still locked around Tain with all her strength. "You bastard," she said clearly. "Don't you ever do that to me again." Then she hugged him hard, tears in her eyes, and kissed him on the lips.

***

Septimus's limousine squealed up to where they stood, Samantha shaking and sick. Septimus's driver hopped out and opened the back door, and the vampire's voice rumbled out.

"Looks like you need another ride." He was squeezed into the far corner while the door was open and didn't lean forward until the two were inside and his chauffeur had safely closed the door again.

Samantha collapsed into the seat that Tain had more or less shoved her onto. Tain lay back next to her and closed his eyes, his face drawn and gray. He'd drained himself, Samantha realized, giving every bit of magic he'd had to closing the portals and getting them down safely. At the moment, he was as vulnerable as Samantha was, and Septimus, one of the most powerful vamps in the world, sat across from them.

"Can you take us to the Malibu house?" Samantha asked tiredly.

Septimus instructed his driver through an intercom, and Samantha relaxed a little. Her panic was wearing off, and she desperately wanted to sleep.

With Tain out cold, Septimus's death magic filled the car, pressing against Samantha's nerves. Septimus's lips had pulled back, his fangs gleaming in the dim light.

"I drank an Immortal once," he said softly.

"So I heard," Samantha said. Leda had told her the story—Septimus had bitten Adrian and given him over to the demon Kehksut, a part of a master plan Septimus and Adrian had concocted, or so Septimus claimed later.

"It was like nothing I've ever experienced, before or since." Septimus's voice was smooth as silk, the powerful vampire at his most seductive. Samantha's body tried to respond to him against her better judgment, as though her blood craved to be caressed by his mouth.

Tain didn't react at all, unconscious in the gently swaying car. The vampire's gaze lingered on Tain's exposed throat, the stark hunter in his eyes.

Samantha tensed. Septimus was an Old One, and deadly strong, but she was paranormal police. She slid her hand inside her blazer to rest on her gun. Bullets wouldn't stop a vampire, but they could hurt him or at least make the driver pull over, where she could threaten Septimus with exposure to the sun.

"Leave him alone," she said sternly.

Septimus laughed. "I could snap you like a twig, Ms. Taylor. What would you do against me?"

"Anything I could," Samantha said with conviction.

Septimus laughed again, and then his fangs receded. "Where do these Immortals find such ferociously protective women? It's delightful."

"I'm not delighted."

"I was testing you. You certainly are devoted to him."

Samantha eased back into the seat, but she didn't relax again. "I'm armed, you know."

Septimus continued to smile. "I could take your gun from you or shatter a stake before you could get anywhere near me."

"Possibly."

"Just so we know where we stand. You're an uncommon woman, Ms. Taylor."

"Glad you noticed."

"You're not glad at all. You only have eyes for the Immortal. What *is* it about them?"

"I don't honestly know," Samantha said. "I'm demon. I shouldn't love him, but I do."

"Ah, love." Septimus shook his head, his eyes taking on true humor. "It makes fools of us all, doesn't it? Is that Shakespeare?"

Samantha closed her eyes, the aftermath of the fall plus her worry about Septimus leaving her exhausted. "I don't remember," she said.

***

Once Logan had assured himself that Septimus had gotten Tain and Samantha safely to the Immortals' house in Malibu, he took on the task of questioning Merrick.

The demon attack had baffled Logan and McKay, as well as everyone else present. But the demons had dispersed again, vanishing into whatever death realm they'd sprung from. Logan hadn't even been able to catch one for questioning.

He'd almost shit himself watching Samantha and Tain fall off the roof, sure he was about to witness the very messy death of his friend and partner. But Tain had pulled it off, and Samantha was all right—or at least whole. Tain had

gone straight into the vampire's limousine, shoving
Samantha in as well, and Logan had decided that the crazy
Immortal seemed to know what he was doing.

Logan had turned away, still shaken, and resumed his
human form and clothes. He'd continued the investigation
as though nothing had interrupted it, knowing Samantha
would expect him to come up with something the two of
them could present to McKay in this insane case.

He drove to Bel Air, where Merrick owned a luxurious
home. Today the demon wore a crisp black business suit
and received Logan in a cavernous living room.

"I'm in the process of screening construction companies
to rebuild my club," he said to Logan, waving him to sit in a
leather armchair. Logan noticed that the paintings from his
penthouse above the club had reappeared here. "I can open
again in about a year, if I'm lucky."

"Great news," Logan said dryly. As usual he felt uneasy
in a demon's domain—Merrick's death magic permeated
every inch of the place.

Merrick sent him a smile. "You don't give a rat's ass
about my club," he said, while a butler served them coffee.
"So, what do you want from me this time, wolf?"

Logan took the steaming coffee, served in a fine porcelain
cup, blew on it, and took a sip. The brew was the best he'd
ever tasted, he decided, a rich roast from some South
American plantation. "Samantha had a question for you," he
said, licking a drop of coffee from his upper lip. "She'd ask
you herself, but she'd a bit indisposed at the moment."

"Ah, yes, I heard the story of her and the Immortal taking
a leap off a downtown roof. He enjoys jumping from heights
to save people, I have reason to know." Another smile.
"Very impressive display of magic, that."

Logan let out a breath and took another sip of coffee.
"Not something I want to watch again in my lifetime."

"I'm sorry I missed it," Merrick said, his large fingers
holding a dainty coffee cup with surprising delicacy. "But
I'm happy to hear our dear Sam will be harassing me, an

innocent businessman, for a long time to come. Tell her that if she ever gets tired of arrogant Immortals, she can give me a call."

"I'll let her know," Logan said. He clicked down the coffee cup and opened his notebook. "The question is about Mindglow and its effects. If, for instance, you were to give it to a demon—not a human—what would happen?"

"Hypothetically?" Merrick asked. "Off the record?"

Logan gave him a nod. "I'm here in a purely friendly capacity."

"*Friendly*, you call it. I suppose you mean you won't be bringing out the hot lights and thumbscrews. Very well. *Hypothetically*, Mindglow would do to demons much the same thing it purportedly does to humans. Make them compliant, easily suggestible, that sort of thing."

"Anything else? For instance, would it weaken a demon to the point that he or she couldn't revert to their demon form?"

"Possibly." Merrick shifted in his designer chair. "But that's not information I'd like to see made public."

"I'm not a reporter," Logan said.

"True, but you feed things to reporters you want the public to know." He lifted his cup again. "I'm not sure what Mindglow would do to a demon for certain—I've never had reason to test it—but I believe it could keep a demon subdued enough to not be able to change at will." He gave Logan a sharp look. "Is that what you think happened to Nadia and the Lamiah matriarch?"

"And possibly the assistant to the leader of No More Nightmares."

As expected, Merrick didn't look surprised by the news of Melanie Atkins' death. Like Septimus, the demon seemed to know everything that went on in Los Angeles thirty seconds after it happened.

"An interesting problem for your police division." Merrick took a thoughtful sip of coffee. "No doubt our dear Samantha will have her teeth in it as soon as she recovers.

That is, if she takes her teeth out of her Immortal warrior long enough to pay attention to anything else. I'll have to wait until Tain dumps her in the dust before I ask her out myself. I'm a snappy dresser and have all this luxury, but I can't compete with muscles and gleaming swords."

Logan let this speech run out before he asked, "What do you know about the demon attack today?"

"Absolutely nothing," Merrick said at once. "I admit it— when I found out Samantha had come into my club as a honey trap, I was hurt, quite hurt. I didn't even realize she was demon—she hides that part of her very well. But I respect her and, like I said, wouldn't mind a little something with her. How you, werewolf, can work side by side with her every day without wanting to jump her bones, I can't imagine."

"I contain myself," Logan said dryly. "Now, about the attack . . ."

"I'd never do anything so crude as open a death realm portal on top of a skyscraper and try to batter my enemies with it," Merrick said. "If I'd wanted Samantha dead—and my point is that I don't—I'd be much more subtle. In fact, if I went after Samantha I'd want to do it myself, make it personal. I assure you, wolf, I have no idea who instigated the attack, though I could find out, if you like."

For a price, Logan was certain. He kept his expression noncommittal and pretended to consult his notebook. "I came to ask you something else as well."

Merrick smiled. "You amaze me."

Logan met his gaze. "I'll be blunt. Who is supplying Mindglow to the demon clubs? To be fair, I don't think it's you."

Merrick made the slightest of shrugs. "I don't know why you'd think I know anything about that."

"You offered Mindglow to Samantha when you thought she was a demonwhore."

"I did no such thing, my lad. I offered her herbal tea, to calm her down. Any Mindglow found in my club was planted there by those who attacked me."

Logan kept his temper in check. He knew he was lucky Merrick had agreed to talk to him at all, and without his cold demon lawyer present, but he'd hoped he could get the man to give him *something*.

"Hypothetically, then," Logan said. "*If* I wanted to get Mindglow in this town, and *if* I found it at a demon club, who would be supplying the club?"

"It would depend on what clan the club owner belonged to. Dealers like to deal within their own clans—they don't trust outsiders."

"All right, say it was a demon club in the Djowlan clan. Who, in theory, would supply them?"

"I'm not familiar with the goings-on of the Djowlan clan, at least with regard to Mindglow. Apparently, I don't even know when they're gearing up to attack me."

"The Lamiah clan then," Logan said, clenching his teeth. "If you happened to know who supplied clubs in the Lamiah clan, who—in theory—would that be?"

Logan didn't really expect Merrick to answer. The man loved to dance around and not say anything while talking a lot—he was a careful criminal. He knew Merrick couldn't afford to be seen assisting the police either, though he could be seen *pretending* to assist them. But whether he would tell Logan anything helpful was anyone's guess.

Merrick laughed suddenly, a deep throaty laugh of true mirth. "You're so much more diplomatic than your partner, Detective. She'd have been threatening me with bodily harm by now, or arresting me to show me that she could."

"I'm not above a little arresting myself," Logan said. "I enjoy it."

Merrick held up his hand. "Peace, wolf. I know you're dying to turn into your beast and tear up the place. Shapeshifters are so predictable. But I'll be fair to you, since you've been fair to me. I'm only surprised you haven't figured it out yourself."

Logan said nothing, not wanting to indicate one way or another what the information meant to him.

Merrick laughed again, softly, shaking his head. "Since she's dead and the route will dry up for obvious reasons, I think it no harm to tell you." He leaned forward. "The supplier of Lamiah clan clubs was the Lamiah matriarch herself."

***

Tain slept. He had no idea where he was, his body an immobile blank.

He dreamed again, of darkness swirling through standing stones. At first he thought this a continuation of his earlier dream, but in this one he was older, his body strong and covered with chain mail. He was far to the north of where he'd grown up, in a crease of tall mountains overlooking a dark blue loch with a square stone castle on the other side. Tain recognized the setting and tried to twist away from the dream, knowing what was coming.

His shoulder rocked from where his brother Hunter had just clapped it, the man walking down the hill, ready to fight the menace they'd been summoned to kill. Unseelies—ugly, nasty, dangerous beasties—had broken into the world, and the brothers had been called to seal them back into their bubble of hell.

Easy work for Immortals with swords and powerful magic. They'd finish the job, retire to the castle for ale and women, and return home to Ravenscroft. This was their life.

Except Tain had headed for the castle as soon as the battle was done, without waiting for his brothers. The dream forwarded to him rowing himself across the loch in a coracle, his sheathed swords crossed in the bottom of the little boat. He left the boat, took up his swords, and climbed the hill to the keep, knowing she waited for him.

The demon woman had dark hair and liquid dark eyes, and Tain enjoyed her. Unlike Hunter, who had a fanatic hatred of demons—for good reason—Tain let himself take what they offered. He knew how to taste without letting their death magic entwine him, knew how to let them imbibe his incredible life essence without becoming addicted to them.

Tain liked to walk with the danger, knowing he could easily walk away again. Kehksut was different, a little more powerful and much more beautiful, although she'd never asked for Tain's life essence. Now she lifted her face for Tain's kiss, and he gave it. Why not? She was one more pleasure in his lifetime of snatched pleasures, a brief respite between battles.

Tain took her on the stone floor of the castle's empty hall, with nothing but furs beneath them. When he finished, he noted how silent the place was. Tain dressed and left the demon woman, climbing to the solar to see if he could spy his brothers coming across the lake. There he'd found the inhabitants of the castle—who'd lain dead and dying across the floor.

He'd tried to heal them, but he was too late. As anguish took him, Kehksut became who she truly was, an Old One, one the most powerful of them. Tain's magic was depleted from helping his brothers conquer the Unseelies and from pouring his healing power into the dying. He had nothing left to fight the unexpected wall of death magic, stronger than he'd ever experienced in his life, that surrounded and crushed him. He awoke imprisoned in pain and darkness, terrified and alone.

"Cerridwen, help me!"

There was no answer, only the sigh of darkness.

Tain called over and over again, begging the goddess to at least soothe his pain, begging his brothers to find him, to release him. No one answered, and no one came, except Kehksut.

"They can't hear you," she'd whispered, her red lips against his skin. "They gave up looking for you. They despise you for taking a demon lover."

Tain didn't believe her. His brothers would never desert him, no matter what—they'd made that clear time and again, Adrian especially.

Kehksut had healed him, made love to him, and then she became a powerful male demon and tortured him, leaving him in a pool of blood and pain once more.

Over and over again, Kehksut healed Tain and then tortured him again, every three days, until Tain lost all track of time and memory of any life before this. He kept waiting for Adrian to find him, kept calling out, pushing his magic to enter his brothers' dreams, but Adrian never came.

As time passed, Tain knew what Kehksut told him was true—they'd stopped looking for him. They couldn't find him, had given up and gone on with their lives.

Tain hated them for that. The memories of them tasted of ash, his love for them had been depleted by rage and pain.

The only way to survive was to make himself believe he liked the torture, embracing it, lowering himself into complete madness. As the years rolled by and Kehksut's sadistic ritual went on, Tain grew stronger. The madness grew greater as well, until the remaining tiny, hot spark of his true self got lost in the whirling vortex.

"You are mine, my love," she would say to him, caressing him with her exquisite touch. "You were born for me."

And Tain believed her.

Tain dreamed he saw her now, her black hair like watered silk, her eyes voids of darkness, her red-tipped fingers raking his skin. She'd never touched the tattoo on his face, the mark that meant something Tain no longer remembered.

"Tain," Kehksut whispered. She touched a kiss to his lips, and he felt the madness swirl around to suck him down yet again.

Another voice came out of the darkness, holding the same taint as the one he'd sensed in the death-magic portal on top of the building. An Old One, calling out to him.

Come to me . . .

Tain screamed and swung his fist, waking in time to see Samantha catch his wrist in a competent grip. She had the same demon-black hair and dark eyes as the woman of his dreams, but these eyes held concern.

"Tain?"

The world stopped spinning. Samantha knelt on a wide bed beside him, wearing nothing but a long T-shirt. Tain realized with a sickening jolt that he'd flailed out at her, and she'd caught his fist just in time.

"Samantha," he said, his voice barely working. Saying the name helped him swim back to reality, to know the darkness was over. This white bed and Samantha was the truth.

Tain gently slid his wrist from her grasp. "Are you all right?"

"I wanted to ask you that." Samantha touched his cheek. "You were dreaming. But everything's all right now."

"No, it isn't." Tain swung out of the bed, standing and looking down at her. His body was cold with sweat, his head pounding.

Samantha put her back to the headboard and crossed her legs. "You saved me today. All those demons would have killed me." She gave a little laugh. "Next time you want to jump off a building, though, warn me. I'll say no."

Her laughter wrapped around him like a balm, but the dream of Kehksut had been too real. Tain could still feel his skin being peeled from his bones, the pain that went too deep for healing. "Kehksut is dead," he said. He needed to say it out loud.

Samantha's eyes widened. "I know. Is that what you were dreaming about? Come here." She held out her hand, her invitation apparent. She wanted to soothe him, help him.

Tain shook his head. "Kehksut's death doesn't mean I'm healed. It was seven hundred years in madness, and my mind won't let it go so easily."

"I know," Samantha said. "That's why you're here with your family and your friends."

"Friends and family I can hurt." He clenched his fists, the remembered whisper of the new demon too near. "Look what I did to you yesterday, when you took my life essence. I was so far gone with it I didn't know I was hurting you. Is that what you want?"

Samantha's throat moved with her swallow. "We can slow down. That's what I wanted to talk to you about."

Tain reached for his jeans and pulled them on over his bare backside. "You said the first time that if you wanted a diet of life essence, you wouldn't start with me. But I pushed you into it, showing you how to take it, knowing you could get addicted to me, and me to you. What if next time I can't stop?"

"We'll think of something." Samantha reached for him again, anguished. "I'm not going to give up on you. We'll think of something."

Tain leaned his fists on the bed, pushing his face close to hers. "Even here, in this house, you're not safe from me. Kehksut made me stronger than all my brothers put together, did you know that? Hunter can't stop me, and Leda can't stop me. Even Adrian, the most powerful of them all, can't stop me. What if I become the killing madman I used to be? What will stop me then?"

"You won't," Samantha whispered. "You're a healer — you've proved it time and again."

Tain shook his head again. "You know nothing about me, Samantha. You know nothing of what I am and what I endured, and I can only thank the goddesses you'll never really understand. Kehksut tried to make me a force of destruction, but I refuse to destroy *you*."

Samantha stared at him, tears beading on her lashes. Tain couldn't pause to comfort her. Comfort might lead to sex, which would lead to her taking his life essence again, and who knew what might happen after that?

He turned around and walked away from her, out through the dark living room to the back door. Samantha didn't follow, and Tain was grateful. Not that he'd intended to let her—he could wall her into the room with a shield of magic if he needed to.

Pickles leapt off the sofa as Tain opened the door to the terrace, happy to be let out of the stuffy house. Tain made his way down the board stairs to the beach, the cat at his heels, the cool sand welcoming to his bare feet.

While Mukasa lumbered out to greet Pickles, Tain strode into the water, embracing the waves that pulled at him. He kept walking, his jeans soaking and heavy, water spilling into them.

Behind him in the house, the light went on in the room he'd shared with Samantha, but Tain kept walking forward until the dark, cold ocean closed over his head. Only then did the whisper of the demon in his death realm cease to call.

Chapter Twenty-One

Four days later, Samantha met with her father to discuss becoming the Lamiah clan matriarch.

She'd been working almost nonstop on the death of Melanie Atkins, realizing she was throwing herself into her work to forget that she hadn't seen Tain since the night he'd woken from his dreams and left her.

At first Samantha worried he'd truly gone insane again, but Hunter didn't seem concerned at all, which told Samantha that Hunter knew where he was. Leda also looked anxious, but she wouldn't talk about it with Samantha, which meant Leda knew where Tain was too, or at least knew that Hunter knew. Neither Leda nor Hunter would share the information with Samantha, which was driving her crazy, but short of arresting and interrogating them, she had to let it go. If and when Tain wanted to communicate with Samantha again, he would.

In addition, Samantha had been feeling sick and weak. She realized it was because she'd stopped taking Tain's life essence — all life essence. Now that she was aware she'd taken it from others, like Logan and her mother, she deliberately tried not to. As a result, she was cranky, tired, and working on a four-day headache. *Like permanent PMS,* she thought irritably.

Fulton had gone ahead with plans to declare Samantha as a candidate for matriarch. Samantha had grudgingly let him, remembering what Tain had told her during the demon attack—the matriarch had set up a shrine to an Old One, and the prostitutes' deaths and No More Nightmares was somehow connected with it.

Melanie had been part demon, as Logan surmised. She hadn't been Lamiah or Djowlan, or from any other Los Angeles clan—turned out, she'd moved out here from the heart of South Dakota. Her clan, Samantha had discovered, rejected all those not of pure blood, so Melanie had been raised human with no contact with her demon clan at all. Logan speculated Melanie had joined the demon haters because of her clan's rejection, but that brought Samantha no closer to finding her killer.

Ms. Townsend had returned to the No More Nightmares office the morning after Melanie's murder, seemingly upset at the death of her assistant and surprised to learn that Melanie had been part demon. She behaved as though her encounter with Tain out in the desert had never happened, and she had an alibi for the time of Melanie's death. She'd been at a conference in Phoenix, six hours away by road, or one hour and however long it took to navigate airports by air. The medical examiner said that Melanie died at two in the afternoon, and precisely at two, Ms. Townsend had been speaking to five hundred people in an auditorium.

Searches of the No More Nightmares offices had turned up no evidence they'd been sending the threatening letters. McKay had sent Logan out to Nevada to meet with local authorities there and investigate the canyon Tain had discovered, but the locals hadn't been very cooperative, and Logan had found nothing.

Merrick's revelation that the matriarch of Samantha's clan had been supplying Mindglow to the clubs bothered Samantha, and she wondered how it tied in with the

matriarch's shrine and sacrifices. She wondered, too, if
anyone else in the clan had known about the shrine, or if the
matriarch's fixation on the ancient demon had been private.
Tain hadn't told Samantha which Old One was involved.
Was it because Tain didn't know, or because he didn't want
her to know?

The afternoon after the matriarch's funeral, which
Samantha had not been invited to, her father called and
asked her to come over to her mother's house to talk.

Samantha arrived and embraced Joanne, who'd also not
gone to the funeral, and then her father. Samantha was still
getting used to hugging Fulton, and he was getting used to
the contact too.

They sat in the kitchen sipping coffee Joanne provided,
while Fulton told Samantha of his plans to put her forward
as matriarch. "The decision must be made soon, or we'll lose
the chance of keeping the rise of the next matriarch civilized.
A battle within the clan right now could mean the
destruction of it. The Djowlans would take the opportunity
to move into our territories while we're busy fighting one
another, and either kill every Lamiah or drive us back to our
death realm."

Samantha shivered. Demon battles weren't allowed in
these times, but that didn't mean demons didn't have them.
And what happened in the death realms had nothing to do
with the human world. The tons of demons pouring out
from the portals on top of the building downtown obviously
hadn't given a damn about following rules.

"This is important," Fulton said when Samantha didn't
answer. "You don't know *how* important."

Samantha thought she understood. If the matriarch had
been dealing Mindglow and sacrificing demon hearts to an
Old One, or at least using No More Nightmares to sacrifice
them, the Lamiah clan was in trouble. Samantha wished
Tain would have left a fully detailed outline about his
findings before he'd disappeared, maybe in a nice file folder
with all the evidence neatly laid out.

Becoming the Lamiah matriarch would give Samantha a prime opportunity to investigate—she'd be privilege to info even the police wouldn't be able to find out. She could possibly crack this case and stop the killings. But then, once she'd closed the investigation, she couldn't simply quit and go home. Samantha would be matriarch for life, giving up all she knew to do it.

"I can't believe there isn't a venerable full-demon woman in our clan who wouldn't leap at the chance to become matriarch," Samantha said to her father. "You don't need *me.*"

"We do need you." Fulton took her hand in a firm grip. "The matriarch wanted you, and I am head of the most powerful family in the clan. If I put you forward now, we can do this. We need a leader, and we need her now."

Samantha disengaged from his grasp and stood up. "I'm not special, and I barely inherited any magical ability. I'm not even full demon."

Fulton's eyes burned with an adamant light. "Samantha, as matriarch you will have far more power than you ever can as a police officer. If you want to keep demons from hurting people, you certainly can do that as matriarch. They'll listen to you."

"And you can have a family," Joanne put in. "You can marry and have children. I always hear that a police career is hard on a family. I know I'm always worried sick when you're out chasing criminals."

Joanne's eyes and Fulton's both held concern, hope, and the need to see their only child happy.

"You want this for me," Samantha said in surprise. "Not for you, for *me.* Why?"

"Because we made so many mistakes," Joanne answered softly. "We wanted to raise you apart from your true heritage, because we weren't sure the clan would accept you, and that you wouldn't accept Fulton as your father. That proved to be a mistake. I never meant for you to despise your own father and hate what you are. We were trying to protect you, and sometimes parents get so protective they become foolish."

Samantha sat down again. "You're trying to get me elected matriarch to make up for my childhood? Isn't that a bit extreme? Just take me out to dinner or something."

"There's more to it than that," Fulton said, not smiling. "Samantha, I want you to be happy, in any way you can, but this goes beyond our own needs."

She spread her hands. "How can I lead a clan I know nothing about?"

"The majordomo will help you," Fulton said. "She's ready to retire, but she agreed to stay on until you can find a trusted assistant of your own."

Samantha gave a sharp laugh. "Telling me I have to work with that ice queen is not a good way to convince me."

Fulton gave her a quiet look. "Ariadne is smart, she's wise, and she knows the clan. She'd be the best help you can have."

"Why doesn't she become matriarch?" Samantha had been wondering how much the majordomo knew about the matriarch's interesting activities and how deeply she was involved.

Fulton shook his head. "She can't. Ariadne's from one of the lowest families, one step above the untouchables. Their line only serves, although they can become very influential in their own way. They like being the powers behind the throne. But you don't have to worry about that with the majordomo, because she really does want to retire."

"There are untouchable demons?" Samantha asked, startled.

"Yes," Fulton said in a matter-of-fact voice. "They mostly keep to themselves and don't interact much with the others."

"Isn't that a bit cruel?"

"Everyone in the clan has a part to play," Fulton said. "You'll learn all about it."

Samantha regarded him and her mother, who were watching her worriedly. "I still think you're both crazy. You want *me*, a human-raised, half-demon cop, to become the matriarch of a clan I know nothing about?"

"I am prepared to give you my full support," Fulton said.

"*You* are, but what about other demons?" Samantha broke off. "Wait a minute, let me try something."

She pulled out her cell phone and tapped a number. "Merrick, please," she said when a smooth-voiced male demon answered.

After a moment, Merrick's voice boomed out. "Ah, it's my favorite policewoman. How did I know I couldn't get through a week without being harassed by you?"

"Merrick," Samantha said, cutting him off. "If I became the Lamiah matriarch, would you support me?"

Dead silence filtered to her from the other end.

"Are you still there?" Samantha asked. "Did you hear me?"

"I heard you." Merrick sounded subdued. "I know the matriarch wanted to put you forward. Are you seriously considering it?"

"I haven't decided. But would you?"

Another silence, then Merrick said thoughtfully. "You know, I think I would. Once I got over the utter shock, that is."

"Why? Support me, I mean."

"Because you're an annoying bitch, but you can think for yourself, both good qualities in a matriarch. You wouldn't take any shit from someone like that majordomo."

"Would *you* work for me?"

Merrick's reply cut off with a squawk. "Me? For you?" He started to laugh, then quieted. "I might consider it. Why? Would your sword-toting boyfriend cut off my head if I didn't?"

"I'm just putting out feelers for now, nothing definite."

"You really are a piece of work, Samantha. I sensed it the moment you walked into my club."

"I love you too, Merrick. I'll be in touch." Samantha clicked off the phone before he could say good-bye.

Fulton raised a brow. "Drumming up favors already?"

"I know Merrick's a thug," Samantha said. "But he'd be a handy person to have on my side."

"The gap the matriarch left must be filled soon," Fulton said. "Our family will meet for dinner on Saturday, on the last quarter of the waning moon. I ask you to please come with me and declare your candidacy." He smiled a little. "Who knows? You might lose."

Samantha toyed with her coffee cup. "Will declaring myself involve me fighting someone to the death?"

"I shouldn't think so," Fulton said, his smile widening but his gaze serious. "That hasn't happened in at least three hundred years."

***

Tain gazed out from his vantage point of the cool green garden to the vista below him — the flat white of a dry lakebed, the sun pounding on it with vigor. He leaned against the low wall that separated the monastery from the sloping desert mountain and contemplated the lakebed — empty, stark, and beautiful.

His brother Adrian leaned next to him in T-shirt and jeans, sunlight on his black hair. A cobra lolled in the cultivated flower bed at their feet, basking in the cool earth.

The two of them — three, counting the snake — had reposed here in silence most of the morning. Now Adrian stretched, his big frame pulling at his shirt and asked, "So are you going to tell me what happened to your hair?"

"Fire," Tain said laconically. "Rescuing a demon."

"Trying to impress a girl?"

"Something like that."

"Did it work?" Adrian asked.

Tain pretended to think it through. "Yes." While Adrian chuckled, Tain scrubbed one hand over his face. "But I might have done more harm than good." He gave his brother a quiet look. "It's not going away, Adrian."

Adrian studied him, his dark eyes still. "I didn't think it was."

"All of it was meant to happen, Cerridwen told me. I get that. I suffered, you rescued me, we saved the world. But it won't stop. I still have the dreams. And I want Samantha. I crave her. When she takes my life essence, it's the only time the pain stops."

Adrian's look was tense, the guilt in his eyes sharp. "Go back to Ravenscroft then. Stay there, heal, and be safe."

Tain shook his head. "I'm not leaving Samantha alone to face what's out there. She needs protection, and I'm the best she can have. I'll have to, as they say, suck it up." He returned his gaze to the splendor of the unmarred desert, eastern California at its most beautiful. "I can't go to Ravenscroft and let the world flow past me," he said, his voice softening. "Samantha will live and change, and be gone by the time I'm able to come out again. I don't want to miss her life."

Adrian watched him, sympathy in his eyes. At their feet, the cobra raised his head. *Such a dilemma,* the snake's voice said inside their heads. *Cobras never have these problems.*

"Ferrin," Adrian growled at him.

We fertilize the eggs and we're done. No moping, no drama, no broken hearts.

Adrian picked up one of Tain's bronze swords and pointed it at Ferrin. "Small snake, large sword."

Ferrin lowered himself into a sulky coil. *I only speak the truth.*

"He's a wise reptile," Tain said, squinting against the glare on the dry lake, white against blue. "But there's more to it than wanting Samantha to take my life essence at any cost." He paused, the desert breeze tugging the ends of his short hair. "When I felt the presence of that Old One, I wanted to go to him, Adrian. It was a powerful reflex."

He'd told Adrian what had happened on top of the building, but Tain hadn't told his brother everything, until now.

"A reflex you successfully fought," Adrian said. "Obviously. You're here."

"It was very, very close." Tain felt a tinge of fear, not because of the ancient demon, but fear of himself. "What if I succumb, and he uses what I become?"

"Then Kalen, Darius, Hunter and I will drag you back to sanity again," Adrian said. "I'm not losing you a second time."

Tain didn't answer. Unlike his brothers, he knew their rescue of him had been Tain's choice. He'd so much power by then, he hadn't needed Kehksut anymore. The demon had become superfluous, and then Kehksut had threatened Samantha. Kehksut daring to hurt Samantha had made Tain sever the ties, enough that he could follow his brothers' collective magic back to reality.

"There's more," Tain said. "I found the portal to this Old One's death realm under the Lamiah matriarch's mansion. I sealed it, but if Samantha becomes the matriarch, she'll have to deal with him."

Adrian stretched his hand to the ground, and Ferrin curled himself around his wrist, blinking sleepily. The cobra twisted all the way around Adrian's bicep then shimmered and became a silver, snake-shaped armband. "You should be there with her then," Adrian said with conviction.

Tain's eyes narrowed, his blood warming. "Oh, I intend to be."

***

For the meeting with her demon family, Samantha bought another dress, a black satin sheath with a mandarin collar that hugged her body and skimmed to the floor. Samantha hoped, as Leda helped her into the dress, that this one wouldn't get acid slimed. The formal rental shop had of course demanded full price for the replacement of the blue silk she'd done battle in, which Samantha paid without fuss.

Fulton reassured her that they were going to a family dinner, no attacks anticipated, but Samantha had learned that you never knew with demons. She'd bought a purse to match the dress large enough to carry her gun, badge, and ID.

She'd also bought a pair of very high heels to complete the outfit, their straps decorated with rhinestones. The shoes would kill her feet, but observing herself in the mirror, she thought the pain might be worth it.

Samantha wanted to look good when she met her father's family — *her* family. But she wanted to look modest good, not like a demonwhore as when she'd staked out Merrick's club or the virginal look she'd gone for when meeting the matriarch. She wanted to be *Samantha*, equal to any of them.

"You're gorgeous," Leda said, hugging her. "You'll knock 'em dead."

"Don't say that about a demon gathering," Samantha warned. "It could happen."

Fulton picked up Samantha in his new SUV, bought to replace the one damaged in the demon attack at the matriarch's. He drove down out of Malibu, heading north and west along the mountains that hugged the coast. Eventually they pulled off into Santa Barbara, and Fulton drove through the small city, up a winding road into the hills, and halted at a wide iron gate. He gave his name to the guard, the electronic gate slowly rolled open, and Fulton drove on under arching eucalyptus trees.

The house Fulton pulled to a stop before was less opulent than the matriarch's mansion but twice as big. It spread gracefully across the grounds in old California style, with arches, tile roofs, and little balconies popping out here and there. Eucalyptus and tall palm trees surrounded it, leaving a space for the wide gravel drive.

A man in white gloves opened the doors of the SUV for them, then got into the driver's seat once they'd disembarked, and drove the vehicle to an open garage.

"He's human," Samantha observed.

"Most of the people who work for us are," Fulton said. "Not many demons live up this way, and our family . . . well, you'll see."

The interior of the house was also old California, with vast Saltillo tile floors, arched corridors, and colorful tiled staircases twisting intriguingly out of sight. Their way was lit with candles flickering in wrought-iron wall sconces instead of electric lights.

Fulton led Samantha along winding halls to a cavernous dining room. A heavy Spanish-style table stretched the length of it, encircled by heavily carved chairs. Well-dressed people wandered about drinking from crystal glasses or warming themselves in front of the white arched fireplace, the evenings this far into the hills cool.

Conversation ceased as Fulton ushered Samantha in, and twenty pairs of dark eyes regarded them with interest. The matriarch's mansion had been intimidating enough, but that house had been built and staffed to serve the needs of one woman. This was a family house, where these people lived or visited as they pleased. There was no atmosphere of a business office—this was their home—and Samantha had come to claim it was her home too.

Her blood was cold, and her skin prickled. Even the stoked fire couldn't warm her.

A darkly handsome demon in a suit held up a glass. "Drink, Fulton? Parker brought a bottle of single malt." Fulton nodded, and the demon went on. "Samantha, for you?"

Samantha swallowed. She'd love to drown her nerves in alcohol, but she shook her head. "No, thanks."

"So this is Samantha," another man who looked much like Fulton said. "We've heard so much about you." His keen look made Samantha wonder what they'd heard.

"My reprobate brother Parker," Fulton said. "Your uncle."

"And who is *he*?" Parker demanded, looking past them. "He reeks. Who let *him* in here?"

Samantha swung around, her mouth opening in shock as Tain came through the dining room door. He wore a modern black suit jacket with a tie knotted at his throat, and a crisp, clean kilt. The hilts of his twin swords poked out from beneath the coat.

The demon in Samantha throbbed, hungry for the rampant life essence he was exuding. It was all she could do not to run to him, grab him, slap her hand over his tattoo, and drink him down. Her cleft tightened, and her previously cold blood flowed hot. She hoped her nipples weren't poking against the thin silk of her dress for all to see.

The human half of Samantha wanted to ask him where the hell he'd been and why he'd left her to *worry* about him like that. As a result, she could only stand numbly, her mouth dry, while Tain took in the crowd of demons staring back at him.

The woman next to her uncle Parker coolly took a sip of her drink. "Maybe he's a gift? His essence is heady." Her eyes darkened.

Samantha sensed others in the room looking Tain over as though he were the first course at a banquet. Tain gazed back at them steadily, standing out like an outlaw biker in the royal enclosure at Ascot. His buzzed red hair and twin swords were at odds with the roomful of people who'd glammed themselves to have dark hair and eyes and elegant bodies that showed off graceful clothes. Tain was dressed well enough, but he still had the look of a thug, one who wasn't worried about a roomful of demons.

"He's with me," Samantha said in a strangled voice. "He's . . . helping me out." In reality she had no idea what he was doing there, and Tain didn't enlighten her.

"I see," Parker said, dark brows rising. "That's not going to sit well with Tristan."

"I don't give a damn what sits well with Tristan," Fulton rumbled.

"Who's Tristan?" Samantha asked.

"Our unfortunate nephew," Parker said. "An orphaned brat who's gotten full of himself."

"He's a little more than that," his wife added, but her gaze was still fixed on Tain.

Samantha couldn't look away from him either. Tain had sprung out of nowhere, looking as devastating as ever, though he bore a half-healed gash high on his cheekbone.

He *would* choose this moment to walk back into her life, where Samantha couldn't take him aside and ask what had happened to him. Or take him aside to hold on to him and reassure herself he was truly back—if he was, and this wasn't some quick visit between disappearances.

Human servants began trucking in carts of food, and the family dispersed to take seats for dinner. Everyone seemed to know where to sit, with Fulton at the head of the table. A place to Fulton's right had been left clear for Samantha, but there was no seat for Tain, and no one offered to bring him one.

Tain made a little gesture for Samantha to sit, then silently took up a stance behind her chair. Questions about what he'd been up to and why would have to wait. Samantha looked nervously around at her family, who'd started eating the first course.

It didn't help that what the servant carefully laid on Samantha's plate was long, gray, and unidentifiable. It was also very gently pulsing.

"*Haggert*," Tain leaned down and murmured into her ear.

"What?"

"It's *haggert*," Fulton said, his dark eyes unsurprised. "A beast found only in certain death realms, hard to bring down. A delicacy."

"Why is it moving?" Samantha asked, gingerly poking it with her fork.

Her uncle Parker answered. "It takes a long time for them to die. Often, their pulse still goes even after they're sliced and roasted. Better that way—full of life essence."

Samantha sat back, letting her fork drop. Parker's wife leaned forward. "You mean you've never had *haggert*? It's wonderful. Although I suppose you'd rather stick to dead cow?"

"Maybe a salad," Samantha said hastily.

"Salads are good," her aunt agreed. "Especially with mushroom grubs and vampire blood."

Parker guffawed as Samantha flinched. "I have the feeling the new matriarch will be ordering out Chinese."

"Oh, I love Chinese," his wife said. "Koreans are quite good, too . . ."

The doors banged open, breaking conversation. The demon who entered wore a tailored suit, but Samantha sensed him ready to burst out of it and shift into a snarling monster at any moment.

"Tristan," Fulton said under his breath. "Your cousin."

"So this is Samantha," Tristan said, gazing down the table at her. "Our half-blood."

In the course of Samantha's career she'd faced down plenty of hot-headed, belligerent, out-of-control criminals. Tristan reminded her of every single one. He looked into her eyes, unapologetic, angry, and unremorseful.

"Sit down, Tristan," Fulton said.

"Who is *that*?" Tristan demanded, glaring at Tain. "What have you brought into our house, Fulton?"

Fulton squeezed Samantha's hand under the table and gazed calmly back at Tristan. "If Samantha becomes our matriarch, it is her choice to bring in Tain to guard her. Considering what happened to our last matriarch, I welcome his help. Are we all still agreed?"

Samantha expected reluctance and resentment, but to her surprise the whole family except Tristan nodded, including Samantha's aunt with the strange food preferences, who smiled at her across the table.

"I can see that Fulton has brainwashed you all, as usual," Tristan said. He moved to the foot of the table where an empty chair waited but he didn't sit. "You would put a half-demon and her pet *thing* over us, instead of my candidate?"

"Candidate?" Samantha asked her father. "This is the first I've heard about another candidate."

"Her name is Ariel," Tristan answered in a loud voice. "A pure demon who knows how to stop the harassment of demons going on in Los Angeles."

"Oh, really?" Samantha said. "How interesting."

"Demons are stronger than humans, no question," Tristan said. "There was a time when humans were nothing but food for demons, and Ariel will bring those days of glory back to us."

Samantha's aunt nudged Parker. "With *him* on top . . . of her." Parker chuckled, and Tristan glared at them.

Fulton observed calmly, "Ariel is from a rival family and is a protégé of the matriarch's majordomo."

Samantha saw distrust of Tristan and dislike of this Ariel on every face at the table, and pieces fell into place.

"I see," Samantha said to Fulton, her anger rising. "You all want *me*, because better the demon you know . . ."

Fulton nodded without shame. "Exactly. Although there's much more to it than that."

No doubt there was. Samantha, young and inexperienced, could be told to put the needs of her demon family over the others in the clan. They wanted Samantha, because they thought they could control her.

Anger flowed through Samantha's body, clean, strengthening anger that chased away the last vestiges of doubt. She knew now what she had to do. She glanced at Tain and saw the same grim realization reflected in his eyes.

Tristan was rambling on. "We demons have stayed hidden too long—assimilating, adapting, letting humans rule us."

"They don't rule us," Fulton said calmly. "Sit down."

Tristan stretched a long finger toward Samantha. "*She* works for those who arrest us, imprison us, humiliate us."

"Only when you're stupid," Samantha said in a hard voice.

Tristan's eyes glittered with dislike. "Half-breed females are good for only one thing. You should serve us whatever we want—on your back, on your knees, however we please."

Tain moved, and Samantha in that moment understood that he'd been holding in the full extent of his power since he'd arrived in Los Angeles.

His life magic whipped through the room in a blinding flash of light. It found and destroyed every warding and death-magic spell that had been placed in here, bursting them with little pops, then it flowed through the house to find all the others. Tain replaced the demon magic with his own white-hot power—strong, protective, deadly. Samantha heard groans of dismay and fright from her family. Even Fulton, who had seen what Immortals could do, shivered.

Tristan tried to launch a stream of death-magic at Tain to stop him, but the small trickle splintered and died in the face of Tain's overwhelming force.

Tain reined in his magic without even breathing hard. The light vanished, and the guests at the table let out their breaths in relief.

"Well," Parker's wife said. "That was a display." She picked up her drink again, pretending nonchalance, but her hand was shaking. "Do you lend him around, Samantha?"

Down the table Tristan declared in a loud voice, "You had no right to bring that life-magic creature here, Fulton. *He* killed the matriarch, and I can prove it!"

Chapter Twenty-Two

The guests gasped or looked disbelieving, and all swiveled their gazes to Samantha and Tain behind her.

"You were misinformed," Tain said calmly to Tristan.

"Was I?" Tristan said. "That's not what the vampire told me."

"What vampire?" Samantha demanded. If Septimus had leaked the information about Tain, he'd see the sharp end of a stake, Old One or not.

"A vamp who works for the one called Septimus," Tristan said. "He followed your lover all over town and sold me the information—I have it here."

"The little rat made copies," Samantha cried, her fury mounting.

Tain's gaze snapped to Samantha, the cold in his eyes chilling. "Show me," he said.

With a smile of glee, Tristan reached into his coat and pulled out a large manila envelope, which he tossed to the middle of the table. No one seemed to want to touch it, recoiling from it the same way Samantha had recoiled from the *haggert*.

Fulton at last stood up, walked down the table to retrieve it, then pulled it open and unfolded papers and photocopies of pictures. He laid them out on the table in front of Samantha, and Tain leaned down to look.

Tain was clearly visible in the photos, which were time and date stamped, catching him at various places around Los Angeles. Tristan waved a hand at them.

"Behold the killer of our clan matriarch and family leader," he said. "Why he did it, I don't know. Maybe he just likes to kill demons, or maybe Fulton put him up to it, to promote his own daughter."

No one answered. Tain said to Samantha, "You knew about these."

The noise of the room receded, and for the moment none of this mattered — not the matriarch's death or the family Samantha was meeting for the first time, or the fact that Tain had popped back into her life as suddenly as he'd vanished from it.

"Septimus gave them to me," she said.

Tain's breath was hot on her ear. "And if I told you I was not in those places in those times, would you believe me?"

Do you trust me?

Samantha looked up at him, meeting his blue gaze, then she returned to the photos spread before her, the evidence of a camera's eye. It was possible Septimus's vampire had faked the whole thing, but she didn't think Septimus would have used him if he hadn't been reliable. Samantha also suspected that the vamp's decision to sell the information to Tristan came after the fact — an opportunity seized, not a planned event.

She looked up at Tain again to see the darkness in his eyes. Something had changed about him, but she couldn't put her finger on what. His shaved hair was still in that silky red buzz she found incredibly sexy. She kept envisioning running her hands through it while he slowly slid his coat and shirt from his body.

"Your hair," she whispered.

Tain's brows twitched together. "What about it?"

Samantha grabbed the photo of him taken inside the matriarch's grounds, time-stamped the evening of the matriarch's death. "I knew something bugged me about this. Look at your hair."

The photo was black and white, but it clearly showed Tain's thick hair rolling back from his forehead to his shoulders.

"The matriarch died *after* the fire at Merrick's," Samantha said. "Your hair had burned, and you'd cut it off. This can't be you, or else the date stamp is wrong."

Tain leaned over her shoulder to examine the picture. "It looks like me."

"Maybe it's a Chameleon," Samantha suggested. She wanted to dance around the table and wave the photo under Tristan's nose, but she retained her dignity.

"Or a demon casting a glam," Fulton said. His gaze went to Tristan, and Tristan's eyes widened.

"Don't look at me," Tristan said indignantly. "I bought all, as is, from a vampire, I swear it."

"I believe him," Samantha said. "I think Tristan bought these in good faith, happy he had something with which to incriminate Tain and me."

"I don't think I need to ask why," Fulton said.

Samantha heaved a resigned sigh. "Dad, if I don't let you put me forward as matriarch, what happens?"

"Tristan and the majordomo back Ariel, the only other candidate."

Samantha's head began to ache. "The majordomo must have been horrified when the matriarch talked about grooming me to take her place. I wonder if *she* faked the photos to make it look as though Tain and I had something to do with the matriarch's death."

"She could have," Fulton said, looking thoughtful. "She's a 'demons should dominate' type. She's not happy with us trying to play well with others."

"But didn't you tell me the majordomo is from one of the lowest classes of our clan?" Samantha asked. "No matter who is matriarch, she doesn't really get any of that power."

"The under classes are amazingly old-fashioned," Fulton answered. "And the majordomo enjoys being the power behind the throne. The matriarch only let her get away with so much, but if a matriarch the majordomo herself has mentored comes forward . . . she pulls all the strings."

Samantha swallowed, her throat tight. "And that's why you asked me to do this?"

Fulton gave her a quiet nod. "One of the many reasons."

Samantha saw her life abruptly splitting into two paths. One led back to her job as a police detective, where she'd arrest vampires accused of turning more people than allotted or do stakeouts on demon bars suspected of dealing Mindglow. Her father's family and clan would remain under the thumb of the majordomo and her trained matriarch, the consequences of which, if the new matriarch gained enough power, would be felt in the world.

Or Samantha could take the other path, fully embrace her demon family and their world, and keep the clan from becoming nothing but a gathering of evil. She could figure out what the old matriarch had been up to and why she'd died, and prevent demon sacrifices in the future. She could come to terms with her need for life essence and figure out a way to get it without hurting others. But the possibility for Samantha to have any kind of normal life would be gone.

She glanced up to find Tain's gaze still on her. If she became matriarch, she'd be swallowed by her clan and their problems, by the people who were Tain's enemies. She couldn't predict what he would do once she was the matriarch, but Samantha knew she'd fallen in love with him. These past few days without him had been unbearable.

Tain said nothing, only watched with his enigmatic blue eyes as Samantha made the most difficult choice of her life. She swallowed the lump in her throat.

Samantha anchored herself with Tain's gaze, which was the most steady and solid thing in the room, as she slowly got to her feet. "All right," she said to Fulton, who watched her anxiously. "I'll be your matriarch."

***

Tain thought he'd never seen anything more beautiful than Samantha standing in front of her father, her black dress as sleek as water, quietly declaring she'd change her life for the good of her clan.

Tain had missed her more than he ever dreamed he would. He'd needed to leave town to clear his head, and he didn't regret going, but when he'd ridden back into Los Angeles with Adrian, his heart had lightened, knowing he was on his way to Samantha again. For the first time since his escape from Kehksut, he'd looked forward to something.

He'd learned from Logan that today Samantha was meeting her family at a formal dinner in Santa Barbara, and Tain knew he needed to be there. So he'd changed into a suit at the Malibu house, and Hunter had driven him to Santa Barbara and dropped him off. Tain had told him not to stay. Hunter hadn't liked that, but he'd let Tain have his way.

At Samantha's declaration, the entirety of her aunts, uncles, and cousins cheered, except for Tristan. Samantha looked down and away, but not before Tain saw the tears in her eyes. The decision had been difficult for her, and Tain was no stranger to hard choices.

"What happens now?" Samantha asked her father.

"We have a clan muster," Fulton answered. "And the clan decides whether to accept you."

"And if they don't?"

"You go home, and we seek another."

"As simple as that?"

Fulton looked uncomfortable. "Not really."

"I see. Will Mother be able to come to this muster?"

Fulton shook his head. "The clan isn't that open-minded. No non-demons allowed in our realm beneath."

"So when will this muster be?" Samantha asked. She spoke in a calm voice, but Tain heard the tremor in it. "I'll have to resign; there's a process . . ."

"The muster is right now," Fulton said. He put his hands on Samantha's shoulders, kissed her cheek, and then moved to the richly paneled wall opposite the fireplace.

"Right now?" Samantha's voice went sharp. "Can't I have time to prepare, or at least fix my hair?"

"Candidates are not allowed to prepare," Fulton said, facing the wall. "Matriarchs have supreme power over clans when they take up the mantle, but before that, the clan has supreme power over them."

Samantha faltered, though her shoulders remained square. "I wish you'd have mentioned this. I'd have worn more comfortable shoes."

Fulton didn't answer. Tain saw in his stance worry that his daughter wouldn't be accepted, his need to protect her warring with his need to placate his family and follow the ancient traditions.

The wall in front of Fulton dissolved to reveal a darkness beyond and a waft of death magic. Tain went cold. He hated the death realms, the lands of demons. Mortals *could* go there, but only with a death-magic creature as a guide. There were realms beyond these surface death realms that were only for the dead, true hell dimensions where Old Ones ruled. Tain had been to those deepest hells, and had survived, but they'd scarred him.

He drew a breath, forcing himself to take in the air of the tainted place, willing the blackness that rose in his mind to dissolve.

Beyond the wall Fulton had opened lay a hall of carved stone, with white marble arches flowing down the cavernous room. The pillars seemed to glow from within, bathing the place in a luminous white light.

Fulton walked by himself to the middle of the room, where a small table with a chime and a mallet on it waited.

He picked up the tiny mallet and struck the chime, sending a sweet note through the stone hall.

Fulton turned back and held out his hand to Samantha. "It is time."

Samantha, fists clenched at her sides, stepped into the room, and Tain moved to follow. Samantha's uncle Parker put himself between Tain and the opening.

"No non-demons at a muster," he said sternly.

Tain gazed down at Parker, immobile. "I go, or she does not."

"Tain . . ." Samantha began.

"I won't let you step into a death realm without me at your side," Tain said in a hard voice. "They manipulated you to get you this far—what else might they have in mind?"

The spark of anger in Samantha's eyes flared, not at him, but at the truth of his words. "He has a point, Father."

Fulton looked back from the table. "Let him pass, Parker. They're coming."

Parker didn't look happy, but he moved aside. Tain walked into the room after Samantha, the frosty chill of death magic clutching him with moist fingers. He held himself rigid, walling off the madness that tapped at him. He had to stay alert, to discover if the portal the matriarch had made was connected to this death realm.

Demons flowed toward them from every quarter, in demon form or in the guises of well-dressed humans. All the demons of the Lamiah clan, Tain surmised, entering from each of their families' strongholds.

They grouped themselves around the room, gathering in disparate clumps, as though each family knew exactly where to stand in the hall. Tain recognized some of the demons—Merrick stood near one pillar in his human form, wearing his customary well-tailored suit and a sly smile. Near Merrick was Nadia, her shorn hair neatened, her look defiant. Tain remembered the matriarch stating that Nadia was no longer of the clan, but perhaps the matriarch's death gave Nadia a chance to claim her part of it again.

Notably absent was Tristan, who had disappeared as soon as Fulton opened the way to the death realm. Also absent was the matriarch's majordomo.

Six men joined Fulton in the middle of the room—heads of households, Tain guessed. Fulton greeted them all solemnly, their breaths fogging in the cold air. All but Fulton looked over Samantha like they might eye a racehorse, wondering if it would bring in the biggest prize for them.

The meeting was simple. Fulton spoke to the six men, formally presenting Samantha as both his daughter and the candidate for matriarch. The household heads went back to their collective groups and murmured among themselves while Samantha, Fulton, and Tain waited at the table.

The chill of death magic was like ice in Tain's blood, and he wasn't sure how long he could stand here. The pentacle tattoo on his cheek burned, and voices in his head began to whisper.

You are a hundred times more powerful than they are. Even in this death realm, you can crush them. You can take Samantha far away and have her as your own, make her yours.

He clenched his teeth against the thoughts. Kehksut had thought that way—*destroy everyone and take what you want. Lesser beings should bow down to the more powerful or be obliterated.*

Now Tain, the being who'd been strong enough to kill Kehksut himself, fought the urge to do as the demon had taught him. He closed his eyes, willing himself to calm, calling words of soothing meditation.

Samantha touched his hand. He opened his eyes to find her at his side, her warm hand in his.

She trusted him. She looked up at him with her soft, dark gaze, believing he'd come here to protect her, believing he'd support her. She'd quickly proved the damning evidence of the photos had been false, supporting *him*. They were holding up each other.

Tain couldn't look away from her. Nothing was more important than the warmth in her eyes, the touch of her hand. Her heat cut through the death realm's chill, soothing him, unwinding the tightness in his body.

He barely noticed when the six men detached themselves from their families again and returned to Fulton.

"We have decided," one of them said. "Samantha, daughter of Fulton, will become our matriarch."

Fulton nodded solemnly, and Tain saw Samantha grow still more rigid. She was uncomfortable here too, but he saw her trying to make herself believe she *did* belong here.

She jumped when Fulton and the six other heads of households drew short-bladed, black knives. Tain stepped closer to Samantha, but the men drew the blades across their palms, each scoring a line of deep-red blood. Then each man stepped in front of Samantha in turn, dipped his finger into his own blood, and traced it across her face.

"I pledge my blood, my loyalty, and my house to you, our matriarch," they intoned.

Each one provided a line that created a seven-sided pattern, Fulton tracing in the last piece. "I pledge my blood, my loyalty, and my house to you, our matriarch," he said in a warm voice.

He whispered something into Samantha's ear, and when he stepped away, she said, "I accept and will protect my clan against its enemies, come what may."

The clan gave a rousing cheer and someone shouted for champagne. Fulton gave Samantha a handkerchief with which to wipe off her face, then kissed her cheek. "Thank you, daughter." He had tears in his eyes. "You've made me so proud."

The clan came to congratulate her. Samantha was surrounded first by her own family and then those that made up the rest of the clan. For the most part they were friendly and smiling, though Tain detected a few speculative and unhappy glances.

Merrick was one of the last who came to pay his respects. He held a champagne flute negligently in one hand and looked Samantha up and down.

"So you made good on your threat. I bow to you, my matriarch." Merrick made a mock salaam. "Perhaps I can make an appointment with you to talk business?"

"You'll have to speak to my assistant," Samantha said, meeting his gaze with a cool one of her own. "Which I don't have yet, so you'll have to wait until I appoint one. But no more Mindglow, Merrick. *This* matriarch is not going to assist in your illegal activities."

Merrick's smile widened. "What illegal activities would those be? I don't think I ever actually *said* the last matriarch supplied me with Mindglow. That would be so wrong of her."

"I'm glad you agree. I don't get to be a cop anymore, but I imagine there's a file on you in the matriarch's office this thick." She indicated a substantial size with her thumb and forefinger.

Merrick only let his smile widen. "I look forward to fencing with you, dear matriarch. Here's to the start of an interesting friendship."

He moved off, whistling to himself, and Samantha's defiant stance faded. The face she turned to Tain was wan and lined with exhaustion. Tain leaned down to her in concern. "Are you all right?" he asked.

"I will be." Samantha drew a breath and gave him a decided nod. "I have to be. But don't let them give me any more champagne. My headache is monumental."

Tain plucked the half-empty glass from her hand and transferred his grip to her elbow. "I won't let you fall," he said.

Samantha's dark eyes were full when she looked up at him. "Thank you," she said. "Oh, gods, Tain, what did I just do?"

He gave her a faint smile. "Chose your life."

Her eyes shone with fear. "What if it was the wrong choice?"

"There are no right and wrong choices," Tain said trying to keep his voice gentle. "There is only what we do with the choices we make."

She frowned. "Oh, great. Of all the Immortals, I had to get stuck with the philosopher."

He lifted one shoulder in a shrug. "It's what happens when you're a prisoner for seven hundred years."

Samantha laughed, and then shivered. "Let's get out of this hellhole. Isn't it making you sick?"

"It is. Serves me right for showing off for your cousin Tristan."

"He needed to be slapped, the little monster. I'll deal with him." Samantha's humor faded, and she put her warm hand in Tain's. "This is what I am, now."

"I know," Tain said, and led her back to Fulton's dining room.

***

"You're the what?" Hunter growled, then turned an accusing green glare on Tain. "She's the *what?*"

"The matriarch of the Lamiah clan," Tain said. "Pay attention."

Samantha stood in the middle of what used to be the matriarch's study in the basement of the matriarch's Beverly Hills mansion. Fulton had sent her here after the champagne had run out, explaining that she'd take over that very night. The majordomo had been terse when Samantha had arrived, but seemed to accept the decision of the clan as final. She'd stated that she still wanted to retire, but she'd help transition Samantha's new assistant, whoever that might be.

Samantha thought the woman's acceptance too quick, especially when she'd backed a different candidate, and resolved to keep an eye on her. Samantha had immediately called Leda and Hunter and invited them down, wanting to tell them in person why she wouldn't be returning to their house that night.

"So you're the leader of the demons now?" Hunter asked, his scowl in place.

"Just of this clan," Samantha corrected.

"Right. Sure," said Hunter the demon-hater. His gaze flicked to Tain and his tone turned to one of concern. "You going to be all right? The death magic is pretty heavy in here."

Tain gave him a brief, stoic nod, folding his arms over his coat. "I'm used to it."

"I know, but I had the idea you wanted nothing more to do with it. Ever."

Tain merely shrugged. He'd been quiet since the muster, staying close while they rode to the matriarch's mansion. He hadn't touched Samantha in the car one of the human drivers had chauffeured, but sat thigh-to-thigh with her, his bulk reassuring. He hadn't offered an explanation of where he'd been for the last few days, but then again, they hadn't yet been alone for a solitary moment.

Tain had been very protective of Samantha tonight, but she knew Hunter was right—Tain didn't belong with demons. He might stay around long enough to know that Samantha would be all right, maybe until they figured out who was cutting out demon hearts. But then he'd be gone, off to protect the next person who needed an Immortal. It was difficult to think about, but she'd have to face that sooner or later.

Hunter and Leda finally departed, Leda giving Samantha a tight hug before she went.

As soon as they walked out, the compound came on alert as a limousine delivering Septimus pulled up to where the gates had once been. Samantha gave word he could be admitted, and received him in one of the ground-floor rooms whose tasteful opulence matched Septimus's quiet elegance.

"This is a first," Septimus said smoothly when they were seated. "And a last. A vampire lord visiting a demon matriarch. Quite unprecedented."

"We can note that for the record," Samantha said. She'd decided on one of her female cousins as her secretary, a smart-looking young woman called Flavia, who even now sat in the room, her stylus poised over an electronic tablet.

Tain had left Samantha's office when word of Septimus's visit had come, saying he wanted to look around. Surprised, Samantha had said nothing, and he'd calmly walked out. She'd thought Tain would want to confront Septimus about the vampire having him followed and photographed, but Tain didn't seem interested—or maybe he had some idea up his sleeve he wasn't going to share with Samantha.

"So you're not with the police anymore?" Septimus asked once they were settled.

"I'll go in tomorrow and resign. But that doesn't mean I won't be in touch with my best friend Logan and keeping an eye on excessive vampire activity."

Septimus gave her an answering smile. "I'm sure you'll keep an even better eye on it now. And I'll be keeping my eye on *you*. I have the vampire interests in this town under my thumb, but you . . ." He leaned forward, his handsome face showing concern. "Ms. Taylor, the other clans will challenge you. You'll have to work hard for their respect, because respect is much more important than fear. They'll want to rule you, if they don't simply try to wipe you out."

"I'm aware of that." Fulton had already briefed Samantha on the other clans and what they could do, and on the strength of the Lamiah clan. The Lamiahs might have let themselves become civilized and citified, but they still had a private army.

"I can help you," Septimus offered. "You can have my strength behind you in an instant. All you have to do is ask."

Samantha sent him a skeptical look. "As smooth as ever, Septimus. Me having vampire backing would ostracize me from *all* the clans, leaving me completely dependent on you. I know what much."

Septimus shrugged, his dark eyes showing the shrewdness of centuries. This was a vampire who'd advised

Julius Caesar on how to take Rome, if Septimus's stories were to be believed. "Ah, well, I had to try." Septimus rose, holding out his hand. Samantha clasped it, knowing that their friendship, such as it was, would be distant and diplomatic now. "I wish you the best of luck."

"Thank you," Samantha said. "And I'll keep your offer in mind. You never know."

"That's true, you don't." Septimus swept her a bow then turned and walked out.

***

Samantha couldn't stand the thought of sleeping in the bedroom in which the previous matriarch had been killed, so she chose a generic guest room on the second floor. One of the staff had startled her when she'd chosen the room by going through the chamber and disabling about a dozen hidden cameras and bugs before letting her in. Apparently, the matriarch had liked to spy on her guests. Samantha had gone through the room again on her own, to satisfy for herself that *all* devices had been removed.

After Septimus departed, Samantha told Flavia good night and retreated to the bedroom, dismissing every member of staff who wanted to accompany her and wait on her, all the way up to tucking her into bed. Samantha very much wanted, and needed, to be alone.

She'd snapped off all the lights and stripped down to her underwear when she heard the locked door open. In a moment she felt a warmth behind her then strong hands on her abdomen, warm through her camisole.

"I hope that's you, Tain," she whispered in the darkness.

"Is that your idea of security?" he rumbled, leaning down to nip her ear. "Asking the intruder you hope it's who you think it is?"

Samantha leaned back against his hard body, feeling the tension in him. "No one else in this place has life magic pulsing like that."

Tain's lips grazed her neck, and Samantha's body responded, as tired as she was, warmth curling in her belly. Samantha craved Tain, and not just for his life essence.

"Are we going to talk now?" she asked. "You'll tell me about your adventures for the last week, and I'll tell you all about settling in as matriarch?"

"Not yet."

Part of Samantha chafed with impatience, wanting to know where he'd been and what he'd been doing, but another part thought maybe it was better if he didn't tell her.

Another nip, this time to her neck. "Tonight, no talking about feelings," Tain said, breath hot on her skin. "No discussing demons, no worrying about tomorrow."

"No?" Samantha closed her eyes, letting the fire of his touch slide through her. "Then what are we going to talk about?"

"You and me."

Samantha tensed a little. "What about you and me?"

"How I want you until I'm crazy with it."

Tain skimmed the spaghetti straps of her camisole from her shoulders and pushed the silk down her body. His lips brushed her neck, unshaved whiskers like fine sandpaper against her skin.

"You have to tell me what happened," she said, though without much conviction now. "I'm going insane not knowing."

She saw him in the full-length cheval mirror across the room, his red head bent to her, his suit coat and tie gone, his shirt a pale smudge in the gloom.

"I thought it would be a relief for you to be without me for a while," he said.

"No, it wasn't. I was afraid."

Tain touched his lips to her shoulder. "Hunter would have protected you from any danger. So would Leda and their pet lion."

"I meant I was afraid for you. I was afraid you'd gone insane again—and that you'd never come back."

Tain kissed the side of her neck. "I admit I came very close."

"Please tell me what happened."

He went silent for a time, kissing her neck, her bared shoulders, her back. Samantha thought he wouldn't answer at all when Tain said, "I was with Adrian."

"You went to Seattle?" Samantha hated to sound like an interrogator, but if she'd learned one thing about Tain, it was that she had to pry information from him one piece at a time.

He rumbled a negative, lips on her skin. "There's a monastery in the desert east of here, quiet and protected, no death magic. Adrian told me if I ever thought I was losing it, I should go there."

Samantha had read about a monastery way out at the foot of a desert mountain range, located at the end of a winding, unpaved road. It had been there since the eighteenth century, and had white arches, cool tiled floors, quiet bells, and silent monks.

"Did Adrian sense you were in trouble, and came to find you?" Samantha asked.

Tain chuckled, his breath tickling her. "No, I called him on my cell phone and told him. He flew down and met me there. We talked about a lot of things."

"Good." A tightness in her released. "I'm glad you weren't alone."

Another kiss, another brush of breath. "We talked about Old Ones and this case. And you."

Samantha tried a laugh. "I'm not sure I want to know what Adrian with the scary snake said about me."

"I will tell you, but not right now." Tain's voice went softer, his lilt pronounced, his breath burning. "You've taken no life essence since I left, have you?"

She swallowed. "You can tell?"

"You need to take it, Samantha. A human being can't go without water and sleep, a vampire can't survive without blood, and a demon can't live without life essence. You'll kill yourself if you go without too long."

"I'm coming to that conclusion." It dismayed Samantha to give in to her demon needs, and her instinct was to fight that. But she'd felt so awful the past few days, exhausted and sick with no relief, that she had to admit he was right.

Tain ceased speaking, and Samantha's camisole fell all the way down her body, crumpling to the floor at her feet. Tain bent to her, lips traveled down her spine until his hot breath touched the small of her back. Samantha shifted, loving the sensation of his mouth.

"Why do I crave it all the time?" she whispered. "I used to not even notice."

Tain sank to his knees and pressed a kiss to each of her silk-clad buttocks, then moved down to her thighs. His whiskers brushed the insides of her legs. "You need to let it come naturally."

He moved down to kiss the backs of her ankles, on hands and knees now, but he was hardly submissive.

"I don't know how to let it come naturally," Samantha said.

"I'll teach you."

"You're guarding me, not to mention you're an enemy of demons. How is it going to look if I'm hooked on your life essence?" At the moment, Samantha didn't much care.

"I don't plan on letting anyone watch. I'm not a—what do you call it in these times?—an exhibitionist."

"In these times? What was it called before?"

Tain's kisses moved to her calves again. "In the old days we called it *not enough rooms with doors.*"

Samantha had to laugh, which came out breathy. "I suppose I'm lucky to have privacy," she said as he continued to feather kisses up her legs. "I always need somewhere I can retreat and figure out how to get through another day."

"We all need a place to lick our wounds."

Right now Tain was licking the inside of her thighs. He hooked his fingers into the waistband of her panties and slid them down her legs.

"Do *you*?" she asked. "Need a place to lick your wounds?"

Tain kissed his way up her back as he rose to his feet then slid his strong hands around her waist from behind again. "Yes, but I don't want to retreat anymore. I want it all back."

"All what back?"

"My strength. My sanity." Tain kissed the corner of her mouth, enfolding her in his body and his warmth. "My ability to love a woman without fear."

Samantha caressed his strong hands where they lay on her abdomen. "Not an unreasonable thing to want."

Tain's voice was low, almost savage. "Everything I ever knew or loved was taken from me."

"I know." Samantha turned around in his arms, wishing she could give it all back to him. She undid buttons on his shirt. "Someone wanted me to think you'd killed the matriarch."

Tain put a finger under her chin to turn her face up to his. "I didn't. Do you believe me?"

Samantha nodded. "You asked me to trust you," she said softly. "And I do."

Tain looked at her for a long moment, his blue eyes unreadable. Then he leaned down to kiss her mouth. Samantha wanted to tell him she'd believed in him no matter what anyone tried to prove against him, but he kissed her until she couldn't breathe, and lifted her into his arms.

Samantha licked the bare curve of his neck, his skin hot and salty, while he carried her across the room. She expected him to lay her on the wide bed, but Tain stood her up in front of the mirror instead.

The mirror reflected not a dignified, powerful clan matriarch, but Samantha, her hair disheveled, her body naked and pale with Tain's strong brown arm across her abdomen. He looked delectable, his shirt parted and sliding off one shoulder, his kilt warm in the darkness.

She reached back to smooth her hand over his hip under the kilt, at the same time he slid his fingers to the space between her legs.

"Gods, you're beautiful," Tain murmured. She felt his teeth on the shell of her ear and his hand at her opening, which was hot and wet. "I used to dream only of darkness," he said, lifting his head to watch her in the mirror. "Now I dream of you."

Samantha's mouth was too dry for speech. She dreamed about Tain as well, about him coming to her hard and naked, making love to her until she forgot the world.

Tain curled his hand around hers and lifted her palm to his cheek. "Take it," he whispered. "Please. I won't hurt you this time."

Samantha hated how quickly her fingers moved to touch his face. She swallowed, nervous, fearing the bright hot pain that had seared her in his apartment.

"Don't be afraid," Tain said, his gaze on her in the mirror. "*Trust me.*"

It had been too long. Samantha's heart thumped as she let him press her palm to his tattoo.

Tain's life essence spilled quickly through her veins, finding and filling her. In the mirror she watched the tips of her breasts tighten and her eyes grow heavy.

"You need me," Tain said, his lips in her hair. "Let it happen."

With a groan, Samantha surrendered. Tain's hand went to his waistband as she pressed herself to him, and he slid off the kilt, baring himself for her.

He slowly moved in front of her and knelt, Samantha's hand still firmly on his cheek. With gentle fingers, Tain moved her legs apart, then he leaned forward and closed his mouth over her.

Samantha gasped and rocked her head back. Tain began to lick, then suckle, and Samantha moved against him, wanting more. His mouth was talented, her skin burning under it.

She'd never talked dirty to a man before, but she heard all kinds of wicked things come out of her mouth—what Tain made her feel like, what she wanted him to do to her. The half-smile on his face told her he heard her and liked it.

All the while he pleasured her, Tain's life essence roared into her. He filled her with what Samantha had denied herself, as though she'd been dying of thirst and was at last drinking cool spring water.

Just as ecstasy spiked through her, Tain wrenched his mouth away and got to his feet. Samantha whimpered, cold at the loss of his heat.

Tain lifted her in his strong arms and wrapped her legs around his hips, his mouth finding hers. She was slick and ready for him, so that when he positioned his tip against her, he slid easily inside.

Samantha arched back in his arms, dragging in a breath as he filled her, his strong embrace around her. His life essence flowed into her in a smooth stream, soothing Samantha's hurts as her psyche absorbed it.

She gave in to the feeling of him stretching her, and to the hot beating of her heart. Tain's fingers bit into her buttocks as he slid in further, filling her with every inch of him.

"I can't," she moaned.

"Yes, you can." Tain opened his eyes, which were nearly black, lights flickering inside them. "You can take all of me. You're so strong, my Samantha."

She ached where they joined, so full and hot that Tain moved easily, his arousal slick and stiff. She moved against him, feeling him drive deeper, and wanted it to go on forever.

Tain moved them to the bed, and Samantha cried out when he slowly lifted her off him, not wanting to lose him. Tain gently turned her over and deposited her on her hands and knees on the blankets.

Samantha lost contact with his life essence, but it didn't matter, because her skin was sparkling with it. Life essence tingled through her and only got better when Tain knelt behind her and thrust himself back inside her.

She dimly hoped the room was soundproof because she began to scream, long, glorious cries of ecstasy. Tain's hands were heavy on her back as he drove into her, his thrusts hard. Samantha came in an exquisite orgasm that went on and on, and still he rode her, building her up into another.

Samantha wasn't clear how long it went on, because she lost all sense of time and place. Sometime later, she found herself breathless and hoarse-voiced on the bed, Tain's large hot body on top of hers. She wanted to cry because it was all over, but Tain wrapped his strong arms around her and held her close.

Chapter Twenty-Three

The next day Samantha resigned her position with the paranormal police. Lieutenant McKay tried to convince her to stay on as a consultant, but Samantha declined, explaining that the rival demon clans wouldn't take well to having the Lamiah matriarch hand-in-glove with the police.

Logan better understood, werewolf packs sharing similarities with demon clans.

"You're one of the good ones, Samantha," Logan said to her regretfully as he walked her out to her truck. "I never thought I'd give a demon the time of day, but you proved me wrong. Are you sure you want to do this?"

"I need to," Samantha said.

Logan turned her to face him and rested his warm hands on her shoulders. "I hope you make time for the occasional werewolf visit."

"Always."

Samantha hugged him, tears trickling from her eyes. Logan held her hard. "Take care of yourself," he growled, and then he let her go.

***

Samantha rode back to the Beverly Hills mansion in the matriarch's limousine. The house was still being repaired from the Djowlan attack, workers fixing the security equipment and parts of the house that had been smashed before Tain had raised his protective shield.

While Samantha had gone downtown to talk to McKay, Tain had returned to the Malibu house to pack his things and hers and fetch Pickles. Samantha had been surprised Tain had let her go to the police department alone, but he'd heavily warded the matriarch's limousine until there were more protective spells on it than any other place in Los Angeles, vehicle or otherwise. Tain was at the mansion to greet Samantha on her return, Pickles grooming himself happily on the windowsill in Samantha's new first-floor office.

Tain's greeting kiss held a hint of the heat they'd shared last night, then said he wanted to poke around the basement where he'd found the shrine to the Old One and the portal to a death realm. Samantha was happy to let him. Portals leading to pissed-off demons or an Old One were not what she needed to deal with right now.

Flavia brought Samantha a cup of rich coffee, and Samantha sipped it as she continued going through mountain of files the last matriarch had left. Not much of the information was computerized, so if Samantha wanted to learn about her clan and its dealings with the outside world, she had to wade through the written files.

Samantha reflected darkly that she'd thought being a police detective required a lot of paperwork, but it was nothing compared to the accumulation of knowledge in the matriarch's offices. Ariadne, the majordomo, was a surprising help for sifting through the information, though she worked with tight lips and an expression of one hoping to get something painful over with soon.

Much of the information in the files concerned other members of the clan—their backgrounds and expertise and when and if they could be called on to help in times of need.

The information went back more than seven hundred years, and Samantha realized that some of the demons mentioned were still around.

There were also files on other clans — bios of their matriarchs, the locations of demon clans throughout the world and their activities. Samantha found information about Los Angeles since Los Angeles had first existed — who was in power in human society as well as vampire, werewolf, and other shifters — Chameleons, and the shamans and skinwalkers native to California.

There was enough information to pinpoint exactly who was doing what to whom at any given time, which, Samantha realized, was the point. The matriarch's power was not so much demon strength but knowledge and negotiation — much like being a good detective.

Samantha didn't find anything about Mindglow, which was suspicious. Merrick had had nothing to lose telling Logan that the matriarch had supplied it, and Samantha believed him. If the majordomo had known about the drug trafficking, she'd likely destroyed the records the night the matriarch died. Samantha said nothing to her now, but she wasn't going to let Ariadne quit before the woman answered some hard questions.

Samantha sipped coffee that Flavia had topped off and read the fat file on Septimus, which offered few surprises. As an Old One, the vampire could afford to be open about his activities, but he was also very diplomatic. He'd be a good ally to have, but Samantha knew that if he ever turned against her, she'd be in trouble.

She yawned as the majordomo set another stack of files on her desk. If Samantha insisted on staying awake all night to have sex with Tain, she mused with an inward smile, she should expect to be tired. Pulling all-night stakeouts with Logan had never wiped her out as much as a night full of sex with Tain. Not to mention how greedily she'd lapped up his life essence.

The life essence should have given her energy this morning. It had jolted through her last night, filling the emptiness inside her. Samantha had awakened alone, Tain already up and out warding the car, but she'd felt refreshed.

Now her limbs were heavy and tired, her thoughts straying too often to Tain kissing her as he made love to her. She'd had the best sex of her life last night. Maybe she and Tain could try to top it tonight.

Samantha found herself leaning back in her chair, her body glowing warm with need. "Has Tain come back upstairs yet?" she asked the majordomo, who picked up a file off her desk.

"No," Ariadne said with crisp disapproval. "I have made an appointment for you with the Djowlan matriarch for three o'clock tomorrow afternoon. She will come here. Tea in fine china, I think, in the front reception room."

"Yes, sounds terrific." Samantha stretched, running her fingers through her hair. She loved how her hair felt against her hands, silken soft, almost erotic. She let it fall against her neck, making a humming noise as tendrils tickled her skin.

"Matriarch?" the majordomo asked, mouth flattening. "Are you all right?"

Samantha blinked and sat up. "What is the matter with me? I was fine when I woke up." Worry worked its way through her strange happiness, and she shot a glance at the cup of coffee she'd just drained. "Oh, gods."

"What?" The majordomo leaned over the desk, her sharp face uglier than ever. "What has happened?"

"Mindglow," Samantha said. Then she laughed loudly. "There was Mindglow in the coffee. Merrick is right—this is wonderful stuff."

Ariadne snatched up the coffee cup and sniffed it. "I don't smell anything."

"You can't smell it. But it makes you . . . oh, so compliant."

Ariadne glared at the cup, glared at the closed office door, and then her eyes widened. "This is the coffee Flavia brought. I drank it, too."

Samantha laughed again, her eyes drifting closed as a pleasant heaviness took over her body. "Well, crap, then we're both screwed." Another wave of contentment swamped her, and through her blurred vision she saw the majordomo put her hand to her head and sit down hard on her office chair. Pickles broke off his grooming and eyed Samantha in concern.

"Find Tain," Samantha whispered to him, and then her lips wouldn't work anymore.

***

Tain went through the hidden door in the mansion's basement he'd discovered on previous explorations and descended the narrow, spiraling stone staircase beyond.

The first time he'd come down this set of stairs, he'd found a shrine at the bottom, set up to pay tribute to an ancient demon called Bahkat. Tain had never met this Bahkat, though Kehksut had talked of him. Bahkat was another Old One of great power, though he rarely ventured out of his hell realm.

Tain had destroyed the shrine, smashing the offering bowl and breaking the altar. The portal to the death realm beyond it had opened, the demons who guarded Bahkat pouring out to attack Tain. Tain had quickly killed the few demons who'd made it out before he'd sealed the portal, then he'd gone downtown to the No More Nightmares building to the destroy the portals he'd sensed through this one.

Now, the altar was back, bearing half-burned candles, a bowl with demon runes on it, and garlands of dried herbs snaking around the candles. The bowl held a heart, black, shriveled, and stinking. Tain covered his mouth against the stench and burned the heart away with a short burst of magic.

He'd thought the matriarch had set up the shrine, she offering Bahkat hearts of demons she didn't like in return for favors from the Old One. But then the matriarch had died by the same method as the demon prostitutes, and someone in the house had clearly re-erected the shrine a week or so after the matriarch's death. Someone was asking an Old One for power, and that spelled grave danger for Samantha.

Tain studied the map that had been pinned above the shrine. To anyone unfamiliar with demons, the map would look like concentric rings radiating from a central point with cryptic runes around each. Tain, on the other hand, knew the map pointed out portals to the death realm that opened around the city and region. Demon script noted that the portals at the No More Nightmares building had been destroyed "by the Enemy." Tain smiled. He liked that they'd capitalized *Enemy*, even in demon.

He stopped smiling when he saw the most distant portal that had been marked on it. That one came out in the canyon in the Nevada desert, high up in the cliff dwellings. His blood went cold. Tain had known there was something very wrong out there, but he hadn't been able to decide what.

It made sense now. Because of the magic drain of the vortex, the portal would be difficult to detect from the desert side and be plenty protected. It also explained the waft of death magic he'd sensed that propelled Ms. Townsend of No More Nightmares across the cliffs — likely someone had opened the portal, and it had pulled her to it, just as the portal above the building downtown had sucked in the last of the attacking demons.

Tain drew one of his swords. It took death magic to open the way into the death realms, and Tain hummed with life magic. But Tain had also spent seven hundred years in thrall to the most ferocious demon Old One of all, and he'd learned to draw on death magic and channel it when he needed to.

He didn't like how easy it was for him to tap the dark magic from both the shrine and the mansion full of demons above him, how painlessly it flowed through him and down the sword.

The sword sliced open the portal to the death realm with ease, and Tain stepped inside.

***

Logan piled what he'd found on a long table in front of McKay. "It's all here," he said. "Tons of clippings of newspaper headlines, paper, glue, scissors, lists of demons all over Los Angeles—names, addresses, family connections, where they work, what they do on their days off—the FBI couldn't put info like this together."

"And you arrested this Tristan?"

"He's in the cells," Logan said. "He wasn't hard to find, and he seemed plenty proud that he sent the threatening letters—or at least got his human groupies to send them where he directed. That's why we didn't detect any death magic on the letters themselves—his human addicts did the grunt work."

McKay beamed up at Logan, her half-Sidhe beauty shining. "Please tell me he confessed to the kidnappings and the murders, named all his accomplices, and then signed the confession."

"Sorry, boss," Logan said, and McKay gave a resigned sigh. "He insists he didn't do the killings or kidnappings, and he wants his lawyer. But we pretty much got him on the terrorizing letters."

"Oh, well. I didn't really think it would be nice and neat."

"He must know who's doing it, though," Logan said. "Lawyer or no lawyer, if we can get him to give away his buddies or whoever employed him, we can close the case."

"He said nothing about the canyon in Nevada?" McKay asked.

"No. I'd swear he had no clue what I was talking about when I mentioned it."

"What has the sheriff there told you?"

"Not a damn thing. She said neither she nor her deputies could find anything out of the ordinary, just another canyon that woo-woo people like to call a vortex. A collection of energies. She thinks it's all bullshit."

McKay grimaced. "Unfortunately, we need their cooperation if it really is something, or we'll have to make it a federal case, which I'm not in a hurry to do. On the other hand . . ." She gave Logan a look. "I can't stop you hiking into a canyon in Nevada on your day off."

Logan nodded. "I'd planned to check it out."

McKay held up her small hands. "Not that I know about this."

Logan grinned. "Know about what?"

As he started to turn away, his cell phone vibrated in his pocket. He pulled out the phone and smiled when he saw Samantha's number on the display. He already missed talking to her.

However, it wasn't Samantha who shouted at him as soon as he lifted the phone to his ear. "They're gone!" a woman yelled.

"What? Who's gone? Who is this?"

"Samantha is gone," the woman said, distraught. "I'm Flavia, her cousin. Someone put Mindglow in the coffee. When I went into the matriarch's office, she was gone—she and the majordomo both."

"Slow down a minute," Logan said, his heartbeat speeding. "What about Tain? Where is he?"

"I don't know. I can't find him anywhere. There was one of those letters in cutouts left on Samantha's chair." Flavia faltered, crying. "It says, *The Final Sacrifice.*"

***

Samantha awoke in pitch dark. Her head pounded and made her sick, not helped by the fact that she lay facedown on something hard, her ankles and wrists tightly bound with what felt like duct tape. She was happy to find she hadn't been gagged, but her mouth was so dry it didn't much matter.

"Damn it," she croaked. "Is this what Mindglow does to you?"

"I certainly hope not," a male voice rumbled. "Or I've been getting ripped off."

"Merrick?" Samantha groaned. "Hell, I'd decided you were innocent of all this."

"I am innocent, sweetheart. I'm lying here trussed up hand and foot, and I have the feeling the next heart in a box will be mine."

Not good. "You can't become your bad demon self and break your way out?" she asked hopefully.

"Oh *gee*, I never thought of that. The answer is no, I can't. I've never felt this weak and sick in my life. All I can do is lie here and spout feeble sarcasm."

"If I can find you, do you think we can get each other untaped?"

"Worth a try," Merrick grunted. "Not that I expect it to do any good. I imagine if there *was* any way out of this pit, they'd have chained us to the walls to keep us from finding it."

"Who's they?" Samantha asked.

"Hell if I know. I never saw their faces."

Samantha spent the next few minutes trying to roll in the dark, hearing Merrick doing the same. It took a long time, but eventually she landed on her side and felt the warmth of him behind her. She groped for Merrick's wrists and found slick tape around them. She felt his fingers connect with the tape on *her* wrists and start picking at it.

"Demon claws would be handy about now," Samantha said.

Merrick growled. "Your warrior lover and his big swords would be handy about now too, even if he did almost cut my head off once. I'll forgive him if he gets me out of here."

"You hit me."

Merrick jumped. "Pardon?"

"In your club, you hit me," Samantha said. "That's why Tain tried to cut off your head. He didn't do it all the way, because a headless man can't learn a lesson."

Merrick kept picking at the tape. "Very, very funny, and anyway, you'd just shoved a gun in my face."

"I was making an arrest for possession of Mindglow."

"*Hypothetical* possession of Mindglow. My club has burned to the foundations now, so it's a moot point. Funny how my life has gotten so exciting since I met you."

"Pure coincidence," Samantha said.

"Really? I wonder. Ah, I think I might have found an edge to the tape. I've always hated this stuff."

For silent moments, Merrick tugged and pulled at the bonds on Samantha's wrist until she heard a hiss of tape being ripped from tape. After an infuriatingly long time, the tape was loose enough for Samantha to pull it free. She lay still, her aching arms at her sides, wincing as circulation returned to her fingers.

"Will you be returning the favor any time soon?" Merrick asked, his voice as rasping as hers.

"Give me a second to get the feeling back into my hands," Samantha said wearily. "It's not like we're going anywhere."

"True."

When Samantha felt well enough to roll to her knees, she groped for Merrick's wrists.

"Once we get out of here," Merrick said as she started working at his bonds, "how about we ditch your sword-toting boyfriend and spend a wild weekend in Vegas?"

Samantha snorted. "I don't think so."

"You think matriarchs don't fool around with their underlings? The previous one certainly did."

"Really?" Samantha asked in surprise.

Merrick chuckled. "Oh, my, yes. When she was younger, especially. She'd host orgies and join right in. She liked sex, with men or women, she didn't care which."

Samantha patiently picked at the tape. "Weird, she seemed so straight-laced when I met her. Very disapproving of Nadia and her sister — even of demon women working in the clubs."

"In her later years she calmed down," Merrick said, grunting when one of Samantha's nails nicked his wrist, "but she certainly got a lot out of her system in her youth. She'd have humans, demons, vampires, shifters — used her position to find the best-looking of the bunch and command them to be brought to her. She had sex with them and sucked down life essences like there was no tomorrow."

"And yet she was so snotty about Nadia," Samantha said, remembering her meeting with the matriarch. "No sympathy whatsoever."

"Ah, but the matriarch didn't *sell* her services or exchange anything for life essence. She wasn't a prostitute. Stayed home like a good girl and used the power of her rank to get whatever she wanted."

"Maybe that's why she was murdered," Samantha said thoughtfully. "Someone whose life essence she gobbled held an old grudge. Or the relative of someone she used."

"Could be. Or it could be the killer knew *you* were likely to be the next matriarch and wanted you in power."

Samantha's fingers stilled. "Why on earth should they?"

"Who knows? Maybe whoever it was wants to control you, like the majordomo controlled the matriarch and planned to control her protégé, Ariel."

"How did you know about that?"

"Everyone knew, my dear. A demon clan is a hotbed of gossip, as you will learn soon enough. You know, this tape isn't coming off by itself."

Samantha resumed the task. "You're an asshole, Merrick."

"But a very shrewd one, don't forget that."

"What am I doing here?" Samantha said to herself as the tape started to give. "A few weeks ago I wasn't doing anything more difficult than staking out demon clubs. All the sudden I'm hunting people who cut out demon hearts and becoming a demon matriarch."

"And screwing an Immortal warrior."

Samantha scowled in the dark. "*That* is none of your business."

"It is my business now that you're the matriarch. We're death magic, and Tain's life magic knocks us over. We demons are wondering when he'll turn around and kill us all — he's nearly killed me already. Besides, if you haven't guessed it yet, an Immortal warrior isn't the kind of man you settle down with."

Samantha's heart squeezed until it hurt. "Neither are you."

Merrick laughed, the sound harsh in the darkness. "I never claimed to be, but I can make that weekend in Vegas the best of your life."

"Save it." Samantha peeled the tape from Merrick's wrists, and he sat up, rubbing them.

Samantha worked on the tape around her ankles, and from the sounds in the dark, Merrick was as well. She got herself free first and massaged her bloodless feet.

"Now what?" she asked, trying to looking around. It was so dark she could see nothing, not even shapes in the gloom. The air smelled close and dank, more chilled than the September weather should make it. "I think we're underground," she concluded.

"You have amazing powers of deduction, my love." The sound of tape ripping told her Merrick was peeling it away from his ankles. "But there must be air coming in or we'd be dead by now."

Samantha got shakily to her feet and instantly regretted it. She held her stomach, struggling for breath, her head spinning.

"I wasn't hard to capture was I?" she said, angry at herself. "They carried me off without a struggle."

"*I* struggled," Merrick said. "Until they shot me with a tranquilizer."

"Who did?"

"I don't know. Obviously someone crazy. They abducted me as I was leaving the muster."

"Someone from the house in Santa Barbara?" Samantha immediately thought of Tristan, her disgruntled cousin. He'd been very angry that Samantha had won.

"No, no," Merrick said. "I never went into the house. I have a portal to the Lamiah realm at my old club. The club might be gone, but the portal's still there. One minute I'm walking out of the club's ruins, minding my own business, the next, I'm waking up here, sick as a dog. I bet there are snakes down here."

"They hibernate when it's cold," Samantha told him, refusing to think about sharing wherever they were with a mass of snakes. "I wonder who else they plan to take." Her heart thumped in fear as she thought of Fulton, head of the most prominent household in the clan.

"There might not be snakes down here," Merrick said as he got to his feet, his clothes rustling in the dark. "But scorpions are highly likely."

Samantha made a noise of impatience. "You're a big, bad demon, Merrick. Are you afraid of a few insects?"

"Ones that sting? Yes." Merrick turned, scraping on rock. "So what's your great plan, oh my matriarch?"

"My great plan is to get out of here."

"Now why didn't I think of that? Any ideas how, brilliant one?"

"No," Samantha snapped. She found a wall, smooth and seamless, and felt her way along it. "Just help me look for a way out."

"You know," Merrick said as he joined her, "in movies, when the hero or heroine gets captured, sometimes the helpful secondary character dies during the escape. To give the film that touch of pathos."

"This isn't a movie," Samantha said abruptly.

"The question is, whose movie is this? Yours or mine?"

"Merrick." Samantha rested her hands against the wall. "We're both getting out of here, neither one of us dying. That's my job, not just to uphold and enforce the law, but to protect others."

"You're not a police officer any more, my dear."

"No, but I'm the matriarch, for better or worse." Samantha's conviction grew as she spoke. "It's my job to keep the clan from falling apart, which means I protect those within it. At the moment, that means you."

"Hmm." Merrick continued to tap on the wall, shuffling next to Samantha. "Then I know what kind of movie this is."

He wouldn't say what he meant by that, and they worked their way around the room in silence.

Chapter Twenty-Four

The chill of the death realm filmed Tain's skin like half-dried sweat. He found himself in a vast room, very unlike the elegant, marble-pillared chamber Fulton had taken them to for the muster. This chamber had crumbling square columns carved with strange square designs, as though someone had decided to mock the clean lines of the Native American petroglyphs etched into the canyon walls outside.

A demon woman stood in the middle of this room, black-haired and sensual, glammed to look young and lush. She wore a gauzy wrap pinned at the shoulder, similar to those depicted in Egyptian paintings, with thick gold bands clasping her wrists and upper arms. Her smile was sultry, but Tain saw in her liquid dark eyes the steel sharpness of the woman who had been Ariadne, the Lamiah matriarch's majordomo.

The woman was not what created the miasma of darkness that filled this room, however. The majordomo was a lesser demon, easy to deal with.

The evil Tain sensed in the darkness behind her was so vast it made his stomach churn. It had been a year since he'd been in the presence of an Old One, but the death magic rolling off the demon called Bahkat was unmistakable. The thick touch of it found Tain, pressing on him, calling to him. The lesser demon woman in front of him was a minute distraction compared to the clamoring need building in Tain to follow the Old One into that darkness.

Tain tried to focus on the majordomo. "Who are you?" he asked.

"Haven't you guessed?" She came to Tain and touched his chest, but her fine-nailed caress did nothing against the death magic beating on him from behind her. "I am the matriarch of the Lamiah clan."

Tain snapped his gaze to her, the surprise of her words breaking his contact with the Old One. The woman looked up at him with glee in her dark eyes, but Tain shook his head. This woman was the majordomo, he was sure of it.

"The matriarch died," he said. "I saw her body—what was left of it."

"No, simpleton. *That* was my majordomo, playing the part I gave her. *I* am the real matriarch."

Tain studied her, able to see beyond the demon glam of the beautiful woman in the Egyptian tunic and gold to the ugly, harsh beast beneath. He'd glimpsed what had been behind the glams of the majordomo and matriarch as they'd stood side-by-side at the mansion—he'd known their demons looked different, but there'd been nothing to tell him which was matriarch and which was underling.

The demon gazing up at him now still held the form of the demon they'd been introduced to as the majordomo. Plus, the woman they'd met as the matriarch and the woman who'd been murdered had definitely been the same. If the majordomo and matriarch had switched places, it had been before her death.

"How long had the majordomo been playing this part?" Tain asked her.

The demon who was the matriarch smiled. "Nearly nine hundred years. She put on pearls and met with the heads of clans while I did as I pleased and went where I wanted, discovering oh, so many things. It was wonderful—having all that power and being able to move about as I wished at the same time. I was very young when I became matriarch. In those days, matriarchs were inaccessible, and in time there were no more demons alive who remembered what I looked like. The new generations had no idea." She laughed. "Ariadne gave me great freedom. Her kind were born to serve, after all."

Tain's eyes narrowed at her glib speech. "If you had so much power and freedom, why did you need to start calling to the Old One?"

The matriarch's smile widened, the black in her eyes spreading to fill the whites. "Oh, I didn't *start* calling to him. I've been with him from the beginning. I've always preferred the company of Old Ones. They know what it is to have all bow before them."

"In ancient times, maybe," Tain said. "Now they hide in death realms and don't like to walk the surface of the earth."

"No thanks to you and your Immortal brothers." The matriarch lost her amused look, her beauty dimming with her anger. "You drove my master underground, and you killed Kehksut, the most beautiful of them all."

Tain couldn't stop his flinch at the sound of Kehksut's name, but he forced his voice to remain even. "It's what I was made to do," he said, sounding off-hand. "Call it my raison d'être."

"Ha. You were Kehksut's slave, and then you killed your own master. For that, you will be punished."

Tain pinned the matriarch with his stern gaze. "You've sacrificed demons of your own clan. The new matriarch is pretty pissed off about it."

The woman gave him a deprecating look. "The new matriarch has no power. The Lamiah clan is weak—more interested these days in buying stocks and shopping the latest fashions than acquiring human slaves and power. They've been *yuppified*."

"And so they deserve death?" Tain asked.

"They deserve to be utterly destroyed," the matriarch said calmly.

"Not all the demons that were killed were Lamiah," Tain pointed out.

The matriarch shrugged, her loose dark hair sliding across perfect shoulders and catching in one of her gold armbands. "I can't help it if the Townsend woman is too stupid to distinguish one clan from the other. But they were good kills, and helped blind the pathetic paranormal police to my true purpose."

"Who sent the threatening letters for you? " Tain asked, wanting to keep her talking while he tried to figure out what the Old One behind her was doing. "No More Nightmares?"

"I got Samantha's foolish cousin Tristan to do it. He was easy to manipulate, wanting more power than he could handle. I promised to back his candidate for matriarch, and he jumped to do anything I told him. I look forward to ripping out his heart."

"And Samantha?" Tain asked, sending the smallest bit of his magic into the corners. "Why did you want Samantha to become the matriarch?"

Tain's magic was weak, dying off before it went very far, the death realm pressing at him. His first instinct was to flee back to the matriarch's mansion and try to seal the portal—if he'd be able to find that exit now that he was in the Old One's realm.

But Tain knew that, if he didn't confront this Old One, the Old One would only grow in power, using his puppet, the matriarch playing the majordomo, to do it. The Old One had a nice thing going out here behind a magic-sucking vortex, a perfect place from which to plot his attacks. If Tain didn't destroy him, Samantha would be vulnerable.

Tain's power, however, was diminished in the death realms, not to mention in the magic-draining vortex outside in the canyon. This could get tricky.

The matriarch laughed. "I needed Samantha because of you, of course. Did you really think I'd want a half blood to take over the clan? She'll not last past the first challenge to her authority. Another reason I told Tristan I'd back his girlfriend was because I knew damn well the rest of the clan would balk at anyone Tristan put forward, and they'd beg Samantha to save them from such a fate. Fulton was easy to flatter, and he convinced Samantha she had to become matriarch for the good of the clan."

"He wasn't wrong," Tain said softly.

The matriarch ignored him. "The *true* reason I chose Samantha in particular—and not just any demon woman in the clan—was because of you. The Immortal warrior who killed Kehksut would be a wonderful gift to bring to my master, Bahkat."

Tain looked down at her from his height, letting his voice grow icy. "What makes you believe I will let you make me your gift?"

"Because Samantha will be the next to die if you *don't* let me." The matriarch touched his chest again, the gold band on her wrist glinting. "You hate demons, but you're addicted to them, and you know it. Why else would you be sniffing at the skirts of a half blood? I know exactly how to make you obey."

Tain said nothing. He knew his love for Samantha had nothing to do with addiction and everything to do with *her*. Kehksut was dead, the ancient, powerful demon master dissolved into dust. Kehksut had broken Tain with pain and loneliness, despair and madness. Samantha had slowly but surely dragged him back into the light.

The matriarch's body shimmered and took on the features of Kehksut in her female form. Tain knew it was a glam, but the matriarch had down to the last detail what Kehksut had looked like in Tain's eyes—the curve of body with plump breasts, the black dress that hugged every bend of her, the long red-painted nails, the fall of black hair that was too much like Samantha's.

"Kehksut was one of my lovers," the matriarch said in Kehksut's seductive tones. "He told me all about you."

The Old One's voice rolled out of the darkness as he came toward them. "Kehksut was one of my lovers too, Immortal. I have brought you here for *my* vengeance."

Tain drew his swords and held them ready, but here the death magic rendered them only so much metal.

He seemed to hear Hunter's voice in his head: *Yeah, but metal with an edge.*

The matriarch smiled, her eyes shining. "Have I pleased you, master?"

The demon Bahkat chuckled, a chill sound. "You have pleased me well. Enjoy him as you wish."

Darkness rolled from the shadows and hit Tain like a heavy weight, and when his vision cleared, time had passed and things had changed. He'd had been stripped to the waist, his hands chained behind him around a square pillar.

"This is what you're used to, isn't it?" the matriarch purred, in her own guise again. She came close to Tain and drew her fingernails lightly down his bare chest. "Kehksut told me about what you liked and what you craved, and how he did it to you." She pressed her palm flat between his pectorals. "Your heart is racing now. Is it fear? Or anticipation?"

Tain tensed his muscles, but the chains that held him were extra thick and spelled with death magic. The blanket of Bahkat's magic over everything made Tain sick and exhausted.

"A little of both, I think," Bahkat said, still in the shadows.

The matriarch reached behind Tain then showed him a long, hooked knife. "I think I'll enjoy this. Feel free to scream when it hurts."

She touched the point of the knife to Tain's neck, and Tain closed his eyes, the comforting black of madness swirling in to coat his brain.

***

Samantha made a complete circuit of the smooth-walled prison she and Merrick were in without finding so much as a crack in the rock. The walls were natural, not manmade, the stone polished by weather and time.

"You see?" Merrick said when she stopped, frustrated. "They knew it didn't matter if we unbound ourselves. There's no way out if you don't have climbing gear or a lot of magic."

"Don't sell me short," Samantha said, irritated. "I'm pretty resourceful—I was trained to be."

"Yes, at the police academy, where you were taught how to bring down demons and hungry vamps." He sounded weary.

"Exactly."

"Did you learn orienteering as well?" Merrick asked, his patient voice grating on her nerves. "As in maybe figuring out where the hell we are? This doesn't feel like death realm, but it doesn't feel like the sewers of Los Angeles either."

"I think we're in the place Tain and Logan told me about," Samantha said. "A canyon in Nevada, in the middle of the desert."

"Wonderful. That means if we do manage to get out, we'll be miles from civilization, with no water."

"One thing at a time," Samantha said.

"If your boyfriend knows about this place, shouldn't he have rescued you by now?" Merrick rubbed his arms. "It's getting damn cold down here. Even demons can get hypothermia."

"Shh," Samantha said sharply.

"I'm merely pointing out that if we don't die of thirst, we will certainly freeze to death . . ."

"*Quiet.* I'm trying to listen."

Merrick snapped his mouth shut, and the darkness went still. Samantha strained for the sound that had come from far above, but she heard only Merrick breathing next to her and the skitter of an insect as it scurried across the rock face.

"Not hearing anything," Merrick said softly.

"Wait."

The sound came again, muffled and far away, but she knew it because it was familiar. Far off in the desert, a wolf was howling.

Samantha's heart beat faster. "That's Logan."

"How do you know?" Merrick asked. "There's probably another werewolf pack out here somewhere. I know there's at least three in Vegas."

Samantha wanted to laugh with joy. "Because every wolf has a unique cry, and that's Logan's. I worked with him for more than a year—I got to know what he sounds like. It was useful when we had to split up while investigating."

"All right, I'll believe you, but how do you know he's come to help you and not bury you?"

Samantha stared at Merrick, trying to see him in the dark. "Why would he do that? I know Logan—he'll rescue us."

"No, you only *think* you know him. It's amazing what we can make ourselves believe when we want to." Merrick touched her hand where it rested on the rock. "Why do you think he's in Los Angeles playing lone wolf? He was forced out of his pack, that's why."

Samantha stopped. "How the hell do you know that?"

"My dear, when you and your partner busted up my club, I made sure I found out everything I could about the pair of you. For leverage, of course. A few phone calls to an old friend in St. Paul, and voila."

Samantha wanted to know more, but she didn't want to hear it from Merrick. Not that she could completely trust everything that came out of his mouth, in any case. "It's none of my business," she said quickly.

"It is entirely your business. As matriarch, you need to learn that any anomaly can spell danger, and to keep your eye on it."

Samantha knew he was right, and knew with a sinking heart that being matriarch gave her the potential of becoming just like Merrick, or Septimus with his network of vampire spies. As a police officer and detective, Samantha had always believed herself to be one of the good guys. As matriarch, though, she had the chance to become vastly powerful, to make her world one where the line between good and evil blurred. That was how Merrick lived his life and Septimus lived his.

She also realized that Tain walked that line every day, deciding whether to help and heal or use his power to destroy.

The howl came again, closer now. Samantha beat her hands on the wall. "I'll never have the chance to be matriarch if I don't get out of here. Logan!" she shouted.

Merrick danced aside, rocks scraping. "Warn me next time you're about to bellow like that. I think you shattered my eardrum."

"Help me, then. It's your ass on the line too."

"Good point."

They both began shouting Logan's name. Far above Samantha, something moved, rock on rock, and then pebbles trickled down on them. Merrick cursed, but Samantha peered upward. Was it her imagination, or could she see a faint outline against a smudge of light?

What she didn't imagine was the solid *click* of a shotgun being cocked and starlight gleaming on a very long barrel pointed right at her.

***

Tain's skin healed rapidly, as it always did, but blood ran in rivulets down his chest and pooled in the waistband of his jeans. The matriarch didn't flay him carefully as Kehksut had—she simply cut his flesh over and over again.

The excessive power Tain had acquired through his captivity, which he'd spent the last year and a half getting used to, now drained away, leaving him weak, but he no longer cared. He'd realized in the last few weeks that magical strength meant little unless you knew exactly how and why to wield it.

Samantha always thought she had very little power, but she was wrong. Samantha had an inner strength that could quiet the entire city of Los Angeles. She'd come to a crazed, out-of-control Immortal who'd been ready to destroy the world to heal his pain, and snapped at him to stop being selfish. Then she'd taken in that same Immortal warrior, who'd been defeated and bewildered, terrified he'd slide back into the dark place, and she'd trusted him.

Samantha kept giving of herself, and that giving was far more powerful than Tain's magic was or ever could be. Tain had to face that she meant more to him than anything else in any world, and that if he lost her, he'd face immeasurable grief.

This was sane, human hurt, and the fact that Tain could feel it was the gift Samantha had given him.

The matriarch wasn't finished. After she cut Tain's exposed flesh in crisscross patterns, she whipped him, her gold bands tinkling with every lash. She knew exactly where to aim each stroke, how to find the welts of his cuts and open them again.

Bahkat said nothing, neither gloating nor laughing. He just stood with his arms folded over his bare chest and watched. He'd taken the guise of a man before he walked out into the light, handsome of course, with smooth skin over a well-muscled body, black hair in a short buzz, and very blue eyes. He wore jeans only, and his naked arms were covered in tattoos, demon runes that contained spells of power.

"Kehksut's killer," he said to Tain in a matter-of-fact voice. "You don't seem up to much at the moment. Why did you kill Kehksut? You loved him."

"You're wrong," Tain said, his voice a rasp. "I hated him."

"He let me watch sometimes, did you know that?" Bahkat asked. "I got to see how he flayed every bit of skin off you, then took a female form and sexed you. You used to beg him for it."

Tain forced his mind to go blank, trying not to remember, but the scenes welled up before he could stop them. Kehksut smiling much as the matriarch was now, the horrible agony as Tain's skin was peeled from his body, the strange ecstasy of sex as his flesh began to heal. Over and over it had happened, until Tain hadn't been able to distinguish pain from joy.

The fact that this demon, Bahkat, had watched Tain's torture for his entertainment made Tain's rage rise. He might be without magical power in this place of death, but he was still a warrior, trained long ago by his father and other soldiers of Rome, some of the best fighting men who'd ever lived.

He twisted his body and kicked the matriarch in the stomach. She lost hold of the whip and stumbled back. "Bastard," she snarled.

Bahkat shoved her aside and stood directly in front of Tain as Tain regained his balance. "You don't understand how to make him pay," he said to the matriarch. "You only play at torture. We will make him so insane with the pain that he'll do anything for us. Then the first thing we'll make him do is kill the pretty half-demon he's been banging like a lovesick rabbit."

Tain's heart constricted. He wasn't certain what he feared more—the two of them hurting Samantha or himself being pushed into madness and hurting her for them.

Never, he thought. *Samantha is my salvation, and I will never let her be touched. This I vow by all the gods.*

Bahkat picked up one of Tain's swords, the bronze that had been forged nearly two thousand years ago by a master Roman sword maker in faraway Britain. The demon examined the weapon, tracing the Roman runes of protection on it, then tested the blade on his thumb.

"Excellent workmanship," Bahkat said. He drew the sword back, his muscles rippling, and drove its point straight through Tain's left eye.

Tain's scream rang through the vast cavern, hollow echoes overlapping each other on the way back to him.

***

"Keep your hands where I can see them," a slow male voice came down to Samantha.

"You can't see anything down here," Merrick returned. "It's pitch black. Are you with the wolf? If not, I'm not coming anywhere near where you can see me."

There was a little silence as though the man with the gun was working through this. "Just don't move."

"Is Logan with you?" Samantha called up to him.

"He's here," the man said. "He can't answer, being a wolf right now and all. You Samantha? Tain's girl?"

"Yes, that's me."

"And her friend," Merrick put in. "Her *best* friend."

"Good thing I brought a rope," the man said. "Looks like that's the only way you're going to get out." He withdrew the shotgun and lifted one hand in a wave. "Hi there. I'm Ed, by the way."

"Hi, Ed," Samantha said in a weak voice.

"You sit tight. We'll get you outta there."

Samantha backed away from the opening as a rope came hurtling down. When she looked up again, she saw a wolf shape outlined against the stars.

"Thanks, partner," she said in relief.

The wolf made a brief huffing noise then backed away, letting the humans do their work.

Samantha knew how to tie a rope around a person so they could be pulled up without hurting them or cutting off their breath. She insisted Merrick be hauled up first, and he didn't protest too hard.

Merrick half-climbed the rock wall as he was towed upward. He made it out safely with only some cursing on his part, mostly about his clothes. When the rope came back down, Samantha fixed it around herself and let Ed haul her up.

When she reached the top, rolling out with the help of Ed and another man, she lay on solid rock and gratefully breathed the fresh, dry air. Stars stretched above her thick and bright, unmarred by pollution or clouds.

Logan bent over Samantha, his lupine nose touching her face. She used Logan's strong shoulder to brace herself while she sat up, still feeling the effects of the Mindglow or whatever drug had been slipped in her coffee.

Two men stood next to Logan, both with graying hair and stubbled chins. The one with the gun, Ed, introduced the other as his buddy Mike.

"Is Tain with you?" she asked them.

Ed shouldered his shotgun. "Nope. Logan here called us, saying he's Tain's friend, and can we meet him outside this canyon? He said Tain disappeared, and he thought maybe you were together. Then Logan changed into a wolf — that was a sight, I tell you — and he hasn't changed back since we walked into the canyon. He told us he might not be able to, because of this vortex thing."

Samantha blew out her breath, her heart thumping in worry. "So we're in the place Tain thought was being used by No More Nightmares."

"Looks like. That's what Logan said anyway. Tain's not with *you* then?"

"No." Samantha felt sick. "Do you have a phone? I can call him."

Ed shook his head. "Logan's already tried to find him, and he said some woman at your place says he'd been nabbed too. Girl was hysterical, he said."

"Flavia?" Samantha felt both worried and a little relieved. She'd liked and trusted Flavia, and she hoped her cousin had nothing to do with this abduction. The majordomo, on the other hand, clearly hadn't been abducted with Samantha. Was the majordomo a victim, or in on the plot?

Samantha looked around. She sat on stone in a box canyon, the walls of which rose high around them. Moonlight glittered on the white walls, picking out black outlines of petroglyphs. "Now what?" she asked.

"We go up to the cliff dwellings," Ed said. "That's what Logan told me we had to do. He also said to give you this. Mike?"

Mike, who'd said not a word, stepped forward, unbuckled a shoulder holster with Samantha's Glock, and handed gun and holster to her. Samantha took it gratefully. She slid out the gun and checked it, finding it loaded, then slipped it back into the holster.

"Looks like everyone's armed but me," Merrick said, sitting down on a boulder. "And here I am with diminished powers. Anyone mind if I wait in the car? If you brought a car, that is, and if you'll tell me where it is."

"That might be a good idea," Samantha said. Merrick couldn't help much in his weakened state, and Samantha felt responsible for him now. "Ed, can you and Mike show him where your car is? Logan will lead me back once we check this place out."

Mike immediately nodded, but Ed needed to be persuaded. He'd taken to Tain and wanted to help find him. When Ed started insisting he go with Samantha, however, Logan got in front of him and snarled, ears flat, muzzle pulling back from his teeth. The snarl wasn't directed at Samantha, but she felt the power of it, the instant authority that told Samantha, more than Tain's and Merrick's speculations could, that Logan was high in his pack.

Ed only saw a giant snarling timber wolf a few feet from him. He swallowed and nodded.

Merrick sighed in relief and followed Mike down a path, Mike shining a lantern flashlight ahead of them. Ed came behind, his shotgun in his hands.

Samantha shouldered ropes and a pack of gear Logan had brought and looked around the canyon. The floor of it was strewn with enormous boulders and rock slabs, as though giants had cast them from a dice cup. Cliff dwellings were tucked on a shelf under an overhang high above Logan and Samantha, the native peoples having the wisdom to protect themselves both from above and below.

"Up there?" Samantha looked in dismay at the rough trail that led more or less upward. "Seriously?"

Logan growled. Samantha knew from experience that he was both impatient and amused.

Drawing a breath, Samantha began to climb, going carefully over the gravel which slid out from under her shoes. She was wearing slacks and nice loafers, clothes for an office, not for clambering around canyons. Her clothes would be in shreds by the time she found Tain—if he was even here.

Logan kept up with her, his huge paws finding purchases Samantha missed. Logan could also leap from ledge to ledge when Samantha couldn't. Before long, she had to pull out the ropes and crampons, tying herself off and pulling herself upward. Logan helped, digging out handholds with his claws, anchoring Samantha with his strength when needed.

When she reached the bottom tier of the cliff dwellings, Samantha sat herself down on a ledge to rest and look around. Logan, after sniffing at her, satisfying himself she was all right, turned away and explored.

These cliff dwellings were crumbling and not well-preserved. Starlight flashed on a faded sign that said an archeology team from the University of Nevada was examining it. The sign looked so old, however, that it would soon be an archeological find itself.

Logan had his nose down as he moved around the bottom of the cliff dwellings. There were no openings here—most cliff dwellings were entered from the top, the ladders or ropes leading to the roofs drawn up for defense when needed.

Logan growled softly and reared onto his hind feet, scrabbling with his front feet on one corner of the rock wall. Samantha heaved herself up and walked carefully to him, shining a flashlight she'd retrieved from the pack into a dark hole that was about five feet high and a couple wide.

The flashlight's faint light showed that the hole led into a cave, shallow, dusty, and empty. Samantha beamed the light around the best she could, stopping when the light landed on an image etched into the cave's back wall. It was a precisely drawn ring of circles within circles, surrounded by square-shaped runes.

"I'm willing to bet that symbol isn't Native American," Samantha said, squeezing through the hole and into the cave. "It's demon, but I can't read it." She moved the few feet to the wall, examining it without touching it. She heard grunting and huffing as Logan pushed himself into the hole. His warm fur touched her, his strength comforting, as he pressed his wolf nose to the wall beneath the image, sniffing hard.

"Do you think they're behind there somewhere?" Samantha asked him.

Logan looked up at her, frustration in his tawny eyes.

Samantha sighed. "I know—you can't tell me. I feel like I'm in an episode of *Lassie*."

Logan growled, his eyes narrowing.

"Sorry," Samantha said quickly, giving him a grin. She pressed her palms to the rock, careful not to touch the symbol. She sensed the chill behind the wall, similar to what she'd felt when Fulton had opened the way to the Lamiah clan's death realm.

"If there's something behind this, I have no clue how to get to it."

Logan sat on his haunches and stared at the wall as though he could dissolve it by glaring at it hard enough. Samantha was tempted to ruffle his fur, but she knew Logan wasn't the "ruffle the fur" kind of werewolf.

"I've never learned how to enter the death realms," she said. "But we have a demon handy who might know how."

Samantha ducked back out of the cave and gazed back down over the cliffs to the canyon floor. She didn't relish the climb down and back up again, but she'd endure a little sweat and sore muscles if it would help her find Tain.

"Be right back," she said to Logan, who'd come out behind her, and began the arduous descent.

***

"They are coming," the matriarch said.

Tain barely heard her through the haze of his pain. His eye socket pounded in agony, blood clotting on his face. Bahkat, still the jeans-clad man with tatts, had taken Tain's eye out, held it in his palm, and destroyed it with a single dart of fiery magic.

"All you have to do is kill the half demon," Bahkat said, tossing Tain's sword, blood-streaked now, and catching it by the hilt. "Sacrifice Samantha to me, and I will raise you up again, help you heal, set you at my right hand. You may have *this* female as your prize." He gestured to the matriarch.

The matriarch didn't seem to mind. She slid her hand around Bahkat's muscled arm. "Join my master and me — we will raise all demons to their former glory. No more white picket fences in the suburbs, no more stock portfolios and business meetings."

Tain said nothing. Even through the pain, he felt a grim joy. Kehksut had never touched Tain's face when he'd tortured him, wanting Tain to always look whole and handsome. Now Tain would be scarred forever — even if he healed from this session, his face would bear lines and creases. He would no longer be the prize Kehksut had sought to keep beautiful. He would survive, kill Bahkat and the matriarch, and finally be free.

Tain smiled, the drying blood on his face cracking. "You forget," he rumbled softly. "What I am."

"An Immortal," Bahkat said. "That means I can keep you alive while I torture you as much as I please."

Tain laughed, a grating sound. "I mean I am a madman," he said, his old Celtic lilt pronounced. "And you never know what a madman will do."

Tain enjoyed the looks on Bahkat's and the matriarch's faces before he let his good eye roll back, and he reached for darkness and the incredible strength it gave him.

***

Merrick collapsed on the top of the cliff dwellings, panting and swearing. "I take it back," he said, gasping for breath. "Your Immortal can have you. You're one sadistic bitch, Samantha. To think, I used to think you were cute."

"Save it, Merrick." Samantha put her hands on her hips and took in the incredible view through the canyon and out of it. The desert beyond stretched forever, empty and pale in the moonlight, stark and breathtaking. "I wouldn't have dragged you back here, but I can't open the portal to the death realm. I don't know how."

"You need magic to do it," Merrick said impatiently. "And if you haven't noticed, the vortex thingee in this canyon sucks magic out of us."

A shotgun landed on top of the rocks, and a grubby pair of hands followed it. Samantha hurried over and helped Ed the rest of the way up, until he lay on his stomach next to Merrick, also gasping. Mike followed more slowly, without breathing as hard, then sat down cross-legged against the rock wall, resting his shotgun across his lap.

"I'm not the most powerful demon in the world, you know," Merrick said. "Good thing, or your Immortal boyfriend would have killed me by now."

Ed sat up, carefully picked up his shotgun, and aimed it at Merrick. "Why don't you do what the little lady says?"

"Oh, perfect," Merrick said. "The demon matriarch and her redneck defender."

"Now," Ed said, and Logan growled in agreement.

Merrick snarled a little more but heaved himself to his feet, swearing again when he examined the ruined remains of his suit.

"Today, Merrick," Samantha said. Her heart beat hard with impatience and worry as she slid her Glock from her holster.

She hadn't taken it out to threaten Merrick, but Merrick eyed the gun in trepidation. "I still haven't decided whether I love you or hate you, Sam, my dear. All right, let me take a look."

Merrick ducked through the opening and stepped to the back of the cave. He pressed his palms to the smooth black rock, as Samantha had done, closing his eyes to concentrate.

"It's an entrance to a death realm, all right," Merrick said after a time. "But I don't know if I can open the way. Depends on the demon clan whose death realm it is, and this one stinks of a lot of power."

Merrick leaned his cheek against the wall, his dark brows drawing together in concentration. Disturbed pebbles trickled from his fingertips, and he frowned harder before sighing and stepping back. "Sorry, sweetheart, this place has drained me. You're going to need a much stronger demon than me—"

He broke off as the wall in front of him dissolved, as did the rest of the shallow cave, and the chill of death magic poured out from a cavernous room beyond.

Merrick took a wide-eyed step back, and at the same time, Tain stepped out, his face and naked torso covered in blackened blood. He swung his bronze swords in strong hands and then brought them around to rest, crossed, on Merrick's neck.

Chapter Twenty-Five

Samantha went rigid with shock. Tain was naked to the waist and barefoot, every inch of exposed skin slashed and covered with blood. His handsome face was ruined, his left eye a mass of blood, his right eye wide and dark with madness. The black tattoo on his cheek stood out amid the blood, almost glowing with light. Manacles encircled his wrists, the remains of chains dangling from them.

"Tain." Samantha's whisper was frozen.

He wouldn't look at her. The muscles in his forearms bunched as he squeezed the swords into Merrick's neck.

"Tain, no." Samantha seized his arm, fingers sliding on his blood. Her heart beat rapidly in pain and desperation as she saw herself losing him again.

She felt a wash of death magic stronger than any since Kehksut, and a demon stepped out behind Tain — a tall man with an impossibly beautiful face, eyes that were pools of black, ancient demon runes tattooed on his arms. He was an Old One, and his death magic wove with that of the death realm behind him and blanketed the ledge.

The bubble of death magic would lend strength to the demon woman with him, but Samantha and Logan were sitting ducks. The Old One's strength might also help Merrick, but whose side Merrick was on was still up in the air. Merrick was an opportunist, not a hero, and right now, his neck was in danger of being severed.

"Start with that one," the demon woman said to Tain, pointing at Merrick. "I will give his heart in sacrifice. Then the humans and the werewolf. We'll save dear Samantha for you."

Logan snarled, fangs bared, saliva dripping from his mouth. Ed and Mike stood against the wall, white-faced, shotguns cradled in their big hands.

The Old One swept his dark gaze over Samantha, and everything in her went cold. Despair and hopelessness caught her in a wave, nearly sending her over the edge of the rocks into the canyon below.

"Tain serves me now," the Old One said.

Samantha held on to her sanity by keeping her hands around Tain's right arm. He might be bloody, but underneath he was warm, strong, powerful. He was Tain.

"Who the hell are you?" she demanded.

"My name is Bahkat, and this is my realm."

"I meant *her*," Samantha said, gesturing with her chin to the demon woman. "Are you Ms. Townsend or the majordomo?"

The woman's lip curled. "And you call yourself a detective. I am the matriarch of the Lamiah clan."

"The matriarch is dead," Samantha said in a hard voice.

The woman laughed. "That's what your boyfriend said. It was easy to drug your coffee, pretend to be drugged myself, and transport you here for safekeeping."

"Why?"

The matriarch sighed. "They always want to know *why*. They can't simply obey." She made a slashing gesture, and Samantha lost her hold on Tain and fell to her knees, rock cutting her through her thin pants. "Because having you is the best way of enslaving Tain," the matriarch said. "*I* want vengeance for my lover Kehksut. Bahkat will provide that, since I am his."

"Merrick was telling me what a demonwhore you were," Samantha said, her voice steady to cover the shock. She shouldn't be surprised this was really the matriarch, she supposed. The majordomo had been too perfectly efficient, too self-sacrificing to be believed.

"Excuse me," Merrick broke in quickly. "Could you *not* piss her off? See the swords in my neck? The blood?"

"Tain is life magic," Samantha said to the matriarch. "His magic can't work in this vortex or amid so much death magic. You can't use him to do anything right now." She hoped.

"Tain doesn't need his magic to cut off heads," the matriarch said. "He just needs all that gleaming muscle." She stepped to Tain and ran a finger down his bicep.

The demon in Samantha growled. Tain belonged to *her*.

"Tain has plenty of magic," Bahkat interrupted. "He has given himself to me, and I make him strong."

Bahkat stepped to Tain and licked his bare cheek. Tain did nothing, only remained rock-steady, his swords crossed over Merrick's throat.

Logan abruptly leapt at the matriarch, a streak of snarling wolf fury, and latched on to her. She went down with a cry of surprise, which was cut off as blood spurted from her throat.

Bahkat gestured contemptuously, and Logan flew through the air, slamming hard against the rock wall then skittering to the edge of the cliff. He made no noise, paws scrabbling in a desperate attempt to save himself. Then he went over.

"You bastard," Samantha yelled, drawing her pistol.

Ed cut off her words by bringing up his shotgun and firing straight at Bahkat. Bahkat twitched his fingers again and the gun swung wide, going off with a roar. The shot clicked against rock above them and pebbles rained down. Ed was lifted from his feet and slapped high on the wall of the cliff dwelling, then dropped. He groaned as he slid back to the ledge, the shotgun falling uselessly from his hands. Mike hurried to him and bent over his friend.

The matriarch climbed to her feet, but Samantha had her Glock in her hand, the familiar weight reassuring. She sighted and fired — one, two, three rounds into the demon woman's body, bracing herself for the gun's kick.

Samantha didn't think the bullets would kill the matriarch, and they didn't, but they did make her stumble. Samantha lunged for her, caught the woman around the waist, and threw her toward the edge of the cliff.

The matriarch stopped herself before she reached the edge and spun back to face Samantha. Her beautiful-woman glam fell away, and Samantha found herself looking at the grim, lined face of the woman she'd met as the matriarch's majordomo.

"Don't cross me." The woman's voice rasped. "I am your matriarch, and I command you."

Bahkat watched them with emotionless dark eyes. "She *was* your matriarch," he said, his voice chill and dark. "She was a good disciple and lover. Now that I have the Immortal I have no more need of her."

He held his hand out toward the matriarch, and then closed his fist. The matriarch morphed back into the lush woman, staring at Bahkat with wide and anguished eyes. Then she screamed.

Her body began to compress, a hidden force crushing her. She fought it, crying out, but Bahkat simply held his hand in place. Blood burst from the matriarch's body, bones shattered with a cracking sound. After a few moments, her screams died to gurgles, and she fell into a broken pile of bones and flesh that dissolved slowly into dust.

Samantha stared, wide-eyed at the swirling sand that had been the matriarch, her hand still locked around her gun. She wanted to be sick but was too dazed and shocked to do much of anything.

Tain finally moved. He lifted his swords from Merrick and sent the demon flying backward on a wave of magic that bore the stink of death. Merrick crashed into the wall beside Ed and Mike and lay still, blood gushing from the wound on his neck.

Samantha looked at Tain and knew she'd lost him. His good eye was blank, the blue swallowed by black, and he regarded Samantha with no recognition.

Samantha loved him, had always loved him, and knew it for a futile, impossible love. Tain was an Immortal and half crazy at the best of times. His brothers might have healed him and helped him kill his enemy, but Tain's mind had been taken long ago.

"Tain," Samantha whispered. "I love you."

Bahkat swung his full attention to Samantha. "That's very sweet," he said in his rumbling voice. "She'll make a wonderful slave if she already loves you, my friend."

Samantha knew she had no magic at all, no power to best an Old One, and her bullets would have no effect on him. She figured she could either throw herself over the ledge and try to run for it—if she survived—or stay here and brave it out.

"Why don't you suck him off, my dear?" Bahkat went on. "I'd enjoy watching that."

Samantha gave him a look of loathing. "Screw you," she said. Then she fired.

The bullets stopped in front of the demon, as though they'd run into a transparent wall, and clinked harmlessly to the floor. Samantha had known shooting Bahkat wouldn't work—Tain had a similar trick when he was being fired at—but it felt good to try. Bahkat flicked his fingers and the gun ripped from Samantha's hand, her palm stinging.

Tain stepped to Samantha. A brush of Bahkat's magic forced Samantha to her knees, and she found herself looking at the waistband of Tain's jeans, the fabric spattered with blood. The jeans rode low on Tain's hips, revealing smooth skin below his navel, a line of dark red hair that disappeared under his waistband. Tain smelled like blood, sweat, and death magic, but also of himself, the warmth of his skin, the strength of his body.

Tain grabbed Samantha around the wrist and dragged her to her feet. "No," he said, voice grating. "My way is better. It will hurt her more."

Bahkat came forward, interested. Tain's fingers clamped harder on Samantha's wrist, forcing her hand to open, and he slammed her palm to his pentacle tattoo.

"No," Samantha cried. She felt the enormity of his magic even before her hand contacted the mark.

The tattoo seared into her palm, hotter than it had when he'd overwhelmed her in the tiny bedroom in his apartment. Tain poured *all* his life essence into her, not slowing it, not preparing her, not stopping it from hurting.

The demon in Samantha at first drank it greedily, and then as the essence continued to gush in, Samantha started to scream. She couldn't take it all at once—it would kill her, burning her from the inside out. She struggled, trying to jerk away from the tearing pain, but Tain held her remorselessly.

Tain's essence filled her with white-hot heat, a magic stronger even than that of the goddess Cerridwen, who had entwined her psyche with Samantha's at the battle with Kehksut. Then, Samantha's real self had become enmeshed with the goddess, and she'd felt enormous power, but it hadn't hurt.

This was unbearable. Samantha felt every cut of Tain's torture, relived the horrible agony when Bahkat had cut out Tain's eye. She was forced to take all of it, every space of her filling with Tain's life essence, his memories, his magic. Samantha's skin began to glow, the power of the essence she'd absorbed lighting the dark cavern.

Bahkat snapped his gaze to her, suddenly alert. He flickered and elongated, death magic pouring from him to surround the life magic now radiating from Samantha.

A roar filled the air, the sound of a shotgun, and Tain's hand tore from her. Samantha stared in shock as Tain fell to the ground, his chest bloody. She whirled to see Mike standing behind her, staring with terrified eyes, the acrid smoke from his shotgun curling around his face.

As she gaped dazedly at Mike, Samantha felt Tain's fingers, slick with blood, on her wrist. She looked down at him, the man she loved covered in blood and in terrible pain, his magic gone. He pressed the hilt of one of his swords into her hand. "Do it," he whispered. "You're strong enough."

Pain burned her, Samantha's head pounding with nightmare agony. Her vision was all wrong too—white lines crisscrossed in front of her, bright points that seemed to stab around the cavern, making the walls sparkle.

Bahkat rose in front of her, huge and dark, his body morphing to his demon form. He filled the cave, a horror with wings unfolding, his eyes red and burning.

Tain's hand closed harder around Samantha's wrist. "Do it for me," he whispered.

Samantha's mind cleared, and she understood. Tain had infused her with the life essence of an Immortal, the essence that had been too powerful for an Old One like Kehksut to take. Tain had trained Samantha, by letting her imbibe him little by little, to absorb that power.

Samantha pulsed with Tain's life magic. His sword was in her hands as Bahkat rose over her, ready to crush her.

"I love you, Samantha," Tain said, then his grasp went slack.

Samantha roared. It was a terrible sound, ringing through the cavern and out into the night. Samantha the demon and Samantha the woman screamed together in rage, and Samantha the matriarch came in for good measure.

She raised the sword. She was full of Tain's beautiful magic that he'd drained himself to give her, Samantha's demon self able to carry it in this place of death magic. She brought the sword down on Bahkat.

Bahkat slid out of her reach, throwing a wave of death magic at her, but the wave flowed around Samantha without touching her. She came at Bahkat again, sword high, laughing wildly.

"Do you know what happened when Tain suffered all those years at Kehksut's hands?" Samantha shouted. "He got strong—stronger than all the Immortals put together. Did you really think you could defeat *him*? He's got more power than any life-magic creature in the world, and your friend Kehksut made him that way." Samantha stalked Bahkat as she spoke, her terrible strength rising in volcano fury. "Wouldn't Kehksut love it if he knew the being he'd created was the one who killed *you*?"

Bahkat came at her, claws out, his body huge and horrific. Samantha drew back Tain's well-balanced bronze sword, made a quick feint, and came up and under the demon's reach to stab him in the neck.

Bahkat screamed. Black blood poured over Samantha's hands, and the demon shuddered violently. Samantha kept the sword in place, holding it hard.

Tain's white-hot magic poured out of her and up the blade straight into Bahkat, shaking him like an electric wave. The huge demon writhed and twisted, trying to get away. Samantha stayed steady, even though her arms felt like they were being wrenched out. She refused to move—she knew from experience it took a long time to kill demons.

A second Roman sword joined the first, this one driving deep into Bahkat's chest. Tain stood beside Samantha, his body shining with sweat, muscles contracting as he held his sword in rock-steady hands.

Bahkat thrashed in panic, and death magic exploded over Tain and Samantha, crushing the air from Samantha's lungs. She lost her hold on the sword and went down, hearing the blade clank faintly on the rock next to her.

Tain landed on top of her, shielding her while Bahkat's death throes went on. The magic cavern began to crumble, the death realm losing its patron, its pillars toppling into dust.

Tain dragged Samantha up and over his shoulder, and he hurtled across the ledge to the ropes that led down. Ed, Mike, and Merrick were gone, having sensibly fled while Samantha fought Bahkat.

Tain half jumped, half fell over the ledge with Samantha, she banging against his shoulder. They landed on a jutting slab of rock below, where Ed, Mike, and Merrick already cowered.

The cave above them exploded, the ancient cliff dwelling going up with it. Bahkat's cries of agony went on, long and shrill, growing fainter as the chunks of cliff dwelling fell to block the hole. Samantha felt the death magic dwindle as the entrance to the death realm was buried and destroyed.

Boulders and pebbles continued to rain down around them, plinking against the rocks like hail. Tain shielded Samantha with his body, never flinching as the falling gravel cut into his bare and already cut skin. The others huddled together, Merrick growling and cursing as the rain of rock went on and on.

After a long time, the pebbles pattered out around them, and everything gradually went silent. The last chill wave from the death realm dispersed into the vortex, and white dust spiraled into the light of the coming dawn.

***

What was left of the Old One Bahkat slithered through the portal he'd opened back into the matriarch's mansion. He'd fled here in blind panic, drawn to the life essences of the group of humans repairing things in the basement.

Bahkat relaxed in relief. He could drain the humans and regain strength, then lie in wait to capture Tain and his half-demon bitch when they returned. He'd kill Samantha and seal the Immortal into Bahkat's hell dimension. If Tain thought he'd been tortured before, it was nothing to what Bahkat would do to him now.

Bahkat crawled out, gasping and half-dead, to the secret room below the house. He would lie here, in human form, until he regained his strength, then he'd seek sustenance.

As his bare human feet hit the floor, he heard a strange whooshing sound, and he looked up to see a flaming sword in front of his face.

A green-eyed, tawny-haired man held the sword's hilt, and behind him stood a lion, a true one, who snarled softly. Beyond the beast was another Immortal glowing with life magic, the snake in his hands just changing to a sword.

"Look, Adrian," the green-eyed one said. "Tain sent us an Old One. This should be fun."

"He's dying," the one called Adrian said. "Put him out of his misery."

The green-eyed one's horrible smile widened. The flaming blade swung around and swiftly and cleanly struck Bahkat's head from his body. The last thing the demon heard was the Immortal saying, "Oh, that was too easy. Tain got to have all the fun . . ."

***

Tain hobbled out of the canyon with his arm around Samantha. His magic was spent, the vortex and the battle sucking him dry, the white-hot essence he'd used to fill Samantha gone. Samantha staggered beside him, insisting on helping him walk, although it was clear she could barely walk herself.

On her other side was Mike, the only one of them still whole, who silently guided Samantha with a hand under her arm, his shotgun clutched in his other hand. Ed and Merrick limped behind them, Merrick uncharacteristically quiet.

They found Logan partway up the canyon, as far as he'd dragged himself before collapsing. He lay still, his fur matted with blood, a hind leg twisted and broken. He looked up with dull eyes when Samantha bent worriedly over him.

"Mike, can you carry him?" Tain asked tiredly. "I can heal him, but we have to get out of this damned canyon first."

Mike nodded, handed Ed his shotgun, and leaned down and hoisted Logan up and over his shoulders. Logan yelped in pain and squeezed his eyes shut.

"Was that really the matriarch?" Samantha asked Tain as they moved on again. He liked having her arm tight around his waist, liked her warmth against his aching body.

"She said she switched places with her majordomo years ago," Tain answered, his voice like broken rock. "There aren't many demons left who remember what she looked like."

Merrick laughed hoarsely. "The vixen. I told you she'd been a wild woman in her youth."

"Well, she'd dead now," Samantha said. She shook her head. "Just when I thought demons could be civilized, one tries to sacrifice me to an Old One."

Merrick chuckled again. "When demons start to age, they get a little crazy. They hanker for the old days, which are gone forever. Live with the times, I always say."

Samantha slanted Tain a glance, not smiling. Tain had hurt her deeply, he knew that, and there was a chance she wouldn't forgive him for it.

As the canyon walls receded, Tain felt his magic return, slowly but surely. After about another mile or so they emerged onto flat ground, a chill morning breeze wafting across the desert floor. The rising sun glinted on the windshield of Ed's pickup a ways off, and on the chrome of a motorcycle parked next to it.

When they reached the washboard road, Tain told Mike to lay Logan on the ground. The wolf shimmered and became a man, naked-and gray faced, covered with blood. Logan moaned, his eyelids fluttering.

Samantha knelt next to him. "Merrick, give me your jacket."

Tain expected the demon to argue, but Merrick slid his suit coat from his shoulders and handed it to her. "Two thousand dollars at Armani on Rodeo. They know my size."

"Shut up," Samantha said, but without much heat. She spread the coat over Logan's body, and Tain crouched next to him.

Magic flowed to Tain's fingertips, tingling and hurting, his own body wanting to heal first. Tain tried to ignore the pain, and sank his magic into Logan, taking comfort in the familiar ritual of healing. He saw Logan's injuries as a jumbled mass of torn muscle and bone, and he let himself straighten the threads of them one by one.

Logan groaned again, moving in pain as his body healed. Then he sucked in a sharp breath, normal color flooding his face. "Hell," he said, looking weakly up at Samantha. "Looks like I missed all the fun."

Tain next turned to Ed, healing the man's abrasions and broken ribs. Next Merrick, whose neck became whole and smooth under his touch.

"You could sell that skill," Merrick said when he'd finished. He fingered his throat. "Maybe when I open my club again, we could work a deal."

Tain ignored him. He turned to Samantha and cupped her face in his hands, letting healing magic flow gently into her. He healed what he'd damaged with his flood of life essence, and allowed the feel of her to soothe his battered soul. He sensed Samantha growing aroused, as she always did when he healed her, and his own body responded even through the pain.

But Samantha said nothing, did nothing, and when he finished, she turned away from him without meeting his gaze.

Chapter Twenty-Six

Cleanup from a case was always a bitch, no less now that Samantha was not on the force. As the Lamiah matriarch, she had to find a way to explain that the majordomo and the real matriarch had switched places long ago. Also that the matriarch had called forth a nasty Old One, destroying demons in her own clan to do it, and that she'd met her death at said Old One's hands.

Logan helped her tell the story to McKay, who listened with a tense look on her face. "And that portal is closed?" McKay asked. "No more big bad demon coming out to wreak havoc in my city?"

"Tain's brothers sealed it up," Samantha said, remembering Hunter's glee when he told her. "And made sure Bahkat was dead. I don't think there will be any more Old Ones popping into the matriarch's house."

"Thank goodness for that. Good work, lieutenant." McKay stopped. "I mean matriarch."

Samantha smiled, always enjoying hard-won praise from her boss, even if McKay wasn't her boss anymore.

Tristan was arrested for sending the threatening letters for the matriarch, charged with being an accessory to murder. Tristan had expected Samantha, as his cousin and matriarch, to provide him with a top lawyer and get him off, and was shocked when she refused. Samantha also refused to supply bail money. Tristan needed to pay for helping the old matriarch cause the deaths of girls who'd done nothing to deserve being turned into demon sacrifice, Samantha decided. He needed to pay for Nadia's anguish and grief, as well. The rest of the Lamiah clan agreed with her.

Ms. Townsend of No More Nightmares was brought in, and coldly confessed to kidnapping the demon prostitutes and presiding over the ritual killings. She showed no remorse at their deaths, not even at the death of her own assistant, Melanie. Once Ms. Townsend had discovered Melanie had demon blood, Melanie had to die, in order to cleanse the organization. It was easy to make Melanie's death look like the others.

Samantha worried that a human jury might sympathize with Ms. Townsend's anti-demon point of view, but Logan said Nadia had agreed to testify and tell the world what she and her sister had suffered. Logan was confident that he and Nadia could persuade a courtroom to see Ms. Townsend's cruelty.

Samantha was exhausted and happy to return home, where Flavia had become very maternal. The young woman felt terrible that the coffee had been drugged and Samantha taken while she'd obliviously worked in the next room. Samantha reassured Flavia that it hadn't been her fault, but Flavia still went about looking guilt-stricken.

Samantha hadn't seen Tain since their long, dusty ride back to Los Angeles in Ed's pickup. Tain had retreated to the Malibu house after Ed had dropped Samantha off at her mother's, Tain saying he needed to spend time with Hunter and Adrian to heal. Samantha longed to be there with him, but Tain told her to return to the matriarch's mansion as soon as she could, to smooth things over, reassure the clan, and keep the peace.

Samantha was surprised the clan still wanted her, now that they knew the matriarch hadn't truly backed her. But Fulton said that Samantha had been chosen legitimately — put forth by a head of household and voted on at the muster — and the clan accepted her as leader. Samantha helping to kill the Old One that the matriarch had summoned, not to mention besting Tristan, only raised her in the clan's estimation.

As for Merrick . . . Samantha learned that, by demon law, he was due compensation, because he'd suffered as a result of assisting Samantha in her role as matriarch. Samantha made a generous donation to the rebuilding of Merrick's club, giving the money directly to the builders instead of Merrick himself. She even bought him a new suit from the shop on Rodeo.

So all was well at the matriarch's mansion, but Samantha went to bed alone every night, her heart aching.

***

At the Malibu house, Tain waited for his Immortal body to close its wounds and return his strength. He soon realized the eye Bahkat had cut out would not regenerate, though the socket scarred over, the flesh itself healing. Leda assured him he looked like a dashing pirate with his new eye patch, but Tain found no humor in it.

He waited until his strength returned in full, then made his way down to the matriarch's mansion. Using spells to make himself unobtrusive, he slipped past Samantha and Flavia talking in the hall and waited for Samantha to return to her office.

When Samantha entered the room and closed the door with a sigh, Tain kept the spells in place and let himself look at her. She wore a classic suit, the skirt revealing her long legs, the jacket hugging her curves. He'd missed the fine smoothness of her face, her beautiful dark eyes, and the way she could roll those eyes whenever Tain said something cryptic and Immortal.

Samantha stood in the middle of the room, gazing out the distant window as she lifted her hair from her neck and let it drop through her hands. Her black hair shimmered as it fell, and Tain's arousal swiftly rose. He couldn't resist coming up behind her and sliding his hands across her shoulders, kissing the silken fall of her hair.

Samantha let out a cry and swung around, eyes wide. "Tain," she gasped, hand at her heart. "Jeez, don't *do* that."

The door swung open and Flavia hurried in. "I heard you call out. What's wrong?"

Samantha stepped out of Tain's arms, flushing. "I'm fine. Tain startled me, is all."

Flavia fixed Tain a cold stare worthy of the old majordomo. "You didn't make an appointment."

"It's all right," Samantha said quickly. "I'll cut him some slack. This time."

Flavia frowned once more then stalked out, closing the door behind her.

Samantha touched Tain's cheek below the eye patch. "Are you all right?"

I am now, Tain wanted to answer.

She swallowed. "You look . . ."

"Like a pirate?"

Samantha gave him a faint smile. "I was going to say normal. More human."

Tain studied her, searching for answers deep in her eyes. "Do you like me more human?"

The smile grew warmer. "Yes."

His heart hammered with relief. He'd half expected Samantha to recoil from him, to gaze in horror at the mass of scars that covered the left side of his face. Tain had welcomed the scars because Kehksut would have hated them, but he didn't want Samantha to hate them too.

"I came to tell you something," he said.

Samantha's expression grew wary. "And that is?"

Gods, he wished she didn't look so delectable in those clothes. He wanted to lick her legs all the way up to the delight between them.

"I'm going to Ravenscroft," Tain made himself say.

Samantha's eyes flickered. "I thought you might be."

"Did you?" Tain asked in some surprise.

"That's what Immortals do, isn't it?" Samantha said stiffly. "You come when you're summoned, you kill the bad guys, you go back home. Problem solved, and you move on. The Old One is dead, and now you're heading out."

"No." Tain stopped, unsure how to proceed.

"You just said you were going to Ravenscroft." Samantha's dark eyes glittered as she moved back to her desk, as though ready to slide into her role as matriarch.

He couldn't do this. Adrian had told him to come here and tell Samantha flat out what he was going to do. Hunter had advised Tain to charm Samantha first, flirt with her until she was melting and compliant.

His brothers were assholes. Tain didn't have the commanding air of Adrian or the flirtation skills of Hunter. When he wanted a woman, he smiled at her, and that did the trick. Or at least it used to. Now his face was a hideous mess, and no woman was going to respond to Tain's smiles ever again.

"Damn it." Tain was across the room and had Samantha bent backward over the desk before she could speak or push him away. Pens, file folders, and little ornaments clattered to the floor, and then he was kissing her, brushing back her hair and taking her mouth. She tasted wonderful, like cinnamon, coffee, and heat.

"Did you mean it?" he whispered against her lips.

"Mean what?" Her dark eyes were wide.

"When you told me you loved me," Tain said. "When you tried to save me from Bahkat, up in that cave, you said you loved me. Or was that just to get me to stop?"

"I thought I was going to die," Samantha said, and she swallowed. "I thought I'd better say it—in case."

"Say it again now that we're safe. I need you to. I need something I can believe in."

Samantha's eyes filled, and her mouth softened. "I love you, Tain."

The words floated around him like fires on a frozen night. "I love you too," he said, his breath not working. "Gods, Samantha, I love you so much."

She smiled, hope in her eyes, and she touched his face again. "Tain."

Words tumbled out of him, coming from someplace he didn't understand. "You were right when you said you saved my ass back in Seattle. For a long time I wandered around thinking the last thing I needed was *you* in my life, when you were exactly what I needed. You could have healed me a long time ago if I'd let you."

"Why are you going to Ravenscroft then?" Samantha asked, her brows drawing together. "If you need me so much?"

"I want to take you with me."

Samantha stopped, her dark gaze searching. "I'm demon. Isn't it a special Immortals place full of life magic?"

"You have Cerridwen's permission to enter, and you'll be with me."

Samantha started to shake her head. "But I'm clan matriarch now, and I have a mountain of work to do. I can't just leave."

Tain tightened his arms around her. "If you want, the goddesses can arrange it so we arrive back here minutes after we leave."

Samantha looked puzzled. "If you can come back in a few minutes, I don't understand why you want me to go with you."

"For a good reason." Tain kissed her again, slowly this time, while he opened the portal that would take them to Ravenscroft.

The matriarch's office dissolved to be replaced by a grassy slope that ran down to a wide, flowing river under bright sunshine. Tain broke the kiss, and Samantha smiled and touched his lips before she realized what had happened.

She sat up with a start. Tain rolled off her to stretch out next to her in the warm grass, enjoying the view of Samantha's legs as she gaped at the meadow, the river, and the long, Japanese-looking building — wood with lattice and paper screens — at the top of the slope.

"Where the hell — ?"

"This is Ravenscroft," Tain said.

Samantha gulped a few breaths of the sweet air. "Shit. I didn't realize you meant you wanted us to come here *right now.*"

Tain grinned at her, feeling happier than he had in a very long time, but he kept his voice gentle as he explained. "When I filled you with my life essence in the cave, I hurt you. You are incredibly strong, but I nearly killed you. I've healed you most of the way, but here, I can finish, to make sure you're completely well."

Samantha sank back down beside him, sunshine on her beautiful face. "It did hurt. But it worked." She touched his chest, her fingertips drawing fire through his shirt. "We weakened the Old One enough so Hunter could kill him — Hunter's told me that story about six times already." She smiled up at Tain, breaking something inside him. "I'd do it again in a heartbeat."

Tain stroked her hair, enjoying it softness under his fingertips. "I hope to the gods you never have to again." He leaned down and nuzzled her. "I'll make *sure* you never have to."

After their next long, tender kiss, Samantha raised her head and gazed at the beauty surrounding them. "How long can I stay? This place is amazing. I'm used to city that sprawls for miles or the barren desert beyond that. I get excited when I see a tree in its natural habitat."

She laughed, but Tain remained serious. "You can stay as long as you want."

"I have to go back eventually, though," Samantha said, sounding wistful. "The clan has accepted me for whatever reason, and they're my family. I have a job to help them now."

Tain gave her a nod. "I'm going back with you. I don't intend to lose you again. I'm going to be personal bodyguard to the matriarch."

Samantha blinked. "Personal bodyguard?"

"To you and to the clan. You need life essence to survive, and this way I can be on hand to give it to you."

"I see." Samantha sounded uncertain.

Tain laid her back down on the grass and covered her warm body with his. Then he did what he'd been longing to, pushed back the lapels of her blazer and unbuttoned her blouse with gentle fingers. "Will you have me, Samantha?"

Samantha traced the pentacle on his cheek. "As a lover? Yes."

"I mean as a life mate. A wife. Forever. The goddesses will make you immortal to be with me . . . if you can stand the thought."

Samantha's eyes were wide. "Of course I can stand the thought. But you just asked me to marry you. Didn't you? You're saying you want to stay with me forever too."

"That's usually what it means." Tain smiled, feeling his scars pull under the eye patch. "I love you, Samantha, and I need you. Be my life mate." He paused. "Please."

Samantha stared at him while his heart thudded with the enormity of what he'd asked her. He waited while thoughts flickered behind her eyes — uncertainty, outright fear, need. Hope. Love.

"My father once told me I'd live a long time anyway," Samantha said in a faint voice.

Tain's body stilled. "Does that mean *yes*?"

Samantha smiled, her eyes beautiful and full of love. "Yes."

Relief flooded him. "Thank you." He collapsed onto her, resting his head against the ground, his body shuddering.

When he raised his head again, his good eye was full of tears, blurring her beautiful face. "Will you say it again?" he asked, voice rasping. "That you love me? I need you to."

Samantha laughed and wound her arms around him. "I do love you," she said fiercely. "I've loved you ever since I first saw you in Seattle—I love the way you smile as though your smile is only for me. I love your deep voice and your accent and your body wet in the shower. And I especially love your gorgeous, tight ass." Samantha's smile shook as she squeezed his backside. "I love how you worried about a demon prostitute hurt and alone in an alley. And I love how you feed my cat junk he's not supposed to eat when you think I'm not looking."

Tain grinned. "You noticed that?"

She gave him a wry look. "You're not very subtle."

"Not my strong point." Definitely not. Tain wanted to get on with the business of making love to her right now, but he dug into the pocket of his jeans and pulled out a small, black velvet-covered box.

Samantha's eyes widened. She took the box from him and opened it with trembling fingers. Inside lay a ring, set with a large, white diamond, which winked in the sunlight.

Samantha gasped and almost dropped the box. "Good gods, Tain."

"Hunter had to take me to the bank and explain how to get out my money again. But he didn't mind—this time it was for a good cause."

Samantha worked the ring out of the box. "Put it on me."

Tain took the cool band between his fingertips and slid the ring onto her fourth finger. He seemed to be shaking as much as she was. "If it doesn't fit, the jeweler said it could be resized."

"It's fine." Tears filled Samantha's eyes. "It's fine."

Tain lifted her hand, kissed the ring, and laid her palm against his tattoo, liking that she didn't pull away. "I used to love so easily," he said. "Teach me how to love again, Samantha."

Samantha brushed her thumb across his cheek, hand still on his tattoo. "I'm not sure I can."

"If anyone can, it's you."

Samantha dragged in a breath, looking scared a moment, then she gave Tain a nod. "I'll try," she said softly. "I promise, I'll try."

"Good." Tain pressed a kiss to her damp cheek. "Now, no more tears, love." He parted the blouse and kissed the tops of her breasts, then slid his hand around to unhook her bra. "I want to celebrate gaining my freedom again." He slanted her a smile. "Do you know how I want to celebrate?"

Samantha kissed his throat. "I'm getting an idea."

Tain pressed his forehead to hers, looking straight into her eyes and letting his smile grow wicked. "I want to make love to you. I want to do it hard and fast, and then I want to do it loving and slow. I want to be inside you, and to savor you, and I want you to feel so good you never want me to stop."

"That sounds nice," Samantha said shakily. "If this is what giving me a huge diamond does to you, you can give me one every day."

"Mmm, Hunter wouldn't like that—he'd have to take me to the bank all the time."

"Hunter can get over it."

Tain laughed, the sound flowing from him, free and strong. "I want to give you my world, Samantha. Because you gave mine back to me."

Samantha twined her arms around him. "Maybe you can thank me now."

Tain seized one of her hands and pressed it to his tattoo again, liking how she immediately started to take his essence gently, not hungrily. He grew harder as he felt the pull, Samantha arousing him as no one ever had, as no one ever could. "Oh, I intend to, love."

"Good." Samantha smiled, her eyes darkening as she tugged him down to her, and Tain surrendered himself to her. She would be his mate, forever, this demon who'd healed him and taught him about love. "You know," she mused as Tain slid his hands under her skirt, finding the heat of her. "I wouldn't mind if you kept always your hair short. It's wicked sexy."

Epilogue

Weeks later Tain sat on a verdant field in Ravenscroft, overlooking a lake, its blue like a reflection of his own eyes. A pavilion up the hill floated with pink and white streamers, and laughter echoed from his brothers — Adrian, Kalen, Darius, and Hunter, and their wives and children, as well as Logan and other friends they'd made during the fight against Kehksut. All were here with the blessing of the goddesses.

Samantha was in the pavilion with Tain's family, being passed around for hugs in her sleek white gown. She and Tain had wed not an hour ago, Tain sliding a plain wedding band onto Samantha's finger next to the diamond ring — a human custom, but one he liked.

Now he lounged in the grass, and his mother, the goddess Cerridwen, stood near him, her red hair swirling in the wind. No longer insubstantial as when she visited Tain on the earth, she was tall and stately, wrapped in gossamer that glittered like starlight.

"This is your ending," she said. "No more suffering, Tain."

4

Tain glanced at the pavilion, feeling the soft scrape of the eye patch he was still getting used to. "She's worth it," he rumbled.

"Nothing is worth what happened to you. I grieved every time you hurt, my love, knowing I'd forced you to that."

Tain looked up at his mother, but the pain and anger had gone from his heart. "It was necessary. Kehksut never would have been defeated otherwise. I understand that now." He let out his breath. "The only thing I would have changed was you and the goddesses not giving me the choice. I should have made the decision myself to submit to Kehksut's torture, walked that path of my own choosing."

Cerridwen raised her fine brows. "If the choice had been yours, if you'd known you had to sacrifice yourself, would you have done it?"

Tain replied readily. "To keep my brothers from having to go through that? Yes, I would have."

"How could you, knowing what would happen to you?"

Tain stood up and took his mother's hands, looking into the swirling silver-blue of her eyes. "Because even if I didn't survive, *they* would. They did. That's all that really matters, isn't it?"

Cerridwen's lips parted as though she saw and understood her son for the first time. "Tain . . ."

Tain shrugged, releasing her hands. "It's no longer worth talking about," he said, his Celtic lilt pronounced. He smiled as he heard renewed laughter floating from the pavilion, Samantha's voice raised above it all.

"This is my redemption, isn't it?" he asked Cerridwen. "To be a guardian of Samantha and her demons—the same kind of beings as the one who tortured me for centuries. Now I protect them." Tain's heart warmed as he laughed. "I like the irony."

Cerridwen started to speak, but just then, Samantha came out of the pavilion and called down to him. "Tain, come up here and explain to your brother that I am *not* carrying a piece under this dress."

Tain waved to her, wondering which brother was teasing the life out of her this time. He kissed his mother on the cheek, wiped away the tear that had leaked from the corner of the goddess's eye, and turned and sprinted up the hill to Samantha's laughter and her waiting arms.

End

Author's Note

Thank you for reading! Tain's book was very special to me—I was glad to give him a happy ending, and I enjoyed learning more about Samantha and her world.

Look for other stories set in the Immortals world from Joy Nash, Robin Popp, and Jennifer Ashley, including *Wolf Hunt*, Logan's story, from me. I plan to write more stories set in this world, so be on the lookout for those as well!

Visit my website (www.jenniferashley.com) for more information on this series and my others, including Shifters Unbound, my *New York Times* bestselling shape-shifter series.

Also consider joining my newsletter to obtain up-to-date information on releases, forthcoming books, and other important news. Go to:

www.jenniferashley.com

and enter your email in the boxes at the top.

Again thank you for reading!

All my best wishes,

Jennifer Ashley

About the Author

New York Times bestselling and award-winning author Jennifer Ashley has written more than 80 published novels and novellas in romance, urban fantasy, and mystery under the names Jennifer Ashley, Allyson James, and Ashley Gardner. Her books have been nominated for and won Romance Writers of America's RITA (given for the best romance novels and novellas of the year), several *RT BookReviews* Reviewers Choice awards (including Best Urban Fantasy, Best Historical Mystery, and Career Achievement in Historical Romance), and Prism awards for her paranormal romances. Jennifer's books have been translated into more than a dozen languages and have earned starred reviews in *Booklist*.

More about the Immortals series can be found at www.immortals-series.com

and more about Jennifer's books at

http://www.jenniferashley.com

Or email Jennifer at jenniferashley@cox.net

CPSIA information can be obtained at www.ICGtesting.com
Printed in the USA
LVOW10s2008180515

438913LV00007B/964/P

Immortals

WHERE VAMPS, SHIFTERS, DEMONS, WITCHES, AND IMMORTAL WARRIORS EXIST, AND THE FORCES OF LIFE MAGIC AND DEATH MAGIC STRUGGLE FOR BALANCE.

For seven hundred years the Immortal warrior Tain was held captive and tortured by a powerful demon, retreating into madness to escape his pain. Set free by his brothers, Tain has wandered the world, but he's drawn to Los Angeles, a city divided by demon lords and vampire masters, the death-magic creatures barely kept in line by strict rules and the paranormal police.

Samantha Taylor, detective in the paranormal division, brings down drug-selling demons and vampires who turn too many victims. On night, her stakeout of a demon club is blown by the appearance of man with amazing power who kills attacking demons with one burst incredible magic.

Samantha realizes to her shock that the man is Tain, the Immortal sh helped rescue, whose healing touch burns her at the same time arouses her.

Tain is back, and he needs Samantha's help. Young demon women a being murdered, and though Tain has no love for demons, h recognizes that they are innocents. He's also powerfully drawn Samantha, a half demon, and fears his pull to her means he hasr healed from his ordeal. Tain reveals to Samantha more about herse than she's comfortable knowing, but thoughshe's falling for Tain, s knows he'll never allow himself to be tied to demonkind again.

ISBN 9781941229699
90000

For more about the author, please visit:
www.JENNIFERASHLEY.com

9 781941 229699